Waiting for Yesterday

D1080872

Waiting for Yesterday

Grace Thompson

CANELO

First published in United Kingdom in 2001 by Severn House Publishers Ltd

This edition published in the United Kingdom in 2018 by

Canelo Digital Publishing Limited
57 Shepherds Lane
Beaconsfield, Bucks HP9 2DU
United Kingdom

A CIP catalogue record for this book is available from the British Library.

Print ISBN 978 1 78863 130 3
Ebook ISBN 978 1 910859 97 1

Look for more great books at www.canelo.co

One

In the Welsh seaside town of St David's Well during the month of April 1941 there was a mood of growing irritation. Everyday objects were becoming scarce and making do and doing without was developing into a routine that people still found difficult to accept.

Cigarettes and, to a lesser degree, pipe tobacco were strictly under the counter reserved for regulars. Sausages were changing their contents to contain less meat and more bread as the rationing made itself felt. People spent more of their time shopping, joining queues and hoping for something interesting to place on their tables. Families were reduced in number by the increasingly urgent conscription of men, and girls danced with girls at the local dances.

Several engagements were broken due to the unsettling effect of the war. Girls coped with the absence of a partner for a while in a limbo of half-made plans and half-made promises, then, on discovering the freedom to please themselves and the advantages of extra money provided by the factories still advertising for bench hands, began to enjoy managing alone.

Men conveniently forgot their promises and found distractions while away from everything familiar and gave in to the temptation of what was offered. Long-standing plans for marriages that would have been relatively content, were forgotten, many with sighs of relief.

At the same time many couples were marrying after a very brief courtship. Life was precarious, happiness short-lived and the growing attitude among young people was to live for the day. Older people shook their heads and said these marriages wouldn't last but the young knew that for many of them, they wouldn't live long enough to prove or disprove the sceptics.

Shirley Downs, who worked in a newsagent and tobacconist shop, lost interest in Freddy Clements as soon as he was sent to join the fighting in some secret location overseas. While he still had the occasional leave to brighten her life she had written to him and even promised to wait for him, but the war was dragging on and she didn't fancy living the life of a nun while the war continued, maybe for another year. The most fun she'd had with him had been taking him away from the boring Beth Castle just weeks before they were to marry.

Men were a way of amusing oneself, she thought cynically. After the way her father had treated her mam, how could she think otherwise? Right now, all she wanted was a man to partner her at the local dances, but with so many young men called into the forces, it was proving rather difficult.

She was certain that Freddy would not remain faithful; she had no illusions about that, so when a man working in a reserved occupation invited her to the Saturday dance, she accepted with delight. Having suffered an injury during his years on his father's farm, Silwyn Davies's left arm was weak but he could still dance.

He took her to several dances but she became bored with his conversation and frustrated at the monotony of his dancing as well as his juvenile attempts at kissing her after walking her home. She needed a challenge. She wanted a dance partner whose skills matched – or preferably bettered – her own.

Until she had met Freddy Clements and encouraged him to leave his fiancée Bethan Castle, she hadn't realised what fun dancing could be. She had fooled around in the living room to tunes played on the wireless and had even sung along with them, but going to a dance hall and seeing everyone enjoying themselves, something woke in her; something that had been lying dormant all her life.

When Freddy had joined the army and disappeared from her life apart from irregular weekends at home, she thought her evenings spent dancing were over. Then she talked to Joseph Beynon, a regular customer in the shop where she worked, and persuaded him to take her. When she realised he was nowhere near good enough for her, she dropped him and braved walking into the dance hall on her own to search for someone who was.

Joseph Beynon was hurt by being dropped by Shirley and his resentment grew, but he was still attracted to the vivacious, dark-haired girl who was so good on the dance floor, and who felt so good in his arms.

She easily found partners, the few men present quickly recognising her talent. Some were good and others better than good, but they were unsatisfactory, only half their mind on the dance, the other half aware of their girlfriend or wife watching them, pouting, in a corner. If only she could find someone to dance with regularly. With the war taking its toll of the local boys she thought it was a hopeless search.

3

Max Moon was an entertainer. He and his friend, Ken Ward, had both been turned down for the armed forces when war began and now, in the spring of 1941, they were occupied travelling around the country giving performances for the forces, and in hospitals and factories. When he was on a visit to St David's Well, he called in to the newsagent and tobacconist, where Shirley Downs worked, to buy a newspaper. Recognising him from a concert he and Ken Ward had given for the children in 1939 when the evacuees first came to St David's Well, she engaged him in conversation. The result was an invitation to go with him to the Saturday night dance.

'It's in aid of comforts for the soldiers,' he began to explain. 'I'm doing a song and dance spot with Ken as part of the cabaret and we're giving a record as one of the prizes.'

'Which one?' she asked, and when told it was the Glen Miller version of 'In The Mood', she gasped. 'I want to win that. I've got the Edgar Hayes recording but the Glen Miller is the one. It makes my feet start tapping just to think about it.'

'Why don't you come with us?' he invited.

'Won't you be too busy to bother with me?' she asked, but her eyes were shining at the prospect of the dance with a partner of her own.

'Ken and I won't be occupied for more than fifteen minutes, for each of our two spots. The rest of the evening is mine.'

Pity he wasn't more conventionally handsome, she thought with mild disappointment. Max was abysmally skinny and towered almost twelve inches above her for a start. Guilty at her criticism when he had been kind enough to invite her, she smiled her special smile. 'Thanks, I'd love to come.' Excited at the prospect of walking into the dance hall with Max Moon for a partner, it was as much as she could do to accept with reasonable decorum. She wanted to shout and scream, do a can-can on the counter. Having walked in to the dance on her own several times, it would be luxury to have her own partner, and to be there with one of the entertainers would make it more exciting still. All the same, it was a pity he was so tall and skinny, and with spiky red hair that looked as though it had been cut with a knife and fork!

The dance band musicians of 1939 had all gone. The young men who played had been conscripted and their replacements were men with grey hair and in some instances, less than nimble fingers. What did it matter. If Max Moon was an entertainer he must be able to dance, she thought happily.

She was abrupt with the last few customers, specially those choosing birthday cards and unable to make up their mind. She was impatient to start getting ready for her night out, her mind racing ahead, planning what she would wear, what make-up to use.

-

The cloakroom, where a spotty mirror was all that was on offer for the girls to touch up their make-up and comb their hair, was very crowded. She squeezed herself against the wall and edged around until she was near the mirror. Her hair needed a bit of adjustment. She usually wore it in a roll around her head, wrapped over a thin scarf and with a few ends pulled provocatively free around her face. Tonight, she wanted to wear it loose.

During the afternoon in the newsagent where she worked, she had covered her head with a bright scarf under which she had her hair tightly fastened in dinkie curlers. She had taken them out but not combed the shiny sausage shapes and separated them into small curls. Now she wished she had. There was hardly room to raise her arms to get a comb in her hair.

There were several people she knew but she avoided starting a conversation. She didn't want to keep Max standing while she gossiped. She was surprised to see Bethan Castle, Freddy Clement's ex-fiancée, who had never enjoyed dancing. She couldn't resist making a comment on that!

'Fancy seeing you here. You wouldn't come when your Freddy asked. Who's managed to persuade you?'

'I'm here to help with the refreshments,' Beth explained coldly. 'We all have to help with the war effort, don't we?'

'The Castle family making money out of the evening by doing the catering then, are they?'

'My mother and father are *giving* most of the food.'

'Good on them.' Shirley sniffed. 'Stuck-up lot the Castles,' she confided to a girl beside her. 'Work on the beach they do, selling buckets and spades and ice cream, and run a common little beach café, no better than peddlers they are and think they own the whole of St David's Well!'

'Terrible snobs some people,' the girl agreed, knowing nothing about the subject and concentrating on a smooth lip line.

After struggling for an age, in a forest of arms and an armoury of combs and brushes, Shirley went into one of the lavatory cubicles and using her small handbag mirror finished styling her long brown hair. She came out with heavier make-up than usual, and with her hair long and sleek over her head before falling in small curls around her shoulders. She left the cloakroom feeling as though she had fought a battle but when she saw Max's surprised and flattering expression she was well rewarded.

'Shirley Downs, you look a picture,' he said admiringly.

At first they danced in a rather subdued manner, Max still looking at her as though he hadn't seen her before.

'What's the matter, Max? Is there something wrong with my face?' she asked pertly.

'Wrong? No, there's nothing wrong with your face. In fact, I can hardly believe my luck having a lovely girl like you for a partner.'

'Come on, then, let's get dancing. I won't break in half, you know,' she said, coaxing him to move more vigorously as a quickstep began its rhythm. Soon they were moving as one, their steps becoming faster and more intricate as inhibitions fell from them. At one point, the floor cleared as more and more people stopped to watch them. For Shirley, it was like the first day of her life. Having these people standing admiring her skill opened something inside her and she smiled up at the red, perspiring face of Max Moon with his intense blue eyes and the tuft of unmanageable red hair and thought he was gorgeous. She laughed in pure excitement and happiness. The admiration of an audience, even as small as at this Saturday dance, was a hunger gloriously appeased.

Watching from the people crowding the edges of the hall, people who had stopped dancing to admire the skill of Shirley and Max, Joseph Beynon was full of resentment. He had partnered Shirley several times and although he knew he was not good enough for her, he had begun to think that their partnership was more or less permanent. Then she had discarded him. Now she was here with Max Moon. What would happen when Max left St David's Well? Would she ask him again? His thin lips tightened and a frown creased his forehead. He was determined not to be used when Shirley needed a partner and then discarded when someone better turned up. Yet he knew that his resolution would falter as soon as she asked him to take her dancing. There was something very special about Shirley Downs.

Beth Castle watched with the rest as Shirley and Max showed off their skill. Max was too tall for Shirley but his natural ability and her instinctive understanding of what he needed made them glide through the numbers as though they had practised together for years. If she felt a tinge of jealousy towards the girl who had stolen her fiancée and was now taking one of her friends, Beth forced herself to ignore it. Losing Freddy Clements to Shirley Downs had not been a tragedy. In fact by flirting with him and causing their engagement to end, Shirley had given Beth back her freedom and enabled her to find a far happier future with Peter Gregory. But she couldn't feel grateful. Taking Freddy from her had been deliberate and unkind. Shirley had started an affair with her fiancé Freddy Clements, when she knew his marriage to her was only weeks away. She clapped their performance with the rest and managed a smile. Dancing was something she had never enjoyed, but she recognised the talent of Shirley and appreciated the competence of her partnership with Max Moon. Freddy had loved dancing and his second love had been the pictures, both of which she found boring. By refusing to go with him, she had enabled Shirley Downs to coax him away from her. Shirley had filled his need to enjoy those things and she had been left behind.

Beth Castle was one of the well-known local family who ran stalls and cafés during the summer on the popular holiday beach of St David's Well Bay. Today, the Castles' catering skills were being used to provide a buffet supper for the dancers. Leaving the dancers to enjoy the final melody before the interval, she slipped through the crowd and joined her mother and her Auntie Audrey in the kitchen.

Max poked his head around the door a few moments later. 'Sorry I haven't said hello, Beth. I'm afraid I became too involved with the music. Shirley Downs is an amazing dancer, isn't she?'

'Very talented,' Beth agreed. 'Are you looking for an early helping of supper? There are some sandwiches on the table if you can get past the waitresses.'

'I won't say no,' he said, giving his cheeky grin. She handed him two plates and promised to come and find him later when she wasn't so busy. She watched him go, much taller than most, his sparse red hair sticking up untidily on his head. What was it that makes a man attractive, she wondered. Max Moon made friends wherever he went, and yet not even a doting mother could describe him as handsome. Somehow his kindness and honesty shone through. Again a small stab of envy, explained not by any attraction Max held for her, but by the fact that she considered Shirley Downs undeserving of him.

It was no surprise when Max and Shirley were declared the winners of the dance competition and Shirley's face glowed as the result was announced. The smile faded quickly when Max refused to accept the prize on behalf of himself and Shirley.

'I am delighted to be chosen,' he said, an arm around Shirley. 'We can't accept of course. I'm a professional besides being one of the organisers. Perhaps you could use the prize in a spot dance?'

As the other dancers clapped his decision, Shirley felt an aching anger around her heart. She wanted that record. And being a winner in a dance competition was something she dreamed about, and Max Moon had ruined it. 'How stupid can you get,' she muttered as he led her on to the floor for the spot dance.

'Sorry, Shirley, I didn't think you'd mind too much. It's only a local affair.'

'It might not have been important to you, but it was to me! I'd have been able to say I'd won a dance competition, wouldn't I? The very first time. Can't you see how disappointed I am?'

The dance with its roving light was a waltz and as they demonstrated their skill she deliberately tripped him up and they had to sit out the rest of the piece.

'What did you do that for?' Max demanded.

'Couldn't have us winning the spot prize as well, could I!' she snapped.

—

In London, an ex-citizen of St David's Well stood in Coventry Street and looked at the huge crater where the Rialto cinema had once stood. Eirlys Price, another victim of a broken engagement, had left home to work in London after her engagement to Beth's cousin, Johnny Castle, had ended. She was staying with the family of Ken Ward, Max Moon's partner in the double act they performed around the country. While Max was visiting St David's Well, she and Ken were spending the weekend together exploring London. Horrified by the damage, they were staring at the ruin, in the basement of which the Café de Paris had been situated, previously advertised as the safest night-spot in London. The bomb that hit the building the previous month had killed many members of the orchestra, including its leader, Ken 'Snakehips' Johnson. It seemed impossible that the area could ever be restored to its previous state.

After discussing the loss of several of the country's talented and popular musicians, he told her, 'I want to make entertainment my career once the war is over. Max and I accept any invitation to perform, and we get plenty of bookings but if were to be professionals after the war, we'll need a slick new act. We both sing, tell the odd joke and play instruments, which is fine for the present, but after the war I don't think sing-songs and old jokes will be enough.'

'There will always be need for laughter,' Eirlys said. 'A comedy act will bring you plenty of bookings, now and after the war.'

'A comedy act, ending with a song. Yes, I think there will always be a place for that, but many will have the same idea. I have to think of something different, unique, something that's strictly Max Moon and Ken Ward, which no one else can do.'

'What about the female impersonation Max does? It's funny because there's no doubt he's a man,' Eirlys suggested.

'Clever of you to realise there are two types, the "beautiful woman" act to deceive, and the Old Mother Riley style of Arthur Lucan, with Kitty McShane as his or her daughter who doesn't set out to fool anyone.'

'I had a letter from Johnny and Hannah last week and Johnny told me that the entertainment the army offered usually consisted of all men. Female impersonators are a necessity and some are *very* convincing.'

Ken smiled at her and pulled her arm through his. 'So Johnny Castle still writes to you, Eirlys?'

'He and Hannah are my friends.'

'And you can cope with that, after you and Johnny almost made it to the altar?'

'No regrets, Ken. I don't think I'd have made Johnny as happy as Hannah does. And somehow, I wasn't as devastated as I should have been. I think it was best for both of us. Probably because I'm an only child without cousins, I was in love with the idea of belonging to the large Castle family. To belong, and to work on the beach watching families come and enjoy themselves, it seemed so wonderful. Long summers filled with perfect days spread out before me. But as I said, it was just a dream.'

They walked back along the streets with the shells of buildings looming threateningly above them, the smell of damp brick and stale air creating that inexplicable smell of old, abandoned and ruined properties filling their nostrils, and caught the underground train back home.

Eirlys Price was aware of Ken's growing affection for her but she was not certain how she felt about him. Being so close to marrying Johnny Castle, becoming a member of that large family, then ending it when he admitted his love for Hannah, had left her wary of love and afraid to trust. Love needed time to grow, and although it was a year ago, it was still far too early for her to think of someone taking Johnny's place.

'Will you write back?' Ken asked, breaking into her thoughts.

'I might, but only a brief note to them both, to tell them how happy I am here, with you and your family.' she said, smiling. Ken nodded; to know she was happy was enough for now. He could wait for the rest.

It had been Eirlys's ambition to open a shop and sell rugs and other handmade items. Leaving St David's Well so suddenly had put a stop to that although, in Johnny and Hannah's letter, they had assured her that her store of wool and other materials, left behind after her hasty departure, was still there if she needed it. She lived in a room in the Wards' busy household and worked in an office dealing with the distribution of foodstuffs. Occasional deliveries of rarer items such as oranges arrived and had to be allocated via ration books, distribution worked out on the various priorities. The under-fives and expectant mothers with green ration books were usually the recipients of such items which, although rare enough, were unlikely to appear for much longer.

Fruit was limited to that grown locally and once the season ended it was less and less likely the public would receive more. Eirlys was at the receiving end of many irate phone calls during which she reminded the caller that seamen had to risk torpedoes and bombs besides the usual dangers of the sea to bring them luxuries like fruit. Sometimes she was shaking when she put down the phone. Didn't they realise how much was being risked to bring food across the sea?

She felt tearful at times and knew it was because she was not happy, in spite of what she told Ken. London was a fascinating place and she knew she would never grow tired of exploring on her own or with Ken when he was free, or with one of his sisters. But deep inside she was homesick for the small seaside town in South Wales.

It was probably the manner of her leaving. The sudden end to her engagement to Johnny and the death of her mother had made it a frenzied decision, taken without proper thought. The unexpected return of the three evacuees who had been taken back to London by their mother, had added to her distress. Teresa Love had been present when Eirlys's mother had been killed and she had brought the boys back to St David's Well, purporting to comfort Eirlys's father, Morgan, and herself. Morgan had been delighted to see them. Stanley, Harold and little Percival filled his life and helped ease the pain of his wife's death. Teresa was a consoling friend. She told everyone she was there only for a brief visit but she had quickly settled in with every intention of staying.

Finding her father in bed with the boys' mother so soon after her mother's funeral had meant Eirlys had felt unable to return home and the longer she delayed a return visit, the harder it was to contemplate walking into the house that had once been her home. She knew that her present confusion was because she hadn't stayed and sorted everything out in her mind before moving on. Perhaps a visit home would help to settle her emotionally and allow her to make a fresh start.

'I think I might go home when I can get a Saturday morning off,' she told Ken as they waited for the train. 'I've left it too long to face Teresa Love and my father.'

'Good idea. You'll feel better for seeing your father, and the evacuees. You miss them, don't you?' He looked at her quizzically and added, 'Good for you to see Johnny too, see how you feel about him.'

'I know how I feel about him! I thought I loved him and now I know it was nothing more than a loving friendship. I hope I'll always be his loving friend. Hannah's too.'

'It's Easter very soon. The eleventh of April is good Friday. Why don't you go then?'

'Not yet. Perhaps in a month or two.'

'Go, Eirlys. When you've seen your father and Teresa and the three boys you'll come back more relaxed about your father's new family. Think of Stanley, Harold and Percival, the three musketeers. You'll be happy seeing them so settled and reunited with their mother.'

'Dadda is living with her. Teresa has taken Mam's place and it was only weeks after Mam died that she moved in. How can I face him and pretend I'm pleased?'

'Blame the war. Everyone seems to be grabbing what happiness they can in case it all ends tomorrow.'

'That's too simple an answer.'

'You father can't cope alone. Most of us need someone, the other half of the coin; we aren't complete in ourselves. With your mother gone and you leaving straight afterwards, well, not many would blame him,' he said softly.

'All right. Ken. I'll go.'

–

Shirley Downs was the first to see Eirlys when she walked out of the station late on Thursday evening two weeks later. Shirley had been delivering some monthly magazines that she considered too heavy for the young paper boy to carry. Eirlys tried to avoid her. The reminder that Shirley had been the cause of her friend Beth Castle and Freddy Clements ending their engagement, overlaid any truth that it had been a good thing. She blamed her. She had to blame someone in support of Beth.

Putting down the last of the magazines in a porch doorway, Shirley ran to to join her. Eirlys forced her stiff expression into a casual smile.

'Hi yer! Come back to open your shop, have you?' Shirley teased, taking the small suitcase from her and walking along beside her.

'No chance of that,' Eirlys replied. 'I chose the wrong time to start something new, with the war and everything.'

'Plenty of empty shops, mind.' Shirley said. 'What with everything getting scarce, leaving some of them with nothing to sell, and women earning more money in the munitions than they'd ever earn in a shop, no one wants them.'

'I'm only on a visit,' Eirlys explained. 'I managed to get this afternoon off and leave early, so I went straight to Paddington and got the two o'clock train.'

'I see your father's lodger is still there,' Shirley said knowingly. 'Teresa Love and her three boys have found a permanent home with your father it seems. Where will you sleep? Teresa will be using your room, won't she? At least till you go back to London!' The words were said with a chuckle. It would be common knowledge that Teresa Love had moved in soon after the death of Eirlys's mother and settled to take her place.

'My father couldn't manage on his own,' Eirlys said sadly. 'I was wrong to leave him.' She forced her thoughts away from the scandal that had caused her so much anguish and said brightly, 'Tell me, Shirley, what have you been doing since I left?'

'Dancing!' was Shirley's brief reply. 'I started going with Freddy Clements as you know, but he's in the army and not likely to be home very often, so I've dumped him and I'm searching for a partner who will be around all the time.'

'You dumped him after taking him away from Beth?'

'Took him away? Came willing he did. Beth Castle's very nice – whatever that word means – but even her best friends would admit that she isn't much fun. She wouldn't dance, wouldn't go to the pictures. Can you blame Freddy Clements for getting bored? But what's the sense in having a dance partner who's hundred of miles away? No, I've got to find someone regular if I'm to get anywhere.'

Eirlys looked shocked but said nothing more.

'I've even started dancing lessons but like everywhere else, I'm expected to partner a girl and imagine she's a tall, handsome man. My imagination isn't that good, I need the real thing! I went with Max Moon a few times. Too tall of course but strong and very nimble. We won first prize at the Saturday dance but we refused it,' she said casually. 'Left it for someone else to win, him being a professional and me being, well, better than most. Max is too tall for me, mind, but very light on his feet. Pity is, he's not here much either.'

'So you'll give him the push too?'

'Yeh. Damned war, eh?'

'Yes, damned war,' Eirlys repeated, thinking of how it had taken away everything good in her life. A loving mother, a father she had adored, marriage to Johnny Castle and it had even taken her away from this town where she had been happy.

'Max and your friend Ken Ward are off to Scotland in a few days' time,' she told Shirley. 'They have a tour booked, entertaining army bases mainly but a few hospitals and factories too.'

'Fond of Ken Ward, are you?'

'Fond, yes. He's like the brother I never had.'

'As fond as you were of Johnny Castle?' She looked towards her companion curiously, but she couldn't read anything in Eirlys's expression. Unable to resist taunting, she went on, 'There's happy there, those two, Johnny and Hannah. A marriage made in heaven if ever there was one.' She looked at Eirlys again but there was no response.

Shirley was grinning as she left her at the shop above which she lived with her mother, Hetty Downs. She knew she was unkind to tease, but Eirlys had been so sure of herself and Johnny Castle, it was only human nature to be a bit pleased when her life turned out to be not as perfect as she pretended.

'See you soon.' she called as she opened the door and ran up the linoleum-covered stairs to the flat.

Eirlys walked on and wondered whether she had made a mistake in coming home. Everyone had moved on. Johnny had forgotten their broken engagement and was happy with Hannah and her two girls in a 'marriage made in heaven', to quote Shirley Downs. Her friend Beth Castle had broken off her engagement to Freddy Clements after discovering his 'carryings on' with Shirley and was now going to marry Peter Gregory. Her father was obviously settled with Teresa Love and her sons. Everyone was frantic it seemed. Engagements that usually lasted a couple of years now seemed to last a matter of weeks. And herself? She had simply run away and taken her disappointments with her.

She slowed her footsteps as she approached Conroy Street. She felt very apprehensive, wondering how she would be received. Would Teresa treat her as a guest rather than someone who belonged there? If she did, would she be able to accept Teresa being the lady of the house? Would her father be easy or was he too anxious about this long-delayed meeting?

She stood outside 78 Conroy Street for a long time before walking up the path to the front door. Normally she would use the back entrance which was never locked but instead she raised her hand to the dull, unpolished knocker. For the first time in her life she knocked on her own front door. She knew she could and should walk in, but some sense of unease forbade it. When Teresa opened the door with Stanley, Harold and Percival crowding behind her, Eirlys pretended to be searching in her handbag for her key.

'Eirlys!' the three boys shouted. Teresa looked back and called, 'Morgan, it's your Eirlys!' She stepped back to allow the boys to swarm forward, all trying to hug Eirlys at once, shouting their greetings, trying to tell her their news. Twelve-year-old Stanley and ten-year-old Harold looked at her as though unable to believe she was there. Percival, the youngest, put an arm around her and wouldn't be separated from her, even to get through the doorway; looking up at her, his pale, solemn face was almost tearful.

Her father came then and wordlessly held her close before taking her bags, adjusting the black-out curtaining ready for lighting-up time and pushing the boys aside to allow her to enter.

'Knocking the door, is it? Since when have you needed to knock the door, Eirlys, love?' he said, his smile as great a welcome as she could have wished. 'Duw, it's wonderful good to see you back home.'

'Come on, Morgan, get the kettle on,' Teresa said brightly. 'Eirlys is gasping for a cuppa, I can see that if you can't.' Teresa, her face thickly made up and her hair an unbelievable blonde, pushed Morgan playfully towards the kitchen.

Everyone talked at once, even Percival who, at 'seven-almost-eight', as he proudly informed her, had something to say. In his solemn manner he told her he had a reading book and would read some of it to her at bedtime.

She had been away a year and although there were no birthdays to celebrate, she had brought them some gifts. As they were Londoners, driven away by the threat of bombing early in the war, she had chosen a few ornaments relevant to their previous home, tiny models of a London bus and a London taxi, and for Stanley, the oldest, a statue of Nelson on his column. Sweets were not yet rationed although some were in short supply so she had filled a bag with their favourites.

Apart from the first greeting in the hallway darkened by the black-out restrictions, she hadn't looked at her father. She was embarrassed, knowing he was sharing a bed with Teresa. A situation that would have been awkward and uncomfortable to deal with if it involved a casual acquaintance, was extremely painful with her own father. Her Dadda blatantly sleeping with another woman. It was like the worst kind of romantic fiction. How could she look at him? How would she cope with sleeping in the room next to the one he shared with this comparative stranger? Why had she come? Why had he allowed her to stay?

She found herself thinking of Ken Ward and wishing he were here to share her discomfort. He was so relaxed about everything, his presence would have eased the situation. His house was one of the few private houses to have a telephone and on impulse, as soon as they had eaten – fish and chips from the chip shop – she made an excuse and went to a phone box to talk to him.

'I shouldn't have come, Ken,' she said as soon as he answered.

'Of course you should. Whatever the situation, he is your father and you love him.'

'But she's living here as – you know – as his wife.' She felt herself redden as she explained. 'Everybody knows. Shirley Downs met me as I arrived and made sure I knew that it was common knowledge.'

'Thank goodness he found someone to look after him. When your mother died he missed her so much he wanted to replace her. If he had been unhappy with her, he wouldn't have wanted to find someone else. It's a compliment to your mother that he found someone to take her place so quickly.'

'A nice thought, Ken, but I don't think the choice was his. Teresa made the decision and moved in, nothing to do with Mam and how he missed her. Dadda was too soft to refuse!'

She returned to the house feeling worse rather than comforted.

Out of a sense of decorum or consideration for her. Teresa slept in Harold's bed and Harold shared with his younger brother. Muted whispers early the following morning told Eirlys that things had changed during the night.

She was the first to rise and she set the table for breakfast and went out for a walk. The April morning was misty and birds were busy flying here and there searching for food for their mates and early broods. The hedges were smothered with the wonderful blossoms of blackthorn, the sloeberry bushes. Flowers before the leaves made it a welcome sight as though the branches were too impatient to wait to display their springtime excesses.

She met Shirley Downs again as she wandered slowly home, giving her father and Teresa time to get up, disguise their sleeping arrangements and start their day.

'Hi yer!' Shirley called, moving the heavy bag on her shoulder to a more comfortable position. 'Don't tell me you slept in the fields! That's taking embarrassment too far!'

'I woke early and the morning was too good to waste.' Eirlys smiled. 'Want a hand with the papers?'

'The paper boy let me down again,' Shirley moaned.

'Why not ask Stanley, he's keen to earn money unless he's changed in the time I've been away.'

'Thanks. I'll call and ask him. Have you thought any more about a business of your own?' Shirley asked as they took it in turns to push the newspapers through letter boxes.

'I've got a job in London and I think I'll stay there for a while longer. Ken's parents are very kind.'

'And Ken, is he the reason you'll stay?'

'You ask a lot of questions, Shirley.'

'You don't have many answers,' Shirley said with a shrug. 'Don't stay with Ken for fear you won't find anyone better.' Then as they parted, she added, 'Too many make that mistake. You almost did with Johnny, remember!'

Smarting under the girl's forthright impertinence, Eirlys hurried home. Shirley was too outspoken to ever be a friend, she thought angrily.

The return to St David's Well didn't achieve much and Eirlys wished she had waited a while longer. She had come back too soon. Her wounds hadn't healed. She and her father were both uneasy with each other and Teresa seemed unable to say anything apart from polite comments about the weather and a few vague remarks about the progress of the war. Then there was the ever present possibility of bumping into Johnny Castle and Hannah. She wasn't sure how she would feel about seeing them together.

She was happiest when she was out with the three boys. The weather was dull but she took them to one of the quieter beaches where, to her dismay, barbed wire and concrete fortifications prevented any serious exploring. As she explained the reason for their disappointment, they wandered back to the sandy St David's Well Bay where preparations were well under way for the summer opening.

Pitches were marked out on the sands, and heavy metal bases were in place on a few sites. These would be covered by canvas-topped stalls selling all the needs of holiday-makers once the summer officially began.

On the promenade, where sand drifted on the ground and people were busy finishing the painting of the shop and café fronts, shops selling inexpensive gifts and seaside rock were already displaying an assortment of novelties ready for business, although the word ice cream had been painted out as that commodity was a victim of the war, no longer allowed to be made. There would be other things to sell to fill in the gaps left by goods no longer available. St David's Well Bay was ready for a summer of fun, whatever shortages they suffered.

Above the beach alongside the cliff path a flag was flying above the café once called Piper's, now bearing the name Castle's; a name that was once to have been hers, until Johnny realised his happiness lay not with her but with Hannah Wilcox and her two young daughters.

On impulse she walked up the steps leading from the beach, the boys following with shouts and a pretence of fear as they made their way up the clanking metal steps, and peered in through the window. The café was empty, although everything was ready for the visitors: china and cutlery dazzlingly clean, the shelves covered with fresh paper and the glasses and windows gleaming.

She didn't call to see Johnny and Hannah. Her disappointment at the sudden end to her plans to marry Johnny still brought her pain. Although she knew that they would never have been completely content, and knew he loved Hannah as he'd never loved her, she wasn't ready to see them together and be reminded of their happiness. She did see Johnny's father, Bleddyn Castle, when she took the three musketeers, as the evacuees liked to be called, for a fish and chip supper at the Castles' fish café in the town.

Bleddyn didn't try to disguise his delight at seeing her. He found them a table at the back of the café and whenever he could spare a moment from serving and cooking, he joined them to hear their news.

The boys, Stanley, Harold and Percival, were still very enthusiastic about their return to the town and considered themselves to be locals. They talked about London but showed no regret at leaving or any desire to go back. Eirlys, who had seen the sad little room where they had lived with their mother, understood why they didn't want to return.

Bleddyn repeated Johnny's reminder that the wool and material she had collected to start her rug-making was still stored in his back bedroom, ready for when she returned.

'I can't see you staying in London for much longer, Eirlys,' he said. 'Take a little while longer to get over the mess of yours and our Johnny's engagement and then come home.

You won't be my daughter-in-law, but I'm still fond of you and I miss you, like a lot of other people do.'

'Not easy to retrace your steps, Mr Castle,' she said sadly.

'Then the sooner you do it the better, young lady!'

Joseph needed to get out, and trying to forget Shirley's previous attitude he went to the newsagent and invited Shirley to go with him to the Saturday dance. He coped with his miserable life well enough most of the time but occasionally the dreary monotony of each day made him need to escape, to be among people and pretend to share the laughter and camaraderie.

She accepted, knowing that Max Moon and Ken Ward were away. Better to have someone to walk in with than arrive alone.

'I won't promise to dance every dance with you, mind.' she warned.

He agreed. It was something he would have to face, for the present.

When she danced three times in a row with a small, energetic soldier, who seemed to be making love to her in the way he held her and stared into her eyes, he couldn't stand it. 'Come on, it's after eleven,' he said, taking her arm and guiding her towards the cloakroom. 'You have to be up at six, and I've had enough even if you haven't. If you don't come with me now you'll have to find your own way home.'

To his surprise and relief, she agreed. They walked home through the dark streets and he kissed her lightly on her warm cheek as she unlocked her door.

'Watch it! No taking liberties,' she warned, and he smiled as he walked away.

On Eirlys's last day she walked with the boys to see Bernard Gregory, who worked a smallholding and ran the donkeys on the beach during the summer. Bernard's son Peter was soon to marry Beth Castle – another hasty engagement following the break-up of wedding plans to another.

'Peter can't ever be sure when he'll get leave so when he and Beth marry it'll be at short notice.' Bernard Gregory told her. 'My son and Bethan hope you'll be able to get home for the celebration, even though you won't get much warning.'

Eirlys thanked him but didn't think she wanted to see her friend on her special day. That might make her seem miserable, but too much happiness was hard to bear while she felt loveless and homeless.

Although she stayed less than four days, Eirlys was relieved when it was time to leave. She stood on the station platform confused and more unhappy than when she came. She had deliberately chosen a time when her father was working and the boys were out. She didn't want them to see her off, she wanted to wallow in her misery. It was not homesickness but something far, far worse. St David's Well seemed no longer to *be* her home.

Coincidentally it was Shirley who saw her go. Working early each morning, she had a few hours off every afternoon before going back to deal with the evening papers. She was strolling past the station when she saw Eirlys standing near the wire fence.

'Come back again soon,' she called cheerfully, as the people on the platform moved closer to the edge as the train steamed to a hissing halt. 'We'll have a night out, just you and me, right?'

Eirlys waved acknowledgement, a pretence of under-standing. Pointless to shout above the noise.

-

Beth Castle picked up the letter from the doormat and at once recognised the writing. It was from Freddy. She was tempted to throw it away and for a moment held it as though about to tear it in half. Curiosity was too much to bear, however, and she slit the envelope and pulled out the small sheet of notepaper – notepaper she had given him in the hope of hearing from him when he first joined the army. How naïve she had been. The few letters she had received from him had been pleas to send him some money.

Surely he wouldn't have the cheek to make the same request now? To her surprise it was a loving note, begging her to write to him, telling her that he had been foolish to leave her for Shirley who had abandoned him. He went on to explain how important it was to have news of home.

At once she was flooded with guilt. She was so happy now she and Peter Gregory had found each other. Although it was Freddy who had messed everything up she felt she was basing her present contentment on his misery. But guilty or not, she couldn't put everything back as it had been. How could she write and pretend they could reverse everything that had happened?

Putting the note aside, she wrote Peter a loving letter telling him how much she longed for the day she would become his wife. As Mr Gregory had told Eirlys, they hadn't set a date. With Peter's unpredictable and secret work, often – she suspected – behind enemy lines, he was likely to be away for weeks and it was impossible to arrange a date and be certain of him being there.

She didn't know exactly what he did but guessed from various words he let slip that he was often out of the country, undercover and in a dangerous situation.

When he had leave they were going to marry by special licence. That sounded more romantic than the grand wedding her family had planned when she and Freddy had named the day. She had given her wedding dress away. For her marriage to Peter she wouldn't be wearing anything like the one she had chosen before. A pale blue suit with a silly frothy hat were her choice and she had chosen them alone.

Being a member of the Castle family, it had been almost impossible to persuade them to allow her to arrange everything herself, but they had. This wedding was going to be one of many war weddings: sensible, simple and sincere.

She looked at the note from Freddy and sighed. Perhaps she would reply, just to tell him about her and Peter's plans. She wrote a letter, gently reminding him that she couldn't promise to write regularly but would sometimes let him know what was happening in St David's Well. Then she put his note aside to show Peter. Peter was very easy-going and tranquil about everything and he was unlikely to be worried, but she didn't want to risk any misunderstandings. Deep down she didn't trust Freddy not to try to cause trouble.

When the letter box rattled again, she went to investigate and found another letter, obviously pushed through the wrong door and delivered by a neighbour. This one was from Peter, and in her usual excited way she ran up to her bedroom to read it where there wouldn't be any interruptions.

The letter was not his usual interesting one telling her amusing stories and reassuring her about his health and safety by means of a code they had devised; it told her not to plan on getting married until at least August. He was going away and it seemed unlikely she would see him for four long months.

–

Shirley Downs saw Beth later that day when both girls were searching the market for vegetables other than carrots and leeks.

'I'd love a helping of spring greens, wouldn't you?' Shirley said, ignoring the fact that Beth did not appear to want to talk to her. She was not a person to be put off by frosty glares or past anger. 'I've heard there's some coming next week. About time too, eh?'

'Yes. Very nice,' Beth said. How could she be expected to chat in such a friendly manner to Shirley, the girl who had carried on with Freddy while she and Freddy were engaged?

'I expect you get plenty from Peter's father, eh? Him with a smallholding an' all.'

'Mr Gregory is very kind, yes,' Beth said. 'Now, I have to go, I'm in a hurry.'

'Oh yes, you help at the fish-and-chip café tonight, don't you?'

'You're very well informed. Perhaps you'd write to Freddy Clements and let him know what's going on!'

'No time these days. I go dancing two nights, then there's the pictures and dance class and besides, Freddy will come to see me when he gets leave. Better than a letter, eh? The real thing?'

Shirley smiled and pulled a face at Beth's retreating back. She had no idea when Freddy would be home, and wasn't interested to learn, but some devil inside her couldn't resist teasing the po-faced Beth Castle. No, this weekend, she had arranged to meet Max Moon and enter a dance competition. More fun that anything Beth had planned, she was certain of that.

Walking around the various stalls, seeing the variety of goods offered, the two girls bumped into each other again, this time near the back entrance where Beth's brother Ronnie and his wife Olive had a greengrocery stall.

Ronnie was Beth's oldest brother. He had served in the forces but had been invalided out. He and Olive now ran the stall and were content. Ronnie had loved working on the sands with the rest of the Castle family but Olive had not been happy. Now with their own business, small though it was, they were content and waiting for Olive's first child to be born in early July.

'Hi yer, Ronnie and Olive,' Shirley said in her confident manner. She never seemed to worry that people wouldn't be pleased to see her. Old quarrels were best forgotten, was her attitude. 'How's the baby coming on? You're looking well and truly plump now, isn't she, Ronnie?'

'You've got a nerve, coming here after what you did to our Beth,' Ronnie growled. Olive put a hand on his arm and shook her head to stop him.

'What I did to your Beth was do her a favour and she well knows it.' snapped Shirley. 'Best for her, finding out what a useless husband that Freddy Clements would have made – if she hadn't already guessed but was too cowardly to admit!'

'Careful what you're saying,' Ronnie threatened, but Beth smiled and said, 'She's right. Ronnie. We all know she saved me from a terrible mistake.'

At that moment a young woman appeared carrying a tray on which there were two steaming cups of tea.

Shirley turned away from Ronnie's glowering face and asked brightly. 'Is one of those for me then?'

'Plenty in the café, it's only a couple of yards away,' the young woman smiled, placing the tray down beside Olive.

Shirley took Beth's arm, waved a cheerful cheerio to Ronnie and Olive and guided Beth towards the market café. There were few customers and in her usual confident manner, Shirley began talking to the owner, Janet Copp. They soon discovered a mutual interest in dancing.

'I've never had lessons,' Janet told her, 'never been able to afford them, but I love both dancing and singing. In fact, my dream was to earn my living at it. Fat chance of that, eh? There's daft it sounds, me serving tea and sandwiches in a market café, wrapped in my pink and white pinny.' She held up the edges of her apron and sighed.

In moments Shirley had arranged to go with her to the next dance. Better than walking in alone and Max was in Scotland. Joseph Beynon had invited her but she had refused. Better to take a chance on finding a partner rather than being stuck with him and his two left feet all evening.

'It's dancing bust to bust, mind,' she laughingly told Janet. 'There are never enough men there, so it's girl partnering girl most of the time. Still, we could perhaps do a sort of demonstration act, just for fun of course. What d'you say?'

'I don't think I'm good enough for anything like that.' Janet frowned.

'How d'you know, eh? How d'you know before we've even tried?'

Two

Janet and Shirley went to the dance and Shirley was surprised and somehow disappointed to discover that Janet was a talented dancer. She was relaxed and moved easily with the music, keeping time and inventive in her movements. Like Shirley, she soon had a group of admirers watching her and enjoying her performance on the floor. Shirley had expected to show her how, be kind to her and have Janet feeling grateful for her kindness, but in fact, Janet taught her a few moves and this was not easy for Shirley to cope with. Since she began dancing and singing, she had been the centre of an admiring group and she was loath to share that with her friend.

When a song she knew was played during the interval. Shirley began to sing and again she was surprised and none too pleased when Janet joined in, her voice strong and true. Competition was good for her. To win was important and competing with others was a part of that, but it had been so unexpected to find rivalry coming from Janet. Then, as she began singing 'Carolina Moon'. Janet began to harmonise and their voices soared as everyone fell silent to listen. She knew in that moment that rather than harm her burgeoning ambition, Janet might be an asset.

Joseph Beynon watched from a dark corner, envious of those close to Shirley, hating her talent without which he might stand a chance of getting close to her.

A glance at the wall clock made him sigh. It was time to leave. Like a schoolboy, he had to get home before the end as it was time for his mother to throw the bolts on the doors and go up to bed. Since the war began, his mother had been convinced that doors had to be bolted securely for fear of German soldiers landing on St David's Well Bay and walking in, choosing their house above all others.

–

Eirlys Price had lived in London for the past year and, until her recent weekend stay, she had not been home since she had walked away from the sight of her father in bed with Teresa Love soon after her mother's funeral. Now she wished she had waited even longer. An only child, used to being the centre of her parents' lives, she had been reduced to being a visitor who put everyone on edge. Words had been considered before they were spoken, there was hesitation whenever their activities were discussed in case she was hurt or offended. Even Stanley, Harold and Percival seemed to treat her like a stranger after their first ebullient welcome.

It wasn't only her father; all her friends had moved on. Like a pebble thrown into the water, the ripples widened then ceased and left no sign of the disturbance. She had no place in St David's Well any more.

Sitting in a café during her lunch hour, she settled down to write letters wondering whether she ought to address one to her father and Teresa, instead of her usual ploy of writing to the boys and letting them tell her father her news. She thought about it, decided she couldn't and wrote to the three boys as usual. She was unable to talk to her father with the previous ease, not even through letters to the boys. Much was left unsaid.

The letter to her father via the boys wasn't the only one she had to write. Although it was difficult with the amount of travelling he did, she kept in touch with Ken, hoping some of the places where he and Max Moon performed would keep mail for him. She had the occasional postcard telling her his news and was glad of the friendship they shared.

They had once been more than friends and she knew that if she gave him any encouragement, Ken would return to their former love. Staying with his family created a kind of closeness she couldn't avoid. Hearing his mother talk about his childhood, and his sisters relating amusing stories about his growing up, brought about an expectation of love and happy ever after that she tried to avoid.

There were moments when she felt tempted to let it happen, but unlike many girls, she knew that marriage to someone compatible and loving was not enough. She wanted to feel a strong bond that nothing would break and so far, both with Ken and Johnny Castle, that was something she had not experienced.

Restlessly she returned to the office for the afternoon and as she left the sunny streets with their sandbagged entrances and the taped-up glass windows, and the distant bomb damage that left a miasma of decay on the air, she felt an aching loneliness like she'd never before experienced. Since her mother's death and the arrival of Teresa Love she belonged nowhere. Why had she gone home? The visit had only emphasised the gap between her father and herself. Didn't people say you can never go back? Now she understood what they meant.

Everything had changed. Her space in the small town that had been her home had been filled by the jostling of others and it was as though she had never been there.

–

The Castle family had once had at its head Granny Molly Piper. Her youngest daughter Marged and her family ran all the stalls and cafés that made up the family business of Piper's. When Moll had died, Marged's husband Huw and Huw's brother Bleddyn ran the business as they had done for many years, but with the change of name to Castle they felt more valued and in control.

Huw and Marged had four children; Ronnie, who ran the market stall with his wife, Olive, Lilly whose child was expected soon, Beth who worked in the sands and the café, and Eynon, who was in the army serving a sentence for going AWOL – absent without leave.

Huw's brother, Bleddyn, was a widower whose wife had committed suicide. His two boys, Taff and Johnny, were both serving in the army so he lived alone. The summer was a busy time for the whole Castle family and Bleddyn was grateful for having the days filled. Irene used to complain about the long hours he worked, but he was glad not to have to spend much time in the house: then as much as now, he admitted sadly. His marriage had not been a happy or fulfilling one.

Molly Piper's other daughter, Audrey, still lived in the house that had been Moll's, running the home and caring for the two girls they had rescued from poverty, Maude and Myrtle. During the summer season she also looked after the small shop on the promenade selling seaside rock and sweets, plus a few postcards and small gifts. Alice Potter helped her there and Audrey left the shop to her more and more as she found herself happily occupied at home.

At the home of Marged and Huw, in Sidney Street, Marged was awake, worrying about her daughter, Lilly. Since the girl's pregnancy had become apparent, Marged had tried to persuade Lilly to stay indoors, exercising only after dark. She knew that people criticised Lilly and the rest of the family for the baby she carried, with no husband in evidence. Marged knew also that several people had shouted names at her daughter in the street.

Lilly seemed either unaware or she simply did not care. She didn't attempt to hide her condition and walked brazenly around in a way that made Marged and Huw embarrassed and ashamed.

It was only three thirty a.m. After drinking a cup of tea, Marged went back upstairs hoping not to disturb Huw and slid back into bed. Huw didn't stir but Lilly was woken and she lay there for a while, then decided she would like a cup of tea. In the ninth month of her pregnancy she was using her condition to persuade the rest of her family to spoil her. 'Mam? Mamma?' she called weakly, knowing that Marged would come running the moment she heard her.

Marged leaped out of bed, bleary-eyed and confused with newly found sleep, convinced that this was it, the baby was on the way. The fact that Lilly had broken into her sleep for at least the last fourteen nights didn't stop her believing that this was the day.

'What is it, love, getting pains, are you?'

'I don't feel well and I'm terrible thirsty, Mam,' Lilly moaned.

After allowing her mother to persuade her that she needed a cup of tea Lilly said weakly that she would try to drink it and maybe have a biscuit or two. She listened as Marged went downstairs and filled the kettle.

Marged felt exhausted. After putting the kettle on to boil, she opened the kitchen door and pulling the heavy black-out curtain behind her, leaned against it allowing the morning air to wake her. Three times that night she had heard Lilly call her and every time Lilly needed nothing more than reassurance, afraid, dreading the pain to come. Compassion vied with irritation as the kettle began to sing. Surely Lilly didn't need twenty-four-hour care? Babies were born all the time and carried with far less fuss than this one, she thought, as she stifled a yawn. How much longer would this baby keep them waiting? Lilly had been vague about its conception and her dates were unsure. Surely they didn't face another month of this?

It was five a.m. In two hours she would be leaving to prepare the café for opening. Huw would be on the beach with Bleddyn unwrapping the stalls and setting up the rides. She would be on her feet all day in the café. Her sister Audrey would stay with Lilly and neighbours would look in to make sure all was well, but her daughter would be on her mind and she knew it would be difficult to concentrate on giving her customers cheerful service. Another hour's sleep would have been nice. Now it was not worth going back to bed.

After taking Lilly her cup of tea and a couple of biscuits, she took out the makings of a cake. No point in wasting time if she couldn't use it for sleep. Chocolate cake that contained no chocolate, a sponge cake using no fat. Nothing was real any more. Everything was 'making do'. Substituting one thing for another, ingenuity was an essential requirement for cooks. Food rationing had made cooking a challenge to produce good food from poor ingredients. Thank goodness she had the grinder to make icing sugar from granulated. She sprinkled a little over the cakes when they were cooling to add interest to a product of which she would normally have been ashamed.

She heard someone walking across the landing and presumed it was Huw. She put the kettle on again. Time to get things moving. Then a scream rent the air and she went up the stairs two at a time and bumped into Huw on the landing.

It was Lilly and this time she was not pretending. Sending Huw for the midwife and the nurse, she comforted Lilly as she took her back to bed.

The cries and occasional screams went on for several hours. Huw had absented himself promptly and willingly to do what he could to keep things going at the café. Shirley's mother, Hetty Downs, had been sent for and she helped organise the café for a few hours, while below, on the sands, men, women and a few children struggled with stiff and unwieldy tarpaulin as they uncovered the stalls and decorated them with sunshades and sunhats, windmills and beach balls, buckets and spades, water wings and flags, and other essentials for a day on the sand.

Huw's brother Bleddyn was there and, as usual, doing the work of two, both uncovering and setting up the stalls and rides, and coping with them during the busy day. He was manning from the roundabout to the helter-skelter to the swingboats, coping with change, collecting money when it mounted up, while at the same time making a note of items to re-order – when they could get them.

Twelve-year-old Stanley Love, one of the evacuees who lived with Eirlys's father, was there, earning a little pocket money before school began. Other children too were occupied with the activities, taking the place of the men who had been called up to fight. Some insisted that the school was closed that day and they could stay. Huw was so desperate to find people to help he pretended to believe them.

With Hetty Downs and young Alice Potter who had been borrowed from the sweet and seaside rock shop on the prom, the café coped without too many disasters. Maude and her sister Myrtle, who had been found living rough and who had been rescued by Beth and her mother, were in charge of a stall as well as the swingboats, supported by Bleddyn when necessary. The Castle family survived another day, but how much longer they could continue, Huw was not certain.

The café was extra busy and, without Marged's guiding hands, throughout the day many jobs had been neglected. When Huw went home, exhausted, at eight thirty, having helped Beth to clear up and leave the café as orderly as they could, the house in Sidney Street was quiet. He didn't investigate; he flopped into a chair and his eyes closed of their own volition.

He thought he must have dozed off because when he next opened his eyes he could hear voices. Pulling his sluggish, sleep-heavy body from the chair he went to the bottom of the stairs. He didn't want to go up until he was sure of what he would find.

'Marged?' he called. 'Lilly? You all right, love?'

'She's as right as rain, Mr Castle,' a strange voice replied. The nurse he supposed. 'I'm Mrs Denver, Phil's mother.'

'Him that called himself Phil Martin and got my daughter in the family way?' Huw bounded up the stairs prepared to shout and rage but when he saw the pink gentle face of Mrs Denver he fell silent. She seemed unperturbed by his anger and he felt the outrage leave him. 'Where's your mam?' he asked Lilly, looking at her for the first time. It was only then that he saw the bundle in Lilly's arms and became aware of her smiling face.

'You've got a granddaughter, Dad. Isn't she beautiful?'

Huw's reaction, quite unexpected and unselfconscious, was to cry, 'Lovely girl you are, our Lilly, beautiful she is, just like you. Oh, Lilly, what a wonderful little girl you've got. What's her name? Where will she sleep? Do you want me to get anything for her? I'll go and fetch your mam, is it? And Ronnie and Olive, and your Uncle Bleddyn will want to know and—'

'Dad, she's called Phyllis Vera Castle. Do you like it? Phyllis is for her father, Philip.'

Clumsily, Huw leaned over and kissed his daughter, then nervously kissed the child. 'Perfect she is. Lilly. Just perfect.' He took a few deep breaths to recover and then said, 'I'll go and find your mam and send one of the neighbours to tell your Uncle Bleddyn.' He turned to Mrs Denver as though just realising she was there. 'What are you doing here?'

'I'm Phil's mother,' Mrs Denver replied. 'I'm the little mite's grandmother.'

'The grandmother. Oh.' Still frowning as though unclear about her presence in his house. Huw went downstairs. Nor knowing what else to do, he put the kettle on and spooned tea leaves into the teapot.

News of the birth spread in the magical way of small communities and by late evening a troop of neighbours and friends had called to congratulate the family, although with some, aware of the absence of a father, their comments were muted and almost sorrowful in their praise of the child.

-

In London, Eirlys heard the news from Lilly's sister Beth by letter and wondered how the lazy Lilly would cope. A letter from her father giving the same news came the following day.

Morgan wrote to his daughter every week although Eirlys had never written to him during the time she had lived in London with the Ward family. This time he had felt certain of a reply. Both the news of Lilly's baby and his own announcement would surely persuade her to address a letter to him and not send news via the boys?

Taking both letters, Eirlys wrote a brief congratulatory reply to Beth regarding Lilly's baby, addressing her friend as Auntie Bethan, and sat looking at her father's letter for a long time. He asked her what she thought about him marrying Teresa and adopting the three boys. Her first instinct, strong and protective, was to tell him 'no'. A part of that immediate response was because she missed her mother but there was also the cold certainty that, at the end of it, her father would suffer more.

She didn't trust Teresa, and was convinced by past events that one day soon her father would have to face disappointment. Marriage would only complicate things, it would not change the likely outcome.

Now she had visited and found the situation at home a firm if irregular arrangement, she knew she had to make a decision. She had a choice between the truth and what her father wanted to hear. She could tell her father exactly how she felt and risk upsetting him, and that reaction would probably be fuel for Teresa to convince him he wasn't loved. If she continued with her disapproval she might never return to the closeness she had once felt for her Dadda. Alternatively she could relax and accept the fact that Teresa was there as a permanent fixture; at least then there was a chance of one day things returning to normal.

Picking up her pen and opening the ink bottle again, she decided on the former. Being truthful, she ignored the fear that her letter would be read by Teresa, and told her father firmly that although she understood his need to have the Loves living there with him, marriage to Teresa would be a big mistake. She wisely gave no arguments to support her comment. Morgan knew the facts about Teresa's dishonesty and her unsavoury past better than she did.

–

Ken came home that evening and they went into the West End to the pictures. Coming home, an air raid began, and they hurried to the shelter where they stayed until the following morning. The noise of the bombing seemed a long way off, muted by the depth of the shelter, but it was frightening just the same. Like many other couples, they clung together and whispered reassurances, telling themselves that Ken's family would be all right, that the raid sounded to be coming from a different direction from their home, that the shelter was a hundred per cent safe – which no one believed – and that it would be over soon – which it wasn't.

The crumping sounds and the wilder explosions that followed continued and their words of comfort became more personal. The kisses that began as morale-boosting soon increased in fervour and Eirlys felt her head swimming with the remembered pleasures they revived. Around them everyone had fallen quiet. The lively chatter, the rude remarks about Hitler's army that always began during the wait for an air raid to be over, had long ago come to an end. Some of the children slept, and in the tube-like concrete shelter the bench seats along each wall held a series of grouped figures in various positions of sleep.

'I still love you, Eirlys,' Ken whispered. 'I know I promised not to talk about us until you were ready, but in the circumstances, with us likely to be blown to smithereens any moment, I want you to know.'

'I love you, Ken, I always will, but not enough. You deserve more than the little I can give you.'

'I'd settle for anything.'

Eirlys didn't reply. She feigned sleep to avoid continuing the conversation, but she was excitingly aware that sleeping in his arms was a far from unpleasant experience.

It was early the following morning before the all-clear sounded, and the disparate collection of people emerged from the underground shelter, their eyes filled with sleep, their movements stiff, and looked around them.

The city was hidden from view by the smoke from a hundred fires. The smell was choking and most held handkerchiefs to their faces. Shouts were heard as the rescue teams went about their business, haste in their voices and movements in the knowledge that there was so little time to find those buried in the rubble of their previous homes.

As Eirlys and Ken walked towards where they hoped to find an underground station, the scene unfolding itself in front of them looked like something from a nightmare. There was nothing they could recognise, with many buildings reduced to dust and rubble and others nothing more than framework that surely could never be rebuilt.

Craters blocked their way and the streets were unfamiliar as they tried to find their way. It was impossible to work out where the underground station was and it would almost certainly be out of action if they could find it. When they asked where they were, the warden refused to tell them. Instructions not to help anyone who might be an enemy sympathiser (or worse) seemed ridiculous but the man wouldn't be moved. Walking in what they hoped was the right direction they set off to walk home.

It was almost an hour before they worked out where they were and Eirlys was on the edge of tears seeing what had happened to the sobbing people who were searching through the debris of their homes, perhaps in the hope of finding a treasured article, until they were led away by the harassed and exhausted firemen, policemen, ARP workers, wardens, ambulance crews and others. Once clear of the worst of the devastation they saw the unbelievable sight of one of London's buses, with the conductor on the platform urging the passengers to, "Urry along inside if you please, ladies and gents, I've got breakfast waiting for me at 'ome. Tomatoes on toast, Gawd 'elp us. Tomatoes! I ask yer! Exciting, eh? Damn ol' Hitler's whiskers.' Whistling cheerfully he rang the bell and came along the aisle selling tickets and with a cheerful quip for many.

The bus deviated several times from its usual route, but as though he had done the trip in its present conditions a hundred times, the conductor put his passengers down at the spot closest to their destination, pointed the way and waved them goodbye as though they were old friends.

'Winston Churchill would be proud of him,' Ken commented with a wry grin. 'London's unquenchable spirit personified.'

The severity of the raid had frightened Eirlys and for a few days she considered returning to the safety of St David's Well. Then memories of how everything had changed returned to worry her, and reminders of the impossibility of living at home with Teresa and her father sharing a bed. She no longer belonged there. She would be an intruder in their lives. The waters had ceased their concentric rippling and her place in the life of the town had vanished. Best she faced it and forgot any hope of going home.

Yet there was still a niggling thought of the shop she had planned, the business she had started to build. Perhaps, one day, but after a year it was still too soon to contemplate.

There was also the growing affection for Ken. She couldn't deny that her feelings for him had changed. Could she walk away from him again? Could she live in close proximity to Johnny and Hannah and their marriage made in heaven? No, better to forget St David's Well with its lilting voices and its friendly holiday atmosphere and settle here, with Ken's family, and treat Dadda and his new family with polite formal friendship. She was Dadda's little girl no longer.

–

Shirley Downs was still searching for a dance partner. There was often someone who danced well but they were either with a girlfriend or a wife, or they were passing through and she would never see them again. It was frustrating. Starting so early in the mornings to get the papers out, she had a few hours off each afternoon. Instead of resting she went to the

45

market café to see Janet Copp and pleaded with her to go with her. She had long since changed her mind about the competition Janet threatened; Janet offered a second route to stardom and stardom was on Shirley's mind.

'Hi yer,' she called cheerfully as she approached the busy market café. 'Come to ask you to come to the Saturday dance I have. You'll love it, the dance band isn't bad and there's always a crowd. We can do a number or two and have a bit of a laugh. What d'you think? You've got quite a nice voice,' she added kindly.

'I don't know.' Janet hesitated. She lacked the ambition that was more and more apparent in Shirley. Singing and dancing were fun, but not important.

'Why don't we ask Ronnie and Olive Castle to come too?' Shirley suggested enthusiastically, nodding towards the fruit and vegetable stall. 'It's always more fun going in a crowd.'

'Fat chance of that,' Janet laughed. 'Ronnie's got a bad leg. Invalided out of the army, remember? And Olive is too shy and besides, she's expecting!' She tilted her head on one side, considering. 'All right, you've talked me into it, Shirley. I'll come. Not this week mind. I'm going to the pictures with a friend.'

'Oh no! Can't you bring your friend with you?'

'Sorry,' Janet said as she poured tea from the large cream enamel teapot.

Shirley couldn't face staying in on a Saturday night so in despair she pleaded with Joseph Beynon to take her when she saw him walking past the shop. It just wasn't the same going on her own and standing waiting, hoping for a partner.

Joseph looked doubtful at first. He knew he was not a suitable partner. Sliding around the floor using his limited knowledge of the steps and the minimum amount of movement was not what Shirley needed and her frustration made his feet even more awkward than usual. And since she had made it clear that she was using him when she had no one better, he had been determined not to take her again. Her pleading persuaded him, however, and it was a pleasant prospect to walk in with a good-looking girl like Shirley on his arm, her shining curls bouncing around her shoulders, her eyes sparkling like stars.

The dance hall was more crowded than usual and there were a large number of uniforms among the dancers. She gathered that there was a group of soldiers gathered for a training exercise and with such a choice of partners, wished she had come alone.

For a while she danced most of the numbers with Joseph but as her skills became apparent, she was in increasing demand and soon Joseph was reduced to standing in a corner just watching. He was disappointed but didn't blame her for taking the opportunity to dance with men with more ability than himself. And at least he would be the one walking her home.

Standing there not dancing, just on the periphery of the fun and laughter, was hardly exciting, but staying at home with his mother endlessly knitting and with the incessant organ music of the wireless interspersed with comedy shows and yet more music, or programmes like 'The Brains Trust', was worse.

Joseph had an easy life, with a doting mother attending to every whim. His father had been the caretaker of the council offices, a faded old man, unimportant in a household that revolved around his son. He had died quietly without fuss a few weeks before. It was what awaited him upstairs that caused his life to be such a tragedy. There seemed to be no foreseeable end to that situation.

Shirley learned a great deal that night. Besides new steps and increasing her ability to read her partner's movements and know what he wanted of her, there was the realisation that she was really attractive. She had had one or two boyfriends previously but now, being universally admired for her dancing and for herself, her confidence blossomed. She danced three times in a row with a soldier called Frank who asked to take her home. She looked into his wicked blue eyes and glanced across at the solitary, boring figure of Joseph and agreed.

They slipped out before the last waltz, while Joseph was searching for her to claim the dance which implied agreement for the man to walk the girl home.

A shy young girl stood near when he had finally given up wandering around looking for her. 'I seem to have mislaid my partner.' he said with a shrug.

'Mine has vanished too.'

'Dance together if you like, no commitment, just the dance.' He smiled and they glided into the throng.

'You dance well,' she said.

'My girl doesn't think so.'

'More fool her then.'

He thanked her formally for the dance and hurried to the cloakroom to collect his coat and wait for Shirley to appear. He waited until the last person left, the doorman had locked up, the night had closed silently around him, then he walked disconsolately home. By the time he reached his street his mood had changed. He would never be humiliated like this again. Shirley had definitely seen the last of him.

The final humiliation was finding the door bolted and having to throw stones up at the window to wake his mother to come down and let him in.

'Joseph, where have you been? After midnight it is. I thought you must be in bed,' she complained gently.

'I had to get out among people, Mam. Miserable I was. I went to the dance and stayed until the end.'

'I understand, son,' Mrs Beynon said, kissing him. 'I really understand.'

–

Shirley's escort pleased her with his obvious attraction; she liked the strength of his arm around her and the way he stopped in the darkness and kissed her before walking on holding her even closer. Then his kisses became longer, more passionate and finally alarming. The way he held her, pressing her body against his, frightened her, and as they approached her home above the newsagent, she ran from him and knocked loudly and frantically on the door before fumbling for her keys.

When she practically fell into the living room, Hetty took one look and demanded to know what had happened, as she put a comforting arm around her.

'I came home with—' She stopped, not wanting to admit that she had allowed a stranger to walk her home through the dark, empty streets. 'He was a bit, you know, amorous. I thought he was going to force me, Mam.' She began to cry and when her mother questioned her she refused to say who had upset her, knowing her mother would presume it had been Joseph. What did it matter; she wouldn't see that stuffed shirt again.

Shirley's father had left them when she was a child and it was only very recently that they had discovered his second family, who had been orphaned when he and his new wife had been killed in a road accident. Her two stepsisters, Maude and Myrtle, were being looked after by the Castle family who had found the sisters ill and undernourished and living in a semi-derelict stable. Bleddyn, Huw, Marged and Audrey were training them to help on the Castles' beach stalls, shop and cafés. For her mother it was still very difficult to look at the girls and know that her ex-husband was their father.

Hetty Downs had been shocked at the realisation that the two little girls found by Beth Castle living rough were her daughter's stepsisters, Now the shock was fading and she realised how unfair she had been to blame them for their father's treatment of herself and Shirley; she wanted to get to know them. The previous summer she had worked for the Castles in the café on the beach. Perhaps applying to work there again would be a sensible first step. After all, she had worked for them before and had helped out for a few hours recently. They knew she worked reliably and well.

With Granny Molly Piper gone, she would have to ask Marged and Huw or perhaps Bleddyn. She decided that Bleddyn might be more sympathetic and called to see him one Sunday morning when he was most likely to be home. Since the death of his wife, Irene, and with both the boys serving in the forces. Bleddyn filled his time with work and was rarely at home.

Leaving her daughter selling newspapers she walked to Brook Lane and knocked on the door. When Bleddyn answered, standing there almost filling the doorway, she forgot the opening words she had prepared, he looked so angry at the interruption.

'Sony to bother you, Mr Castle, but could I have a word?'

'Come in, Mrs Downs.' he said, standing back to allow her to enter.

'I shouldn't be worrying you on a Sunday, but I know how busy you are, and—'

He led her into the rather gloomy living room and gestured towards the chair beside the fire. 'How can I help?' His voice was quiet and there was no sign of that first irritation on his bearded face.

'You know that Maude and Myrtle Copp are my husband's children.' she began, and when he nodded she went on. 'I want to get to know them, help them perhaps, if I can. I was very unkind to them when they first appeared but their birth wasn't something they could help, was it? And, well, I want to make it up to them, just in a small way, mind. I don't want to take them from Marged and Huw.'

Bleddyn sat opposite her and asked, 'How can I help?'

'Could you find me a job for the summer in the café at the beach? I worked there last year and, well, I'd get to know them informally, without any great drama, working alongside them. We could find out whether or not we could be friends.'

'What about Shirley? She's your daughter and could be hurt if you make too much of Maude and Myrtle.'

Surprised at his thoughtfulness, she smiled. 'It was Shirley's idea. She told me she'd like to think she has stepsisters who can become friends.'

'You have to forgive your husband first,' Bleddyn insisted. 'Any bitterness would be distressing for the girls and they've had enough trouble in their short lives.'

'I've thought it through, Mr Castle, and I know I'm ready for this. After all, Paul – my husband – left us a long time ago.'

'Will you answer something before I decide?' Was there a twitch of humour in Bleddyn's dark eyes?

Her quick mind guessed what his question would be. During the previous summer she had fastened a kipper behind the drawer in the café kitchen to pay Marged and Moll back for accusing her of not cleaning properly. 'No more kippers,' she said, grinning. 'I promise.'

He laughed aloud then and offered her tea. They sat and talked for a surprisingly long time, the conversation wandering over husbands and wives, their virtues and vices, and their infidelities. They talked of their children and their fears for them during the conflict, relaxing then into favourite music and films, and radio programmes on which they both agreed that Tommy Handley's ITMA was the unbeatable best. Hetty went home in a happier mood than she could remember. When she walked into the shop, Shirley asked, 'Did you get the job?'

Hetty laughed; she and Bleddyn had talked about everything except that. 'I don't know,' she said, adding, 'and for the moment, I don't care!'

–

Bleddyn felt happier after Hetty's visit that he had for a very long time. He stood in the living room and her departure had made him see how gloomy the place was. Irene's chair was close to the fire, blocking the heat and light from the rest of the room and the curtains were almost closed, as she had preferred. He pulled back the curtains and moved the chair away from the fire, opening up the room, and he felt better still. He wished he had invited her to stay for another cup of tea and wondered vaguely what excuse he could find for inviting her to call again.

−

Since the air raid during which she and Ken had sheltered for most of the night, Eirlys had felt more strongly attracted to him. It was a revival of their past romance but caution must prevail. It had been the moment, she told herself sternly, nothing more. Yet she failed to talk herself out of the emotional excitement that had been engendered that night. She had thought herself in love with him once and the feelings she had at that time had lain dormant, ready to spring back into life. She was frightened by the intensity of her feelings for him and tried repeatedly to convince herself it had been the romantic if uncomfortable closeness of that night, wrapped in each other's arms among strangers and with danger all around. Nothing more than a romantic interlude she told herself, coupled with her loneliness, but her body told her something different.

Fortunately Ken was away for much of the time and she immersed herself in work and tried to put from her mind the memories of that night.

She liked her job, dealing mostly with the distribution of limited supplies of certain commodities. Yet she wished she were back in the council offices of St David's Well, where she had been given such responsibility. Mr Johnston and Mr Gifford had trusted her with important jobs, given her more and more responsibility, and her present position was mundane in comparison.

Everything she was given to do had rules to be precisely followed. 'A monkey could be trained to do it,' she complained to Ken in her letters. In one reply he suggested she went back home.

'It was that last air raid that made me think about it' he explained when he came home a few days later. 'You could have been killed. Why stay here in a job that bores you when you could be doing something more useful and worthwhile in a town that's safer?'

'I'll miss you and your family,' she said, hurt by the suggestion that she leave him. Hadn't their increasing closeness meant anything to him?

'Since that night in the shelter, I've realised more and more how important you are to me,' he said then. 'I want you safe, and living among your friends and family.'

She shook her head. How could she go back? Where would she live? She could never go back and live in the same house as her father and Teresa. No matter how badly she wanted to return, she had no home to go back to, not with Teresa there, and she didn't seem inclined to leave.

'No, Ken, I want to stay here with you and your family,' she said firmly, then less confidently, 'unless I'm in the way?'

'They love having you here,' he assured her quickly.

He was home for three days, which he and Max Moon spent rehearsing a new song Max had written, a weepy called 'Waiting For Yesterday', which told of a soldier's girl's memories of wonderful carefree days filled with love, to which she hoped to return.

> 'To my happiness you hold the key,
> Yesterday, oh yesterday,
> Please come, bring him back to me.'

Ken stared at her as they sang the sentimental words as though they were meant for them alone. Could they go back to their yesterdays, she wondered. The look in Ken's eyes told her they could.

–

Bleddyn called into the newsagent's shop and left a message for Hetty with her daughter Shirley.

'Tell your mother that if she wants to work in the café during the summer, there's a job for her. She'll be cooking food and serving alongside Marged and Beth.'

Hetty was pleased. Although she was past forty, she could still be called to work in one of the factories in the area and she preferred the happier atmosphere of the beach.

Hetty smiled and looked at her daughter. 'I promised him there'd be no more kippers.' She grinned.

'Mam, as you're in such a good mood, can I ask a favour?' Shirley asked.

'You want me to close up the shop this evening so you can go out?' Hetty surmised.

'Thanks, Mam. There's a dance at the RAF camp and there's a bus to take us and bring us back.'

'Who are you going with?'

'Oh, that Janet Copp, you know, the nice girl who works the market café.'

'All right. I'll come down at four, so you can get ready.'

'Thanks, Mam.' Eating the sandwich Hetty had prepared for her lunch, Shirley dashed out. Now she had to ask Janet!

Janet was surprised by the invitation and intrigued enough to accept. The bus picked up twenty girls at six o'clock and took them to where a dance was arranged to begin at seven.

Food had been prepared for later and it looked as though the evening would be a good one.

Unfortunately, the band, who had been playing at a school that afternoon, failed to turn up, having become lost in the narrow lanes in the coastal area around the camp.

All signposts had been removed in case they helped enemy invaders and no one would help for the same reason, so they went round and round the lanes in their van until they ran out of petrol and when one of them had the belated thought to make a phone call, they were unable to tell anyone where they were, so their would-be rescuers also drove around in a search that lasted for hours. It wasn't until one of the musicians had the bright idea of playing their instruments, loudly, that they were found.

While the search went on, and the dance organisers gathered together some records. Shirley approached the man who seemed to be in charge and offered to sing.

'Come on, Janet, let's start with "For Me and My Girl".'

'But I don't think I know all the words,' Janet protested. Shirley grabbed her hand and led her towards the microphone. 'Just hum,' Shirley whispered to her doubtful partner. She knew she had enough voice on her own and if Janet couldn't join in it didn't matter. Just as long as she got on that stage, nothing else mattered.

As often happens, as soon as they began to sing, with a pianist quietly trying to accompany them, the words came back and they sang in perfect harmony as though they had sung it together a hundred times. The pianist realised they didn't need him and sat with the others to enjoy the unexpected performance.

The applause was enthusiastic and they were encouraged to sing some more. Harmonising came naturally to Janet and even without the support of music they were surprisingly impressive. When records finally arrived and the dancing began, the two girls were excited at their success. Later, with the band playing and a microphone to give them more confidence, they sang again, daringly putting in a few simple dance steps between verse and chorus.

On the bus coming home they felt like entertainers rather than a couple of girls out for a few dances and a bit of flirting. Everyone praised them and told them they should be professionals. It was exhilarating, the most exciting thing they had ever done, and hard to believe when they had never rehearsed an act before.

'Janet, I want to do this again, don't you?'

'Yes. And soon.' Janet agreed. 'I think we should sign up for some singing lessons too.'

'Let's talk to Max Moon before we decide anything.' On this they agreed.

-

Writing to Eirlys was the simplest way of contacting Max and when Eirlys received their letter telling of the triumphant debut, she showed it to Ken.

'I don't think they should get too excited, Eirlys,' he said, after reading the letter a couple of times. 'We can rarely judge our own work honestly. Max and I have had quite a few hopefuls auditioning for us and you'd be amazed at how hopeless many of them are. Specially if they're pretty. An audience can be very kind to pretty girls – the hopeless ones as well as the moderately talented. Several who have sung for us have been quite unaware they are practically tone deaf.'

'But you will help them?'

'I'll see them and listen to their act when I'm next in St David's Well.'

'They said in a PS that they are prepared to come to London to see you both,' she prompted.

Ken shook his head. 'I want to let them down lightly; bringing them all this way might give them hope I can't reinforce.' He turned to her and suggested. 'Why don't you come with us next time we go down? We're performing at that same RAF camp in two weeks' time.'

And so it was arranged.

-

Shirley and Janet met whenever they could and practised three songs. Their harmonising improved and they added a short dance sequence halfway through their second number, Jerome Kern's 'All The Things You Are'. They were determined that Ken and Max were not going to be disappointed.

-

Joseph heard about the girls' success but showed no interest. He bought his newspapers from a different shop and when he walked past the place where Shirley worked he looked determinedly to the front. He was offended and wanted everyone to know this. When he was honest with himself, he knew he was fooling no one. Shirley didn't care or was even aware of his displeasure.

Instead of going out to the pictures or to a dance most evenings, he stayed home. He would leave work, eat the meal his mother had prepared for him, wash and change then go into the bedroom, where his sick wife lay, waiting for him to come to her. He would read her favourite books until she fell asleep, then tiptoe out to his own room and lie awake for hours, staring at the ceiling and wondering what he had done to deserve such a life.

Three

Lilly Castle didn't enjoy being a mother. She considered baby Phyllis a grumpy child and once everyone had admired the child and congratulated the mother, she soon grew tired of soothing and rocking and feeding and changing. She was shocked to learn that her mother expected her to wash the napkins as well as the baby clothes. She soon had that organised.

Inviting Phil's mother to visit her granddaughter at the time when she was starting on these unpleasant tasks, resulted in Mrs Denver dealing with it under the pretence of showing her how. This became a regular daily routine, something of which Marged and Huw were unaware, so they constantly told people how proud they were of the way their daughter had settled into motherhood and all its exhaustive activities.

Everyone gave her advice and she ignored it all. She found that walking Phyllis around the block in her pram encouraged her to sleep and although the constant walking was tiring for someone like Lilly who had spent much of the past months sitting around being waited on, she found it less exhausting than trying to sit down and ignore the cries.

Mrs Denver went out with her when she was able and her gentle face wore an expression of such pride and happiness. Lilly felt momentary guilt at the way she was using her to do the tasks she hated. Only momentarily: the thought of a bucket filled with napkins soon made common sense prevail!

Walking down the road towards the beach one day and following a different route, they found themselves in a neighbourhood Lilly rarely visited. To their alarm several women came out and began calling Lilly unpleasant names.

'Fancy one of the posh Castles being so brazen.'

'Stupid you are, as well as a snob.'

'Got what you deserved, didn't you, tart?'

'Stuck-up lot! How did you explain this to your gormless father, then? Thinks you found it under a gooseberry bush, does he?'

The words 'disgusting' and 'shameful' were repeated until Lilly couldn't take any more. Grabbing the pram from Mrs Denver she ran, leaving the old lady to fend for herself. She was crying when Mrs Denver caught up with her, unable to see for the huge tears in her eyes.

'How can anyone hate a baby,' she sobbed.

'Don't let them upset you, dear, some of them haven't the right to criticise a decent young girl like you. Husbands in the forces, they have, and the way they carry on, several of them will have some explaining to do when the men get home, for sure.'

They hurried home, Lilly convinced that she would never step outside the door ever again. She had been so sheltered by her loving family and spoilt into believing that everyone was the same, that it had been a shock to discover how unkind people could be. Any criticism she had previously encountered had been innuendo or sarcasm and it had not registered. Subtle insults had missed their mark completely. Lilly was so used to doing what she wanted and used to the family accepting her behaviour, whatever she did or didn't do.

'They said such awful things. As if I chose for Philip to die and leave me to look after his baby,' she sobbed. 'They were really unkind.'

'Plenty of that I've had in my time,' Mrs Denver told her. 'You get hardened to it after a while. Ran out on me, that's what my man did, and bringing up Philip on my own started the tongues wagging wherever I went. They didn't stop to gather the facts, just made up their own explanations and spread them. Get used to it, you will.'

Lilly wasn't so sure. If only she could run away. But having to work and earn enough to keep herself and her baby was impossible. She'd just stay at home, except when she went somewhere with her mam and dad. No one would be rude to Marged or Huw.

–

Joseph watched Lilly and Mrs Denver hurrying back to Sidney Street and mused on the unfairness of life. Lilly would not be the only young woman to have a fatherless child. Mrs Denver wouldn't be the only mother to lose her only son. He was stuck in a loveless, hopeless marriage that would drag on and on without a chance of a better future.

Life had been so full of hope when he was younger. He had been fortunate enough to have parents who could afford for him to have a good education and when he reluctantly left college he settled into a position as the manager of a hotel in Cardiff.

He did less and less work, delegation being his favourite word, and when the organisation fell apart due to lack of control he frantically blamed others, causing two men and a young woman to lose their jobs without a reference. Then as the truth of his laziness had become clear, he had been ignominiously sacked.

He now worked as a clerk in a food store and, apart from the hours spent at work, did little else. Mrs Beynon looked after her only son devotedly and he had only to ask for something for it to appear. Soiled shirts were discarded and miraculously reappeared washed and immaculately ironed. She even allowed him to keep his wages and offered extra money when he had the need.

It was when his father became ill and the prospect of managing without his parents when they grew old and died that made him decide to find a wife. Before that he was too lazy to think further than the next meal presented to him and the clean clothes stacked neatly in his bedroom drawers.

He had met and married Dolly after meeting her at a dance. Neither were keen on dancing and they had rarely gone after their first meeting. Their courtship was brief and Dolly had arranged to move in with Joseph and his parents. Life would have continued in the same way, his mother teaching his wife how to care for him for the foreseeable future, and for Joseph that was perfect.

Unfortunately, just before their wedding his bride had been taken ill and was now confined to bed almost permanently. Now he was faced with the prospect of caring for Dolly and his parents. Why had life treated him so unfairly, he wondered gloomily.

When she was no longer able to go out, Dolly had been very understanding. She told him she didn't mind him going out and having fun, but she made him promise not to get serious about another woman. She begged him to swear never to leave her for someone else. 'Have fun, look, but don't touch' was his interpretation of her permission to go out and about.

—

Eirlys didn't know how she felt about visiting her father and Teresa and the three boys again. She knew the reason for her father asking her to come home was to get her blessing on his marriage to Teresa, but how could she give it? On the other hand, why should she not? It was her father's life and he had to live it the way he chose; she hadn't the right to insist on his staying single. However she felt about it, he was a free man. If only it was someone other than Teresa Love.

She was comforted by the knowledge that he asked for her approval and knew she would have been more hurt if he had not, but she still couldn't tell him it was all right. Visions of her returning to the house unexpectedly so soon after the death of her mother to find him in bed with Teresa still caused pain. Until that vision faded how could she welcome Teresa as her stepmother? She simply had to stay away.

'No, Ken,' she said when he reminded her of her intention to go with him to St David's Well, 'I can't come, not this time.'

Ken left for St David's Well alone. While he was there he heard Shirley and Janet sing and he was impressed. He telephoned Eirlys and told her.

'It isn't just getting the words right and hitting the right notes,' he explained. 'There has to be real energy to make a song work and the singer has to involve the listener and touch their emotions.'

Eirlys was pleased for them. She wasn't a close friend of Shirley but it was always good to hear of success.

A week later, while Ken was still away, an emergency happened at her office and in the absence of her boss she dealt with it. She was pleased with the way she handled it and in her mind imagined how pleased Mr Johnston or Mr Gifford would have been in similar circumstances, so it was a surprise when she was called into the manager's office and reprimanded.

One of the girls had cut her hand badly and after sending someone with her to the hospital, Eirlys had asked a girl who worked mornings only, to stay for the afternoon. The work was different from that usually handled by the part-time assistant and she had sent wrong information to one of the local suppliers of office equipment.

Eirlys realised quickly what had happened and had rectified the matter in her usual efficient way but her manager had been furious.

'You take too much upon yourself, Miss Price,' he began. 'I'm afraid we'll have to move you to a different position where you can't do any more harm.'

Eirlys stared at him in utter disbelief. How could they complain when she had dealt with everything so sensibly? Again her thoughts flew to Mr Johnston who always praised the way she used her initiative.

'We were short-handed and there was work to complete so I used my initiative,' she said, using the word as Mr Johnston would have done. 'I expected you to be pleased.'

'Initiative is not for office girls, Miss Price, and please don't forget it,' the man said firmly. He handed her a piece of paper detailing her new position and its lower wage. 'You can go home now. Come back on Monday, nine o'clock promptly, and report to Miss Pool.'

Stunned by the events of the past few minutes, she stumbled back to her desk, collected her belongings and left the building. She was stinging with embarrassment and a pall of homesickness covered her like an invisible shroud.

The weather was perfect: a warm gentle breeze, a blue sky and bright sun, the war-torn buildings a backdrop hardly noticed as people became accustomed to the awesome sight. The brightly dressed office and shop girls walked to the park to eat their lunch and she followed, needing to sit and think about what had just happened.

The grass was scattered with cheerful groups of men and women. Laughter filled the warm summer air and floated towards her. Small groups of baby birds fluttered their feathers urgently, to attract the attention of their parents in the hope of food. An errand boy was whistling as he edged his bicycle between men at work mending a water main near the park gates. She saw none of these things: all she could think of were the words of her boss and his pompous criticism. With a few days off and a new position to start on the following Monday she had been virtually sacked!

When she reached home some hours later there was a letter waiting for her. It was from Beth Castle asking her to come to her wedding on the following Saturday. Beth and Peter Gregory had explained the difficulty of arranging their wedding in advance. It would happen as soon as Peter managed to get home for a few days, by special licence. When Beth added the request for Eirlys to be a witness, she could hardly refuse. She packed a bag and two days later, on 9 May, she caught the train and went home.

–

While Eirlys was travelling through Swindon. Beth received a message from Peter: his leave was cancelled, the wedding would have to wait a while longer. Hiding her disappointment, Beth went to the station to meet the train she expected Eirlys to have caught.

'The wedding's delayed,' she said as cheerfully as she could, 'so what shall we do? I've got the whole weekend off.'

Seeing that sympathy was not the right approach, Eirlys said. 'Cardiff for some shopping? A walk in Roath Park? Then a meal in some café, if we can find one that doesn't serve chips?' Laughing, they went to Sidney Street, where Eirlys had arranged to stay with Beth's Auntie Audrey and Uncle Wilf and the two young girls, Maude and Myrtle, to deposit Eirlys's case.

She made a brief visit to her home but there was no one in. She looked with dismay at the untidy garden and at the muddy area where her father was obviously trying to make a vegetable plot from what had once been a lawn. It had always been so neat and now it was filled with broken toys and abandoned rubbish. She sadly recognised her old doll's pram which her mother had put in the loft, hoping one day to see it used by a grandchild. Its wheels were missing and the side dented and scratched.

The first person she saw when she and Beth alighted on to the platform in Cardiff Central was her ex-boss Mr Johnston. That he was pleased to see her was in no doubt. 'Eirlys! Does this mean you're back in St David's Well? Your job is still waiting for you, you know.'

'How are you all?' she asked, ignoring what she thought was nothing more than politeness. Pushed along by the impatient passengers they edged slowly towards the exit steps.

'In need of your organisation skills, we are, Miss Price. We've tried three girls in an attempt to fill your vacancy but we've yet to find someone half as efficient as you.'

She was smiling in a deprecating way and he looked at her. 'I am serious, Miss Price. If you would consider coming back you'd be welcomed with great sighs of relief all round. A better salary too,' he said, and Eirlys realised he was serious.

'Can I telephone you at the office on Monday?' she asked, although the idea fizzing in her head was far from a definite decision.

Mr Johnston took a piece of paper from his pocket and wrote down the number. 'In case you've forgotten,' he said, smiling.

As he walked away with a polite lifting of his trilby she turned to Beth and was surprised at the wide smile on her friend's face. 'Eirlys, I'd be so pleased if you came back.'

'It's strange, Beth, but if I'd had that brief conversation a week ago my answer would have been different,' she said. Then she explained about the undeserved ticking-off she had received the day before.

Although she was so near, Eirlys didn't try to visit her father again during that weekend. Every time she decided to go home she felt her heart racing with anxiety, and changed her mind. On the train going back to London there was a great deal to think about if she were to return home, top of the list being how she would deal with her father. Second was having to face Johnny and Hannah, see them regularly and be happy for them without allowing a tinge of regret to show.

That brief conversation with her ex-boss had given her a greater sense of her own worth and she knew that going back and giving her notice would not be the worry it might have been. The criticism that had knocked her confidence so badly had now been overlaid with the realisation of other people's better opinion of her and this had given her strength.

Third on her list of things to consider, was where would she live? Not at home with Morgan and Teresa, that much was certain. Tired, and becoming less rather than more sure of her plans, she dozed until the train reached Paddington, then freshened her make-up, combed her hair and prepared to face the rest of the tedious journey back to Ken's family. They would have to be the first to be told of her leaving. At the same time she would write to Ken.

That night one of the worst air raids of the war took place in London. Over five hundred German bombers dropped hundreds of bombs and thousands of incendiaries in a short but horrifying raid. More than a thousand people died. Westminster was hit and the House of Commons was reduced to a shambles. In all this devastation, the people of London proudly said that the dome of St Paul's survived and Big Ben continued to chime the hours correctly. It was a symbol, they said, of the determination of the British people not to be bowed or beaten.

Eirlys looked at the photographs the following day and wondered how the place would ever recover, until she read the comments of the people. She knew then that whatever happened, London would survive.

For a while, running away seemed her real reason for returning to the comparative safety of St David's Well, but only for a while. The danger from bombs was greater here, but what she had run away from at home was far harder to deal with, she decided. But deal with it she would.

–

Hetty worked alongside Bleddyn more often as the summer season began to build up. More and more visitors arrived to enjoy the pleasant beach and the many amusements the town offered. With holidays at home a serious commitment on behalf of the council, many new and enterprising enter-tainments were appearing.

Dancing on the Green was popular when the weather allowed, but with the black-out to remember the dances finished when the musicians could no longer see their music, the lights snapping off without warning as the wardens began their nightly prowl. Competitions abounded, with skipping and whip and top and even hopscotch coming into their own. The skating rink and the swimming pool were full from the moment they opened until the evening, and the dance hall filled any spare moments with tea dances and even tap and ballet displays from the town's children.

Crowds materialised for every event advertised and the place groaned as all available rooms were filled to capacity. Every train that steamed into the small seaside station brought more visitors, some for the day and others hoping to find accommodation for a longer visit.

'So much for persuading people to stay home,' Huw grunted to anyone who would listen. 'Damn silly idea expecting people to stay home and miss all that this place has to offer.'

With Marged and Beth dealing with the beach café, and because of the demise of his usual boat trips around the bay due to anti-invasion blockades in the sea, Bleddyn concentrated on the fish-and-chip shop and restaurant in the town. Whenever she was able, Hetty Downs helped him.

She still hadn't made much progress in her attempt to make friends with Maude and Myrtle. Maude was now almost sixteen and worked in the canteen of the munitions factory. At thirteen, her sister Myrtle was still at school. They both helped out on the sands at every opportunity, Myrtle much happier now she was confident with handling money and had lost some of her shyness. It was only rarely that either girl appeared at the fish-and-chip café in town and when they did, Bleddyn stepped back and encouraged Hetty to deal with whatever they needed.

One day Maude called in on her way home from work when they were just starting to heat the dripping ready to cook. Hetty went to see what the girl wanted and Maude stepped back. She was still unsure of the woman who had been married to her father and who had treated her so coldly when they had first met.

'How are you?' Hetty's conventional greeting was to allow her time to gather her thoughts, but it went unanswered as Maude glanced towards Bleddyn.

'Auntie Marged asked me to ask if you'd bring some fish and chips home tonight for a late supper,' she said.

'Tell Hetty what you need and I'll bring it when I finish,' Bleddyn said, disappearing into the back preparation room.

'I'm sorry I was so unkind to you and Myrtle when we first met', Hetty said, 'I know I should have said this before, but knowing that my husband had a second family was a terrible shock. You're old enough now to realise that, aren't you?'

'He was our dad and I don't know anything about the time he lived with you,' Maude said nervously.

'I don't intend to criticise him,' Hetty promised. 'I would like to talk about him sometimes, to tell you what he was like and perhaps you can tell me a little about the years he spent with you.'

'Come and see us at Auntie Marged's,' Maude said in a spuriously adult tone. 'I'd like to know what he was like before he was our dad.' She added softly, 'We miss him something awful, me and Myrtle.'

'I'll ask Marged when it's convenient,' Hetty said.

When Bleddyn reappeared, she said sadly, 'I can see so much that was Paul in that girl's face; her eyes are like his and something about the mouth.'

'I'd like to think you can be friends, you and Shirley, Maude and Myrtle,' Bleddyn said, smiling.

—

Hetty had once worked alongside her daughter in the newsagent but when a new owner arrived he had kept Shirley on and managed the rest of the time himself. He had no objection to Hetty filling in for her daughter when Shirley needed a few hours off and it was becoming a regular event for Hetty to be there late on Wednesday afternoon, when they reopened on the half-day to deal with the evening newspaper deliveries. Her hours working for the Castle family at the beach were varied, and it was easy for her to arrange to be at the shop when Shirley needed her.

It was also on Wednesdays that the market closed for the afternoon. After the encouragement given by Max when he heard them sing, Janet and Shirley had arranged weekly singing lessons and spent the rest of the afternoon practising songs and also some dance steps to go with the popular songs of the time.

'In The Mood', the signature tune of Joe Loss, was a current favourite and the version they danced to was the Glen Miller recording. Full of enthusiasm and energy they fitted their steps to the lively melody, making much of the stops and restarts near the end. Hetty smiled and hoped they would at least be successful enough to have some fun.

Hetty was in the shop one Wednesday when Bleddyn called. 'Oh, this is what you do when you "mitch" from work, is it?' he teased, his strong, bearded jaw thrust forward as though in disapproval.

'Mitching is it? I'll have you know, Mr Castle, that I worked from dawn to get your café smart and fit for business,' she said, then laughed to show she was teasing too.

'Your Shirley gone to her singing class?' he asked.

'I don't suppose it will lead to anything but I want them to try. At least they'll have a few laughs.'

'From what I hear they're very good. Dancing as well as singing. They need a name for themselves though. Shirley Downs and Janet Copp doesn't roll off the tongue. What about the Beach Belles or the Sand Swingers?'

'You're probably right. I'll suggest it when they come home. They usually come back here and practise some more.' She shook her head. 'I wish I had their energy.'

'So do I! We've been extra busy. Young Beth arranged to take the weekend off for her wedding and she's so disappointed with the cancellation she took a few days off anyway. You don't know how much one girl does until you have to cope a day without her. Grand girl, my niece Beth.

I'm going home to change, then off to the chip shop to work till eleven. What a life, eh?'

'I'll help if you like, once the shop closes,' Hetty offered. 'I can serve fish and chips or work in the café.'

It didn't take Bleddyn long to agree.

–

Morgan Price walked home from his factory shift. It was two thirty and he was hungry. When Eirlys's mother was alive, she would have been there with a meal freshly cooked, waiting for him in a neat, orderly house. Life with Teresa was not the same as with Annie. He loved Teresa, or thought he did – he certainly liked the way she filled his bed – but she didn't know the first thing about running a home. The only thing she could cook was boiled potatoes, and the only variation from that was chips from the chip shop. She didn't know and didn't want to learn. If only Eirlys would come back to look after them all, then everything would be perfect.

'I heard your Eirlys was home for the weekend and she never came to see you.' was Teresa's greeting as he walked through the door. 'Unkind I call that, Morgan, love. Here, you make a cup of tea and I'll open a packet of biscuits. The boys'll finish them off if we don't help ourselves before they get home. Devils for biscuits they are.'

'Eirlys home?' He frowned. 'I wonder why she didn't let us know?'

'Easy to answer that one, Morgan. She can't bear seeing you happy, that's why. She thinks you should go on grieving for her mother for the rest of your natural.'

'Come on, Teresa, Eirlys isn't that petty-minded, but I think we *are* the problem. She hasn't got over how fast we got together.'

'Like I said, hates seein' you 'appy.'

74

'No, I didn't mean—' He gave up and asked instead, 'Is there anything cooking?'

'I haven't had a minute all day. Morgan. I was upset, hearing about your daughter treating you like that and I forgot about food. Come 'ere, and let me cheer you up, eh?' She opened her arms but he turned away, something he was doing more and more frequently.

'I can't think of that. I want to think of a way to bring Eirlys home,' he said.

''Ome? 'ome 'ere? You can't mean it, two women in the kitchen, that'll never work!'

In a rare burst of anger, he said, 'Two women in the kitchen? One would be a novelty!'

Teresa shouted back in anger and within moments they were having a raging row, he accusing Teresa of being lazy and Teresa telling him she was not there as a drudge. He laughed at that and the row ended in seconds.

'Anything less like a drudge than you is hard to imagine,' he said, hugging her. 'Beautiful you are and I don't think St David's Well has ever seen anything like you before. I'm the envy of all my mates.'

'Come on then, show me off, make 'em all jealous. Take me out and treat me to something nice.'

She was dressed in a smart two-piece suit in black, the skirt a fraction shorter than fashion dictated, with a red blouse, red shoes and a silly little black hat on top of her curled hair. Her make-up was always immaculate if a trifle heavy, and she turned heads wherever they went. He had never seen her less than perfectly dressed and admired her for it. Even at night she wore expensive nightgowns and a small amount of make-up on her smooth skin. But why couldn't she combine her attractiveness with a few housewifely skills?

It was about the lack of activity in the kitchen that Morgan wanted to talk to Eirlys. He wasn't having any decent meals except when they ate out and with five of them to pay for, the money didn't allow for that to happen very often. Aware that she was dressed to go out, he belatedly asked, 'Where were you going when I came home – somewhere special? You look very nice. Too nice for shopping.'

'I thought of calling for that Hetty Downs to go to the pictures. You don't mind do you, Morgan? I was going a bit early to look at some dresses, but if you fancy a bit of a rest, and spare half an hour?' She tilted her head and looked at him provocatively and he smiled.

She was lovely and by the time he had washed and changed the boys would be on their way home. He would have spoilt her afternoon.

'Go on, you, enjoy yourself.'

After she had gone he went to the pantry to see what he could find and was disappointed to see that the cupboard was practically empty. He would have to go shopping before the boys came home from school. They couldn't eat from the chip shop again. He dug deep into his pocket and found enough to buy potatoes and carrots and a few items from the cake shop. There wasn't any meat and he decided to appeal to the butcher and get a few scraps to add a bit of taste to the gravy. Searching through his pockets he found an extra three shillings in mixed change and he set off. He managed to buy two meat and potato pies. Half each would have to do for Teresa and the boys tomorrow. He would eat in the canteen if he could borrow from a friend or raise an advance on his wages again. Today they would have eggs.

He handed his wages to Teresa each week less a little pocket money for himself, as he had with Annie, but he had a suspicion that the money was not stretching to Teresa's spending. If only Eirlys would come home and run the household or teach Teresa to do so, he would be a very happy man. In the meantime, he was worried about the scrap meals he was offered, and bills that arrived and which were swiftly snatched away before he could examine them. He was beginning to realise they were in deep water and it was getting deeper.

He knew he should take control. After Annie died he had managed to cook a few simple meals for himself and he knew that with a little advice from friends and neighbours he could cook on a regular basis, but Teresa refused his help. The ingredients he needed were never available, and the ration of items like butter and cooking fat and sugar rarely lasted the week. If only Eirlys would come home, she would have everything sorted in a couple of weeks.

He went to see Bernard Gregory, who explained about Eirlys's unexpected visit to attend the wedding of his son, Peter, to Beth Castle: the wedding that never happened. Morgan didn't want to think about it. His daughter had come home and hadn't called. He had never imagined such a thing could happen. Everything in his life was a mess. He was having to choose between Teresa and the boys and his daughter, it seemed.

He bought a dozen eggs, and, when Teresa came home, he made them all some scrambled eggs on toast with the addition of a few tomatoes and a few leftover potatoes warmed under the grill. Stanley ate his and half of Harold's and when Percival complained that there was skin on his tomatoes and brown bits in the egg, he ate his too.

'What's for afters?' he asked hopefully.

'Bread an' jam!' Teresa retorted.

'I 'aves a bit o' bover with bread an' jam. There's pips and I 'ates pips. I only like puddin's.' Percival complained. 'Unless you takes the crusts off.'

Morgan sighed. He had to find a solution and quick, or the boys would go down with rickets! He took out pen and paper to write to Eirlys again. It was time for some honesty.

—

Joseph Beynon went to the dances and often saw Shirley there, recently with Janet Copp. He never asked her to dance and, unless they actually came face to face, he ignored her. He was still angry at the way she had treated him. One night she left early complaining of an upset stomach and when Max Moon came looking for her he saw Joseph and, recognising him as a friend of Shirley's, asked him to convey a message to her.

'I have an audition arranged for Shirley and Janet next Wednesday. Well, a competition really but there's an agent who promises to be there and I think they should be heard. I'm just off to the station. Would you call in to the shop and give her this?' He handed Joseph a sheet of paper. 'It's the venue and time and how to get there.' Hardly acknowledging Joseph's doubtful expression, he thanked him and dashed off to catch his train. Joseph read the information and tucked it in his pocket.

Walking home he argued with himself about whether or not he would deliver the message. It was utterly unkind not to and, he told himself, it wasn't in his nature to behave badly, but she had been more than unkind to him, treating him with such indifference when they had gone to the dance together. He threw it on to the pavement and scuffed it with his foot and walked on home. Then conscience struck and he turned around, picked it up and wiped it clean.

He went into the shop where Shirley was serving someone with a birthday card.

Waiting patiently, he watched her as she dealt with the customer. Quick, efficient with a smile for everyone.

'Hi yer,' she called cheerily as though they had never had a disagreement. She always thought it best to forget arguments as soon as they were over. No point lumbering yourself with guilt. She eyed him nervously though, afraid perhaps that he was going to make a scene. Amused by her embarrassment, he waited for her to speak.

'Joseph, I've been meaning to call and apologise,' she said, her face glowing a little as she looked at him with her special smile. 'I was very stupid and rude leaving you at the dance. I did look for you to explain but in the crush at the end I lost sight of you and—'

'You left before the end,' he said mildly.

'What a mistake that was,' she said, ignoring the challenge to her lies. 'This soldier said he was with ENSA and could get me an audition. Promised me a tour with some professionals he did. And there was me foolish enough to believe him. I'll never be that stupid again, Joseph. Fancy the Wednesday dance?'

'You can't go on Wednesday,' he said, handing her the grubby note. 'Your friend, Max Moon, asked me to deliver it,' he explained.

'Lucky you aren't as unkind as me, or you might have thrown it away,' she said, unpeeling it with difficulty in its fragile state.

'I did throw it down,' he admitted. 'Then I thought that wasn't the action of an honest person, and picked it up again.'

She read the note and her face flushed again, this time with excitement. 'It's an audition! Me and Janet!' She did a whirl and added more calmly, 'Well, an amateur night competition really but there'll be an agent there and this might be a big step forward for us, if he likes us, of course.' In her excitement she grabbed hold of Joseph and danced around the shop.

Trying to hide his pleasure, he said, 'If you like I'll come with you. You won't want to be travelling home alone late at night, will you?'

'Thanks, Joseph, Mam will be more willing if you come with us.'

–

'No! You *don't* go!' Hetty said firmly. 'Certainly not with that Joseph Beynon who upset you when he brought you home from the dance!'

Too late, Shirley remembered the lie she had told to cover her stupidity at walking home with the unknown soldier. It was a long time before she could convince Hetty that she had not told the truth about the soldier walking her home. Hetty threatened to see Joseph and his parents to hear the story from him. Fortunately he came into the shop just then and he didn't try to cover up for Shirley. He told the truth convincingly, so it was agreed that he should escort the two girls to the audition.

'Stick to the truth,' he said to Shirley when her mother left them to make their arrangements. 'You aren't clever enough to lie! If you don't want to tell it, don't. Right?'

Looking suitably contrite, Shirley nodded.

Shirley and Janet were experienced at competitions by this time and they had learned to read an audience and chose their material to suit it. They rehearsed their songs but were prepared to change them and select others from their briefcase filled with song sheets at the last minute. With many older people filling the crowded hall they sang sentimental songs, old, well-loved favourites. They included one for the girls separated from their loved ones. 'You Came Along, From Out of Nowhere', which they knew would touch hearts.

It was a surprise to no-one when they were awarded the first prize.

They were invited to attend an audition for a concert to be given a few weeks later, and the following day, with Beth looking after the market café and Hetty at the shop, they arrived at a cold, empty room above a café.

They sat in the dingy place, huddling together for warmth, and watched as a long stream of performers took to the stage and offered their talent. They were very poor. Most were comedians who stood and rattled off a long line of well-used jokes, with a few singers who lacked talent and murdered a few lovely melodies, and, unbelievably, a cornet player who lacked rhythm and constantly missed the notes. All stood waiting for applause from the other contenders, with hope on their faces.

'I don't think we should do this.' Janet whispered. 'I don't think it will help us if we take part in a concert with this lot.'

Shirley stared at her friend, then nodded. Waving cheerily to the harassed man sorting out the hopeless from the downright impossibles, they headed for the toilets, then dashed to the door and made their escape.

'I'll kill Max when I see him next!' Shirley said as they ran for the bus.

'No. I want to do it!'

'No, let me!' They laughed helplessly most of the way home. Buoyant with confidence, they were aware that they had passed a certain level and were on the way up.

–

Huw and Marged's youngest son, Eynon, was due home from the army prison where he had been punished for being absent without leave the year before. Marged was so excited at seeing him again she could hardly contain herself. Besides stocking up with as much food as she could buy, scrounge or swap for other things, she cleaned the house, and even made Huw paint the front door. It had been so long, yet in her mind was the picture of the sixteen-year-old, innocent boy she had last seen. Huw tried to warn her that he would have changed but she didn't, couldn't believe him. He was her baby and he was coming home.

Eynon Castle had joined the army before he had reached the age when conscription claimed him. In a mood of bravado, he and Freddy Clements, then engaged to his sister, Beth, had walked into the recruitment office and signed on as regulars.

He expected the other young men to become friends; working together as a team was what the army was all about, wasn't it? In fact he was an outsider straightaway. His accent, the fact of his being shorter than the rest, and his over-anxious expectation of friendship all added fuel to the need for a few of the others to find someone to bully.

Instead of friendship he found himself alone, picked on by several but most severely by a quick-tempered man who had done a little boxing, called Kipper.

Kipper had taken it upon himself to teach the boy a lesson, although why and for what were never explained. It was partly to show the rest how dangerous he was and how wise they would be to treat him with respect. Eynon's clothes went missing, his kit became dirty just before inspection, he was kicked and beaten for any real or imagined slight and when an opportunity offered itself, after a particularly bad session of the man's cruelty, Eynon had absented himself from his group on a cross-country training exercise.

For weeks he was on the run and when an accident burst open an earlier head wound, giving him the excuse to plead lost memory, he gave himself up.

Whether the medical officers believed him or not, the severe cut on his head gave credence to his story and he was given a sentence that was less than he had feared. In addition, his fellow soldiers seemed to have gained a little respect for him. Now, in June 1941, he was given leave to go home and see his family before being sent back to rejoin his group.

In Sidney Street, preparations were under way in readiness for his arrival. Marged and Huw hadn't seen their son since he signed on and Marged was more than a little tearful, partly because they were unable to meet him in Cardiff, not knowing the train on which he would be travelling.

'He must know what train he'll be on, we should be meeting him in Cardiff,' she complained several times. 'He'll think we don't care.'

Huw and his brother Bleddyn soothed her, reminding her that Eynon too would be feeling emotional about the reunion and must be allowed to do things his way.

–

Eynon stepped off the train at six o'clock on a Friday evening and there to meet him, as he had arranged, was Alice Potter who worked with his Auntie Audrey in the Castle family's rock and sweet shop on the promenade.

They were both hesitant to hug each but grinned widely. They walked along side by side, not touching. Eynon carrying his kit and Alice with a small, home-made shoulder bag.

'Your dad, is he all right?' Eynon asked.

'Still about the same. That punch he received in his last fight ruined him, and I doubt if he'll ever get any better.'

Alice's father had been a boxer and brain damage had disabled him. He couldn't walk upright without support and the injury had made him very wild at times, Alice often bearing the brunt of his violent temper.

'I've felt a few punches from a boxer and they didn't feel too good either,' he said ruefully. 'Never fancied that as a way to cam my living. Sissy I am, I'd rather sell ice cream and buckets and spades on the beach!' The laughter broke the ice and they strolled the rest of the way to his parents' house, through the busy streets, arm in arm and close as they could get and still manage to walk.

Once, while he was still on the run, Alice had sheltered him and allowed him to clean himself and get a good night's rest and he reminded her of how grateful he had been.

'That simple night's rest in safety and comfort was the most luxurious experience of my life,' he said, kissing her cheek and making her blush.

As he had expected, the whole family was squeezed into his parents' house and, for the first time, his granny Molly Piper wasn't there with her arms outstretched. She had died while he was on the run. The others made up for it though and for a while Alice lost sight of him as he was surrounded by his brother and sisters and the rest. Then the baby cried and he looked at his sister, Lilly.

'Come on then, let's have our little sprog out and ready for inspection!'

Marged tried to hide her shock at the sight of him. He was thin and pale and there was a look of hardness, a toughness, a 'seen it all' coldness in his eyes. There was even a touch of grey in his short dark hair where a scar stretched almost down to his left eye. She stared at him as he laughed and joked and admired his little niece but she hardly recognised the young boy who had left home to join the army.

'How long are you home for?' Bleddyn asked.

'Why, Uncle Bleddyn?' he replied cheekily. 'Don't say you've got me down for a shift on the ice-cream stall?'

For a moment, amid the laughter, Marged saw the boy he had once been, but the expression quickly faded and she wondered if she had imagined it.

'No ice cream, boy,' Bleddyn replied when the laughter had subsided. 'We aren't allowed to make it any more. But there's the helter-skelter if you're free, mind!'

'Dammit all, and there's me thinking I'd spend the weekend in bed.'

'I saw Eirlys on the train,' he told them later. 'She's coming back and her job is waiting for her. Great news, eh?'

Hannah smiled at her father-in-law and said softly, 'That's good news. I was afraid my marrying Johnny had kept her away.'

'Eirlys is too sensible to keep away because of you,' Bleddyn reassured her. 'It's more likely to be that Teresa Love, moving in with her father.'

'Morgan made a big mistake, from what I hear,' Huw told them. 'Debts all over the place and no decent food. Poor silly sod.'

—

Eirlys went straight to Shirley Downs's flat above the shop when she reached St David's Well. Hetty Downs had agreed to her staying there for a few weeks while she found somewhere to live, and most of her luggage was being held by Ken's family until she had a permanent address.

Joseph Beynon was there ready to escort Shirley to a dance. Eirlys was invited to go with them but she declined.

Dancing was not a favourite occupation and from the look on Joseph's face he was quite happy having Shirley to himself.

In fact the occasion was not a dance but yet another talent competition. Amateur entertainment was popular and inexpensive, with many people tempted on to a stage who would never have been brave enough before. 'I can do better than that,' was a phrase often overheard.

This competition was one about which Shirley had declined to tell Janet Copp. Joseph knew nothing about the competition either, having been told by Shirley that Janet was not free to go and that it was only a boring old dance in a church hall that wouldn't attract more than a few.

When they got to the door Joseph could see that Shirley hadn't been completely truthful. Girls were dressed in long skirts and with their hair carefully arranged. Some of the men were in evening dress, their shoes highly polished.

'What's going on?' he asked. 'I thought you said it was only a dance.'

'Oh, nothing. They've sold more tickets than I expected, that's all.'

Ignoring her casual reply, he asked someone in the crowd waiting to get inside and was told about the competition. Turning to Shirley he demanded, 'Did you tell Janet about this?'

'She wasn't free, I told you that.'

'Where does she live?'

'Oh, I don't know. Why are you making such a fuss? She didn't want to come.'

'Janet Copp,' he called. 'Does anyone know where she lives?'

'Stop it, Joseph, you're making everyone stare.'

'Where does she live?' he asked again.

Someone called out, 'Janet Copp? D'you mean her from the market café? She lives at Seven Oldway Street.'

'Thank you,' he replied, then turning to Shirley, he said sharply, 'You wait here until I get back.'

'Joseph! If you think I'm going to wait out here, you're mistaken!'

'I have the tickets and I said wait!' Leaving Shirley seething with anger, he hurried away.

Oldway Street was not far and within minutes he was knocking impatiently on the door.

'The dance tonight includes a talent competition,' he told a surprised Janet. 'Grab a dress, comb your hair and come.'

'Why have we only just heard?' she asked as they ran back to the hall. 'Shirley heard it was only a small dance for a youth club or something like that.'

87

Joseph said nothing and waving an irritable hand then glaring at a disgruntled Shirley, he ushered them into the hall.

Shirley went into the cloakroom with Janet and waited while she changed her dress and combed her hair. 'Lucky we heard in time, wasn't it?' she said to Janet. 'Just chatting in the queue while we waited, we were, and when I realised it was a talent competition I begged Joseph to go and fetch you. He's so kind, isn't he?'

'I must tell him how grateful I am. Specially if we win.'

'Don't say anything, Janet, he'd be embarrassed. There's no need. I'll remind him of how grateful we both are later,' Shirley said with a wink.

They discussed the song they would sing and rehearsed, very briefly, the steps they would do in the middle before stepping out to rejoin Joseph.

He had entered their names and they were near the end of the list, so they sat watching the other acts, discussing their good points and relishing their bad. The competition was not daunting; they both felt confident of winning.

They had chosen a sentimental number. 'When I Grow Too Old To Dream', Janet easily harmonising for the second chorus, and it went down well, with so many of the audience thinking of loved ones far away. Choosing them as winners was a popular choice and they hugged each other as they ran up to receive their prize.

'Thank you, Joseph,' Janet said excitedly.

Joseph looked at Shirley and said slowly. 'Thank Shirley, not me. She learned about it, didn't you, Shirley?'

Shirley hugged her friend and did not reply. Her eyes were glittering with the excitement of their success, tempered by the thought that if Janet hadn't come, the success would have been wholly hers. If Joseph thought he could shame her he thought wrong! She was going places and nothing would stop her, certainly not loyalty to Janet or stuffy Joseph Beynon!

–

Eirlys went to see her father on the Sunday before she started back in her old job at the council offices in St David's Well. It was eleven o'clock in the morning and her mother would have had meat roasting and vegetables prepared even if the meat was no more than a couple of measly chops. But there were no tantalising smells as she opened the back door and called to let them know she was there. In fact the remains of a previous meal were spread across the table and the sink held unwashed dishes and pans. The strongest smell was of Daddies Sauce which had spilt across the stained tablecloth.

The boys, Stanley, Harold and Percival, came running to greet her and to her surprise they were still in their far from sweet-smelling pyjamas.

'What's this?' she said, laughing. 'I was hoping you'd be ready to come with me to see Mr Gregory.' Teasingly, she turned as though to go back out. 'If you don't want to come then I'll go on my own.'

Stanley and Harold shouted, pleading with her to wait. Solemn little Percival said, 'My 'jamas is boverin' me. The cord's knotted itself and I can't get out.'

As she helped undo the cord and the others ran upstairs to dress, Teresa appeared and said firmly, 'Sorry, Eirlys, but you should have told us you was comin'. The boys ain't going nowhere without a bit o' breakfast inside them. It ain't right to go off with an empty stomach.'

'I'll wait.' Eirlys smiled, giving Percival the ends of his cord to hold so he could run after his brothers and get dressed. She sat down in the chaos of the kitchen and crossed her legs. She wouldn't start clearing up. It would embarrass Teresa and she didn't want to do that.

As her father came running down the stairs, having been told by the boys of her arrival, Teresa said, 'If you want a cup of tea you'll have to wash a cup. One for me an' your father too while you're at it.'

So much for shaming her, Eirlys thought wryly.

It was Eirlys who made toast and washed the dishes, and who ironed a shirt for Stanley when he couldn't find a fresh one to put on.

Teresa and her father sat, telling her about some of the mishaps the boys had caused and how well they were doing at school.

'When we manage to get there,' Stanley muttered. 'Mam oversleeps and we get up too late sometimes.'

Teresa thought that was funny too.

When they were finally ready to go on their walk, Morgan said he would go with them. At first Teresa complained. 'Who's going to help me get our dinner?' she demanded.

'I'll bring back some more eggs,' Morgan promised.

'Thank Gawd they ain't rationed yet.' She sighed. 'We'll 'ave 'em boiled so I'll cut some bread, shall I?'

'That'll be great,' Morgan said, as though she had offered to prepare a five-course banquet.

When they were on their way with the boys running ahead, Morgan said, 'You can see how it is, Eirlys love. Is there any chance of you moving back and taking over? The boys are suffering, not having proper food, and they need shoes and there's no money. Stanley has outgrown his and he's going to school in claps,' he said, using the local name for plimsoles.

'Dadda, you know I can't live there with you now. I love the boys and I want to help, but I can't give up my job and take over the organisation of Teresa's family. You can't ask me to do that.' She was tempted to remind him that the mess was of his own making but she didn't. Instead she called Percival back and held his hand, pointing out the many wild flowers that grew in the fields and hedgerows.

'There's the money too.' Morgan said in a low voice. 'I'm not even sure the rent's being paid.'

'You'll have to handle the money yourself. Be fair, Dadda. If you're expecting Teresa to suddenly be able to run a household of five people with all its complications after the way she lived, you must be crazy. Tell her you'll be managing the money and make sure you really do manage it. I don't want to criticise her but she seems able to do exactly what she wants without a thought for you, or her sons.'

'Mum loves us. "Love be name, and love be nature", that's what she says,' Percival chanted solemnly.

'You're so lucky to have a mum that loves you,' Eirlys said in alarm. She had forgotten the child was there. 'I'm talking about someone else, a lady I know who doesn't love her children enough to care for them properly, they aren't lucky like you and your brothers.'

'Can we have custard for puddin'?' he asked.

'We'll get fresh milk and eggs from Mr Gregory as soon as we've said hello to the donkeys, and I'll make you some,' she promised, bending down and hugging him.

As he ran off to tell his brothers about the custard, she turned to her father and hissed, 'No shoes for the boys, but her clothes are all new, aren't they? Get it sorted, Dadda, or she'll make you homeless then hop it back to where she came from!'

Four

In the way of most families during the difficult war years, the Castles exchanged news and often gave their letters to other members of the family to read and share the pleasure of the often brief communication.

Shirley Downs and Alice Potter were exceptions. Shirley heard from Freddy Clements but had no contact with his parents, so she read his letters then put them aside to read again later.

For Alice it was shyness that made her hide the fact that Eynon wrote to her. Shyness and the loving content of his regular letters. He talked of his love for her, and they made plans for when the war ended and they would marry. Although he had never actually proposed, it was accepted by both of them that they would become man and wife as soon as they were able.

Shirley read Freddy's letters with greater interest than she had at first. Before he had joined the army he had been a convenience, a way of exploring her talent for dancing and then singing. He had been casual about it, treated it as nothing more than a bit of fun, an added interest to their evenings out. Now he was taking her more seriously, not praising her successes overmuch, but wanting to hear her latest news.

She began to look forward to telling him about the auditions, making a joke out of the bad ones and trying to be casual about the ones which went well. At least he was interested enough to ask, and that pleased her.

For Alice, Eynon's letters were the highest point of her week and hiding them from her father the most fearful need.

Hannah wrote every day to Johnny and when she received a letter from him she shared the joy of it with her father-in-law, Bleddyn. She still tried to interest her parents in their son-in-law but they refused to accept the end of her previous marriage. 'In the eyes of the church you are living in sin,' was the regular response when she tried to talk to them. She never gave up. One day they would face facts and accept that her first marriage to a man whose priorities were violence and drink, was over.

–

Eirlys settled back into her former position at St David's Well council offices, but not without some difficulties. Several girls had been employed and none had stayed long, but before leaving they had changed the filing system that Eirlys had kept so meticulously and rearranged the lists of suppliers, cancelling some and adding new ones.

Her first task was to put things back in a way she understood and which would allow her to find what she needed quickly. To this end she worked into the evenings, leaving the building with the escort of the nightwatchman, a replacement for Bob Beynon, Joseph's father. It took a week of busy days and long evenings working alone before she felt confident that she had everything returned to its previous order.

The normal work of allotting food and supplies was a full-time job but on top of that she was given the responsibility for local entertainments. 'Holidays At Home' was the overall title given to a summer of activities intended to keep the local people from travelling to another holiday destination. Posters to that effect were distributed through every town in the country, not just the places that normally attracted visitors but small towns in which there was no tradition of catering for families having fun.

In her absence many of the things she had originally set up had been neglected and on her return, her first action was to get in touch with Max Moon and Ken Ward. What she needed initially were more ideas.

It was already well into the season and the busy month of August was approaching fast. All these arrangements should have been settled earlier. Much had been discussed but very little actually arranged, she thought, as she read through the list of dances, competitions, cricket matches and novelty games.

With Mr Johnston's co-operation she organised a meeting of all the local people involved with guests and day-trippers. There were the expected complaints at interrupting the busy business people, but a large number came.

Bleddyn Castle was there with his brother Huw, and Marged. Marged's sister Audrey came with her husband Wilf. Others who worked on the sands were there too and besides the beach people, the hall was packed with hoteliers and guest-house proprietors, shopkeepers and many of the casuals like the photographer, the fortune teller and Bernard Gregory who ran the donkeys. Nervously, Eirlys began to address them.

At the end of the evening she had a list of possible events and went back to Hetty and Shirley's flat to try and make sense of it. In the office next day she handed ideas to various members of staff for them to investigate and asked them to come back to her with their findings. Her own list included a visit to the school.

After discussing her idea with the headmistress she was invited to address the children in the school hall and when they came in, two by two, she saw an excited Stanley waving at her. Looking around the sea of faces she soon spotted a bored-looking Harold and a suspicious Percival. 'What have we done?' Percival mouthed at her. 'I ain't done nothin'.'

Smiling encouragingly, she asked them all to sit.

'I want you to form a choir,' she began, 'We expect to have lots of people this summer looking for some really good entertainment and you are going to take part.'

There was a groan from some of the children sitting cross-legged in front of her. Smiling. Eirlys went on. 'I want you to have a really grand Sports Day. A day that everyone will enjoy. I want to arrange a bicycle race and a swimming gala and, also, the biggest picnic ever seen. Mums and dads if they can come, grannies and granddads, visiting friends, everyone is invited.'

'It always rains on picnics,' said a voice that could only be Percival.

'Not on this one it won't,' she said firmly.

It was the beginning of a very hectic few weeks and Eirlys wished she had come back sooner so things could have been set in motion without such a tight time limit. She welcomed the work. Since her return she had not passed a night in relaxed and undisturbed sleep. Living so near Hannah was difficult. She hoped that by filling her days so sleep would come might stop her dwelling on their happy marriage, and also be an excellent excuse not to become involved in her father's problems. But although she packed the hours with work, the nights were long and she watched dawn break day after day.

Her thoughts were random and confused. It seemed such a waste of time to lie waiting for sleep that wouldn't come. Most of the thoughts were about things already done and however she worried, nothing could change them. One thing she did think about during the sleepless hours did have a satisfactory outcome: she had to find herself a permanent place to live.

With so many men and women away from home, and most of the evacuees returned home, there were plenty of houses offering rooms to let, but with her good salary and the desire for privacy, she decided on a flat. Of these there was a scarcity but she managed to find one not far from the office and, with grateful thanks to Hetty and Shirley Downs for their help, she moved in at the end of June a few weeks after her return.

Her first visitor was her father. He called late on her first evening after finishing his two-till-ten shift and, after admiring her new home, slumped down in her one and only armchair, a picture of dejection.

'What is it, Dadda? What's wrong?' she asked, certain she knew the answer to her own question.

'Teresa has bought a new three-piece suite on the never-never and I don't think we can afford it.'

'You must have agreed. She can't sign for you, can she? She isn't your wife.'

'She said the old one is dangerous, the arm is weak and one of the boys might harm himself.'

Irritated, Eirlys said, 'And you fell for that? You must be crazy. There was nothing wrong with that furniture and you know it. Mam only bought the best.'

'We're in debt, Eirlys. She doesn't feed us properly and I don't know what to do.'

'Like I told you before, take charge.'

'I've never had to deal with housekeeping. I don't even know how much she'd need for food.'

'Ask her, then give her half of what she asks for!' Eirlys didn't try to hide her dislike of Teresa. 'Either that or tell her to leave.' She knew she sounded hard but there was no soft approach where someone like Teresa was concerned.

'I can't tell the boys to go, they're settled in school and with friends, and I'd be all on my own if they left and I don't think I could cope with that.'

It was tempting, but Eirlys held back a promise to return home if they went. Dadda had to make this decision on his own; embellishing one side of the solution was not the answer.

She made him some food, guessing from the few comments he made that there wouldn't be any supper waiting for him, filling him with tinned soup and some crusty bread. She felt utterly cruel as he walked off into the night, back to his problems which she knew she could help solve. Hardening her heart she closed the door and began to clear up in her tiny kitchen.

She lay awake as usual, her thoughts dwelling on her father, wondering if she should go back and help. He was her father and she loved him. Her mother would have expected it of her. But her mother could not have foreseen the complication of Teresa Love and her children.

When Eynon Castle's leave ended, he went on an earlier train than necessary. He had to travel through London and the risk of delays was a worry. He didn't want to be even a few minutes late returning. He couldn't face more punishment. He spent his last few hours with Alice Potter who had been given the morning off from serving in the seaside rock shop on the promenade. Her father was subject to moods and could be violent for no apparent reason, but when Eynon knocked on the door of the dingy rooms behind an empty shop where Alice and her father lived, she invited him in.

As he stepped into the narrow passageway he heard the shuffling gait of Colin Potter and stood waiting for him to appear. Colin was bent like an old man and he needed to lean on the wall to support himself as he walked. The side of his sleeves were worn with constant rubbing against walls. His dark eyes flashed with anger and he snapped, 'Alice! Who's this then?'

'It's Eynon, Dad, you've seen him before. Eynon Castle.'

'You a boxer then?'

'No fear,' Eynon said, laughing, then seeing the anger strengthen in the sick man's eyes, quickly added. 'Not brave enough to fight. That takes real courage, Mr Potter.'

Satisfied, the man lurched away through the passageway and disappeared into the living room.

Alice led Eynon into the lean-to kitchen and made them tea. Opening a storage tin she offered him a slice of cake bought earlier as a special treat.

'Queued for half an hour for that,' she told him as he took a bite of the gaudy yellow mixture.

They didn't stay long. Eynon's train would leave in an hour and they wanted to spend the time talking freely, so they went to the park.

Children were playing chase among the bushes, they could hear the lop-lop of a tennis game in progress and couples strolled along the paths enjoying the mild weather. They ran out of things to say, both aware of the nearness of their parting. Unimportant comments were exchanged: 'I think I'll have my hair cut,' Alice said after a long silence began to make her edgy.

'No, Alice!' She was surprised at the vehemence of his reaction.

'Why not?'

'Because I want to remember you and know you look the same. I don't want you to change until I'm back home for good. I'll be going overseas soon and I need to have a picture of you in my mind. Just as you are at this moment.'

She understood and smiled. 'I promise I won't change a thing. I'll be waiting for you just as I am this moment.

An hour later Eynon would have had difficulty recognising her. As she walked through the door, her father grabbed her by the long hair she had thought of cutting and dragged her into the living room. 'Weak little soldier!' he shouted, repeating it again and again as he hit her. 'Keep right away from him, d'you hear? Coward he is, not having no guts for a fight, what use is he to anyone, eh?' His fist cut her lip and bruised her eye and as she tried to stem the blood running from her nose she wondered if she would ever escape from her father's frustrated anger.

In June, a few days after Eirlys had taken possession of her flat, there was another attempt on the part of Beth and Peter to arrange their wedding. As before, the plan was aborted only hours before the event. Beth put away her wedding dress for the second time and went with Eirlys to her flat where Eirlys provided a meal. 'What's the opposite of celebration?' Beth asked sadly. 'Whatever it is, this is it.'

'Nonsense, it's just another rehearsal, and a house-warming for my new home.'

Having been given the evening off in preparation for the wedding, Beth suggested they go for a walk. Inevitably their footsteps took them to Peter's father, Bernard Gregory, who was walking home through the lanes with his donkeys. Teresa's three boys were with them and ran to greet Eirlys with affection.

'Where's your mam?' Eirlys asked.

'Rowing with Uncle Morgan.' Harold grumbled. 'Can't stand all that shouting so we went to the treehouse, but it's rotting and Uncle Morgan says he'll repair it but he doesn't.'

All this came out in a rush and Eirlys looked at Stanley and smiled. 'Never was the most tolerant of people, your brother, was he?'

Mr Gregory promised to talk to Morgan about repairing the treehouse and they ran back home discussing what was needed, while Eirlys and Beth followed the dainty-footed animals back to Sally Gough's field and their evening meal.

Comfortably at home in the cottage on the smallholding that was Bernard's home, Beth made a pot of tea and set out the small cakes Eirlys had brought. Her first cooking in her new fiat, they were sticky, shiny, fatless sponge cakes. She exchanged news of Peter with the small man and, with a little prompting, Bernard produced his photograph albums and led them through Peter's childhood, revealing facets of the local families too.

It was late and, although it was not yet dark, Bernard insisted on taking them home. The horse was harnessed and they clip-clopped through the lanes on the back of his cart, the long way around, enjoying the peaceful journey, allowing the quiet countryside and the slow pace to relax them.

The atmosphere in Bernard's cottage had soothed her, made her problems shrink into a manageable size.

'Working with animals teaches you patience,' Bernard said. 'They won't be rushed and you have to accept their ace. For the first time since her return, Eirlys slept right through the night.

—

The preparations for the summer holiday period were going well. The schools in the town and the surrounding area were all contributing several children from each class, and the choir, under the baton of a retired bandsman, were rehearsing regularly for the six Saturday concerts they would perform. Max and Ken came once or twice and began to plan a Grand Concert in aid of Red Cross parcels to be sent to the prisoners of war in Germany. To their delight, Shirley and Janet were included in the list of performers. Dancing to 'Two o'Clock Jump', the Harry James number, they rehearsed at home and whenever they went to a dance and could persuade the compére to play the record.

One Saturday evening when Bleddyn was not working at the chip shop he invited Shirley's mother to go with him to the dance. 'Not to perform,' he added quickly. 'I haven't danced for years. I thought we could sneak in and watch Janet and your Shirley without them knowing we're there.'

–

Shirley received another letter from Freddy Clements, her first dance partner, the one who had introduced her to the joys of dance, which in turn led to her singing in public. He had joined the army on the same day as Eynon, and for a while had expected her to wait for him. Knowing how easy it had been to take him away from Beth Castle, Shirley had no illusions about his loyalty.

The letter didn't mention her singing, just told her the few things the censor would allow about his daily activities. Irritated, she threw it aside. She wouldn't write back; it was better not to hang on to the past. The future with its promise of great things was what she dreamed of, encumbrances of the past were not for her. Freddy was boring. A man with an uninteresting past and no future. Dragging failures along, trying to find them a place in constantly changing fortunes was for losers. She had to forget the past and move on. There was a time to let people go. If they didn't want the same thing, or could cause you to miss chances, they had to be abandoned like a dress that was no longer the right style.

She was already becoming irritated by the constant companionship of Janet. Their partnership had been all right for a while and she knew they stood a good chance of making a reasonable success of their singing and dancing act. It just wasn't what she wanted. She wanted to stand on stage and accept the applause knowing it was hers alone. Janet had outgrown her usefulness. The night she had tried to enter the contest without her and had been cheated by Joseph still rankled. She didn't want to finish with Joseph, although he was not a part of her future plan. She needed him for a while yet, to take her to places when she didn't feel confident going alone.

Joseph did very little apart from escorting Shirley and Janet to their concerts and to dances. When he wasn't needed as their escort, he came home from work and, after cleaning himself up and eating the meal provided by his mother, he would sit and read to his wife. It was weeks since Dolly had felt well enough to get out of bed and come downstairs so he spent more and more time up in her bedroom.

Besides reading, he talked to her about Shirley and Janet and others who frequented the dances. Unable to go and resigned to that fact, Dolly enjoyed hearing about the music and the people he met, reminding him sometimes when she began to feel afraid, of his promise not to become too fond of anyone else.

He flattered her, told her she was too lovely to ever fear a rival.

'I'm too boring to attract someone else.' He would smile, repeating the reassurances as often as she needed them. 'Don't you think I realise how lucky I am to have found a lovely girl like you to love? I wish you would get well a bit faster, but apart from your illness, there's nothing in my life I want to change.'

He knew he was lying; she knew he was lying; but the game of pretend helped them to cope.

The Saturday dance was a regular arrangement with Janet and herself but Shirley learned from Eirlys that on the following Wednesday there was a special evening which included a talent competition organised by the council entertainment committee. There would be someone there looking for acts for a prestigious open-air variety show on the promenade once every week during the peak holiday month. Besides local talent, professional performers would be invited to take pan.

Singers either solo or in groups were required as well as dancers. Shirley wanted to dance solo and sing too. As confidence in herself had grown so had her voice. Janet was definitely not needed.

On Wednesday morning she asked her mother to mind the shop for an hour and went to the market café. Holding her head and putting on a dramatic expression, she announced to Janet that she had a 'real bad head'. 'I can't go to the singing lesson or practise the dance,' she complained sadly. 'I doubt if I'll be well enough for tonight, so why don't you go on your own?'

'I won't do that, we're a double act. No, we'll miss it if you don't feel up to it. There'll be other chances. I'll go and see some of my friends. I've neglected them these past weeks.'

'Thanks, Janet, you're a real good pal.'

Relieved that her plan had worked, Shirley walked sorrowfully until she was out of sight, then picked up speed and ran back to the shop to prepare for the singing lesson. She would be picked for the display, she just knew it. She would think of an excuse for Janet later. She had a momentary twinge of conscience for the way she was cheating her friend, but it soon passed. No one ever achieved anything worthwhile without being strong-minded, and she knew she wanted this badly enough to risk Janet's friendship.

An audience had been invited to watch the rehearsals and a small fee charged in aid of one of the war charities. No opportunity was lost to make money to help the army, navy and air force at this time.

When she walked into the dance hall, which was now filled with rows and rows of occupied seats, the first person she saw was her mother. Hetty and Bleddyn had found a place in a dark corner but it was close to the cloakroom and Shirley bumped right into them.

'Mam? Mr Castle? What are you doing here?'

'We hoped you wouldn't see us,' Hetty said. 'We wanted to watch you and Janet without you knowing we're here, not to make you nervous, you see.'

'Janet? Huh! Janet's let me down,' Shirley said. 'I'm having to perform on my own and I don't think I'm up to it. In fact I think I might as well go home.'

'Of course you are, love,' Hetty said.

'Don't do that, treat it as a challenge,' Bleddyn said.

'You think I should try?'

As though persuaded by them, she went to where the master of ceremonies was organising his acts in order of appearance and pleaded to be near the end. As the final act, her voice would stay in the minds of the audience for longer.

'My mam has turned up,' she confided. 'Embarrassed I'd be and if I'm last she'll be gone home.'

She was given the final spot.

As usual the acts were varied: many were singers, most were dancers, others tried their hand at a comedy act. Shirley chose not to dance, using the excuse that her partner had let her down. She stood in the wings going through the song she had chosen in her mind. It was the song Max Moon had written, 'Waiting for Yesterday'. She would amaze them with her voice, she would move them and she would make them cry.

When she was called to the stage she walked on having given the band leader her music and stood quietly waiting as the introduction was played.

'On life's stage, yesterday is waiting in the wings, come, bring him back to me...' She sang powerfully and with much emotion, a sob in her voice as she pleaded with the fates to listen to her plea. As the song came to an end she stood with arms out, palms up. 'To my happiness you hold the key. Yesterday, please, bring him back to me.' The last note was strong and she held it, swelling and filling the hall with its wonderful sound, then allowed it to fade to a whisper before she bent forward as though grief-stricken.

Everyone in the audience felt the emotion of the words. There were very few who didn't want to relive their yester-days, the days before their loved ones had been taken from them. The applause was deafening and, as Shirley had hoped, there were tears in the eyes of many.

She cried a little too, whether from the emotion of her successful performance or the feelings she had felt through Max's words and music. Her mother and Bleddyn took her home while the murmur of admiration continued around them.

Near the doorway, Joseph stood and watched as she left. His feelings were mixed. He guessed she had dumped Janet once again, but with the voice she possessed, could he blame her? Janet had been a stepping-stone the same as he had been, and Freddy Clements, and the farmer who had taken her when she needed an escort.

As he walked home he thought of the quiet voice and the hesitant actions when she had first sung, accompanied by Janet. They'd had a simple routine and had kept to it, stiff, predictable and unsure. Their voices had been pure but weak and somewhat tremulous. Shirley had been a fledgling and now she had learnt to fly.

He went into the shop the following day to congratulate her and asked why Janet had not been there. She stared at him for a moment, then, as though making up her mind, said, 'I wanted to sing that song on my own. I know I was selfish, but as a duet it didn't really work and I knew that I could put it over in a way that would touch people. There, so I admit it, I'm selfish and unkind. But I want to dance and sing, I want a career as a performer and whatever you think of me, I won't give up on that.'

'Have you told Janet about your success?'

She looked away. 'No, I haven't decided what to say. However I put it she'll think badly of me and, surprising as it might seem, I don't want that. I still want to sing and dance with her, we get on well and as a duet we're fine. It isn't enough though. I want a solo career.'

'You want everything, Shirley.' He spoke without anger. 'You treat people badly and want them to remain your friends, you want to hang on to Janet in case your solo career fails, and what about me? I'm useful as an escort to get you home safely at night – except when you meet someone more interesting.'

'I'm sorry, Joseph. But I can't offer you anything more. You're right, I do need you. But as you say, only as a support, not as the love of my life.'

'Have I asked for more than friendship?' he demanded and she was surprised at the harshness of his voice. 'Have I ever given any indication of wanting more?'

'Well no, but—'

'Don't flatter yourself! I am concerned about you travelling home alone at night, that's all. Right?'

'Joseph, I'm glad of your friendship and I value it. I'll never treat you so rudely again. I don't want anything more, there isn't room in my life for love affairs. I want a career more than I want anything else. Love is for later. You can understand that, can't you?'

'Just don't step on too many people or travel alone for too long, or you'll find one day that it's too late to find love. Success can offer years of fame and glory followed by years of loneliness.'

Suddenly angry at his preaching disapproval, she said. 'I'll take that chance! I could have years of success followed by more years of success, have you thought of that?'

'Hold on to some friends, Shirley, just in case.' he said quietly as he left.

She felt a bit tearful after he had gone, his words a reminder of the need to go and explain to Janet, but what could she say?

A letter came on Monday asking her to attend a meeting during which the programme for the concert would be arranged. Taking it with her, she went to see Janet on Sunday morning. On the way she went through a series of inventions and unconvincing stories in her head, and in the end told her friend the truth.

At first Janet looked hurt but then she relaxed her shoulders and said, 'I don't really blame you. I know I'm not in your league.'

'Janet, don't be so nice about it! I treated you badly and I'm ashamed.'

'I am hurt by what you did. I just wish you'd told me how you felt. I'd have come to support you, I'll be proud of the small part I played if you are a success. I don't have your ambition; for me it was a bit of fun.'

'Will you come to the meeting? I put our names down as a song and dance duo.'

'I don't think so.'

'Please. We can do our usual dance routine, know it backwards we do.'

'We didn't take part in the audition so how can we be included?'

'I put our names down. I told them it was a condition of my taking part.' She was lying but what did that matter if it was a comfort to Janet? 'And another thing, I think I should change my name to something more snappy. What about Jane? Jane and Janet, The Two Jays, what d'you think?'

They went on the following evening and once again, it was Joseph who went with them as it was likely to finish late. Hetty was there and again Bleddyn accompanied her.

As uninvolved onlookers, Bleddyn and Hetty thought the whole thing was chaotic. There were people pushing their way through the crowd of anxious would-be performers first one way then another, hands filled with sheaves of papers, calling for various people to identify themselves. A pianist strummed a few bars of a tune then someone would ask for something different and he would shuffle his papers while answering shouted instructions from one or another of the organisers. In a corner, Shirley and Janet practised their steps, bumping into others doing the same. Although it was a confusion without any semblance of order, there was something very exciting about it and for Hetty, knowing her daughter was an important part of it, the mood was intoxicating.

No one sang or performed their complete act. A few sang a couple of bars just to get the correct key. Shirley and Janet did a brief introduction to their act as it hadn't been seen by the compere, and gradually the list was made up in order of performance. They were all asked to attend more rehearsals over the following few days to ensure that the standard was high enough.

'I hope Mam can cover for me in the shop.' Shirley whispered. 'How will you manage at the café?'

'I'll manage – somehow,' Janet said, pulling a face as she thought of the useless Lilly and wondered if Mrs Denver might oblige.

As Shirley and Janet were leaving, Max walked in having been invited by Eirlys to hear some of the acts.

'I hear you sang my song for the audition and you were marvellous,' he said, kissing Shirley on the cheek.

'Wonderful song,' she said with a smile.

They all walked home together and Joseph. Bleddyn and Max were invited into the flat for a hot drink and to discuss the situation. Joseph seemed ill at ease and stood in a corner as though anxious to be gone. He didn't stay long and after promising to be the girls' escort if needed, waved at them all and left.

Max promised to be there for Shirley's rehearsal and she determined to do her best, just as though she were singing to an audience. His song deserved the best she could give.

She was so excited she knew she wouldn't sleep. Even the thought of her early start dealing with the newspapers wouldn't work tonight. She curled up in bed and wrote to Freddy. She had to tell someone, boast about her success, or she would burst.

Teresa Love was angry. When Morgan had come home from work so late on the day he had visited his daughter, he had been subdued. He had said very little but she knew Eirlys had made him think about Teresa's presence there and maybe advised him that she should leave. He didn't speak except to complain, and made it clear that their food was not what he'd been used to when Annie was alive. He criticised the untidiness in the house and said he couldn't go to work again with a shirt that was unironed apart from the bit that showed underneath his jacket. She had been as nice to him as she could, making him a sandwich which he didn't eat and leading him up to their bedroom with promises that normally delighted him. He wanted nothing to do with any of it, turning on his side away from her and pretending to sleep.

In the days that followed things hadn't improved. Now she was facing the fact that her time here might be over. She wasn't going to beg him to let her stay. It was time she moved on anyway; it was never a good idea to stop in one place too long. A year was beginning to seem like a lifetime. Better to get out before the roof falls in, was one of her expressions. This time 'the roof' was the mountain of debts she had built up that would soon crash down on her.

After sending the boys off to school, she took money from Stanley's money box and went into Cardiff. Instinct told her where to go and within four hours she had earned enough to put Stanley's cash back and buy herself a good meal in a smart restaurant, where she picked up another client with whom to spend the night. Let Morgan worry, it might make him appreciate her a bit more. If Eirlys thought the worst of her, well, what did it matter if she proved her right? Superior little bitch, she wasn't important and, if he kept up this miserable mood, neither was Morgan!

She stayed out all the following day and narrowly avoided an arrest when talking to the driver of a car, lifting her skirt to entice him. Weary and ready for a row, she walked into the house to find Eirlys there with roasted potatoes being lifted out of the oven and some sausages sizzling on a serving dish, with vegetables being drained by Morgan. The three boys sat at the table, scrubbed and ready to eat.

'Where have you been?' Morgan demanded.

'Having some fun!' she retorted.

'Mum loves a bit of fun, don't you, Mum?' Percival said in his solemn manner.

'Shut up and get on with yer dinner!' she snapped. 'I don't want none of that muck. I'm going out for a decent meal.' She went upstairs, threw off her clothes, redressed and went out.

The meal was eaten in silence broken only by Percival's half-muttered complaint about the hard edges of the potatoes boverin' him, but he was hushed by Stanley and, head down in misery, he ate them, a protest in every movement of his little jaw. Eirlys said nothing. She didn't want to be there and certainly didn't want to have to explain to Teresa that her eldest son had come to her flat begging her to help when his mum had disappeared.

–

Joseph went home one day and was surprised when his mother was waiting for him at the door. She was tearful as she told him that Dolly had become much worse. The doctor had been and warned her that Dolly might not survive more than a week, two weeks at the most. In a state of shock, Joseph stared at his mother. Knowing Dolly was terminally ill hadn't really prepared him for her death. It wasn't something that could be rehearsed. When it happened it would be a shock, just as the warning that her days were numbered was a shock. Warnings like this were not in any way a rehearsal; there was always the thought that a miracle might happen and she might recover. No one could rehearse grief, he thought sadly.

'I should have been here,' he groaned, hurrying through to the front bedroom where she lay. Mrs Beynon stood back while Joseph knelt at the bedside of his wife, stroking her white hand and murmuring apologies for his absence.

Dolly was asleep and Joseph watched her for a while. He felt calm as he went to where his mother stood folding things that didn't need folding and smoothing things that were already smooth.

'Well, Mam,' he whispered. 'We're going to have to face it. I'm going to miss her more than people would imagine.' He held her tightly and said sadly. 'After all the hours I've spent with her, reading, talking, or just watching her sleeping, it will be empty here without her.'

'Don't talk as though she's already gone,' his mother whispered back as they left the room. 'The doctors don't know everything. Miracles do happen.'

'Not this time they don't. We have to stop pretending, Mam.'

As he lay in bed that night, he thought about the freedom that would be his when Dolly had gone. He didn't feel free; he felt bereft.

Unable to sleep he got up, dressed and went for a walk. He didn't have any destination in mind, but found himself outside the newsagent, looking up at the windows of the flat above, where Shirley lived with her mother. He turned away and wandered through the town and out to the popular beach where the humped shapes of the canvas-covered rides were barely visible in the uncertain light of the morning.

There was no one about and he sat for a while on the sea wall, staring unseeing towards the sea. Below him the rides were locked up and silent. One or two of the stalls had toppled slightly in the soft sand; somewhere there was the tinkling sound of a toy windmill blown along the promenade by the slight breeze.

The smell of the wet sand brought to his mind childhood memories of summers when the pinnacle of achievement was a well-built castle with a moat. He smiled as he remembered the endless and futile trips to and from the edge of the tide, with buckets of water to fill the unfillable channels.

He went slowly back home, passing the newsagent where he guessed Shirley would be sorting out the morning deliveries. He was tempted to go in and talk to her but decided against it. He wasn't ready to talk about Dolly, not yet. Besides, he was needed at home where Dolly would probably be waking. He began to hurry. He wanted to be there when she opened her eyes. Her eyes glowed when she woke and saw him beside her.

—

Eirlys was kept busy with the routine of the office and the added burden of plans for the summer of entertainments. She passed responsibility for some of the smaller events to others so she could concentrate on the larger, more important occasions, like the grand open-air concert. There were the school choirs' concerts, pet shows, baby competitions and the fun day in the park with many sporting events booked: a women's football match with the players wearing long skirts, a Donkey Derby courtesy of Bernard Gregory with Ronnie Castle giving the commentary, plus dozens of other plans in which streets arranged their own fun.

Already the atmosphere in the town had been lifted, although the telegrams continued to arrive telling of death, injury and imprisonment of loved ones. At least the activities helped to take people's minds from the dread of further bad news. The Union flag and the Welsh Dragon were displayed and many shopkeepers filled their windows with what goods they had to sell, interspersing them with photographs of local heroes and the most encouraging items of news cut from newspapers and magazines like *Picture Post* and *Illustrated* and *John Bull*.

When Eirlys wrote to Ken, she told him of these things and he wrote back and told her that although he missed her dreadfully, she had been right to return. She was helping the people of her town. The war was not only fought on the battlefields, he told her, repeating the words of others.

Using the excuse of long hours spent at work, Eirlys didn't see much of her father, although from her occasional meeting with the three boys, she knew that things were not going well.

'Can you come and cook us some roast 'taters again?' Harold asked one day when she saw them on their way home from school.

'Better than that, ask your mother if you can come to see me on Saturday and we can have a meal, then go and see what's happening over on the beach.'

This was arranged and she called for the boys without actually going inside the house that had once been her home. She was upset at the untidy appearance of the boys.

116

Their clothes had been carelessly washed and showed little evidence of ever having seen a iron. Percival's shirt lacked two buttons and she wondered if the limited contents of her sewing box would include replacements. In case it didn't, she stopped at the draper and bought buttons and thread and a few other items she thought she might need.

Back at the flat, where a tempting aroma of rabbit stew filled the air, she persuaded the boys to allow her to iron their shirts while they waited for the food to cook. To her surprise they ate everything she placed before them, even Percival.

'We ain't 'ad no breakfast,' Harold informed her. 'Mam says we'd waste your food if we didn't come real hungry.'

With lips tight with disapproval, Eirlys refilled their plates.

They went to the beach and Eirlys gave them money for several rides before Bleddyn spotted them and allowed them several more without charge. Tired, sticky and contented, they caught the bus back into town, then walked the rest of the way home.

Teresa opened the door as they approached. She was dressed immaculately in a summer suit of pale pink with a hair ornament to match, and high-heeled shoes over silk-stockinged feet. Eirlys wondered again how she could spend so much time on herself and so little on her sons.

'Morgan ain't 'ere,' Teresa called as Eirlys stopped at the gate. 'No point you comin' in.' She began closing the door behind the boys as they waved goodbye, and Eirlys walked disconsolately away.

She knew that the factory no longer closed down at weekends and her father often had to work Saturday and Sunday, but she had hoped to see him. It was no longer possible for her to call without a reason. The excuse of taking the boys out had seemed to be a necessary one for visiting her home. She went back to the flat disappointed. If she had asked what shift Morgan was working she might 'happen to be passing' the factory when he left, but she couldn't walk back and knock on the door; Teresa Love had made it quite clear she was unwelcome. Perhaps she would try again next weekend, she thought as she went home. But she didn't have to wait that long.

It was the following day when she saw her father. It was almost three o'clock and she was at home working on some financial lists she had brought back from the office and was about to stop and make herself a late lunch when the loud knocking alarmed her. As she opened her door, papers and pencil in her hand, her father pushed past her and closed the door behind him.

'She's gone. She's taken the boys, and she's gone.'

Eirlys saw then that he had been crying.

She didn't know what to say. It was hardly the time to tell him it was for the best; he clearly wouldn't agree. She folded her papers away and stood there while her father sobbed and told her how he had returned home after his six-till-two shift, to find the house empty, and a note propped against the teapot telling him they were gone and were never coming back. Calming himself, he said slowly and with a bitter laugh. 'Blames you she does. She said I've never been happy since you came back.'

'I'm sorry, Dadda, I should have been more under-standing. I had no right—'

'No, love, you aren't to blame. I would have realised soon enough what a fool I'd been. Truth is I already had but

I didn't know how to get out of the mess I'd made. Specially after this.'

He handed her a post-office book which showed that the account had been emptied and closed. 'Stole it all, she did. Money your mam had saved for when you got married so we could give you a real good start. It was money that belonged to you, Eirlys love. I never touched a penny of it, no matter how difficult things were. There was enough for a deposit on a house.'

'But how—'

'Forged my signature, she did. Easily done I suppose. Your mam always said it was like the scrawl of an eight-year-old.'

She tried to persuade him to go to the police but he was adamant. 'No, even after everything that happened I can't put the boys through anything like that. She knew I wouldn't. She knew she was safe from an old fool like me.'

Together they went back to the sad, neglected house in Conroy Street. Eirlys looking around wondering where to start getting it back to its original neatness and wondering if it were even possible.

For the rest of that day, late into the night, Eirlys and Morgan pored over accounts and bills and overdue statements to assess the damage. With an aching dismay, Eirlys realised she would have to commit most of her wages for the coming months to clear the debts Teresa had left.

'Thank goodness you came back home,' Morgan said.

For a fleeting moment. Eirlys wished she hadn't.

Five

Eirlys paid rent to the end of the month at the flat and began to pack her belongings ready to move back into her father's house. She went to look around in advance of moving back, hoping things would not be as bad as she feared. She guessed there would be washing and cleaning needed as Teresa's idea of housework was not like her mother's had been. She began by making up her bed in the room the boys had used, then concentrated on the kitchen.

She didn't go into the front room at first. It was a room they only used at Christmas or when they had visitors. When she did go there to look for something in the sideboard, where Annie had once kept previous bills and receipts, she was surprised to find the room practically empty.

'Dadda?' she called, staring at the wide expanse of empty carpet. 'What's happened to the furniture?'

'Teresa sold it,' he said, shamefaced.

'But she can't have sold it, it isn't even paid for!'

'Fool I've been, haven't I? Besides all the other debts, now I have to pay for a three-piece suite that I don't even have any more.'

'You'll have to get the police.'

'No, Eirlys, I can't do that! I couldn't face it. I feel enough of a fool already.'

Reluctantly, Eirlys agreed.

She was too busy to start sorting out the house; her work often kept her at the office until long after five-thirty. Yet in every spare moment, she collated the piles of unpaid bills into some kind of order. By date, then in order of importance, then shuffled them again into the various areas like coal, light and rent and rates, local shops. Which to settle first? Once she threw them into the air in frustration, watching them fluttering down to cover the carpet and all the space where furniture had once stood.

There were so many unpaid bills she really didn't know where to begin. Head in her hands, elbows on her much scribbled-in notebook, she frowned as she wondered which was the most sensible way of dealing with them. One thing was certain: they wouldn't all be cleared for several months.

She decided finally that honesty was the best way and she wrote to some of the people to whom her father owed money and explained, as kindly as she could, something of what had happened.

There was no doubt her father's affairs were going to take a long time, Eirlys sighed as she began placing money on to red-printed bills that most urgently needed payment. The rent was in arrears and the ominous warnings on the coal and gas bills were also priorities. There was also the new three-piece suite to be paid for, even though it was no longer there. Teresa had sold it, but the balance still had to be paid. She had acted illegally but Morgan accepted the debt as his own.

Digging into her own rather slender savings was unavoidable. So was staying in her flat. Having to come home was disappointing, but the rent she had been paying would help sort out the financial mess. They needed all the money they could find to clear the debts left by Teresa.

'Dadda is more important than my independence,' she explained to Beth when she told her what had happened. 'He's so unhappy. Teresa hurt him terribly by getting into a mess and then running away leaving him to deal with it all. Besides the realisation of how she cheated him, there's the loss of the boys too. Losing the boys is very hard for him.'

'Losing Teresa too,' Beth said. 'I think he believed she was there for life. Thank goodness he didn't marry her.'

It was Bleddyn, and Johnny's wife Hannah, who helped Eirlys move back in the following weekend. Using the firm's van, Bleddyn carried her few possessions from the flat and, seeing the mess the house was in, Hannah stayed and helped with the cleaning. By the end of the first day, it was beginning to feel like her home once more, although, she admitted to Hannah, she grieved for her brief foray into living as an independent woman.

She didn't have much time to nurse her disappointment though, with so much work to be done. She would get home sometimes as late as seven thirty and when her father was working and not in need of a meal, she would make a sandwich and listen to the wireless, glad of Arthur Askey and Tommy Handley and other comedians making her laugh, and the extra programmes of organ music to hum to as she dealt with the chores. If she felt lonely she brushed the thought away. She was one of the lucky ones: so far none of her closest friends had been seriously injured, she was doing a job she enjoyed, living among friends in a town she loved.

Many would envy her, and be grateful for such luxuries.

–

Despite being worried about his wife, Joseph's attraction for Shirley was growing and as he left home each morning, leaving behind his sick wife, he felt the guilt surround him at every step. This morning he hadn't spent as much time with Dolly as he usually did, making excuses about cleaning shoes, chopping firewood they didn't need, and going to the shop to buy an extra paper and spend a few minutes with Shirley.

If he were honest, he didn't believe there could be a future for himself with Shirley Downs, but the promise he had made to his wife about not getting involved with someone else was becoming increasingly impossible to keep. No actions, he had avoided even touching her, but his thoughts about her seemed almost as disloyal.

'I've met a girl,' he told his mother that evening, and before she could comment, he added quickly. 'No, nothing has happened, not even a kiss, but because of how I feel, I'm afraid to stay long with Dolly in case she guesses. I don't want her to have a moment's doubt about me.'

'Then stop behaving like a guilty man, Joseph. I bought a new jigsaw puzzle today. Try and persuade her to sit up for a while and help you with it.' She looked at him with affection. Life had not treated him well and she longed for him to have some normal, good-natured fun. Marrying Dolly so soon after finding out that she was seriously ill had been a devastating blow and now he was a prisoner in a marriage that had no foundation in love. Pity was a poor substitute.

'Perhaps I should stay away from dances. Better if I don't see her at all.'

'I think you should go and have fun, be happy for a while. You enjoy dancing and the crowd and the music and laughter are a tonic for you. If you're happy you bring it home, then that happiness helps Dolly too,' she advised.

Throughout June and early July, Shirley and Janet were busy with engagements. Their reputation was growing and they were booked for cabaret at dances and for the occasional businessmen's dinner dances.

Calling themselves The Two Jays, Shirley calling herself Jane, had started a good run of success. They sang duets and danced together, and they would include a solo from Shirley which was always a highlight of their act. She usually chose a sentimental piece, which everyone needed; the reminder of their boys far away from home had an appeal that rarely failed to please. Like tears of grief after a death, the sadness was in some strange way a comfort. Max's song, 'Waiting for Yesterday', was a regular request.

Keeping to their early mornings at work and the late evening bookings was hard for them both. Shirley used most of her afternoons off to rest, but on Wednesday, when Janet too was not working, they practised, talked over their ideas, and dreamed their dreams.

Joseph still escorted them, and Shirley hugged him once or twice when they had received extra applause and praise, but he never responded. He told them both how well they had done but there was never anything more. Shirley wondered why and for a while suspected that it was Janet he liked and they were perhaps meeting without telling her.

'D'you know where Joseph lives?' she asked her friend one day. 'I know it's Oakley Road but it's a long straggle of houses, miles of it.'

Janet shook her head and Shirley stared at her, trying to decide whether or not her friend was being truthful. 'We don't know much about him at all, do we?' Janet said. 'Just that he failed the army because of his eyesight and lives with his mam.'

'I might walk up there one day and ask a few people where they live.'

'No, we couldn't do that! What if he opened the door, what would we say? He'll tell us if we ask, there's no secret, he just isn't a Chatterbox!'

'Aren't you curious? You do like him, don't you?'

'I don't think about him any more than as useful company when we walk home late at night. I don't think he wants any more than that. Strange though.' She frowned.

'Never no mention of family, no brother or sister.' Shirley lowered her voice and in a frightened voice added. 'Perhaps he's murdered them all and put the bodies under the floorboards!' She laughed at Janet's expression.

'Stop it, Shirley, or I'll never sleep tonight!'

'Come on, he's boring but not dangerous!'

Satisfied that Janet had had no more luck in interesting Joseph than herself, she let the subject drop. She wasn't interested in Joseph as a serious boyfriend, but just curious at his lack of interest in herself, except as their escort.

–

Morgan was depressed. The house seemed so empty without the noise the boys created and everything was orderly when he had become accustomed to clutter. The few items Teresa had left behind, Eirlys had folded away and put in an old suitcase on top of her wardrobe: clothes the boys might need if they ever returned, and one or two school and story books.

At her suggestion Morgan had rented an allotment. It was too late for most crops but he built a small shed with windows on three sides where he planned to start next year's seedlings. Other allotment holders were generous and he soon had a few sprouts and leeks in neat rows. Lettuces were transplanted and radishes were sown. He knew it was more to keep busy than with any real hope of success.

Eirlys found him there one Sunday evening, leaning on a hoe, talking to another gardener. The last few days had been dry and very warm and loosening the soil helped to keep down the weeds and refresh it.

'It needs watering, any volunteers?' he asked when Eirlys approached.

They went to where a stream flowed deep in the ground and had settled into a pool, and lifted off the cover of the area they used. The rich, earthy smell met their nostrils and Eirlys found it pleasing with half-forgotten memories. The ground was damp and thick with wild flowers, mostly herb Robert. Thoughts of other, sun–filled days flooded back as Eirlys filled her nose with the pungent perfume which many disliked but which she loved. Whenever she smelled that unmistakable aroma it took her back to hours spent helping her father in the community of gardeners not far from her school.

They worked steadily for a while, passing a comment occasionally with one of the other gardeners. An elderly man whom she remembered from when she was a child tending her own small plot, called across.

'I found this the other day, Morgan. It belongs to one of your lads. Harold I think.' He held out a wooden boat which Morgan had carved, the mast still intact but the sails shredded. 'I found it near the water, it's rotted in the damp earth,' the man explained. 'I'll make some new sails if you like. I made several of these for my boys years ago.'

Too choked to reply, Morgan looked at Eirlys for help. She looked at the boat and smiled at the man she had once called Uncle Malcolm. 'Thank you, he'll be pleased to see it repaired.'

Eirlys finished watering the plot alone. Her father had hurried home to hide his distress.

An account arrived the next morning from a store in Cardiff. Before she left, Teresa had spent a lot of money replenishing her own and the boys' wardrobes. Eirlys showed her father, then without comment put it with the rest.

'How she managed to carry it all puzzles me,' he said with a shrug.

Eirlys thought Teresa would not have any difficulty persuading people to help her, but she said nothing. Everything had been said, time and again. Now her energies must be spent putting her father's life back together.

–

Eynon Castle received a disturbing letter from Alice soon after he returned to camp. She attempted a joke, telling him that her father was unimpressed with Eynon's lack of aggression. She mentioned that he had hit her but it was casually said, as though the blow had been nothing. She had stayed away from the seaside rock shop embarrassed by a cut lip and a heavily bruised nose.

'I didn't want to put the customers off and I didn't want your Auntie Audrey writing to worry you by telling you I'm off work sick,' she told him. 'I'm fine, just a bit sore so don't worry about me. Dad has calmed down now and if the pattern follows as usual, he'll stay that way for a few weeks. He can't help it, he loves me really,' she had added.

Alice had never made a secret of her father's violent temper, but Eynon's growing love for Alice made it unacceptable.

If only he could get home, just for a few hours, to see her and reassure himself she was all right. Being caught out of camp without permission was a serious offence, particularly for him with his past record. Yet he knew he had to try.

He felt that fortune was on his side when his group was taken to a place on the Brecon Beacons to camp and train for an unknown destination. Once he was overseas it was unlikely he and Alice would meet for months, if not years. He had to get away and get safely back without his absence being discovered.

He had suffered no bullying since his return to his group and, taking a chance, he asked the man who had once made his life so miserable to help him.

The camp was set up in a valley, where a sparkling stream, icy cold, straight from the mountains, meandered slowly through on its way to join the River Usk.

He and Kipper were on guard until late at night and leaving Kipper to do what was necessary to cover his absence. Eynon ran south and headed for the road that would take him to Merthyr Tydfil, Abercynon and eventually Cardiff. He was fortunate with lifts, convincing the lorry drivers he stopped that he was on manoeuvres and was having to use his initiative to get to his destination.

Used to travelling at night after his months on the run, he knocked on Alice's door at three a.m.

Reassured by seeing her, he spent an hour in her bed, filled his pockets with food and began to journey back. Before he left, he woke Colin Potter and warned him not to hit his daughter again. 'Or you'll find yourself back in the fight game, with me as your opponent,' he warned. 'You'll find I'm not so mild as I pretend. Right?'

He avoided public transport. It was too slow, and besides, he knew his face would clearly reveal guilt if any redcapped military policemen appeared. Using the same story about a journey using any means available, he begged lifts and completed the journey with only minutes to spare, walking casually back into camp with a detail sent to draw water from the stream for the breakfast tea urn. At a roll-call unexpectedly made later that morning, he stood beside Kipper and shouted his name as present, sharing a grin with the friend who had once been an enemy.

–

'Who was that bloke you brought home last night?' Colin Potter demanded of his daughter. 'It was Eynon, and I didn't bring him home, he had a brief leave and called to see if I was all right,' she explained. Colin aimed a blow at her, leaning back on the wall to regain his balance as he staggered forward. 'Behave yourself, if you know what's good for you,' he threatened. 'I will, Dad, don't worry,' she said submissively.

–

Freddy Clements was on the move. A letter containing only a printed form with spaces for him to add a word or two, was delivered to Shirley and she wondered whether he was moving nearer to home or further away. She was surprised at how the thought of seeing him again pleased her. Freddy had been great fun, his lack of loyalty and careless attitude, his generosity with money that didn't really belong to him, had all been assets during their time together.

She hadn't been the recipient of his selfish, thoughtless behaviour and it really had been fun. She knew how he had cheated on Beth Castle when they were engaged to be married, and how he had used their savings without telling his fiancée. Shirley doubted whether even a spell in the army would have changed him.

She took out the letters he had written and read them, and became aware as she went through them that in fact Freddy had changed. At first it was all fun and scrounging was a way of life. Gradually the letters had become more serious. They were still filled with humorous anecdotes but he talked about his plans for the future with a determination that surprised her on reading them one after another. He wanted to open a shop selling men's clothing, like the one in which he had worked before joining the army. Reading his words and hearing his voice in her mind, saying them, she felt certain he would succeed. She put the last one down, the impersonal printed form stating simply that he was well and that a letter would follow at the first opportunity, and wondered whether they might have a future together.

–

Beth Castle and Peter Gregory were eventually married at the end of July 1941. In a hastily arranged ceremony, followed by a simple meal provided at the café on the beach, which closed to the public for less than two hours, they said their goodbyes to the few friends and family who had attended, and hurried off for a forty-eight hour honeymoon in West Wales.

Seeing them off in Peter's car for which he had managed to save some petrol, Eirlys wished them luck and wondered how many hours they would have together in the following weeks. Not many, if previous months were a guide. Whatever work Peter did, it kept him out of uniform and far from home for weeks on end. Not an ideal start to a marriage, yet she envied Beth - in a non-malicious way - for having someone with whom to share love.

Her thoughts went to Ken Ward and she wondered whether they would eventually marry. Sometimes it seemed impossible and at others it was inevitable. Childishly she hugged the thought to her of someone coming into her life and sweeping her off her feet as in the best fairy stories, then she laughed at her own stupidity and went into Castle's café to help clear up the debris of the make-shift wedding breakfast.

–

Shirley's mother attended the wedding but not as a guest. She sometimes worked at the café and was there on that day as waitress, handing around trays of bite-sized snacks and wine as well as the ubiquitous cuppa. The two young girls were there, Maude and Myrtle Copp, and although Hetty had been reasonably friendly on the occasions they had met, they were still nervous of her.

Hetty's husband Paul Downs had left her when Shirley was a child, to live with another woman in a town several miles away from St David's Well. When the orphaned girls, Maude and Myrtle, were found, it was eventually realised that they were the daughters of Paul with his new 'wife' - now both dead. Since then Hetty had been through every emotion including shock, humiliation, disgust and even hatred of the innocent children, and her own mortification had seemed to be there to stay, wounding her every day, reminding her of her stupidity at not realising what was happening until it was too late. Now she had accepted that Maude, now sixteen, almost seventeen and Myrtle, now thirteen, could not be in any way responsible for the manner of their birth, and had tried to become their friend.

At first her own unease had shown, causing them to see her as gruff and suspicious, and succeeding in making them wary of her attempts to talk. Gradually she was winning them over and the day of Beth and Peter's wedding saw a big stride in their progress.

Standing in the kitchen of Castle's café overlooking the sandy St David's Well Bay she had joked and teased and gradually they started to respond. She asked questions and answered theirs as fully as she was able. Most of their questions were about Paul, their father; little things like his favourite sweets and why he hadn't smoked like other fathers, and what was he like in the morning. Maude remembered him better than Myrtle, the younger child depending on Maude's memories to make her own.

Cautiously Hetty asked about their mother and learned that she was always teasing Paul and playing tricks on him, hiding one of his shoes and producing it after the three of them watched him search in apparent frustration. They seem to have laughed a lot and a worm of envy disturbed her peace of mind when she imagined them together.

Now she smiled at Maude and asked her how she was enjoying working in the factory canteen.

'Not much. I like the hours working on the swingboats, roundabouts and helter-skelter best,' she told Hetty. 'The fares are easy to collect, not like the stalls where everything's a different price. Our Myrtle is best at arithmetic,' she added proudly.

'I can read and write and I make out Auntie Marged's shopping list every week,' Myrtle said with equal pride. 'And I have a Saturday morning job delivering for the grocer. Only until eleven, then I go over the beach,' she added.

'How do you deliver them?' Hetty teased. 'Not old enough to drive a van, are you?'

'She uses the carrier bike, but it's too heavy and she takes one order at a time and pushes the bike instead of riding it,' Maude laughed.

'Perhaps you can come and help Shirley in the shop during the winter, when the beach closes. She's always looking for someone good at figures to work a few hours.'

'All them papers and magazines? And the cigarettes and tobacco? That would be a bit hard for me.'

'It never would! Clever you are, young Myrtle. Why don't you come and talk to Shirley about it?'

'Perhaps. When summer's over. And we've got weeks and weeks of it yet.'

'Then come to tea on your day off. Shirley can show you what's needed. That'll give you plenty of time to think about it.'

Hetty wanted to be a part of the girls' life. With Shirley out most of the time she spent many hours alone: seeking the company of Paul's children could be a pleasant way of filling them.

–

Lilly Castle's baby was growing and Lilly was growing too, fatter and more slovenly as weeks passed, and she made no attempt to do more than look after her child. The washing which her parents had insisted was her job had first been given to Mrs Denver, Baby Phyllis's other grandmother. Now it was gradually slipped into the big family wash done either by Lilly's mother, Marged, or Marged's sister Auntie Audrey. Shamed by seeing Mrs Denver dealing with it, they had given in.

Using a pram given to her by Johnny's wife, Hannah, Lilly would walk to the park and sit with other young mothers to compare notes and discuss the children's progress. About once a week she walked to Queen Street to visit Phil's mother. It was usually on Wednesday when the shops closed and there was nothing particular to do. Mrs Denver welcomed her and always had a little gift for the baby.

'Come to me for a *cwtch*, fach,' she would say. Then taking the little girl from her pram and cuddling her, she would wrap her in a Welsh shawl close to her body, and with both hands free she made tea and set the table with whatever goodies she had managed to find.

They would admire the child and declare her the cleverest they had ever known, and Lilly would complain about how tired she was and how her family didn't understand her inability to work. Sympathy was showered on her, Mrs Denver telling her she was an exceptionally caring mother, and Lilly would walk home content.

If Phil hadn't been killed in action, she knew they would have been so happy, herself, Phil as the doting father and their beautiful daughter, supported by Phil's mother. Life would have been perfect. In a glow of melancholy she strolled home to where Auntie Audrey and Maude would have a meal waiting for her, having invited her to spend the evening with them so they could admire the baby. Perhaps, as she'd had such a lovely afternoon out, she might offer to deal with the washing-up. Unless it was roast potatoes – she hated scouring pans. Wednesday was sometimes a roast potatoes day.

Roast potatoes weren't only for Sundays. To make a meatless meal more interesting and when there was a little fat to spare, many housewives put part-boiled potatoes in the oven. The meal on this Wednesday was salad and a little grated cheese, with boiled potatoes; so she volunteered.

–

Lilly's brother Ronnie and his wife, Olive, were running their vegetable stall in the local market and on that Wednesday afternoon when the market closed, Ronnie suggested they walk out to Mr Gregory's smallholding to see if he had anything for sale which they could buy for their stall. There were plenty of customers in the busy market but irregular supplies of anything but the basics sometimes meant they had nothing to sell to them. Olive, with the birth of her baby drawing near, wasn't sure about the walk.

'I feel a bit tired. Ronnie. I think I'll lie on the bed for a while. You go, I'll be all right on my own.'

With the intention of not being away from her long, Ronnie set off quickly on his bicycle. Their child was due in a couple of weeks and he was unhappy at Olive being on her own. On impulse he changed direction and called at his mother's home in the hope that someone would be there. He intended to ask if someone could stay with Olive for the half hour he would be away. His parents were out. The beach entertainments didn't close for half day like the shops. There was no sign of his sister Lilly; he'd have settled for her even though she would not be his first choice. Going a few doors further up the road to the house where his grandmother had lived, he knocked and walked in, calling for Auntie Audrey.

No reply. He was angry with himself for wasting time. If he had gone straight to Mr Gregory's he would be halfway there by now. There was a fair chance that Mr Gregory himself would not be home, so he had written a note and intended leaving it on the kitchen table. The Gregorys' door, like many others, was never locked.

He hesitated for a moment, wondering whether to go back home and wait until someone could stay with Olive, then, his mind made up, he went as quickly as he could to the smallholding, left the note of his requirements and raced back. In the yard. Mr Gregory saw him am've and, when he reached the house, saw him racing away.

He read the note and frowned. Unusual for him not to wait.

He always had a kettle on the boil ready for making a pot of tea and Ronnie was known to be a 'teapot', in constant need of a brew. He looked at the note again. It was a request for delivery of potatoes, carrots and the rest of the regular twice-weekly order, plus chicken and duck eggs: a PS added. 'And anything else you have for us to sell.'

He left what he was doing and walked up to the field. There might be a few greens ready for cutting. Better to wait for them to grow a bit larger but by then everyone else would have plenty and the price would drop, he reasoned.

Taking his notebook from its usual place, he made a list of what he would take and tucked it back inside the lining band of his hat. Then he remembered that Olive was close to her time and decided to take the horse and cart and go to see if she had given birth. It would explain Ronnie's haste and if the child was born it would be something interesting to tell Peter when he next wrote.

Ronnie stood on the pedals to give himself more power and raced along the quiet route towards the town, the tyres humming on the surface of the lane. He cut across corners, saving himself a few yards and went hurrying on, his thoughts on Olive and the time she had been alone. He knew he was being foolish – everyone said that babies didn't arrive within minutes of the first warnings – but he still felt she had been alone too long.

–

Another of Bernard Gregory's customers was walking towards the smallholding. Joseph had decided to treat Dolly to a chicken dinner. She ate very little, and he knew that the full meal would not be easy for her to manage, but the broth and some chicken meat put through the mincer and softened with gravy might tempt her poor appetite.

The afternoon was fine and he wasn't in a hurry. Any excuse to get away from the sickroom was to be enjoyed. The hedgerows were richly coloured with the wonderful summer display of wild flowers and he was tempted to collect some to take back to Dolly, but he remembered from previous experience that their beauty did not last more than a few hours. He found a small clump of yellow toadfiax growing in an old wall, with its small snapdragon mouths, and gathered a few. They might stay open for a few days and give Dolly some brief pleasure. She had always loved wild flowers. He was smiling as he tied them into his handkerchief when, without warning, Ronnie's bicycle hit him.

Joseph's mother heard the call from Dolly and went up the stairs.

'Where has Joseph gone?' Dolly asked. She was hot and highly coloured, her eyes enormous in the sunken cheeks. 'He promised he'd only be half an hour.'

'He's probably met someone and is having a chinwag,' Mrs Beynon soothed. 'He has to go out sometimes, Dolly. He needs a break even though he loves being with you.'

'He goes dancing, and he's out eight hours a day at work.' Tears filled her beautiful eyes and she added softly, 'I can't help being ill.'

Mrs Beynon hugged her. Dolly rarely complained, and she had never asked where Joseph had gone, or worried about his late return before. She glanced at the bedside clock. He had been gone rather a long time. To the smallholding to order a chicken for the weekend shouldn't have taken more than an hour. Even allowing for him to stay for a cup of tea with Bernard couldn't stretch it to more than two hours. Joseph had been away more than three.

'Go and find him, Mam,' Dolly pleaded. 'I'm frightened that he's been hurt.'

'Nonsense, love.' Mrs Beynon touched her daughter-in-law's shoulder, patting it gently, aware of its frailty. 'Our Joseph will come through the door any minute.'

Another half hour passed before Mr Gregory knocked at the door.

'Don't get alarmed, Mrs Beynon, but your Joseph was hurt in an accident. Not bad, mind, just a few scratches and a whopping great bruise. Knocked down by young Ronnie Castle on his bike he was. I went past only minutes later on the horse and cart and scraped them up, dusted them down and took them both to the hospital. The doctor is checking him over and he'll be home in the morning.'

'I'd better go and see him,' Joseph's mother said, reaching for her coat.

'In that case I can give you a lift.'

She ran upstairs and in a reassuring voice explained to Dolly what had happened.

'Off to see for myself, I am, and I'll be back in a hour to tell you everything, right?'

She tucked the clothes more firmly around the small wasted body and kissed the hot cheek. With a wave she hurried out. 'I'm locking you in, Dolly, so you've nothing to worry about,' she called. Then to Bernard Gregory she added, 'Scared of being on her own she is. She's so weak it makes her feel vulnerable, although what she imagines could happen to her in her own home I don't know.'

Dolly lay in the bed listening to every sound. She was terrified both of knowing she was alone in the house and the thought that Joseph wouldn't come back.

–

Ronnie was relieved to see that Olive was perfectly all right and his panic and the resulting accident were for nothing. He made a joke out of it all so she didn't know how painful his bruises were, or how embarrassed he felt at giving Joseph such a shock.

–

Joseph was feeling very uncomfortable. There were bandages on his hands and plasters on his face where branches of the hedgerow had caught him as he fell. His hip was one great ache and when he saw his mother walking in, his first words were, 'No dancing for a while, eh?'

He reassured his mother that no damage had been done, they were just keeping him in for observation because his neck was stiff where he had fallen and hit his head on the ground. 'Go back to Dolly, Mam, you know how frightened she'll be on her own,' he urged, when told that Dolly was alone. Kissing him gently on one of the few areas of his face not scratched or plastered, she had a word with the doctor and then left for home.

–

Dolly was trying to retrieve her clothes from the wardrobe. Everything was such an effort. The key wouldn't turn, the hangers wouldn't leave the rail. Crying in despair at her feebleness she sat on the bed to recover. A second try resulted in her finding shoes, a dress and a thin summer coat with which she painstakingly slowly dressed herself. Holding the handrail she edged down the stairs and out of the house.

It was strange being outside after all the months in bed. The sunlight was harsh and holding on to the wall with one hand she shaded her face with the other. The air was cooling to her feverish cheek, the touch of the rough stone wall somehow reassuringly familiar. She curiously touched the scars where the metal railing and gates had been ripped out months ago in the drive for scrap metal. Touching these things, feeling the sun on her face were pleasant, half-forgotten sensations.

She heard the sound of her own feet, hesitant and slow, tapping softly on the pavement, and further off, the rumble of a cart and the hooves of a plodding horse came to her ears.

She imagined the touch of the animal's coat, smoothing it somewhat fearfully as she had as a small child. There were people in the distance, vague and unaware of her. She tried to call out to them, suddenly afraid and alone. Her weakness had intensified and she wondered tearfully how she would get back to the house only a few yards away. She went on, telling herself that if she walked as far as the corner, Joseph would be there, smiling, lifting her and carrying her back to the dim safety of her room, away from the glare of the bright sun. She had to stop every few yards to catch her breath and rest her legs by leaning against a garden wall. At the end of the road she gave a sigh of disappointment and fell.

Jumping off the bus, anxious now she was close to home. Mrs Beynon saw the crowd at the end of the road and hesitated at her gate. She almost went to investigate but instead she went in and ran up to Dolly's room, calling as she went. 'Dolly, love. It's all right. Joseph isn't hurt bad, he's only got a few—' Her voice faded as she ran into the bedroom and saw the empty bed. She went through the rest of the house, then the garden, calling, sobbing with fear, guilt at leaving her, a sharp and very real pain in her heart. With rising dread, she went out of the house to where the crowd had increased and had been joined by an ambulance and its crew.

–

Joseph signed himself out as soon as he was told about his wife's collapse. He went to the ward where she had been taken and stood, looking down at the small insubstantial body under the smooth covers, this unmoving child-like girl who had once been a vibrant, energetic young woman. Her skin was perfectly lovely and he reached out to touch her cheek, willing her to open her eyes and look at him.

A nurse hovered and once gave Dolly a sip of some liquid that Joseph thought might be a medicine or a drug she was taking regularly to ease the pain. When they were alone he talked to her, reminding her of their long-ago yesterdays when they had fun and the days were filled with plans and ambitions and laughter, so much laughter. Max's songs came into his mind. 'Life is a stage and waiting in the wings is yesterday.'

She died early the following morning when he had left her side briefly to stretch his legs by walking along the corridor and back.

'Why did I leave her?' he wailed when the nurse confirmed his fears. 'I should have stayed. She shouldn't have died all alone.'

'They sometimes prefer it and will wait until there's no one with them, so they can relax and gently slip away,' the nurse told him comfortingly.

–

Shirley read the local paper but she didn't notice the announcement of Dolly Beynon's death in the columns dedicated to those items. It was a part of the paper she rarely glanced at, being too young to worry about such things. Besides, if she had read it the name would not have registered with her; she did not know of Dolly's existence.

Joseph had failed to turn up to take them to the Saturday dance and had not been in to apologise.

'Seems he's got fed up with us,' Janet sighed.

'Then book yourselves a taxi.' Shirley's mother insisted. 'You can walk to the hall but I don't like you wandering around late at night. With this nuisance of a black-out you can't see a hand in front of you and you could have an accident.'

The girls were becoming well known for their singing and dancing and would often be asked to perform at the local dances. On this night they had danced and sang three numbers and later were approached by a man who told them they should audition for ENSA, the organisation that travelled around entertaining the troops.

'I couldn't do that,' Shirley laughed. 'I've got to be there in the mornings to get the newspapers out!'

'And the stall-holders in the market wouldn't thank me for not being there to serve their tea and coffee,' Janet added.

The man introduced himself as Henry Thomas and gave them a card on which he had written his address and telephone number. Janet took it and tucked it into her handbag. She shrugged and said to Shirley, 'You never know. Things might change.'

'I think I'll write to Max and ask him if he knows anything about this Henry Thomas,' Shirley said thoughtfully as they waited for the taxi to take them home.

–

Joseph didn't go to work and he stayed out of the house as much as possible. He knew it was hard for his mother: all the caring she had done had filled her days and now she was left with a house that echoed with the hollowness of sad memories. He should stay with her, help her, but he couldn't. Walking into the house and not running up to talk to Dolly seemed to be a constant punishment.

He didn't escort Shirley and Janet to the dance the following week either. Instead he pushed a note through the shop door telling them only that he was unable to go due to family commitments.

The Two Jays were chosen to open an old music-hall style 'Singalong' that week and in great excitement the girls went back to Shirley's flat to look through some old-fashioned clothes they had been offered and to discuss costume and music. It was as Shirley was opening the door for Janet to leave that she saw Joseph.

'Hi yer, Joseph, where have you been'? What d'you think! We're opening the prom concert in August and now we've been asked to do some old music-hall numbers dressed for the part an' all. Good, eh?'

He didn't walk across to congratulate them; he just waved and called a greeting.

'Hey, come on, you old misery! Come and congratulate us properly,' she called as she ran towards him. It was dark but even in the blackout on that moonless night she could make out the armband on his pale jacket sleeve.

'Joseph, you've lost someone? The war, is it? Oh, not your mam I hope,' she said at once, showing concern. This must explain his absence.

'Not my mother, but someone who's been ill for a couple of years. It was Dolly, my wife.'

'Your wife?' Shirley gasped.

To his utter disbelief, she then slapped him hard across the face, again and again.

Janet ran over and held her as she rained repeated blows on him.

'Shirley.' he gasped, trying to hold her arms. 'What's all this for?'

'Not telling me you were married, that's what! Sorry I am that she died, but not as sorry as I am for you. Joseph

144

Beynon! Carrying on, dancing, enjoying yourself, and with a sick wife waiting for you at home!'

'What business is it of yours?' Joseph asked coldly. 'Have I ever done anything, said anything to you that my wife couldn't have heard?'

'You lied!'

'You wouldn't understand,' he said as he hurried away.

'I risked getting a bad reputation because of you,' Shirley shouted after him. 'People will accuse me of being a tart, carrying on with a married man!'

Janet shrugged, guiding her friend back inside. 'I suppose he's right. He only made sure we were safely home, never a hint of more.'

'He still should have told us!' She turned to go back inside. 'I shouldn't have hit him, mind, should I?' Shock and dismay turned to laughter and giggles as they went back up to the living room to discuss it.

'I don't expect he'll get a worse response than yours when he tells people his news,' Janet agreed, trying to stop the inexplicable merriment caused by shock and not lack of concern. '"My wife is dead." Thump. "Oh, is she? Then take this." Thump.'

Laughter faded as quickly as it began and they cried in shame for their reaction and for the woman called Dolly whom they had never known.

Joseph walked home hating his life and hating Dolly, momentarily, for becoming ill and then leaving him.

Shirley constantly watched the door waiting for Joseph to walk in the following day. She was trembling with humiliation, dreading seeing him but at the same time wanting to get it over. How could she have done that? How could she have hit him after being told he had just lost his wife? What crime had he committed by escorting herself and Janet to a few dances without telling them he had a wife?

She was serving a customer with cigarettes; foreign cigarettes as the supply of the well-known brands were sold out until the next allocation arrived. She knew it was Joseph standing in the doorway and tried not to look in his direction. When the customer left she couldn't ignore him any longer. She lifted the flap of the counter, walked through and stood facing him. 'Joseph, I'm so sorry. Sorry for the loss of your wife and sorry I hit you. I don't know what got into me.' Then his arms were around her and they were kissing, half hidden by the door, and her head was swimming in a whirlpool of sensations that were completely new.

Close to them people were walking past and she was unaware of them. Her world began and ended with Joseph's lips and his arms pressing her against him.

When he released her, she stepped back and stared at him. She couldn't speak, didn't know what to say.

'I've wanted to do that from the first time I saw you,' Joseph whispered, pushing the door shut as a customer tried to enter. Foolishly, Shirley muttered something about having to serve and, after staring at her for a long moment, he stood aside and allowed the door to open.

'What time d'you close?' he asked.

'I don't know. I mean—' Bewildered, some part of her mind told her she must not allow this. With a wife so recently dead it was not right. 'I don't know,' she repeated. 'Janet and I are going—' In vain she tried to think of where she and Janet were going but the words wouldn't form a sentence. How could a kiss addle her brain like this?

'I'll be here at six and I'll tell you all about Dolly,' he said, as two women came in and began looking through the magazines.

'No, I can't, it's too soon, it's wrong, Janet and I are going—' she babbled.

'I'll be here at six,' he said softly, as the two women looked at them with curiosity creasing their brows.

When her mother was not back from Castle's beach café by five minutes to six, Shirley locked the door, pulled the shop blinds and black-out curtains and hurried up to the flat. She didn't answer his knocking.

Six

Eirlys seemed to be running around in circles. The more tasks she dealt with, the more piled up waiting for her attention. The activities included in the Holidays At Home season were slowly coming to an end, but now her time was spent catching up with routine work at the office she had been forced to neglect. And all the while there were her father's affairs to sort out.

She juggled their finances and managed them with such skill, she thought she could deal with the National Debt. Gradually she was getting things under control.

Her life seemed to be spent buried in books and lists of debts. She rarely went out and only letters from Ken and Max and their occasional visits kept her in touch with the outside world. She was not discontented; as always she relished a challenge and making sense of the chaos left by Teresa was certainly that, she told Ken in one of her letters to him.

Ken's letters were usually filled with amusing stories about the various concerts he and Max organised. One was different. It was short and contained only one subject. He asked her to marry him.

As she sat reading and rereading his words, she was tempted. To have someone with whom to share all the problems that life threw at her seemed like bliss. She stared into space over the table, filled as always with sheaves of papers and lists, and yet more lists, and dreamed. To be free of her father, to have a place of her own, that was the dream, but it was one she could never achieve. She knew she could never leave him. She was certain too that she couldn't accept Ken's proposal. If she did, she would be marrying him for all the wrong reasons and he deserved more than that.

She replied affectionately and told Ken she was flattered, but needed time to think about it, time to get her father's life in order.

–

For several days following the strange meeting with Joseph that culminated in a kiss, Shirley pleaded ill health and stayed away from the shop. She hid upstairs in the Hat and didn't answer the door to anyone except Janet. The owner stood in for her and when she was not working for the Castles, Hetty did a few shifts too. Being supposedly ill meant Shirley couldn't go dancing either, and Janet came each evening and kept her company.

They practised a few new numbers and wondered wistfully whether one day they might be brave enough to go to Drury Lane Theatre and audition for ENSA, join a troupe and entertain the armed forces. The thought of leaving home and everything familiar was a bit frightening even though they were at an age when most women were married and had children and had, in some cases, moved far away from their families, and the women's services had taken many young women to fight alongside men. They thought of these things and knew they weren't ready. Not yet.

After a week, Janet went to a dance on her own. She knew enough people there to feel comfortable walking in unaccompanied. The same crowd went most weeks, and girls dancing with girls had become the norm since so many boys had been called up. And, she reminded herself, she could always go home if she didn't enjoy it.

Max came in at half-time, when drinks and a few snacks were being served. He seemed very pleased to see her and took both her hands and demanded, 'I want the next dance and the one after that. I've been travelling all day to get to an appointment early tomorrow and I'm off again tomorrow afternoon. Dancing with you will make a boring couple of days into a holiday.'

They were persuaded to sing halfway through the second half, their voices blending sweetly in two Hoagy Carmichael numbers, 'Stardust' and 'I Get Along Without You Very Well'. He sang the second song to her, looking at her so lovingly that she wondered how she could possibly continue to sing. The audience loved it.

'I can't sing like Shirley,' she said as they danced later. 'She can really get a number over to an audience. She puts everything into her dancing and singing.'

'Your voice is different. Softer, more intimate, and tonight the crowd loved you.' He held her closer, bending to touch his lips to her cheek. 'And as for dancing, I love the way you dance, Janet.'

–

Joseph tried to write to Shirley to explain why he hadn't told her about Dolly but the words refused to come. He threw away the latest effort and went to Dolly's room to start the painful task of clearing out her belongings. He found it strangely embarrassing looking through her things. They had never lived as man and wife and it was as though he were prying through the life story of a stranger.

There were a great many books. She had been an avid reader until the last few months when holding a book had become wearisome. It was then he had begun to read to her regularly, and her request was usually for books she had read before, reminding herself of past pleasures through the familiar words.

The clothes he had bought her, hardly worn, he thought his mother could take to the Salvation Army. They would be sent to cities and towns where bombing had destroyed houses and people had lost all their belongings. Many of her personal items such as the dressing-table set and the toys she had kept since a child would go to one of the sales being regularly organised to raise money for various war charities.

When he got to the drawer in which her correspondence was stored he hesitated. He needed to look through the letters so he could write to her friends and tell them of her death, but it would feel even more like prying. Letters continuing to arrive for her would be upsetting both to him and his mother. Taking pen and paper he listed the names and addresses of everyone who had written, then, when he thought he had finished, he found a sealed envelope at the bottom of the drawer addressed to himself.

It was a long time before he could face opening it. Would it be criticism of his behaviour? He had thought many times since her death of the hours she had spent alone while he was working, or out dancing or just walking around to avoid spending too much time in her presence, hoping she would be asleep before he returned.

He felt ashamed. Why hadn't he been more caring, less selfish? Taking a deep breath to prepare himself for the hurt that must be revealed on the pages, he slit open the envelope. Dolly's words, so poignant coming after her death, moved him to tears. She did nothing but thank him, tell him how blessed she had been to have had such a husband. The letter ran to three pages and on the third the writing changed, became more ragged as she told him that she hoped he would quickly find someone else and marry her.

'You need a wife, a home and children to make your life complete, and I beg you not to allow any feelings of loyalty or guilt to hold you back from those wonderful things. I can't be there to share them with you, but as I write this letter I hope and pray that you will achieve them soon.'

Joseph showed the letter to his mother. 'I'm confused between a growing love for Shirley and guilt for not deserving such praise from Dolly. I didn't love her, not as she loved me,' he said sadly.

'With no family of her own she needed you, Joseph. Dependence, that was the core of her love for you; it had to be, she was young, vulnerable and afraid. It's what love becomes in a situation like yours. Everybody moves on, but she was held in a timewarp, she was still the bride waiting for life to begin.' She hugged him and whispered, 'Poor Dolly. She had all she needed from you. However much you tell yourself you let her down, you made her happy.'

That evening, Joseph was at last able to write to Shirley, to explain about Dolly and the marriage that never was.

–

Shirley had been disturbed by Joseph's kiss but she was unable to talk to him. He came into the shop several times but she ignored him until he left. When a letter arrived and she saw his name at the end of it, she replaced it in the envelope unread. When she felt able to return to the dance hall with Janet, she looked out for the farmer, Silwyn Davies, and asked him to accompany them. He hesitated at first then stipulated that he would take them and walk them home.

Shirley agreed. 'No coming in for a cup of tea, mind,' she warned. 'I have to get up at five a.m., remember.'

'So do I! Cows don't have a lie-in on Sunday mornings any more than newsagents do.'

Silwyn called for Shirley then they walked to Oldway Street where Janet was waiting for them. They each bought their own ticket as arranged but when the manager of the hall saw the two girls walk in he immediately gave them a refund.

'I hope you'll sing for your supper,' he told them. 'You've been missed these past weeks.'

They sang two numbers and included their dance routine to much applause. Afterwards, they were approached and asked to perform at two other venues during the coming week. Silwyn walked them home proudly, talking about their success as though he were a part of it and agreeing to escort them whenever they had a booking.

Throughout the rest of July and the beginning of August, they went out regularly, earning small sums of money which they used to buy more stage clothes and Leichner make-up as they began to feel more and more like professionals.

–

Eirlys went to see them perform several times, and once when Ken was in St David's Well with Max Moon, staying with Ken's grandparents, the five of them went out for supper afterwards. She had still not given Ken an answer and he never gave any sign of expecting one. She was beginning to enjoy dancing, recognising it as a valuable relaxation from the hectic hours she spent keeping things running at the office and dealing with the heavy load of the summer entertainments plus getting everything under control at home.

In spite of such an irregular life, both Ken and Max fortunately happened to be there for one of the crazy events they had dreamed up. Shirley and Janet came too as it was a Wednesday afternoon and they were free.

Hannah and Bleddyn had organised races for children. In the final one, Bleddyn gave a commentary in which he persuaded them to run faster and faster through deep soft sand with their legs tied together just above the knees. A simple idea which was hilarious as the children tried to take longer steps and quickly overbalanced. With an audience shouting encouragement, those taking part found it impossible not to laugh and most ended up falling over and being disqualified. Eirlys couldn't help thinking of how Stanley, Harold and Percival would have enjoyed it.

Bleddyn rewarded every child taking part with an illegally-made ice cream, a misdemeanour for which he happily paid a small fine.

Max went off with Shirley and Janet, and Ken walked Eirlys home.

'I keep thinking of how much the three boys have missed this summer,' she said as they strolled through the crowds and headed for the bus stop. 'I miss them but Dadda misses them more.'

'He loved having the house filled, didn't he?'

'I'm worried about him, Ken. He's so quiet, and I think he's deeply unhappy. He misses Teresa and on top of grieving for them all he feels such a fool. That isn't an easy thing to deal with. I don't know how best to help him,' she said as they reached the straggling queue for the bus.

'Marry me,' he said. 'We can have lots of babies, grand-children to fill the gap left by the boys. That will cure his blues, won't it?'

'Shush,' she whispered, laughing, as people stared at him having clearly heard his words. She squeezed his arm affec-tionately but shook her head. Rushing into marriage might be the fashion right now, but something held her back.

–

Because she was so ungainly with the baby due so soon, Olive felt too shy to be seen, even with her shape partly disguised by a coat much too large, wrapped around her like a blanket. She rarely went out during the day. At night, she and Ronnie wandered around the streets, enjoying the quiet darkness, talking endlessly about their plans and the excitement of having a child. For both of them, those weeks were specially happy. Ronnie's wounds didn't worry him a great deal and they were thankful that he would not be recalled to serve in the army. They approached parenthood with impatient delight.

–

Dancing on the Green was always a popular event and they had been fortunate with the weather, only having to cancel once because of heavy rain. Janet and Shirley were there for the final dance and, before they left home 'dressed to kill', as Hetty put it, Shirley read Joseph's letter.

Tears filled her eyes as she began to take in the words. How could she have been so cruel to him? The description of his life during the short time he and Dolly were married saddened her as nothing else ever had. She saw that his address was at the top of the letter and decided to visit him now she knew where to find him. She had never been interested enough to ask before and he had never volunteered the information. Now she understood his reticence. She needed to tell him she understood why he hadn't told her about Dolly before and explain that she had only just read his letter.

He had never appeared at the dances since he had written to her, probably believing that her lack of response meant she didn't care. She had to put things straight, but tonight she was going to the Dancing on the Green, not far from St David's Well Bay, and there wouldn't be time. Tomorrow, she promised herself, and sat for a while wallowing in the romantic story of Joseph's lost love and his unrequited love for her. Putting the letter back into its envelope and tucking it into her handbag, she sighed in a mixture of melancholy and joy. Then, putting all sentimental thoughts aside, she prepared for the dance.

–

Janet danced with Max for most of the night, singing along with some of their favourite melodies. Shirley had plenty of dance partners. Now she and Janet were so well known, most of the men were flattered to have her as a partner. They had arrived without Silwyn, convinced of being able to find a taxi. But he was there, unseen by the girls, not dancing, content to watch and to know he would be the one to walk them home.

Ken encouraged Eirlys to leave her official place making sure everything was running smoothly, and dance with him.

She glided around the floor in his arms and the closeness was not hard to take. Did she love him? Perhaps she was expecting too much of love. The romantic scenes favoured by novels and film might have led her to expect more. Now, the sensations his nearness were reviving were exciting. She looked up and they shared a smile and she wondered why she had ever left him.

Standing amid the circle of people on that late summer evening, Joseph watched and wondered if he would ever again be the one to take Shirley home. Perhaps, now she knew the truth about his sad marriage, she would not want to see him again. His unhappiness dropped another notch and he thought that for him, at the age of twenty-eight, his life was over.

Being the final dance, the event had attracted a larger than usual crowd, most of whom were not enthusiastic dancers but were there to watch, enjoy the music and occasionally join in. Some sat on chairs that had been brought on the back of a borrowed and well-scrubbed coal lorry, most were standing.

There was a murmur of excitement as Shirley and Janet walked to their place beside the small orchestra, took the microphone in their shared grip, and sang. It was getting late and the mood had softened. All the lively dances were done and they chose a smooth, slow Jerome Kern number, 'All The Things You Are'. Joseph stayed hidden amid the crowd and applauded with the rest.

The day had been sunny and it was light until ten o'clock. When the band could no longer see to read the music, the couples refused to go home. It was Max playing piano accordion, plus one violin player that accompanied the last few melodies. Shirley and Janet sang the number before the final waltz. An invitation to this 'last waltz' was a tacit way for a boy to ask a girl if he could walk her home. As couples drifted back into the circle and waited for Max to play, accompanied by the lone violinist, Joseph moved forward. He had to talk to her, see whether there was a chance of them becoming friends, if nothing more. The death of his wife had caused a shyness that was like a pain as he made up his mind to speak to her.

Janet danced with Max and Eirlys danced with Ken, and Shirley wished they had invited Silwyn as escort. She wondered anxiously whether Janet and Max would walk her home, while she played 'gooseberry' to their growing attraction, or would expect her to walk home alone. A hand tapped her shoulder and she turned to see Joseph. She slipped into his arms and under cover of the kindly darkness they kissed.

With darkness almost complete, the couples drifted away. Cars, barely seen in the fading light, moved away and the sound of horses and carts could be heard amid the voices and laughter. The sounds drifted away into the night and Eirlys's friends helped to gather the chairs and clear the remnants of the supper into the Castles' van, then stack the chairs on to the lorry.

Joseph felt doubtful of Shirley's apparent pleasure at seeing him there. A lack of confidence or a thought based on previous experience made him wonder if she had been glad to see him from genuine affection or simply in case she had to walk home alone. He didn't know about Silwyn.

It was as Joseph was guiding Shirley towards the road where a few taxis still waited that Silwyn approached them.

'Shirley, I'm here to take you home.' Silwyn said.

'Oh. I didn't think you were still here, Silwyn. Look – thanks and all that, but I don't need an escort tonight. Joseph is here and he'll see me safely back.'

'But I came specially. I gave up my evening to walk you home.' He turned and in the darkness Joseph felt the man's angry stare.

'Sorry, but I didn't promise and I'm going home with Joseph.' Shirley turned away, almost bumping into Joseph in her hasty movement.

'No, you're not. Shirley!' Joseph said loudly.

'Joseph! I thought—'

'You thought you could abandon this man who'd put himself out for you when you no longer need him. Well, you're wrong. I don't want the company of someone who treats people so badly.' He walked off.

Everyone else had gone, and she called anxiously for Silwyn, but he seemed to have disappeared too. What could she do? The faint, hooded tail lights of the last taxi were fading from sight and she was all alone in a park a long way from the flat.

A figure loomed in front of her and she screamed.

'It's all right, Shirley, it's only me,' Joseph said. 'I waited in case Silwyn didn't come back.'

'What are you playing at!' she demanded angrily.

'Trying to make you more thoughtful of others,' he snapped back.

Swallowing her anger, Shirley chided softly, 'I prefer your company to Silwyn's and you're complaining?'

He put his arms around her. 'I don't know why I said what I did. I'm confused about the way I feel about you. I keep telling myself I shouldn't love you, with a wife so recently dead. But I can't deny it any longer.'

With a long dark walk ahead of her, Shirley swallowed the angry reply that she was bursting to say and took his arm.

'You love me?' she said, as though in wonder, and turned her face up for his kiss.

'You know I do and I hope one day you'll tell me you love me.'

Inside she was angry. Frightening her like that, making a scene over poor Silwyn. Love him? He'd be lucky! But she would use him to take her home when she needed company late at night. It was no worse than the way he'd just toyed with her, leaving her here alone to prove his point. In any case, that's what men were for, to be used. The way her father had treated her mother had taught her that.

Brought up on her mother's reluctance to approve of any man, Shirley had developed the attitude that men were useful but untrustworthy, and a woman was stronger when she taught herself never to need them. To link herself to someone like Joseph would ruin her chances of a career and she needed a career more than she needed a man, except for the occasional pleasure, she thought, remembering how she and Freddy Clements had found delight in their secret meetings until he joined the army and left her.

She held Joseph's arm and walked beside him, taking off her high-heeled shoes and walking barefoot along the dark streets. He changed position and placed an arm around her shoulders, stopping at intervals to kiss her forehead, her cheek, until unable to resist, he pulled her close and in the shadows kissed her firmly, possessively, on her soft submissive lips.

The romantic story of his unfortunate wife was still fresh in her mind and she had felt loneliness as she had watched

Janet and Eirlys walking off with Max and Ken. Her head was filled with music. The night sky was gloriously clear with stars so close she imagined she could touch them. The air was caressingly soft and warm and his nearness revealed a sudden urgent need.

She unlocked the door of the flat she shared with her mother and listened. No wireless playing, the only light a low wattage bulb on the stairs, everything was quiet. Taking his hand she led Joseph to her room.

–

The alarm woke them and Shirley looked outside her bedroom door to make sure her mother was still in bed, before Joseph slipped, silent as a shadow, down the stairs and out into the street. She washed and dressed before following to take in the newspapers waiting in the shop porch and begin marking them ready for the paper boys to deliver.

A few cars passed and there was the usual sound of footsteps as people made their way to begin the early shift at the factories of the town. She smiled as she worked, wondering why the morning seemed so ordinary after such an extraordinary night.

After that unexpected and delightful interlude, Joseph became a constant part of her life. He came with them to dances and concerts where Janet and she were performing. If Janet minded she didn't complain. After all, they did need someone to make sure they got home safely and Joseph had never complained at walking Janet to 7 Oldway Street first.

Shirley began to mind though. Janet's presence was an intrusion, both when she and Joseph were together and, more importantly, at their performances. She wanted to be a solo performer and, while Joseph was so considerate of

Janet, so determined to make her considerate of others, the problem would not be solved. Occasionally she sang alone, but Janet usually accompanied her whenever they were asked to sing. Only with the dancing did Shirley really come into her own. She was good. Far better than Janet who, she insisted untruthfully to Joseph, was inhibited and stiff. Janet happily stood and watched, knowing she lacked sufficient talent or ambition to compete.

'Perhaps if I start getting bookings as a dancer I can gradually include singing until I'm accepted as a solo artiste.' Shirley said to Hetty one evening as they ate their meal with Bleddyn, who was becoming a regular visitor to the flat above the newsagent. Bleddyn advised her to find herself an agent.

At first this seemed impossible. What agent would want to audition an unknown girl from a small seaside town in South Wales?

'What does Janet think of the idea?' Joseph asked when she mentioned it.

Typical, she thought with rising irritation. Joseph says he loves me but his first thought is what does Janet think! 'I haven't discussed it with her. Why should I?' she demanded. 'Bleddyn Castle only mentioned it today.'

'She'll want the chance too, won't she?' he said reasonably. 'Well, yes, but I don't want to discuss it with her yet. I'll get more information first. Pity to raise her hopes.' Magazines were her business and a stage periodical gave her the names of several agents who were looking for fresh talent. She wrote to three, and two replied. Talking to them on the telephone on the square in the middle of the town, she arranged an appointment with them both for a week later and went back to the shop to ask her boss for the day off.

It would be a very long day, with the journey to London taking more than five hours. The bombing regularly closed roads in the cities, bus routes would be difficult to work out. Digging into her savings, she took out enough to take taxis. The time and frustration saved would be worth the money. At least air raids were less of a worry recently, according to the papers, although even Hitler's Luftwaffe wouldn't have stopped her going. She couldn't wait for peace before trying to get a name for herself. Life didn't work like that. She had to do it now, and this was the first step. She said nothing to Joseph or Janet and swore her mother to secrecy.

—

Olive Castle who, with her husband Ronnie, ran a fruit and vegetable stall in the market, was anxious. Her baby was overdue and she was afraid she would begin to give birth without anyone there to help her. Although Ronnie had to attend to the stall every day, she was rarely alone, sharing a house with Auntie Audrey and Uncle Wilf and the two girls, Maude and Myrtle.

One morning, when Audrey was working at the seaside rock shop, having given Alice a day off, and Wilf was out visiting friends, there was only Lilly to keep her company. Bored with sitting in her parents' house, Lilly had taken baby Phyllis and plonked herself beside Olive to complain about life in general, hers in particular.

When the pains began, Olive ignored them at first. There had been a few, which her mother-in-law Marged had said were rehearsals for the real thing. As they grew stronger and more regular, she knew it was time to prepare for the birth.

Frightened now, she asked Lilly to help her to her bedroom and send for the midwife.

Almost throwing her baby at the pain-racked girl, Lilly ran from the house and left a message for her mother, then ran on to the house of the midwife. She was out but Lilly told her daughter to send her as soon as she could. For good measure she also called into the surgery and told the clerk there what was happening, then she ran back, quite exhausted with her efforts, to Olive.

Olive cried out and gripped Lilly's hand for comfort and, in panic. Lilly ran out again, this time with her baby, saying she was going to look for help, and Olive was on her own.

She didn't know what to do. She felt as though her back was breaking and when the pain transferred to the lower part of her body and intensified, tearing her apart, she knew that there was no time to go out herself and seek help. She was crying, both with the pain and for the fear of giving birth alone. In her imagination she convinced herself that both she and the baby would die. She called for Ronnie and for her mother-in-law but no one came.

An hour passed and still she was on her own. The pains had continued but they no longer made her cry out. She lay on her side and begged someone to come and help her. When help came it arrived in the form of the midwife, closely followed by the doctor, and Olive cried again, this time with relief.

The baby, a girl, was born an hour later and the first thing Olive said, when her mother-in-law ran up the stairs and hugged her, was, 'I'll never speak to Lilly again. Not ever.'

'Oh, I will,' Marged said, tight-lipped with anger. 'I'll have plenty to say to our Lilly.'

Lilly was sitting in the park. The weather had turned cold and she was shivering. No chance of going back home for a coat; she couldn't face getting involved in all that screaming again.

There were other mothers sitting in the park, pushing prams or running after lively toddlers. One pushchair with a lively youngster in it was held by a young man. He was pale and from the way he walked, leaning heavily on one side and quickly taking the weight of his left leg, she guessed he had been wounded and was home recuperating.

'Let him play on the grass,' she advised, as the man tried in vain to pacify the struggling child. 'Safe enough here, he'll be.'

'I don't know,' the young man said doubtfully. 'My sister's boy he is and I can't run after him if he gets into trouble.' He slapped his leg. 'Shrapnel, see,' he explained.

'Tell you what, you rock my pram and I'll watch your little boy for a while, how's that?'

An hour later, when Lilly braced herself for the situation at home, she and the young man she now knew as Sam had made a date to meet later that evening. Lilly prepared a contrite expression and went to face her family.

–

Eirlys and Ken still wrote regularly to each other while he was away from St David's Well, and he went less often to London on his free time, preferring to stay with his grandparents and spend time with Eirlys. He tried not to press for an answer to his proposal but Eirlys knew that she had to make up her mind. It was a time of rapid change. Overnight everything could be thrown out of order; things you could once rely on were no longer certainties. Love could wait, but why should it? The present attitude of grabbing happiness while you could had affected the most unexcitable of people. Everywhere there were friends who were jumping into situations with little thought. Ken could be leaving to work overseas at any time, so why should she hesitate?

Since parting from Ken some years previously, she had met, fallen in love and become engaged to Johnny Castle and would have married him, even though she was beginning to realise it was a mistake. Discovering that Johnny loved Hannah had been a shock but a short-lived disappointment. But a part of her still wondered whether they would have been as happy as most if they had married and ignored their doubts.

How much of a happy marriage was acceptance, she wondered sadly. The conviction that a man was the only one for her couldn't be true, or why had she felt that conviction for Ken, and then Johnny, without it lasting in either case? And how could her heart retune itself to loving Ken once that love had faded and died?

Ken had a suspicion that her doubts were in part because of her previous love for Johnny and, in an attempt to help, on hearing that Johnny was home on unexpected leave, he suggested Eirlys invite Johnny, Hannah and the two little girls to tea on Sunday. Believing Ken had suggested it in an attempt to cheer up her father, who still missed the evacuees, she agreed, although with some trepidation. Would she be able to face seeing Johnny and accept Hannah, her long-time friend, as Johnny's wife without feeling the strain? For her father she was prepared to try.

Ken was apprehensive too. What if it proved that Eirlys still loved Johnny? It could end all hope of her saying 'yes' to his proposal. He knew he had to take the chance and he entered into the plans for providing tea for the guests.

Eirlys managed to bake a few party cakes with some duck eggs from Bernard Gregory. Hen's eggs had been rationed since June but duck eggs were still exempt. To the small cakes she added some sweets for decoration, stuck on with a spot of jam in the absence of icing sugar. There were sandwiches of spam and when Mr Gregory heard about the tea-party he delivered an extra couple of goose eggs, hard-boiled and sliced, to impress the children with their size, and a ridge cucumber, nobbly, ugly but delicious in sandwiches. He also gave Eirlys a two-ounce bar of Cadbury's chocolate which she grated over a small sponge cake. The table looked festive and Marie and Josie were impressed.

It was a happy occasion, her father enjoying the company of the little girls. The conversation was lively with no uneasy pauses. Ken watched Eirlys, admiration clear in his eyes. Made for family life, he thought fondly. Efficient, orderly, yet with such a relaxed approach that no one would guess she had worked so hard. No wonder she was so valued as an employee and it was not surprising that she had so many friends, either.

He wanted to be a part of her life, supporting her in whatever she wanted to do, sharing her problems, adding to her joys. For him there was no doubt about Eirlys being the one person for him. No one else had ever come close.

As Johnny and Hannah walked back home with Marie and Josie, Johnny said, 'D'you think Eirlys invited us to show me she was back with Ken?'

Hannah smiled knowingly. 'No, my darling, I think it more likely that Ken wanted to show her she was over loving you.'

Eirlys discussed Ken's proposal with her father that evening.

He was delighted and hoped she would accept. 'I've always liked Ken and I'm sure he'd make you happy. Your mam and I were upset when you called it off.'

'I think I love Ken, but having known him for all these years there wouldn't be the excitement. In other ways too, rushing into a marriage would be a disappointment. I'll miss the build-up, the fun of collecting things for our home.'

'You've done all that,' Morgan said ruefully. 'With Johnny and partly with Ken before. Perhaps a rushed marriage would be better.'

'But everything is so grey these days.'

'Nonsense, love, you'll make a beautiful bride, however frantic the arrangements.'

She hugged her father but wasn't convinced.

Johnny, Hannah and the girls met Eirlys again the following weekend. It included the last of Eirlys's arranged entertainments. The Donkey Derby was to take place on Sally Gough's field where the donkeys spent their leisure time and where they overwintered in the stables built for them by Bernard. No children rode them on this occasion; this was an event intended to make grown-ups look silly, with a commentary by Bernard Gregory aided and abetted by Eirlys's father, Morgan Price.

As the line of animals set off at a leisurely pace, ignoring their jockeys' attempts to make them hurry, and aiming vaguely at the winning post against the furthest hedge, the two men took it in turns to invent a racing commentary out of the disobedient animals' actions.

Some turned and ran back to where their owners were tempting them to disobey by offering hay, others walked across the field and tipped their riders off into the stinging nettles before trotting on towards the finishing post. Being ridden barebacked was something most of the donkeys were used to but today they didn't like it. Some had never been ridden at all, and they too were not hesitant in letting their riders know of their displeasure.

Eirlys laughed with the rest, standing near Hannah and the girls while Johnny ran about helping unseated jockeys to remount and on one occasion being chased from the field by the bad-tempered Charlie belonging to Bernard Gregory. Charlie liked children riding him and, as long as he was leading the string, was amiable and patient. A race like this tried his patience and he let them all know it.

The crowds drifted away and the men set about clearing the field. Ken took Eirlys's arm and led her towards Johnny, Hannah and their two daughters.

'I hope you're taking Eirlys home for a quiet evening,' Hannah said. 'You've done a wonderful job this summer, Eirlys.'

'That's right. A quiet evening being spoilt is what she deserves, don't you agree, Ken?' Johnny agreed.

'After the the way she's worked to make Holidays At Home a success, she deserves more than a quiet night in! It's time for a celebration of a job well done,' Ken said. 'I'm taking her out.'

'Where are we going?' Eirlys smiled. She liked the idea; everything was already beginning to feel flat after these busy weeks and she didn't like the sound of a quiet night in.

Ken kissed her cheek and hugged her affectionately. He was relieved that she didn't object, sure now that her feelings for Johnny were no more than affectionate friendship. 'I'm so proud of her. With her team of assistants, she's given us a summer we'll never forget.'

'And I'm already preparing for the next one,' Eirlys groaned in mock despair.

'Make it the summer we'll never want to forget, Eirlys my beautiful love,' Ken said as they walked away. 'Marry me.'

This time, she said yes, and immediately wondered why, after hesitating for so long. Perhaps it was the mood of euphoria at the approach of the end of a busy season, or the realisation that Ken was the one and, perhaps, had always been. Then she remembered the unfinished business of her father's disasters. She couldn't marry anyone until they had been sorted. 'But not yet,' she added as he began to speak.

'Why? There's nothing to stop us, is there?'

'First, I have to clear Dadda's debts,' she added sadly. 'I won't have the money to do anything until all his bills are paid.'

'Then let me help.'

'I can't do that!'

'Why not? If we're to be man and wife won't you expect us to share everything, bad as well as good?'

They went back to the house and before Morgan joined them they went through the accounts which Eirlys had neatly written out to see exactly how they stood. The following day, they cleared every overdue account except for the three-piece suite bought – then sold – by Teresa, which they agreed that Morgan should manage on his own.

They discussed dates. There was no need to search for accommodation; they both agreed to move in with Morgan.

'To make sure he doesn't fall for another needy, greedy woman,' Eirlys said ruefully.

With the hectic season of entertainment over. Eirlys took a week off from work and spent the time preparing for her wedding. She went first to see Marged and Huw Castle to ask them to organise the wedding breakfast. She wasn't even certain of the numbers at this stage and she laughed aloud at the effect the wedding plans was having on her normally clear-thinking mind.

–

When Shirley reached London on the day she had arranged to meet the two agents, she hesitated at the station and looked around. Paddington Station was huge compared with the stations in the town of St David's Well, and she wondered how to get out of it with so many alternatives on offer. The steps leading down to the underground were solid with people and she thought she would wait until the bustle had eased. She imagined that once the train had discharged its load, the place would be empty but trains continued to arrive and depart, and people continued to pour up and down the steps.

Taxis waited near one of the roadways and people were pushing their way through the hovering crowd determined to get there first. She checked the address of the first appointment and walked towards the taxi queue. She wished she hadn't come.

When she eventually emerged from the dark cavern of the station she stared around her in disbelief. The scenes that met her eyes as they drove through the streets were like something from a nightmare. Many buildings were nothing but piles of rubble, the sun shining through jagged gaps in the walls, and what should have been rooftops was a motley of broken walls and sagging timber. Outside buildings that had survived serious damage, the entrances were surrounded by high walls of sandbags. The roadways had been cleared and red London buses drove through, finding their way, stopping at bus stops which were nothing more than temporary posts standing amid acres of rubble fields, people jumping on and off as though everything was normal.

Newspapers had shown pictures of the devastation caused by the Blitz which had ended a couple of months previously but had not prepared her for the shocking reality. She alighted from the taxi clutching her bag and the folder containing her sheets of music. She was early so she walked around taking in the sights, wanting to tell people when she got back how fortunate they had been to have escaped such terrifying air raids.

The debris of people's homes had been moved away from the roads to allow life to go on. In the absence of pavements, people were walking along the edge of the roadways, men carrying newspapers and briefcases, mothers with children and shopping bags, schoolchildren, a postman, the police. Several ARP wardens stood in a group gesturing towards one of the buildings, making notes, discussing the ruins. An old man pushed a tattered handcart gathering wood which was scattered among the rubble and she saw the policeman wave him away, no doubt aware of the danger of more of the buildings falling. She felt like an intruder, a voyeur looking in on other people's grief.

She was still early for her appointment but she went to the address where she had arranged to meet the first of the two agents.

The address was above a baker's shop, where a queue of tired-looking women stood patiently waiting, hoping for a few of the cakes that the proprietor had managed to bake. Shirley was hungry but she had sandwiches in her bag and couldn't take anything from these people who needed treats more than she did.

Pushing her way through the patient, good-natured shoppers, she knocked on the door.

The interview was brief. The three people present asked her a few questions about her experiences and seemed less than excited by her answers. She sang two numbers to piano accompaniment, but she was nervous and didn't give her voice its usual strength. They told her abruptly they would contact her when they had something to offer. She left convinced that was very unlikely to happen.

Disappointment hit her hard but slowly left her. She had a second audition and surely she couldn't fail to please the second one?

Another taxi took her to the place where she had arranged to meet the second agent, Mr Desmond Green-Hamilton. She read the name and checked the address unnecessarily. To her alarm, she was set down in a street of ruined buildings.

'This can't be it!' she exclaimed to the driver.

'Sorry, love, but London ain't what it used to be. If I ain't mistaken there's your appointment right there, waiting for yer.'

Paying the taxi driver, Shirley apprehensively stepped out into the silent and empty road with damaged and abandoned houses on both sides.

The man was standing near the wall of what had once been a grand building. He wore a smart suit and was smoking a cigar, holding a briefcase in a beringed hand. His hair was slicked back like a second skin, black and shining, curling on his neck, and his bright darting eyes were assessing her as she approached. He waited until she reached him, eased himself from the wall and offered a hand.

'Miss Shirley Downs? Pleased to meet you.'

'Mr Green-Hamilton?' She looked around her and, gathering strength and confidence from her anger and disappointment, convinced she had wasted her time, said, 'I hope you don't expect me to audition here in the street!'

He casually waved a hand up at the mined façade of the building and shook his head. 'That was my office, Miss Downs, but it'll be a long time before I can audition young ladies there again. No, we have to use my flat.' As she hesitated, he added casually, 'My secretary will be making us some coffee, as the junior is off sick this week, so, if you'll follow me.'

Desmond Green-Hamilton had never had an office. The bombing of London had given him the wonderful opportunity of inventing one: a smart office with an exceptionally good address. All he had to do was meet his clients there amid the ruins of these fine buildings, sigh with deep sadness at the trials of wartime, and leave them to imagine the rest.

Foolishly Shirley envisaged his flat like those seen in Hollywood films, so the drab, poorly furnished room into which she was led fifteen minutes later was a shock. Did she imagine it or did he use his hands more than necessary as he helped her out of her coat? His hands touched her neck and she felt them around her waist. She was decidedly nervous, looking around for the promised coffee supplied by a secretary, both of which failed to materialise.

He coaxed her to relax, take off the cardigan she wore under the thin summer coat and she wished she had worn something more flattering than the sleeveless, fitted dress she'd had the summer before.

'Some of my stage dresses would have looked the part,' she said, 'but I didn't think a train journey to London was the place to wear them. All I'd expected to do was sing, not dance as well, like I usually do.'

There was a piano and taking one of her music sheets he began to play, nodding to invite her to sing. He stopped her after a few bars and coaxed her to loosen a button at the top of her blouse.

'Pretend I'm someone you love, flirt with me through the song,' he said. 'Dance, show me how you move.' This had the effect of making her more, not less inhibited.

Through the next hour he persuaded her to move more sinuously. 'Tell yourself you're a cat, a tiger. Don't walk, slide from one place to another. Lean towards me, don't be afraid of showing what you've got.'

She relaxed and tried to do what he asked, but all the time she was hoping to hear the door open and the mysterious secretary appear. When someone did come in, it was a photographer.

'Carry on singing, Shirl, we just want to check on how photogenic you are.'

'Shirley,' she corrected.

She became more and more nervous and after singing the two songs three times, told them she had to leave.

'Leave? What d'you mean? We've got a lot of work to do before I can book you at some of my nightclubs. Best spots in London and they expect the best performers.'

'I have a train to catch.'

'Not today? You weren't planning on going back today? I'd planned for some studio work tomorrow and my wife has our spare room all ready for you. Ain't that right 'arry?' The photographer nodded agreement but Shirley didn't believe them. She didn't want a studio test or any more photographs, or to sing another song. All she wanted was to get out of this situation safely. Pleading exhaustion and promising to come back and stay for a few days, Shirley escaped.

She hurried towards what she hoped was a busy road where she could find a taxi to get her back to Paddington. She had only spent a few minutes there but Paddington represented safety; it was from where the train would leave to take her back to St David's Well and home.

There were tears in her eyes. She was crying for lost hope and for her own stupidity. Why had she insisted on coming alone? If Mam had been with her, or Joseph, there wouldn't have been the danger of things getting out of hand. Sitting on the train she was aware that she had been fortunate to have learned a lesson without losing more than the train and taxi fares.

Hetty was waiting on the platform with Janet when she stepped off the train. It was almost midnight; she was tired, hungry and dejected. 'Mam, I've been so stupid,' she sobbed.

'As long as you're safe, everything else can be worked out,' Hetty soothed, when she had heard something of Shirley's story.

Janet left them as they passed Oldway Street and Hetty explained why she had been at the station.

'I couldn't settle, knowing you were on your own so far away. I went to the market at lunchtime and told Janet where you were. She came to the flat after work and we waited together. We've seen four trains come and go but she insisted on keeping me company.'

'I expect she was angry at me trying to do this on my own. Partners we're supposed to be.'

'Not angry, just worried. "I should have gone with her" was what she said. She knows you have a talent and will go further without her than with her. She enjoys what you two do but has no dreams of being a star.'

'I don't deserve a friend like her.'

'She wouldn't agree. She loves being your friend; you've brought her a lot of fun and excitement, and when your career takes off and she's left behind, she'll still be a friend. I'm not so sure about Joseph though.'

'You didn't tell him?' Shirley gasped.

'Janet did. She presumed he knew and once she'd mentioned it he had to be told the full story.'

'I wish he had gone with me. I'd ask him another time. It was scary on my own.'

'From the way he spoke when he came into the shop, you might have lost the chance!'

'Good! If he's so possessive, starting to think he owns me, I'm better off without him.' It was bravado; she really did want him to remain her friend while she needed an escort.

She knew she was using him, but that thought didn't make her feel guilty. She needed his help and he was willing to give it, wasn't he? If he was hoping for more she had made it clear that was not to be. Hadn't her mother always told her men were to be used?

Seven

Shirley waited for Joseph to call in the days following her unfortunate visit to London. All day she watched the door whenever a customer entered, a half smile ready to greet him, but when she closed the shop door at six o'clock he hadn't appeared. She helped her mother prepare their meal in silence, wondering with some anxiety what Joseph would say about her stupid trip to London, at others asking herself why she cared.

Joseph was soaking wet and seemingly unaware of the discomfort. His mind in turmoil, he had walked around in the rain for hours. When he stopped to shelter and decide where he was going and why, he at last realised that his feet were wet and squeaky and he was very chilled.

He wondered why he felt so confused about Shirley. The death of his wife hadn't helped as he'd thought it would. Dolly was present in death more than she had been in life, and beside that problem that wouldn't go away, there was Shirley's singing. If only she could forget it, accept a normal life keeping house and caring for him like most women did. He decided to give it one more try; surely she was ready to listen to reason?

In the flat above the newsagent, at seven o'clock, the doorbell rang and Hetty answered it. Shirley heard her mother's voice blend with Joseph's as they climbed back up the stairs. Half afraid to look at him, Shirley said, 'Hi yer, Joseph. Fancy a bite to eat?'

'What were you thinking of going to meet strange people on your own? I'd have gone with you if you'd asked.'

'Or talked me out of it, like Mam tried to do,' she retorted unreasonably; he had never strongly discouraged her from singing or dancing, just tried to warn her of the disappointments she might face.

'You're right, I wouldn't have wanted you to go. Performing around here, having fun in places where you're well known is one thing, disappearing to strange towns and mixing with the people involved in the entertainment world is another.'

'What's the difference?'

'Safety!' he snapped.

'Shirley is sensible, she knows how to look after herself,' Hetty interjected.

Joseph turned swiftly and said angrily, 'Of course she isn't sensible! She wouldn't have gone off without me if she were!'

'What are you so angry about? It's none of your business,' Shirley retorted, lifting a casserole out of the oven and standing holding it and glaring at him. 'Don't expect me to do what *you* think's best for me. I know what I want and if you don't like what I do you can get lost, and stop dripping all over Mam's carpet!'

'But, Shirley—'

'Get lost, I said!'

He left without another word.

'Best for him too,' Shirley said, slamming the vegetable casserole down on the table.

Hetty went out later. It was one of the evenings when Bleddyn didn't work at the fish and chip shop and she had arranged to meet him and go for a drink.

The evening was a miserable one. Rain fell almost silently but relentlessly on to the dark pavements, splashing up and chilling Hetty's legs.

'I'll be glad to get in out of the wet.' she grumbled as they approached the façade of the public house that stood shrouded in darkness, no glimmer of light to suggest it was even open, let alone offering comfort and bright, cheerful company.

They noticed a poster on the wall advertising a talent competition for the following weekend.

'We'll tell your Shirley,' Bleddyn said as he pointed it out to Hetty. 'The more she performs the more chance of someone noticing her and helping her to make progress.'

'D'you think she will make a career for herself?' Hetty asked.

'The only thing that can stop her is Joseph. If he persuades her to marry him and give up on it, she'll have lost her chance. She's young and rather beautiful, with her long dark hair and those expressive eyes. In a few years, even if she did try again to recover what she has lost, her chances would be far less.'

'I think I'll put her name down now. Tell them she'll sing Max's song "Slide Down a Rainbow". She can always cancel later if she doesn't want to do it.'

'Something else for Joyless Joseph to worry about.' Bleddyn grinned.

'I wish she'd tell him to get lost,' Hetty frowned, then she laughed, remembering that Shirley had used those words only a couple of hours previously.

They didn't stay long. The fire in the huge grate in the bar room was low, the publicans conserving fuel for the weekend when there would be more customers to enjoy it and, after sitting as close as they could to the smoking wood for half an hour. Bleddyn suggested going to see Marged and Huw.

Hetty was pleased to see that Maude and Myrtle were there. They were struggling to rescue the remnants of lipstick out of a tube and add it to another, getting into a real mess.

'Have you got an egg cup?' Hetty asked Marged and, when one was produced, she used a nail-file to put the remnants of the two lipsticks into the egg cup and stood it in boiling water to melt. The resulting liquid was poured carefully into a lipstick case and left to dry.

'Not perfect and I've no idea what the colour will be, but better than what you were trying to do, eh?'

'That's clever, Mrs Downs, thank you,' Maude smiled.

'Where did you learn that?'

'I saw it in a women's magazine and I've been longing to see if it works.'

'Thank you.'

'You're welcome.'

'I think I earned a few points this evening,' she told Bleddyn as they walked home.

'I just hope it doesn't fall to pieces when Maude tries to use it tomorrow!'

–

Joseph didn't go home. He was uncomfortably wet but continued to walk for more than an hour around the streets and dark lanes, stopping at intervals to sit on a bench, crouched inside his sodden raincoat and umbrella, almost enjoying the discomfort that matched his mood, lost in his thoughts. He had to decide what he should do next. He wanted to marry Shirley. But he couldn't cope with her travelling around from town to town singing in concert halls and theatres and in nightclubs. He knew she was good, very good, and she might be successful, for a while. Just long enough to make her unhappy, he told himself.

He knew he had a choice: he would have to give up on his own life and travel with her, or stay at home and spend occasional days with her and the rest of the time alone. Their marriage would be a series of telephone calls. From a wife who was constantly ill for the whole of their married life, to a wife who would be constantly absent. Hardly an improvement, he frowned, his thoughts welling up in self-pity and creating a sullen look. Didn't he deserve a better future than that?

At nine o'clock, still unable to make a decision on whether to leave her or stay, and hope the show-business dream would fade away, he went into a public house. There was a notice on the wall advertising a talent competition for the following weekend that Hetty and Bleddyn had noted. The landlord told him who was organising it and, seeing the man at the bar, pointed him out. Joseph went to talk to him.

'Have you got many acts booked yet?' he asked.

'Only seven so far,' the man replied. 'Mostly singers, one comedy act and one accordion player.'

'Is one of the singing acts The Two Jays?'

The man shook his head.

'Shirley Downs and Janet Copp?'

'No, no Janet Copp.' he said, checking a list taken from his pocket, 'but there is a Jane Downs. She's singing a song called "Slide Down a Rainbow". It's new, written by a friend of hers.'

'That's her, a friend of mine,' Joseph said. 'Shirley she is, but she calls herself Jane Downs.'

'I can be co-operative, mind, if you want her to win,' the man said with a wink.

'What's it worth to make sure she loses!'

'Spends too much time on singing and not enough on you, is it?'

Joseph looked thoughtful for a moment before replying softly, 'Something like that.'

—

'Slide down a rainbow into my arms,' Shirley sang as she opened the shop on Saturday morning. 'Come with the magic and come with good luck charms.'

'Blimey, Shirley, you're cheerful this morning!' her first customer gasped. 'You can hardly open your eyes most days. Had an early night for a change, did you?'

'Tonight will be a late one.' She laughed. 'There's a talent competition at the pub and I'm going to win.'

'Good on you, girl.'

The steady stream of customers calling for their papers and cigarettes kept her busy until nine o'clock, when she stopped for a cup of tea. Everyone going to work had passed through by that time, the shoppers had not yet begun to trickle in. Taking out the sheet music and going over the words, singing softly, she didn't see Joseph coming in until he spoke.

Looking up, she continued to sing, but this time she sang the words aloud.

'It's the end of the rainbow where treasure is found, meet me my treasure my joy my delight, Slide down the rainbow, meet me tonight.'

'I will if you like,' he said, with a hesitant smile.

She shrugged. 'Only if you want to.'

'Are you entering the talent show?' he asked innocently.

'Yes, I am. Janet and I are going with Mam and Bleddyn Castle so we don't need a chaperone.'

'I'll call for you at half seven, shall I?'

She shrugged again. 'If you like.'

He left the shop more than a little worried. He was in danger of losing her. He had to persuade her to give up her ambition, but how? Then he remembered the man who was organising the talent competition. Perhaps there was a way. Show business was all about confidence, wasn't it?

–

Janet wasn't singing with Shirley in the competition that night. She knew that for Shirley their double act was not enough. Shirley needed a career and Janet didn't think she was capable of rising to stardom with her and Janet told her so.

'I'll sing and dance with you whenever you want me to. I love it. It's fun. When you want to audition on your own I'll go with you and clap louder than anyone because I know you have talent and you need to concentrate on going it alone.'

Shirley hugged her. 'Janet, I don't deserve a friend like you. I'm selfish, and pushy, and greedy, and—'

'All right, don't go on or I'll change my mind and sulk instead of helping!' Janet laughed. 'Now, what are you wearing?'

Since clothing rationing had started in the previous June, stage clothes had become a problem. Appearing in a number of dances and concerts close to home it was unacceptable to wear the same dress repeatedly. Shirley took her dresses to Hannah, who restyled them. Tonight she was wearing a long black dress she had been given by Eirlys. It had been Eirlys's mother's and was very old, but the material was beautiful.

Hannah's nimble fingers set to work removing sections of the full skirt to make a stole which was edged at each end with scraps of fur. It was now a sleek, figure-hugging gown, glittering with sequins from a dress bought in the second-hand shop. Make do and mend didn't only refer to basic clothing; it was even more important to entertainers who had to create dreams.

When Shirley stood on the makeshift stage in the church hall where the competition was held. Joseph felt a surge of admiration and love – and jealousy. She was beautiful and her voice filled the hall and touched every heart. He glanced around at the faces of the audience and possessiveness was his greatest emotion. She had no right to be up there pleasing these people. She belonged to him, not this crowd gawping at her, he thought savagely. She wasn't meant for this, she was meant for him, his reward for the years he had suffered, caring for Dolly.

To his surprise Janet went on next. She was singing with Max, a light-hearted song, undemanding and very successful. When it was announced that Janet and Max had won, the applause was far from enthusiastic and Joseph felt ashamed. Paying the man to make sure Shirley lost had been despicable.

He took her home before the others and they went to her room. His loving and soothing words consoled her. When he told her she should give up on her dreams, she sobbed bitterly, and when Hetty and Bleddyn came in, he stayed and slept beside her till morning. The joy of comforting her was worth the pain of guilt, he smiled, as he silently left her and went back home in the early hours of Sunday morning.

–

As he was a professional entertainer, Max and Janet refused the prize and the hamper of fruit was auctioned, the money going to the Red Cross. They walked home with Bleddyn and Hetty discussing the unlikely result. When they left them at the shop, Max asked Janet, 'How do you feel about joining our concert party?'

'Give up the café, you mean?'

'Yes. You're good enough, you know. You put over a song well and your smiling, friendly personality is as much a gift as your voice.'

'Max, I think I'm too afraid. To let everything go when you have a family to come back to is bad enough, but for me, if I left St David's Well, I wouldn't have a base.'

'I understand, but what if you could have a base here, keep your home firmly rooted, what then?'

'How can I do that? I'm an orphan with not even a distant cousin to call my own.'

'That's easy. Marry me.'

She stared at him as though the words were unclear. 'Marry you?'

'I know we haven't known each other long but it's wartime and we don't have time for long engagements. I know we'd be happy.' He looked down at her with his bright blue eyes, his untidy red hair surrounding his face.

She knew that he was right. They would be happy and, in the uncertainties of war, there was no advantage in waiting.

For a fleeting moment she thought of Ken Ward, someone who had been filling her thoughts more and more as they now worked in such close proximity. Had she imagined that glimmer of interest for her in his eyes? She brushed the romantic image aside. Ken wasn't for her and she knew it was little more than physical attraction she felt for him. Besides, he was going to marry Eirlys. She looked at Max again and felt the warmth of his love enfolding her. He opened his arms and she fell into them, his strength, security and desire enveloping her. She had someone to love and would never again be alone.

–

It was to Ronnie Castle in his fruit and vegetable stall that Janet went first to spread the news of her engagement. Olive was there with their baby daughter, Rhiannon, and Janet said, 'Max proposed last night and I accepted. What d'you think of that, eh? Pity you aren't old enough to be my bridesmaid, little Rhiannon Castle.'

Their congratulations were loud and enthusiastic and several other stallholders including Sally and Arthur from a rival fruit stall, came over and joined in with good wishes. Max himself appeared later that morning and at once the ribald remarks were flying.

'Our Janet's a popular girl, mind,' one of them warned. 'You make sure you take good care of her, or you'll have us after you.'

'Her happiness will be my life's work,' Max said, smiling.

Wherever she went that day people smiled at her news. There was so much to bear that was sad, that happy news was welcomed. It was not until she called on Shirley, after she had closed the café, that she had a different response.

'Getting married? What are you thinking of, Janet?' Shirley demanded. 'What about your career? You'll end up supporting Max and following him around or sitting in a soulless room all on your own until he comes home for a flying visit. You're an orphan – surely you'd want a man who stayed with you? Haven't you spent enough of your life alone? Think about your talent. Janet, and don't waste it.'

'Entertainment isn't my life as it is yours. I'll be happy supporting Max,' Janet replied. The disappointment of her friend's reception of her news was surprising and hurtful.

'You and I can really hit the top if we give up on happy families, Janet,' Shirley persuaded. 'Think of it, singing in the best theatres, on the London stage, it's all possible if we dedicate ourselves.'

Janet stared at her and knew that the words were not intended to give her good advice but to make sure she was there for Shirley Downs, or Jane Downs as she wanted to be called.

'I'm thrilled to be marrying Max. I love him and he's the kindest, most thoughtful man I've known. I'm so lucky that he feels the same way I do.'

'Well,' Shirley said doubtfully, 'I wish you luck, really I do. I think you'll need it, mind. But, Janet, don't give up on your singing. You won the competition the other night, didn't you?'

'We both know you should have won,' Janet said. 'What the judges were thinking about I don't know.'

Shirley looked at Janet thoughtfully and added, 'Mam wonders if someone paid the judges to make sure you won.'

'You don't think Max—' Janet gasped in disbelief. 'How could you think him capable of such dishonesty? Or me? I'm your friend and I expected you to win!'

'Everyone there that night believed I should have won.'

'That doesn't mean that Max was involved.'

Janet left the flat and walked home, running at times, wanting to cry for the disappointing reaction to her news and for the accusation against Max. Shirley's ambition was distorting everything else in her life. It soared high above friendship.

She had ignored Shirley's dishonesty several times in the past, pretending to believe her, making excuses, but now her selfish ambition was making it difficult to consider her a friend. With a shock she realised that, having faced up to Shirley's selfishness, she had no one she could really rely on apart from Max, and Shirley wanted to spoil even that.

Max's family lived in London, not far from Ken Ward. 'You'll have to manage a weekend off and come to meet them,' Max said that evening, after Janet had told him about Shirley's disappointing reaction to her news. She said nothing about Shirley's accusation regarding their being chosen as winners. It was so unpleasant it was not worthy of repeating.

'I suppose she was miserable about us winning that competition,' he said. 'That's understandable with someone as determined to succeed as Shirley.' She nodded thoughtfully but didn't reply.

'Forget Shirley for tonight and let's talk about us,' Max said. 'You and me singing together. I think we have a good future, but only for as long as you want it. I can do something else. Teach perhaps; I'm a qualified teacher, I can teach music in schools, give lessons on the piano and I can write songs. My dream is to write a musical one day. But you are more important to me than any of this. I'd like to stay within the world of entertainment but not if you are less than content.'

'I'll be happy sharing your life wherever your talents take us,' she said happily.

Beth Castle and her sister Lilly agreed to run the café for Janet the following weekend and Janet travelled with Max to meet her future in-laws.

The devastation in London horrified her and she felt vulnerable, as though there was a threat hanging over her in the skies, hidden in the brightness of the late summer's day.

The meeting was a success and Max's family welcomed her, hugging her more like a long-lost daughter than a stranger who came and announced her intention to become their daughter-in-law. Max's father was tall and thin like his son but without his unruly red hair. His mother was small and neat and seemed to wear a constant smile.

She and Max spent most of the weekend talking to each other, slowly learning a little about their different back-grounds, their dreams and ambitions, either strolling through the streets or sitting in the pleasant garden behind the house.

He wrote two songs that weekend, both love songs, his quick mind writing the melody and the words, humming sometimes and discussing his ideas with her in a way that delighted her. They were going to be so happy with their interests shared.

Aware of the fact that Janet had no relatives, Mr and Mrs Moon suggested that Janet might like to be married from Max's home and invite several of her friends from St David's Well to come for a weekend stay. 'So many weddings and so little excitement these days,' she said sadly. 'Being married from here with friends to wish you well might make it a little more special.'

'We'll certainly do everything we can to make it so,' his father assured her.

'That would be wonderful,' Janet said. 'I'll invite them as soon as I get back.' She began listing them, hand spread, a finger tapped for each of her friends, wondering whether Shirley still counted as one of them.

In the brief visit, they managed to send out invitations for the wedding booked for September, and even chose a dress which Mrs Moon promised to alter for a perfect fit.

On the morning they were leaving, Max decided to go to a friend's house to pick up a guitar he had bought.

'It's only around the corner, it won't take me long. It'll be useful for concerts when there's no piano,' he explained as he pulled on his coat. 'I'll teach you to play if you like. It's easy to pick up a few chords to accompany songs. Great for a singalong.'

Janet had brought a dozen fresh eggs for Mrs Moon and in return, Max told her, his mother had made a sponge cake with some butter illegally bought from the grocer, butter gleaned from the scrapings of the paper in which the bulk delivery was packed.

'Tastes a bit funny but better than the awful fatless sponge,' he said with a laugh.

While Max was visiting his friend, Janet spent the last half hour sitting in the garden discussing with Mr and Mrs Moon the possibilities of a brief honeymoon.

'You have decided to stay on in the market café?' Mrs Moon asked.

'I think it's best, at least until the war's over. Then we'll live where it's best for Max. London probably.'

'You won't mind moving away from all your friends?'

'I'll go anywhere with Max. He's talented and I want him to achieve all he's capable of. No point marrying a man like Max if you aren't going to support him. He is a bit special, I'm well aware of that.'

Mrs Moon hugged her and said she was happy for her son. 'I know he's chosen wisely and I'm thrilled with his choice,' she said, smiling.

The air-raid siren sounded then and with a sigh, Mrs Moon led her to the Anderson shelter in the garden. It looked like nothing more than a mound of earth until you walked around to the entrance. Jumping down into the dark, damp place, Janet shuddered, the thought of beetles and spiders more of a worry than bombs, of which she'd had no experience.

'What a place to have to spend nights,' she said as Mrs Moon unfolded a chair for her. The door, which was halfway up the wall as the corrugated building was partly buried, was closed. It was pitch black until Mrs Moon lit a candle placed ready beside a small cigarette lighter. 'Matches soon become too soft to strike,' she explained, as she struck the wheel with her thumb. Revealed in the candle's flickering light, Janet saw two rolls of bedding, a small primus stove and a second chair. Once the beds were unrolled there would be no room for anything else. 'The chairs go outside when we sleep here at night,' Mrs Moon explained.

Janet had never experienced bombing raids, her only knowledge second-hand from newsreels and the sight of the ruined streets that had met her when she reached London. She was apprehensive, aware that for this area the raids were more severe than at home, where an air-raid siren only meant planes passing overhead on their way to destroy other, distant homes. There were no important targets for the enemy to destroy in St David's Well.

'Don't worry. Janet dear. It's probably a couple of German aeroplanes on their way back home. The siren goes often but the worst of the raids are over. Hitler is too busy in Russia and is giving us a rest, for which we are grateful!'

The scream and the crump that developed into the loudest bang Janet had ever heard, came unexpectedly and was immediately followed by two more. Dirt and dust from the seams of the shelter filled the air, the candle went out, the door fell in and everything shook, a trembling that seemed, like the roar of the explosions, to go on and on endlessly.

The two women clung to each other until the sound subsided and the temporary deafness they experienced had eased. Soon afterwards, while dirt still trickled on to their heads and the wail of ambulances and fire engines could be heard in the distance, the all-clear sounded.

They stepped out of the shelter to an unbelievably changed world. Every window in the house was broken, the frames hanging at odd angles, curtains torn and limp. The chimney pots teetered and, as they watched in horror, fell into the garden not far from where they stood.

'Max!' they both uttered. Stumbling over the fallen bricks and wood that littered the garden, they went into the street. A house further down the street had collapsed. Probably the long, continuous rumbling she had heard, Janet thought. Everywhere people were emerging from houses, staring around them in disbelief. Most were stunned, many were crying, a few were calling for help or shouting the names of people they had lost sight of in the chaos. As Janet and Mrs Moon watched, their thoughts paralysed by shock, people were struggling to carry victims from the ruins of once neat houses. They knew they should help but were unable to move. 'Max,' Janet murmured again.

'He'll be safe,' Mrs Moon said. 'He's certain to have found a shelter.'

The sound of engines and sirens drew closer as did the shouts of men and women bringing assistance to the stricken area. The momentary immobility that had affected Janet and Mrs Moon left them and they began to join others, calling for Max, asking for news of him from neighbours hardly recognisable with the dirt and dust on their faces.

There were a few bodies, already covered with curtains or bedding or whatever came to hand. Every part of Janet's body shook as they examined each one, fearful of recognising Max and sighing with undisguised relief with each false alarm. No thought then for the tragedy that belonged to someone else. That would come later when they had found Max safe and sound.

They found him after about fifteen minutes, hope growing as the moments passed and they had almost reached the house of his friend.

He had died in the street, walking home in defiance of the warning, with the guitar which he wanted to include in his act for those occasions when there was no piano.

–

Joseph was sitting in his wife's bedroom, planning to redecorate when he could decide on a colour that would obliterate the memories of Dolly's last months.

He still felt a mixture of relief and guilt when he thought about her. But as the weeks passed relief became the stronger. He was twenty-eight, with a safe and easy job and, he told himself, quite good-looking.

His mother could not be described as rich, but they owned the house in which they lived and another besides, where his grandparents had once lived. He had enough to live on without having to work hard. An easy job without too many responsibilities suited him, and he'd be able to give Shirley a good life, once he had broken her away from the idea of a career in show business.

'How could she imagine being a success in something like singing?' he asked his mother. 'People like us, nobodies born of nobodies, we don't climb to the heights except in films and romantic stories.'

'Come on, Joseph, you know that isn't true. People who are gifted will rise to the top no matter how lowly their beginnings. You only have to read about the famous stars of film and radio and theatre today to know that. Talent is a gift and should be developed. I think you should support Shirley in what she's trying to do.'

'Mam, she sells newspapers, she hasn't any training except for the lessons she had from a failed singer in Rock Terrace! What chance does she have?'

'Not much perhaps, but some. If you love her, you'd want her to have the chance.'

'She can't be that good. She lost in the talent competition last week.'

'She won plenty of others.'

'I want to be there for her when she fails. She'd be devastated if she lost again,' he said, looking away from his sharp-eyed mother in case she saw the expression on his face. An expression not of concern but something more malicious. If only he could devise some means of arranging another failure. He couldn't be fortunate enough to meet the judge and find him sympathetic a second time.

The opportunity came sooner than he expected. When he called at the newsagent, Shirley was out and her mother was standing behind the counter. She looked upset. After serving the two customers with their magazines, she took a letter from her pocket and beckoned to Joseph in a confidential manner.

'This came for Shirley,' she told him. 'I haven't told her in case it's bad news.'

'What is it? Nothing about her job here?' he asked, aware of the possibility of their losing their flat if Shirley no longer worked for the newsagency.

'No, it's from London, from one of those agents she met. If he's turning her down she'll be so upset. Since losing that talent contest she's very despondent.'

'Would you like me to read it? I can throw it away if it's bad news,' he offered. At that moment, Shirley came back from her errand and when she went through to discard her coat. Hetty handed the unopened letter to him and he hid it in his pocket.

When Shirley came back, tying the belt of her overall, she glanced at him, hardly acknowledging his presence. 'D'you want anything, Joseph?' she asked, sounding offhand and slightly bored.

'I was wondering if you'd like to go to the dance on Saturday.'

Shirley shook her head. 'I don't think so, but when Janet comes back from London tonight I'll ask her.'

'I'll call later, shall I?'

She shrugged. 'If you like.'

'You don't fancy the pictures?'

'No, I fancy a night in to wash my hair and things.'

'I see.' Waving to Hetty and patting his pocket with a conspiratorial nod, Joseph left.

'You could have been a bit kinder to poor Joseph,' Hetty said. 'It's hardly his fault the judge chose Janet and Max.'

'Janet had no right to enter with Max. He's a professional.'

'They've done it before, Max and Ken have both entered. It increases the standard you told me, having professionals taking part.'

'This time it was different. I think Max talked to the judge to impress Janet before he proposed, and to bring me down a peg or two.'

'Ridiculous! Don't quarrel with Janet, or Max, Shirley love. And certainly don't finish with Joseph. You'll need them all when you're a success. Friends to support you are essential, believe me. Otherwise the life can be a lonely one.

'You really think I can do it? Become a star of the stage?'

'I believe it and so do you, so stop pouting at the world and get on with your life.' She smiled and added, 'You never know, there might be some good news just about to burst in on you.' She crossed her fingers as she spoke, hoping to see Joseph return with the news for which Shirley desperately hoped: a contract with a London agent.

–

Joseph's heart leapt when he read the letter. It was the offer of a contract giving Shirley a small part in a musical extravaganza, rehearsing in preparation for a tour of provincial theatres. The money was more than he had ever imagined would be paid to an unknown on a first engagement.

He thought about it briefly, then tore it up and scattered the pieces along the street like confetti. She would never know. It was kinder for her never to know.

Later that evening he called again at the newsagent, knocking at the door of the flat and being let in by Shirley's mother. There was something wrong, he sensed it in seconds.

'What's happened?' he asked.

'Janet's home. Max was killed on Sunday.'

'What? Oh, poor Janet! They were thinking of getting engaged, weren't they?'

'More than that! The wedding was booked for the twentieth of September.'

He ran up the stairs to comfort Shirley.

'They had arranged the wedding and moments later he was dead. I can understand why no one waits or makes long-term plans these days,' Shirley said sadly. 'Max, dead. I can't believe it. All that talent gone for ever.' She looked at him and seeing the glittering sadness in her eyes, Joseph took a chance on being snubbed and took her into his arms. Over Shirley's head he looked at Hetty and slowly shook his head, telling her wordlessly that the letter had not contained good news.

Hetty sighed in disappointment and disappeared into the kitchen.

'I want to sing more than ever now,' Shirley told Joseph. 'I want to be a success and sing his songs so his memory will live. I know I can succeed and I've a greater need to do so now. I haven't heard from that first agent I saw. I'll write again. I'll go up and pester him until he finds me some bookings.'

Joseph pulled away from her. There was a cold expression in his eyes as he said softly, 'The agent did write, Shirley love. I didn't want to tell you, but I can't let you go on to further disappointments. Sorry, my dear, but he turned you down.'

'What? When did you hear?' She turned and called to her mother. 'Mam? Why didn't you tell me?'

Hetty stepped out of the kitchen and said sorrowfully, 'Sorry, Shirley love, but I didn't know how to deal with it. So I asked Joseph to open the letter. He shouldn't have told you today. Not today,' she repeated, glaring at Joseph. 'Hearing about Max was enough to cope with in one day.'

'What did he say?' Shirley whispered.

'That you lacked the − er − the charisma needed which together with a first-class voice would enable you to rise above the averagely talented.'

Without a further word, Shirley went to her room and shut the door.

'Thanks for being so diplomatic!' Hetty said, pushing Joseph towards the door.

'I didn't think it fair to tiptoe around the edges, and try to let her down softly. Best to face the truth and then deal with it '

Hetty pushed him harder and once he was outside, closed the door and locked it.

He heard her say, 'Stupid, unfeeling idiot!' before he walked away. He was smiling.

She would soon get that nonsense out of her head now she knew the truth. The London agent would have probably exploited her for purposes of his own. He had saved her from disappointment and worse, hadn't he?

−

Janet returned to work on Tuesday morning. She would go back up on Friday for the funeral. She wanted to be there before that day but she feared she would be an intrusion into the family's grief. She had known and loved Max, but not long enough to be given the right to share the family's mourning. Besides, the Moons' family home was damaged and they were in temporary accommodation until repairs were carried out and she couldn't face staying in a hotel on her own. The loneliness would have been a painful reminder of what she had lost.

She told Ronnie Castle what had happened and, at lunchtime, his wife Olive and their baby called at the café and offered their sympathy.

'If I can persuade Ronnie's Auntie Audrey to look after Rhiannon, and bring her in to me for feeding, I'll look after the café for you on Friday and Saturday,' she offered. 'There'll be plenty of help if I mess things up. The market stall-holders are a friendly bunch.'

Janet accepted her offer, insisting that she would expect her to serve only cold snacks. She was still talking and acting normally, as though the funeral in London was nothing more than a slight inconvenience in a busy week. She was in a vague disbelieving state, sometimes convinced that Max would walk in and smile and tell her it had been a mistake. At those moments, reality would hit her hard.

How could there be a mistake, who else could have that tall, skinny, subtle body or that impossible red hair? Tears would threaten, the overwhelming loss hard to accept, and she would scrub one of the shelves or display cupboards and turn her head away from her customers until she was once more in control.

Shirley went to see Janet and they talked about Max and his kindly nature and Shirley hid her own distress, unable to talk about it to anyone, specially Janet to whom she had boasted so often about the career she knew would be hers one day soon. As Janet talked, her mind drifted back to the audition, wondering what she had done wrong. She hadn't been completely at ease, she knew that, but it had been so important to her. She couldn't have been so hopeless that the man had dismissed her so harshly and finally.

'His music must be kept alive,' Janet was saying and Shirley nodded. It had been her opinion too.

'I want to sing "Slide Down a Rainbow" one Saturday night,' Janet went on. 'On my own, just on my own.' Getting no response she repeated, 'One Saturday, on my own. Max's song. Shirley nodded again. 'Yes, on Saturday. I'll sing with you.'

'No, Shirley, not this Saturday, you aren't listening. This Saturday I'll be coming home from his funeral. I won't want to sing, will I?'

'I don't want to sing ever again!' Shirley sobbed and believing her friend was crying for her, Janet sympathised. 'Sorry, I've been thinking only of myself. You'll miss Max too, won't you?'

'I don't want to sing, ever again.' This time it was Janet who wasn't listening.

–

Lilly met the disabled soldier, whom she now knew as Sam Edwards, several times as summer drew to a close. He was often sitting on the bench she favoured where he could catch the last of the sun's rays when the day had been pleasant and was sheltered by tall privet bushes when the wind was keen.

Their first date had been a disaster. No one had been willing to look after Phyllis, and instead of a getting-to-know-you session, they sat in a café with the baby in her pram. They talked a while, with Lilly complaining about her unfeeling family and Sam commiserating in a soothing manner.

Once or twice as she sat down beside him it had begun to rain and he had suggested going to find a cup of tea and somewhere warm and dry to pass an hour. Since then there had been many such afternoons, spent talking and learning about each other in a cosy café in the centre of town. She told a much-edited story of herself. Her family was a wealthy one, she explained, so there was no need for her to work. Her parents owning half of the entertainments was more than a slight exaggeration but he seemed impressed at the time and the fleeting moment was all Lilly worried about. If necessary, there would be time for explanations later. Making up stories was fun. She told him about her daughter and her dead 'husband', Phil, who had died a hero without ever having seen his darling daughter, and if he was puzzled by the fact that her name was still Castle, he declined to comment.

Sam Edwards described his widowed father and his sister, and suggested that one day she might like to meet them. Soon afterwards she had arrived at 'their' bench to see an older man sitting beside him, whom he introduced as his father. Samuel Edwards.

'Same name, that must be confusing.' she said, laughing as she took the older man's hand.

It was September when she first visited Sam's home and a week later when he showed her to his bedroom. While

Phyllis cried, they made love. Then he watched as she fed the distressed child, before making love again.

When she reached home, there was no one in and Lilly settled the baby into her cot and relaxed in a bath before going to bed herself, to dream of lasting happiness with Sam.

–

September was the tailing-off of the season's activities. The weeks of Eirlys's heavy responsibilities were over and she was looking for something with which to fill the hours. Ken was away for much of the time and although she had the house to run as well as a full-time job, she was never one to sit and do nothing. As with most women during that time, when she did sit to listen to the wireless she always had some handwork to keep her fingers occupied.

A couple of years before she had planned to open a shop and the idea recurred from time to time with growing interest. The rugs she had made had been popular and some were still in her bedroom, wrapped up and waiting for a buyer.

Between knitting socks and scarves and helmets for the forces, she made toys. Some were knitted, many were sewn, fashioned out of the remnants of coats and skirts she had been given to make into rugs. When she was offered a short jacket of imitation fur she took it to Hannah and asked for her advice on making toy rabbits with it. With Eirlys cutting out from a pattern they devised and Hannah busy with her sewing machine, they made several. Then they had to be stuffed and the final seams sewn by hand.

'This is the part that makes or ruins them,' Hannah explained, patiently going over each seam and pulling out the tufts of fur to hide the stitching and give the toys a professional finish. 'Stuffing them evenly and neatening the seams will have to be done properly if you're to make a business of it.'

'How would you feel about us going into partnership?' Eirlys asked. 'I'll do as much of the work as I can, and I'll find out the cost of renting a small shop, or perhaps to start, a shop window to display what we make. What d'you think?'

Hannah's calm eyes brightened. 'I'd love it. I have to continue with my dressmaking, of course, it's my living, but making these toys and gifts is fun.'

Predictably, Hannah's father-in-law at once offered to help and he found a small shop with no living accommodation, simply a lock-up, right on the main road, and he agreed to pay the first six months' rent for them.

'Worth it just to get Eirlys's stack of wool out of my back bedroom,' he said when they protested.

It was surprisingly easy to get the rental. The owner, Mrs Dace, who had sold chocolates and sweets, lived behind the shop and had closed it at the beginning of the war. Mrs Dace was delighted to see it used and the rent was nominal for the first year.

During the month of October, Eirlys and Hannah worked hard building their stock. The rugs Eirlys made with a sewing machine were quickly produced and they soon had a selection to display. Beside their handmade items, with their contacts with suppliers of gifts and prizes for the beach stalls, they were able to obtain generous terms and a six-week payment arrangement on other gifts and toys to add to the variety of what they could offer.

Hannah moved her sewing machine into the shop and worked there during the day on her dressmaking. She soon found this was unsatisfactory. Not being able to work at home in the evening meant a slowing down of her production. A second machine, found and paid for by Bleddyn, sorted the problem.

Besides her normal work. Hannah concentrated on toys and household gifts, aware that with the approach of Christmas people would be glad to have some choice. Shortages were becoming severe and they knew that even little things like novelty tea cosies and egg cosies that would amuse, would sell well as Christmas 1941 approached and the panic to find acceptable gifts began.

They also invited people to bring their work in to sell and devised a system of numbering so they would know whom to pay at the end of every month. Organisation was Eirlys's metier and she and Hannah worked well together.

Bleddyn's plan in getting rid of the collection of wool and material he had stored for Eirlys was twofold. He wanted to help Eirlys and Hannah to build a business for themselves and he wanted to empty the room so he could decorate. It was time he obliterated all memories of his dead wife and started to live again.

–

Shirley refused to go to any dances and when invited to sing at local fund-raising concerts, made excuses not to go. Sometimes she agreed to accompany the still-grieving Janet, then at the last moment would send a note explaining that she was ill.

Joseph spent many evenings in the Downs's flat but Shirley hardly seemed aware he was there. When Hetty and Bleddyn went out and they were alone, she allowed him to kiss her and sometimes would respond enthusiastically, ending up in her bed. Other times she would lie limp in his arms, unaware of him, lost in shattered dreams.

He proposed to her several times but she refused. Knowing the singing career she had envisaged would no longer be hers didn't stop the aching need to perform.

One night she wasn't there when he called and Hetty insisted she didn't know where she had gone. Shirley was standing in the crowd at the dance, watching as a comedian went through his well-worn routine and ended with a song. Sadness overwhelmed her. He wasn't even moderately good, yet he was up there, confidently pulling the audience into joining in. Why hadn't that agent seen her capabilities? Why hadn't he recognised her potential?

She slipped out and walked along the empty street, her heels ringing on the pavement, an accompaniment to the song she was silently singing in her heart.

Instead of going home she went to call on Janet. She had been very neglectful of Janet since Max had been killed. Not much of a friend, am I? she scolded herself, determined to spend more time with Janet even though she would never sing with her again.

Janet answered the door and smiled a welcome.

'Shirley, it's good to see you! You've been hiding away and I don't know why. Have I upset you? It wasn't that stupid judge giving Max and me first prize was it? The man was a fool, Max said so and I agreed.'

'You know that agent I saw in London?'

'Yes?' Janet's eyes lit up hoping for some good news. 'You've heard?'

'I heard some time ago. He said I had moderate talent but nothing to lift me above the ordinary, or some such phrase. I don't remember the exact words, something about a lack of charisma, I think. Whatever he said, he made it clear that I had no chance of being a singer-dancer.'

'Have you got the letter?'

'No, Joseph read it and threw it away. I think he wanted to let me down lightly, but he didn't. He just told me what the man said, coldly and harshly.'

'He would.'

'What d'you mean?'

'Joseph was probably delighted. He doesn't want you to have a singing career, does he? That much is clear to anyone who isn't half asleep! He shows so little pleasure in your success. I bet he was pleased when you didn't win last time, wasn't he?' A glance at Shirley's face told her she had been right in her suspicions. 'He wants you to marry him and spend your life looking after him.'

'He has asked me to marry him and I think I'm going to say yes.' Shirley was still upset at her friend's engagement to Max and wanted to prove she too had received a proposal.

'Why don't you give it one more try? Say nothing to Joseph or anyone else. There's an audition for a pantomime in Cardiff this month. You and I could apply. Why not?' she coaxed, seeing the doubt in Shirley's eyes. 'There won't be any disappointment to report if no one knows except us.'

'We couldn't accept if we did get a part. You work all day in the market café and I have to work in the shop or Mam and I lose the flat.'

'So what? If we do get offered a part we can tell them the money's not good enough or we don't like the look of the leading man. It'll be fun. Come on. Shirley, say yes and I'll write off now this minute.'

'All right. Why not?'

Janet was relieved to see the glimmer of a smile.

Eight

The desperate need to marry continued to affect the town as more soldiers left to serve overseas and more girls grieved for them and feared the appearance of the young telegram boys on their bicycles, wearing their red-trimmed, navy pork-pie hats and carrying the bag of yellow envelopes.

Eirlys and Ken's wedding took place with little excitement, although she tried to make the occasion special by inviting all her friends, and having Ken's sisters as her bridesmaids.

They were married in church, with Eirlys wearing a hastily borrowed white dress and veil and silver sandals. She contacted the beach photographer for some informal photographs to remember the day.

There was no honeymoon, just an afternoon in Cardiff which ended up as a shopping trip and a visit to the cinema: neither of them could spare more than those few hours. Ken moved into 78 Conroy Street carrying only a small suitcase and the whole day was an anticlimax. They were uneasy with each other; the wedding being so casual meant they didn't really feel married.

She also missed her mother that day and thought of the difference Annie being there would have made. It was nothing more than a strange interlude at the beginning of a new stage of their lives and Eirlys regretted the hasty decision, and wished they had waited and built up the excitement, made it more of an occasion.

The following evening, her father made himself scarce, realising their need to be alone. To Eirlys's disappointment Ken wanted to go to the local dance and, hiding her dismay, she agreed. She sat there, forcing a smile, watching others having fun and wishing she were home where there was so much to do.

–

Arranging to attend the audition for the Cardiff pantomime was easy for Janet. Beth was in between jobs having finished at the beach and not yet having found winter work. She enjoyed working at the market café which was busy but simpler than the Castle family's café on St David's Well Bay. Myrtle was used to going there to help after school to help washing dishes when she wasn't delivering groceries on the bike. With Myrtle's help and being used to a busy café, Beth had no difficulty coping.

'My brother Ronnie's just around the corner if I meet any problems,' she said. With Janet's willing permission she moved a few things around to make them convenient to the way she worked and she was ready to take over.

The customers were mostly shoppers, resting for a while between their endless searching and queuing for food, any food that was extra to the rations. A few scabby-looking apples were delivered to her brother Ronnie's stall and at once people appeared as though by magic to form a patient, orderly queue around the nearby stalls, accepting Ronnie's allocation of a pound per customer to give as many people as possible a share.

Beth took her brother his morning cup of tea and was promised a few apples for herself.

'Thanks. I'll take them to Hannah for Marie and Josie,' she said at once.

Besides the regular clientele of shoppers who stopped for a rest and a meeting with friends, the market stall-holders looked to Janet's café for lunch as well as their morning tea and toast, and afternoon tea with a piece of cake. When she was there, this was Myrtle's job and the thirteen-year-old squeezed through the shoppers with a loaded tray, calling for them to 'make way', delivering to each stall. Janet collected the money at the end of each week.

For Shirley to leave the newsagent was different. Unless her mother could be persuaded to take over for the day she would have to plead illness and she didn't like tempting fate by pretending her health was anything but robust. Her mother worked for the Castle family, mostly in the chip shop in the town. It opened all the year round and was a café as well as selling fish and chips over the counter. As their friendship had grown, Bleddyn had come to depend on her for help.

Hetty was working at lunchtime on the day they were planning to go and Shirley knew that the only way to persuade her mother to help her was to be honest.

'Mam, I want a day off and I need your help.'

Hetty looked at her quizzically. 'Not London again? You won't do anything like that again, will you? At least until I can come with you.'

'I might try again, one day, when my wounded pride has recovered, but not at the moment. No, they're looking for people for the panto. Cardiff, not London. I don't feel confident enough to try London again at the moment,' she admitted sadly. 'Or even Cardiff really. I'm going to this audition for Janet's sake, that's all.'

'Don't let anyone put you down, Shirley. You have a great voice and having one agent refuse you isn't the end of the world. When you're ready, start again. I have a feeling you'll make it.'

'Thanks, Mam. At least you think I'm good enough, but the opinions of mothers and favourite aunties don't count.'

'I'll arrange for someone to do my shifts. Perhaps Bleddyn can ask Beth,' Hetty said.

'Perhaps not!' Shirley said with a laugh. 'Beth is taking Janet's place in the café!'

'Don't worry, we'll think of something. Go and have fun and don't be disappointed if you aren't chosen. I bet there are dozens trying and even the best can be overlooked sometimes. And you, my darling girl, are the best.'

Hetty was right. The entrance to the theatre where the auditions were to take place was heaving with hopefuls. Mothers with small children, giggling schoolgirls, perky boys fighting and fooling, and on, right through the ages to quite elderly men and women hoping for a pan.

They waited for three hours and felt their spirits and energy waning, but as soon as they were on stage their tiredness left them and they prepared to sing and dance. As with all the others, the group of casting directors, singing coaches and producers said very little. They scribbled comments about the previous act in their notebooks and sat, looking bored, as they waited for the next in the long line of performers to rouse them out of lethargy.

Janet and Shirley began together as usual with the verse of the song, then when Shirley's solo began, the line of assessors jerked up their heads, their interest roused. She sang confidently and well, her powerful melodious voice ringing out across the auditorium and even persuading smiles to appear on the solemn faces sitting in row eight.

Unlike most of the other acts they were shown around the backstage area and were allowed to look at the costume designs and meet some of the professionals already chosen to take part. Shirley's eyes were shining with the wonder of it. A different world and one in which she knew she should have a place.

They went home smiling happily, both having been offered a role in the forthcoming production, and on the train they discussed whether or not they could accept.

'If I give up the café for the run of the panto, I'll have nothing to come back to when it's over,' Janet said sadly. 'I'd love to take part. All the fantasy, the colours, the outrageous costumes, the songs with the audience joining in, it would be a wonderful experience.'

'I feel exactly the same,' Shirley sighed. 'But if I gave up the shop I'd be making Mam and myself homeless. The flat goes with the job. Mam and I have lived there since my father left us, when I was twelve. I can't take the risk no matter how much I want to.'

They were silent for the remainder of the journey, oblivious of people getting in and out of the carriage. Shirley was troubled by doubts about her ability. Perhaps she was good some days and not others. Perhaps she wasn't as note-perfect as she believed. Tone-deaf singers didn't always know they were out of tune. Why else had that judge chosen Janet and not her? Her confidence dropped lower with every turn of the wheels.

Janet was thinking of Max and how thrilled he would have been. They would have had such a wonderful life together, both involved in show business, sharing each other's joys and successes. Why was life so cruel? Abandoned as a child and brought up in a children's home, alone in the world, then meeting Max and losing him so soon after falling in love.

When they reached the door of the flat where they knew Hetty and Bleddyn would be waiting to hear their news, they wordlessly agreed to put on an act, and burst into the living room, talking as soon as the door opened, excitedly telling Hetty and Bleddyn about their wonderful day, wildly exaggerating the fun they'd had, prepared to laugh off the idea of them taking the parts, which for both of them was impossible.

'So you've both been offered parts?' Hetty said, sharing in their excitement.

'Yes, they wanted us but neither of us can take the job,' Janet said, trying to hide their disappointment. 'It was a great laugh. We enjoyed it, didn't we, Shirley?'

'We knew we couldn't take the parts before we went, but it was fun going to the theatre and seeing the costume designs and everything,' Shirley added. 'We wouldn't have missed it, would we, Janet?'

'We might do it again. We know we're wasting their time but so were most of the so-called singers.' Adding to their attempt at hiding their dismay, they began telling Bleddyn and Hetty about some of the acts, exaggerating the poor quality of them.

Amid the laughter, Bleddyn said solemnly, 'If you really want to do this, I think you should. I've been fortunate in my life, I've always been able to do what I wanted, which was work on the sands. If you two want this as badly as I think you do, then I believe you should make it happen.'

'But how? I can't close the café for months. I'd have nothing to come back to,' Janet explained, laughing falsely at the ridiculous idea.

'If I don't work in the shop Mam and I have to leave the flat,' Shirley said brightly. 'I don't mind, really I don't. It isn't that important. Besides, if I lost a local talent competition and was turned down by two London agents, what's the point of dreaming of a career in showbiz, eh?'

'We enjoyed today but we knew it was only a d—' Janet was about to say 'a dream' but changed it to '—a bit of fun.'

Hetty looked at her daughter in disappointment, but Bleddyn smiled, patted their shoulders and said, 'Don't give up just yet. I have a few ideas that might make it possible. Even if it's only a few months and you don't get another offer when it's over, you'll always have this to remember. Just give me a few days, is it?'

Shirley and Janet hugged each other. For a while at least they could dream.

–

Eirlys already knew that her marriage to Ken Ward had been a mistake. They had moved into her home with her father and it was more like having a lodger than her being a newly married woman. Nothing in the routine of her life had changed and the wedding had lacked the excitement of finding a home, choosing furniture and curtains and gathering together all the necessary utensils needed to equip a kitchen. There had been no time to fill her 'bottom drawer'.

Everything she had saved for her marriage to Johnny Castle had either been discarded or used in her home. Shortages and finding time in their busy lives had prevented them even bothering to decorate the bedroom they were to use.

It had been hers after the boys had returned to London, and its familiar shabbiness was now hers and Ken's with nothing changed apart from new bedding and a hastily scrubbed linoleum-covered floor. Besides, having sorted out the debts left by Teresa Love, money was a problem too. They hadn't been able to consider replacing any furniture, not even the bed.

There had been no experimental cooking, working out meals to please the new man in her life. Rationing had been partly responsible for that but also she was so busy that cooking was a hasty affair at the end of a hectic day, with the hope that Ken would like what they usually ate rather than her trying to find his favourite food as most newly-weds would do, seeking praise and admiration.

Ken was away from home a lot, leaving her with her father, continuing in the same routine as though nothing had changed at all. He was in concert parties and was often absent for several days. Since their wedding he had refused bookings further afield which would entail absences of several weeks, not wanting to leave his bride so soon. Eirlys was filled with shame as she realised she looked forward to their partings more than his homecomings.

She was often exhausted, with her job at the council offices and filling the shop with handmade items, as well as a few fire-watching duties during which she knitted or sewed in every possible moment. 'Make Do and Mend', the posters demanded and it meant women's hands were never idle. Life was frantic for her as for everyone and Ken's visits were more and more an interruption instead of an eagerly awaited joy.

When he was home at a weekend he wanted to go to the dance where there were still local acts performing during the interval. The performers were older and less talented but their enthusiasm was enthusiastically applauded. They had been given a new lease of life and were happy, and it showed.

Eirlys went once or twice, to sit and watch the rest dancing, applauding with them when the singers and comedians entertained, or when Ken himself sang a comedy song at the piano. All the time she sat there, she wished she were at home where there was so much to do, trying not to count the hours before he left her to get on with her life.

For Morgan it was equally difficult to adjust. His daughter and her new husband needed time alone so he went out when Ken was home, leaving them together, and he spent hours in the public house trying not to spend too much money, as he still had debts to pay. Debts he now owed to Ken instead of to others.

When the weather was kind he went to his allotment where he was growing vegetables. He'd had a good crop of onions that year, surprisingly as he had been late planting them. As he harvested them, he thought he could offer them to Ronnie Castle to sell on his stall. He knew they were in short supply and if he could wait until Christmas drew near they would be even more popular. He sat in his shed one day, tying them into lengths, remembering the 'Johnny Onions', the French onion sellers, who, until the war, had come each year to sell their crops, and he wondered sadly how they were coping with the Germans occupying their homeland.

He heard someone approaching and looked up, expecting to see one of the other allotment holders. To his surprise it was Bleddyn Castle. He at once became nervous. Before she had died, Bleddyn's wife, Irene, and he had had an affair.

It was his constant dread that the large, powerful Bleddyn would one day find out and come to take his revenge. To his relief, Bleddyn was smiling.

'I want a bit of advice,' Bleddyn explained as he sat outside the shed on an old wooden seat.

'You've come to the wrong place then,' Morgan joked. '*Twp* I am, you can ask anybody. Without our Eirlys to run my life for me I'd be done for.'

'Have you ever thought of remarrying?'

'You know I have. I wanted to marry Teresa Love and adopt her three boys, but I was a fool, as usual. She took everything she could then hopped it back to London.'

'But if you found the right woman?' Bleddyn persisted. 'Would you marry again?'

'I like to think I won't be spending the rest of my life alone,' Morgan conceded, 'but I'd have to be real sure. Easy to make a dreadful mistake it is, like I nearly did.' He put down the onions he was trimming and looked at Bleddyn. 'Besides, with Eirlys and Ken living with me, the place would be too damned crowded. No, it doesn't seem very likely. Not for me. You think you've found someone special, then?'

'I've been seeing a lot of Hetty Downs. We get on so well and I care for her, you know. I want to look after her, see that she's all right, her and her daughter Shirley.'

Morgan chuckled. 'Better man than me, then. I want someone to look after me!'

'She used to hate the Castles, convinced that they'd cheated her grandfather out of the business or something, but she was bitter about so many things then. You know about her husband, Shirley's father, running off and having another family, don't you?'

'Yes, young Myrtle and Maude Copp. Hell of a shock that must have been for Hetty, mind, to find out who they were.'

'It was, but now she's letting all that go. The thing is, if she married me and came to live at my place, Shirley could try for a career on the stage.'

'Sorry, you've lost me. I told you I was *twp*.'

'If Shirley gives up her job at the newsagent, they lose the flat.'

'Are you thinking of marrying Hetty because you want to? Or to help Shirley's career?'

'Because I want to, that's for definite, but helping Shirley would be a sort of bonus. What d'you think?'

Morgan thrust out a brown-stained hand. 'I wish you luck, Bleddyn boy, and I hope I'm as fortunate as you one day.'

Bleddyn left him and headed off to visit his daughters-in-law. He wanted their approval next. Hannah, Johnny's wife, hugged him and gave him her blessing, assuring him that Johnny would be as happy for him as herself. Taff's wife Evelyn was not as pleased.

'Dad, you can't really want to remarry? And someone like Hetty Downs!'

'Why not? I'm not *that* old. I hope that you and Taff, Hannah and Johnny will be happily involved in your own lives and I don't want to be hanging around waiting for you to spare me an hour or two. I want a life of my own, so you don't have to worry about me.'

'You're talking like an old man entering the twilight of his years.' She tried to laugh but she was clearly upset.

'No. I'm not. That's exactly it. I'm only forty-eight and I don't want to live like an old man for a long time yet.'

'But why do you want to marry? It doesn't sound right. Johnny and Taff loved their mother and they might be—' She hesitated and Bleddyn finished for her.

'Might be disgusted?'

'I wasn't going to say that!' she protested.

'Weren't you?'

'They'd be upset.'

'Perhaps, until they thought about what was best for me.'

Evelyn had always been difficult about change. She objected strongly when Johnny announced his engagement to Eirlys Price and he had often wondered why. Perhaps she was afraid he wouldn't think as much of her if there were others to share. She had been unhappy too about Hannah and Johnny, insisting that Johnny had made a mistake marrying an older woman with two daughters, but her reaction against Hannah was less serious than her dislike of Eirlys. Perhaps one day he would ask her to explain, but not yet. He was fond of Evelyn and knew she made his son, Taff, very happy, but he didn't feel confident enough to ask her about Johnny and Eirlys, not yet. One day he would ask her to explain her resentment towards Eirlys. It had been puzzling at the time.

If Morgan Price had known that Bleddyn was even thinking about getting to the bottom of Evelyn's resentment when Johnny planned to marry his daughter, he wouldn't have slept for weeks. Evelyn's dislike of Eirlys was because of his affair with Bleddyn's wife, Irene!

When he left Evelyn's home, Bleddyn went back to Brook Lane and wrote to his two sons. He began each letter by saying he had just seen Evelyn and Hannah and they were well, then told them about his intention to ask Hetty Downs to marry him.

Posting the letters he knew he might not receive a reply for several weeks, and hoped to follow up the letters with another, bearing the news that Hetty and he were engaged. Now he had to ask Hetty. All the preamble might have been unnecessary; she might refuse him, he thought, as he pushed the letters into the post box and headed for the flat above the newsagent.

—

Shirley and Janet relaxed their decision to keep secret their Cardiff audition. It didn't matter now they had been successful and had been offered parts in the show. Gradually the news spread. Joseph's reaction to Shirley and Janet's offer of parts in the pantomime was disappointment presented as concern.

'Shirley, don't you think you'd be making a mistake? You could give up your job and this small part you've been offered could be the only one ever. You could lose everything for a few months of being a small cog in someone else's wheel. A bit part, no glory, no fame, just a lot of work and with nothing to follow. Having a small success like a part in a panto isn't enough to risk everything.'

'You don't have any faith in me, do you, Joseph? Can't you imagine a better outcome? I might be offered other, better parts. I could be seen by talent scouts and given parts in London shows. Can't you even try to imagine that?'

'What about travelling home every night on the late train?' he asked, ignoring her plea for support. 'What if there's an air raid and you're miles from home?'

Exasperated at his determination to undermine her happiness she snapped, 'What if I'm a success? What if I get dozens of offers? What if they make me a star'? What then, eh?'

'Pigs might fly!' he retorted, his fear of losing the argument making him childish.

'Stand by with a popgun!' she retaliated, equally childishly. 'We'll have to shoot for bacon!'

When Bleddyn knocked on the door, Joseph was leaving.

'Try and talk some sense into Shirley for me, will you?' Joseph said in response to Bleddyn's polite greeting.

'Since when has Shirley been incapable of making her own decisions?' Bleddyn asked in surprise.

He walked into the large room above the shop which was simply but comfortably furnished. Hetty was sitting near the fire and Shirley went to sit near her.

'Shirley, I know it's an awful cheek but would you mind disappearing for a while? I have something to discuss with your mother.'

'Of course I don't mind. I'll go and see Janet,' Shirley said. Kissing her mother, she grabbed a coat and left.

'Hetty, will you marry me?' he said.

'What did you say?' a startled Hetty asked.

'Will you marry me, come to live with me in Brook Lane? You and Shirley can do it up as you want to, make it your home, and if Shirley wants to try to build a career in show business, she'll have a safe secure place to work from. What d'you say?'

Slowly, Hetty shook her head and, at once, Bleddyn said, 'Don't tell me yet, think about it. I won't rush you. There are so many rushed weddings happening in the town, but we can take our time. I want you to be happy. You and Shirley.'

She reached out her arms and they clung together but Bleddyn didn't attempt to kiss her. She had been surprised by his words and he wanted to allow her time to recover.

'I can't leave the flat, not until Shirley's made up her mind about this stage career. She needs the shop and we need the flat, at least until she's decided.'

'She can live with us until she's able to manage on her own. I'll support you both. You can work if you want to or stay at home if that's what you prefer. I want you to do exactly what you choose. I – I'm not very good at saying this, but I love you, Hetty. I want to spend the rest of my life caring for you. When the boys come home we'll be one big happy family. They'll be proud to have your Shirley as a stepsister. As proud as I'd be to have her as a daughter. I hope one day soon you'll realise you feel the same about me.'

It was a long speech for a usually quiet, unemotional man and when he stopped speaking and Hetty gave no response his spirits dropped. She was unimpressed, she was going to say no.

'I'd love to marry you, Bleddyn, but I can't. Not yet.'

'Then we'll wait,' he said, looking at her and smiling. 'We'll wait until you can, right?'

'I promise not to keep you waiting too long before I can say yes.'

She lifted her face for his kiss and they sealed their promise.

One way of dealing with the pantomime season was to ask the owner of the shop for four months' leave for Shirley, with Hetty taking her place. This was refused.

'I might have known it couldn't be that easy,' Shirley sighed. 'And next week there's a first rehearsal. What shall I do, Mam?'

'Go, of course,' Hetty smiled. 'Lie if you have to. I'll take your place and lie as well. One way or another you're going to take that part.'

–

Alice still wrote regularly to Eynon although for a long time she didn't know where he was stationed. His letters to her were short and the few lines he had written were further reduced by heavy blue-pencilling. She went on writing, hoping that his lack of response to her questions and comments were due to the heavy restrictions on what he could write and not because her letters failed to arrive.

She visited Eynon's family and shared the little news she received, each time hoping that the Castle family would have some for her. She didn't show them his letters – they were too personal for sharing – but passed on news that she thought would interest them. They discussed the embargo on information and surmised that he was in training. But for what and where they were unable to guess.

Lilly listened to the discussions and in her vague way worried about her brother. But her thoughts were more on her own war. Every time the news came through about the loss of a local man, she said at once. 'Stop it! Stop it. It brings it all back. I know how his wife feels. My baby's father died a hero, remember.'

They had long ago stopped trying to tell her that other women suffered too and in most cases were married to the man, but Lilly insisted that her family should think of her and not mention such tragedies. Instead she wanted to tell them about Sam and how kind he was to Phyllis. When it was suggested that they meet this wonderful person, she made an excuse.

The plans to open the gift shop were going ahead but it was difficult to find the time to deal with it all. Eirlys and Hannah had employed Sammy Richards the carpenter, who also played accordion, to make a display area in the windows and make a few shelves for the walls.

Bleddyn had posters printed and distributed, telling people that the shop would open soon, and had placed an advertisement in the local newspaper. Behind the white-washed window panes the cleaning and planning went on. Passers-by stopped and screwed up their eyes trying to peer inside, curious and hoping to be among the first to know what was happening.

With a weekend of hard work ahead of them, Hannah, Eirlys, Bleddyn and Morgan arrived at the lock-up shop prepared to wash and scrub, and paint and fix shelves and, with luck, fill the small window with a display of their rugs and handmade gifts.

Beth and Ronnie's sister Lilly was supposed to be helping too, but she was so slow and so adept at being absent when something was urgently needing attention that they sent her back home to make sandwiches for their lunch; an excuse to avoid more strenuous work which she managed to stretch out to more than two hours.

Lilly had never been overfond of work and with the rest of the Castles involved with the beach during the season and doing whatever work they could find during the winter, she had managed to reach the age of twenty-eight without exerting herself overmuch. Since the pregnancy and then the birth of her daughter, she'd had the perfect excuse for taking it easy. Mrs Denver, whose son Phil was the father of Lilly's child, had taken on the role of mother-in-law and she encouraged Lilly to do as little as possible. She wanted to make sure they remained friends.

Mrs Denver's son, Phil, had two other illegitimate children, both boys, neither of whom she had seen. Once her son had told the women he denied parenthood and wouldn't help, they had gone away and refused to allow her to see the children. Although Lilly denied it, Phil's reaction had been the same with her and it was only his death that had allowed her to pretend that he was going to marry her.

Knowing this was her last chance of watching a grandchild grow, Mrs Denver had befriended Lilly and made sure she did nothing to upset her. Whatever Lilly wanted that was in her power to give, Mrs Denver gave. She flattered Lilly and encouraged her in her laziness simply to ensure she was allowed to stay close and share the joy of baby Phyllis.

'Go on, Lilly love,' she would frequently urge. 'There won't be another time in your life when you have such a good excuse. Pretend you're suffering and men don't like to ask questions. Enjoy it while you can. Once this little darling grows up you'll never have another chance of a bit of sympathy.'

Using the excuse that baby Phyllis needed some fresh air after delivering the sandwiches of tomatoes with a thin sprinkling of grated cheese, Lilly strolled through the town to sit in the park. She looked towards her favourite bench and saw not the young man she usually met but an older man. She sat down and waved a rattle in front of Phyllis's face. She didn't look closely so didn't recognise Sam's father.

'Hello, Miss Castle?' the man said politely. Lilly stared at him, frowning, half recognising him, different clothes and hat misleading her. 'I'm Samuel's father,' the man reminded her. 'I'm Sam Edwards too. What a stupid idea, wasn't it?'

'Where's Sam – I mean, your son?' she asked.

'He has a hospital appointment. They're trying to assess whether or not he has to return to his unit. I'm hoping that he won't have to go.'

'I don't blame you. If they tried to take my child, however old she was, I'd take her away and hide her!' She smiled and they began to admire the baby. With Sam telling her how beautiful Phyllis was and what a wonderful mother she seemed to be, the afternoon passed pleasantly.

Mrs Denver lived alone since her son Phil had been killed in action. To earn a little money she baked cakes and pies for a local baker's shop. She usually managed to make an extra cake or two out of the ingredients she was given and kept them for Lilly on her weekly visits. Lilly had one in her bag which she had intended to give to those working in the shop but she had forgotten and proudly handed it to Sam Senior. If he thought she had made it, she couldn't help that, could she?

Marged sent her out again almost as soon as she got home. She was told to deliver more sandwiches and flasks of tea.

'Will you give a hand displaying these rag dolls?' Ronnie asked, handing her a large cardboard box. She did so without attempting to hide her reluctance and when the simple task was almost completed, afraid of being given something else to do, she suddenly announced she was leaving and told them she had a feeling that Mrs Denver needed her.

The others didn't take much notice of Lilly's dramatic remark. Lilly's 'feelings' were well know to be an excuse to leave something she didn't want to do!

'Just as well,' Eirlys sighed. 'She only gets in the way. Thank goodness she brought the food first!'

They had finished scrubbing the wooden floor and intended to stain the boards before leaving that evening. The shelves were now painted a cheerful green and the walls a pale yellow. The transformation from the dingy, neglected premises they had rented was amazing. Tomorrow, when they displayed the rest of their goods, it would be better still.

Hannah had been rather quiet all day and as they packed up their cleaning tools ready to paint the floor before leaving, Eirlys said, 'You go off home, Hannah, the girls will be missing you. I'll finish staining the floor.' Tired as she was, aching in every muscle, she was determined to finish the floor that day.

'It's all right, they're safe and happy with Johnny's Auntie Marged,' Hannah said, but there was concern on her gentle features that Eirlys wrongly interpreted as worry about her daughters. Until she had married Johnny, Hannah had never left the girls for so long.

'You're right, they'll be having a lovely time, don't worry.' Hannah sat on the edge of the window and her shoulders drooped. 'It isn't Josie and Marie. I haven't heard from Johnny for weeks.'

Bleddyn heard her and added, 'Evelyn hasn't heard from Taff either. I expect the boat with the post has been delayed. We have to keep writing and hope our letters get through. It's more important for them to hear from us at home, remember.'

'I know. I write every day,' Hannah said. 'I'm being silly. No news is good news, isn't that what they say? Bad news travels fast, and we'd have heard if—' She couldn't complete the sentence.

'Come on, let's get this finished.' Bleddyn said brightly. 'I can't wait to see Johnny's face when he sees this place.

Imagine you becoming a businesswoman, Hannah love. So proud he'll be. I always knew you were talented. Bring out the hidden talents of a lot of women this war will. Yes, indeed it will, eh, Eirlys?'

'I wouldn't be doing the job I've been given if the men hadn't been called up,' Eirlys agreed, 'but right now I'd go back to being an office junior if it would bring them all home safe.'

'I bet we'll hear before the end of the week,' Bleddyn said. 'Now come on, no slacking, let's deal with this floor and if either of you paint yourself into a corner you'll stay there till it's dry, right?'

When Eirlys finally reached home, tired and stiff and longing for a bath followed by bed, Ken was there. She tried to appear pleased, as she hugged and kissed him and asked what he wanted to eat, but he told her that he wanted to go and see Janet and Shirley to find out how they got on at their audition.

'Did they get it?' he asked.

'I think so. But, Ken, don't you want to see the shop? We've been working on it for days, every moment we could find, and it's looking really smart.'

'Oh, yes, well done. We can go on the way back from Janet's if you like.' Seeing disapproval on her face he added. 'I have to take an interest in Janet, because of Max. You do understand, don't you. Eirlys?'

'Of course. We'll look at my effort when it's too dark to see anything, shall we?'

'Stupid of me. I forgot. We'll go there first,' he amended.

It was tempting to tell him not to bother but she held her tongue, managed without a bath, made an omelette with the crusty remains of their cheese ration for her father and wearily set off with him to see Janet and Shirley.

Her emotion was disappointment, not jealousy. She had achieved something and there was no one with whom to share it. Surely it was not that unreasonable to hope for something more from a marriage than the uninterested, dull relationship that Ken offered? He was extremely busy and spent a lot of time travelling; she knew and understood that, but instead of his hectic life making their time together more precious, she was increasingly certain that Ken felt the same as she did, that their time apart was more exciting than the moments they were together.

She sat in Janet's small flat, her muscles stiffening and the longing to sleep almost overpowering her, and listened while Janet went through every moment of the day she and Shirley spent in Cardiff and joined, in artificial enjoyment, with Ken's congratulations.

At Shirley's home it was a repeat of the same and she kept thinking of a long, warm bath and the last of the bath salts she had been saving for something special. Preparing her shop for opening was something special, but not for Ken; for him, the audition of Janet and Shirley had the edge.

The shop opened, and for the first few days business was brisk. Many people came just to look but there were plenty who either bought or asked for items to be put aside ready to hide away for Christmas.

There were very few goods in the shops towards the end of 1941 and the simple toys made by Hannah and Eirlys filled a need. They put a notice in the front of the window asking for anyone with goods to sell to bring them in for possible inclusion.

The appeal for more goods to sell was not a great success. Most of the soft toys, knitted garments, cushion covers and the like that they were offered were not good enough. The owners were sent away disappointed and in some cases, offended and even angry.

'If we aren't careful we're going to run out of things to sell!' Hannah sighed as she picked up her sewing and finished off the seam of yet another rabbit.

Beside the rugs, Eirlys's speciality was dolls and dolls' clothes and once she had made patterns for the clothes to fit the dolls she made, these were fairly quick to run up. The body, head and limbs were sewn on a machine but the finish was done by hand. Because she did a better job, Hannah stuffed the dolls and did the embroidery that completed them. Each doll was unique, Hannah's nimble fingers managing to shape the heads into pretty little faces with a variety of features and hair styles.

Eirlys still worked long hours at the council offices and called after work to discuss progress with Hannah and decide what they needed to make. She sat up until late every evening at the sewing machine or knitting small dolls and teddies. Like most people at that time, she rarely wasted a moment; there was always something to be done.

—

Beth went home one evening to the cottage she shared with Peter's father, and Bernard Gregory came out to meet her as she cycled towards the gate.

'Got a surprise for you,' her father-in-law smiled, clamping his teeth down on his old pipe. 'He's home.' He held her arm and added softly, 'He's been ill, mind, so be prepared to hide the shock of seeing him. We don't want to upset him, eh?'

Throwing the cycle carelessly down, Beth hardly took in his words. She gave a shout of delight and ran into the house. Her husband was leaning against the fireplace and he looked ghastly ill. His face was sunken and his hair was flattened against his head. Even his eyes were lifeless until she called his name and he looked up.

'Darling Peter!' she said as she ran to him. The sight of him made her careful not to be too enthusiastic. He looked as though she might easily knock him over. She pressed her head against his chest, thankful of the opportunity to hide her tears.

'How long?' This was always her first question and was usually rewarded with the reply, 'Not long enough'. Today, however, he smiled weakly and said, 'Quite a while I think.'

'Wonderful, your father and I can fatten you up.'

'I've been ill,' he said.

'Are you allowed to tell me about it?'

'No, but I will. I think you should know at least something of what I've been doing these past years.'

'I've guessed some of it. Like – you've been behind enemy lines, haven't you?'

'Trying to form escape routes and helping the underground to create fresh ones every few weeks to protect the brave supporters from being caught. As you guessed, my work was in enemy-held territory.' He sank back into a chair as though he hadn't the strength to stand. 'This time I was taken prisoner and I escaped and needed the routes I'd been planning for myself. Holed up for days unable to show myself was pretty sordid, Beth my darling, and I don't want to come near you until I've been able to clean myself up.'

'I'll help you,' she said at once.

'Not this time.' How could he allow her to see the marks of the brutality he had suffered, or smell the filth that seemed to ooze from his skin?

Easing himself out of the chair and away from the fireplace, he moved towards the stairs. 'Please, darling, I need to sleep alone until I feel more human. Please don't think I don't want to be with you, I do, desperately, but not for a while.'

'Let me help you upstairs, at least let me help that much,' she begged. Together they climbed the stairs and into the bedroom where he collapsed, still dressed, on to the bed. He fell deeply asleep at once and she pulled off his clothes and covered his dirt-stained body and left him, trying to hide her tears from his father.

When he woke the afternoon of the following day, Beth was sitting beside the bed, having refused to leave him for a moment. She called down to Bernard who came up the stairs with a bowl of soup and some freshly baked bread.

They helped Peter to sit up and eat a little, before allowing him to go back to sleep. On the following day he was able to sit up and although he protested, Beth and his father insisted on washing him. When he turned over and they saw his back it was almost impossible for them not to cry out in horror, but keeping her voice calm, Beth washed him and soothed the dreadful injuries with ointment and begged him to let her send for a doctor.

'No doctor,' he said. 'No one must know what I do or where I go. It's imperative that my work is secret.'

Two days later he rose at dawn and dressed and stood in the garden looking out at the slowly wakening day. Beth found him there and slipped an arm into his.

'I have some bad news,' he said, putting an arm around her and drawing her close. 'If I tell you, you mustn't repeat it.'

She waited in silent dread for him to tell her.

'It's your cousin, Taff Castle. He was in the same escape party as me. We escaped as we were being taken from one prison camp to another. I got away but, sorry, my darling. Taff was shot. There was nothing I could do. If I'd stayed to see what had happened, I'd have been caught again too.'

'He was wounded?' she asked, even though the look on his tired face told her different.

'I – I'm sure he was killed. I expect Evelyn will have the dreaded telegram soon, but I can't prepare her or his father, warn them, although I wish I could. I mustn't let anyone know what I do, or many more good and brave men and women could die.'

Later the following day he felt strong enough to go out and although the season was over, he walked with the troop of his father's donkeys to the beach, strolling at their haphazard pace, wearing clothes that hung on him, a battered old panama hat of his father's on his head.

The beach was empty, summer long gone, but he walked the length of the bay across the sands as though dreaming of better days to come when laughter would be the strongest emotion and fear only experienced by children on the rides.

Beth watched him surreptitiously, and thought he looked older than his father. What had happened to him she would never know, but she shuddered as her imagination ran riot. Two weeks later, as October brought cold winds that knocked the leaves from the trees in a glory of autumn colours, Peter went back. Beth returned to help in the shop and grieved.

Nine

The Castle family were devastated by the news of Taff's death. Bleddyn heard from a distraught Evelyn when she ran to Brook Lane with the telegram held in her trembling hands.

'Read it. Tell me it isn't true, that there's a chance they're mistaken,' she sobbed. Bleddyn felt a cold chill run through his body but knew that at that moment, his task, his final duty as Taff's father, was to comfort Evelyn. His crying, hidden inside, would erupt later.

Sitting her down, making the inevitable tea, he called a neighbour to sit with her while he went to find Beth. After walking Evelyn back home and making sure Beth could stay a while, he went back and threw himself on the bed and cried, asking why Taff had to die fighting in some foreign land when all the boy ever wanted was to work on the sands and enjoy watching others having fun. Innocent and carefree and now gone for ever.

Within hours the rest of the family were told. Bleddyn's brother Huw came and stayed with him, Marged made food and wished there were a magical wand to take away the pain. Taff and Johnny, cousins to her own four, Lilly, Ronnie, Beth and Eynon, had grown up together. Bleddyn's loss was no less hers and Huw's.

For a while friends and family were afraid to enjoy themselves. The mourning was a balance between life going on and grief for the young life lost. Having no formal funeral to end the first stage of grieving made it worse. Like thousands of others, they were in limbo, waiting for some finale to Taff's short life which didn't come.

Lilly was crying when she met Sam Edwards in the park and he walked her home to Sidney Street. When she stepped inside Marged saw the young man and asked Lilly who he was. As Sam was leaving, Marged called him back and invited him inside.

There were introductions and the usual politenesses as Marged and Huw offered him tea to thank him for looking after their distressed daughter.

When he had gone, the questions began. 'Who is he?' 'Where did you meet him?' and 'Is he married?' being among the first. Enjoying the attention, Lilly told her about Sam and his injuries and his interest in her and Phyllis. Every detail she had gleaned was trotted out and embellished and before the day was out, several members of her family had the impression that there was a strong romance in the making, an impression Lilly did not deny.

Having no one to love her was sad. Wherever she looked there seemed to be couples, and men in uniform with girls on their arms made her solitary state very obvious. Having a pleasant young man, and a wounded hero at that, to call her boyfriend was better, even if it was little more than pretence.

She met him the following day and invited him home for tea. Then he told her he was recovered from his injuries and was going back to his unit. She cried after he had left and at once her mother offered sympathy.

'Just when I thought I'd found happiness, he's leaving me,' Lilly wailed.

'You can write. Sam seemed very fond of you and he'd love to have someone to write to,' Marged said. 'And he'll have leave. Just think how exciting it will be, looking forward to letters and his visits. It's very romantic having a boyfriend in the forces.'

'Oh yeh? Think what happened to our Taff.' She felt ashamed when she saw her mother's face crumple with distress and added softly, 'You know how upset we all are, Taff was like a brother. I wouldn't want to get fond of someone and lose them like we lost our Taff, Mam.' She thought too of Philip, the father of her child and whom she had believed she might have one day married.

For a while she tried to avoid Sam, determined not to become what her mother called a grass widow, having to be loyal to someone she rarely saw and who could disappear overseas any day. Then, one rainy day, she went out, pushing Phyllis in her pram, and headed for the park. She didn't think Sam would be there, but sitting on 'their' bench under a large umbrella was a man in a dark raincoat and trilby. She thought it was Sam and went across. She had missed him and was sorry she had avoided meeting him over the past three days.

'Sam,' she said, but when she drew close she saw it was Sam's father.

She shared his umbrella and he told her that at his son's request, he had sat on the bench every afternoon for three days, hoping she would come.

'Sam was called back with only hours' notice. There wasn't time to tell you he was leaving and I didn't like to call on you at home in case you thought it impertinent,' he explained. 'I wasn't sure how friendly you two were.'

'I'd like to write to him,' Lilly found herself saying, regretting the words almost as soon as they were uttered. Now she would have to write and she was Sam's girl and would have to wait for him. It was definitely romantic but also a restriction on her hope of finding someone who wasn't going away, who would accept Phyllis, and marry her.

Sam Senior was telling her how pleased his son would be and when he offered to give her his address, she smiled and said that would be lovely.

'If you walk home with me now, I'll write it out. I can't remember it,' the man said ruefully. 'All those initials and numbers get me confused.'

Lilly went in and stood while Sam Senior searched for pen and paper, her coat and Phyllis's pram dripping on the hall carpet. She looked around her at what seemed to be a very comfortable home. Sam's attractions were increasing minute by minute.

She knew that Sam's mother was dead, and wondered who did the housework. She suspiciously wondered whether Sam might propose just so they had a housekeeper. That thought did not appeal, but perhaps they were wealthy and employed servants. It all smelled nicely of lavender polish.

As she walked home, indifferent to the continuing rain, Lilly began to dream.

–

Shirley and Janet attended further rehearsals and were given their parts. Shirley's a surprisingly important role, which included a solo. Janet was contented to be told she would appear in the chorus.

'All those pretty dresses!' she said delightedly.

'Janet, I don't know whether I can face it!' Shirley said, her hands covering her cheeks, her eyes wide with alarm. 'Me up there all alone on a stage in a huge theatre filled with mothers and kids, and singing with a proper orchestra. I'm terrified! I'll have to write and tell them it was a mistake and I can't do it.'

'Of course you'll do it and enjoy every moment.'

'What if Beth can't mind the café?'

'We'll get someone else.'

'What if I forget the words?'

'Then hum!' Janet laughed. 'Come on. Shirley, it isn't like you to suffer nerves.'

'I know, but this is IT. I could be heading for great things and if I mess it up—'

'I'll give you a job washing up in the market café. There, that threat should make you do your best!'

Joseph called that evening and as she was excited about the part she had been given and felt the need to boast. Shirley invited him in. Her mother was out with Bleddyn, comforting him and trying to persuade him that life was continuing for the rest of the town's widows and bereaved fathers and it had to for him too.

'I've come to say I'm sorry,' Joseph said, offering her some Dairy Box chocolates, 'and to wish you luck with the pantomime and anything else you're offered.'

'Thank you, but why the change of attitude?' she asked with a suspicious frown.

'I realised a few nights ago that my attitude was down to jealousy.'

'Rubbish! You don't want to sing or dance, so how could you be jealous of my success?'

She hadn't invited him to sit and he stood in the doorway undecided whether or not to walk into the room. 'I've worked in the same job for years with no prospect of promotion. I've never been further than Cardiff. London might as well be a foreign country. I think I was jealous of your determination to do something most would think impossible.'

She gestured towards a chair and went forward to poke some life into the fire.

'Let me do that,' he said, taking the poker from her hand, grasping hers for longer than was necessary. He piled more coal on to the freshened fire and stood beside her as the flames slowly began to lick around the new fuel.

'Will you forgive me, Shirley? Can we start again?'

'I won't have time to see you once the panto starts so what's the point?'

'You'll need someone to escort you if you're going to live at home and work evenings in Cardiff. I'll be there every night, I promise. I love you, Shirley, and I truly want to look after you.'

She turned towards him and she slid her arms around his waist, lowering her head on to his chest where she could hear the beating of his heart, more because she wanted him to see her and Janet safely home than because she needed the comfort. He'd played enough games with her – why shouldn't she do the same? An illusion of love wasn't a bad thing either. Better than loneliness, and she had missed the fun she'd had with Freddy.

A few days after their reunion. Shirley received a letter from the entertainment committee asking her and Janet to sing and dance in a concert the following weekend. The organisers had been let down by two acts and The Two Jays had been recommended to take their place.

'I don't know that I like us being substitutes for other acts,' Shirley said when she and Janet discussed it later that day.

'If it was for anything else other than for the Red Cross I wouldn't do it.' Janet agreed. 'Damned cheek! But it is a good cause, parcels for prisoners. Max would have done it without hesitation. I say we should. Agreed?'

'Agreed.'

Joseph called into the shop and was told about the Saturday evening concert.

'I'll be in the audience,' he promised Shirley, 'and I'll be there to walk you and Janet home.'

Janet was not as confident as Shirley. As she lay in bed the night before the concert she wondered if she could survive it. Before going on stage she always had to prepare herself, talk herself into the excited mood that the audience saw and loved. To sing and dance without nerves, without inhibitions, took a few minutes of confidence building that no one apart from Shirley would ever know, except Max, and perhaps Ken, who understood her so well.

Since Max had gone, this building-up was more difficult and knowing that tomorrow she was going to sing one of Max's songs would be hard for her. She told herself she was singing for him, singing his songs to keep his memory alive, but she would never again sing 'Waiting For Yesterday'. Her yesterday was no longer there for her, however long she waited.

The report of Taff's death, and seeing Ronnie and the rest of his family with their faces distorted by grief, had brought memories of Max's death flooding back for her. Yesterday had been filled with promise but it was gone for ever. She thought for a moment about Ken. Perhaps if he hadn't married Eirlys they might have become more than friends. They had so much in common that a partnership would have been exciting and— She stopped there. Thinking about Ken Ward was stupid and could lead to nothing but trouble. Although it was painful, she forced herself to think again of Max.

She longed to be able to go back to yesterday, to see him pushing his way through the crowd, towering above the rest, his eyes, filled with desire, locked on to hers as he hurried, arms widening, to hold her close. Tears fell and sleep was a long time coming.

–

When Shirley and Janet discussed their clothes for the concert, they were influenced by having seen some of the pretty costume designs for the pantomime. This made them more daring and they wore shorter skirts and more skimpy tops than they previously would, in a cheerful red.

They painted their legs with fake tan, brushing it on in brisk strokes with a piece of sponge. Then they each carefully painted on the seams for the other. Having seen and been involved in more professional dance routines, they had changed their act a little too. Bending forward to offer glimpses of cleavage, kicking their shapely legs that little bit higher. After no more than the early rehearsals for the pantomime, they were already considering themselves professionals and a class apart from the other performers.

From the wings, they watched as an elderly couple of ballad singers went on, and a juggling act and Sammy

Richards the carpenter, appearing tonight as a Tyrolean accordion player, and they knew that when they ran on to the stage as they usually did, their entrance would make everyone take notice.

Their act came just before the interval and they performed a song and dance act they had rehearsed thoroughly. They had an encore and the applause lasted for a long time as the enthusiastic audience begged for more.

'I don't know which I like best, dancing or singing.' Shirley said as they ran, breathless with excitement, and headed for the changing room.

Joseph was so furious he couldn't think straight. How dare Shirley embarrass him so? She and Janet had flirted with the audience and made themselves look like cheap tarts. He overheard some young soldiers remarking on their beautiful legs. Legs were for private moments, not for exposing for anyone to see. How could she do it to him? Still fuming, he made his way to the entrance and waited, with anger bubbling inside, bitter and destructive.

They didn't come out, and he heard the band start the introduction to the second half. Surely they weren't waiting till the end? The Two Jays indeed. Her name was Shirley Downs and if she behaved herself she would one day be Shirley Beynon, but not if she continued to behave in such a disgusting manner.

Nerves jumped at the thought of not making her his wife. He deserved her and wanted her to be a normal wife, running his home and caring for him. After putting up with Dolly all those years, he was entitled to have a wife who was fit, strong and, he added grimly, one who would behave herself.

Slipping back inside he heard the master of ceremonies announce that The Two Jays. Jane and Janet, who were rehearsing for the Cardiff pantomime, had generously agreed to sing another number just before the final act.

Joseph went to the nearest pub and drank until the time the concert was due to end. Repeatedly he glanced at his watch as his fury increased. She was making a fool of him and it had to stop. But how? He had discouraged her and told lies about the agent and that hadn't stopped her, so what would? He didn't care how she was stopped but she had to give up on this sordid prancing about half naked in front of men.

Inside the theatre the girls were given a great send-off and their eyes were sparkling with the success of the evening as they ran for the second time to the dressing room.

'Any doubts have gone after that,' Shirley said, her face glowing with happiness. 'London, here we come, eh?'

'Good luck. Shirley. You've got a fantastic voice and you'll go far. I'll follow as I can but it's you with the talent.' Janet hugged her friend. 'I wish you every success, I really do.'

'What's this nonsense? You'll be with me.'

'I'll be there for as long as you want me,' Janet promised and they were continuing the conversation in friendly argument as they left the stage door.

They were among the first to leave, not stopping to change out of their stage clothes, using their long coats to cover their bare legs, protecting themselves against the chill. It was dark, no lights escaping to help them find their way, and they pushed through the crowd emerging in a chattering flood, heading towards the corner where Joseph had promised to wait for them.

Shirley and Janet ran towards him, expecting him to be bursting with praise, but he took Shirley's arm and pulled her somewhat roughly towards where he had a taxi waiting.

'A taxi? Why? It isn't that far to walk,' Shirley protested as they half ran, trying to keep up with his long angry strides.

'You can't walk through the streets dressed in that disgusting outfit!' he said as the taxi driver opened the door for them.

'What? Joseph, why are you angry? Didn't you see how well we went down? It was wonderful and the costumes were perfect for the numbers we sang.'

'Numbers, is it? Not songs, it's *numbers* now.'

Pulling on Janet's arm, Shirley pulled herself away from Joseph's grip and stepped away from the open door of the taxi. 'Come on, Janet, we'd be better off walking than riding with a madman!' Leaving Joseph calling after them they hurried off.

Neither spoke as they hurried through the chattering crowds and headed for home through the dark damp streets; Janet because she didn't know what to say, and Shirley because she was close to tears.

Determined not to be upset by Joseph's reaction to their performance, Shirley and Janet went to the Saturday dance. Janet hated going, knowing she would never again dance with Max, but Eirlys had told them that Ken was due home. He might be there and he was always a great comfort.

Joseph paid and went in but he didn't show himself to the girls. He stood in a dark corner and watched. Janet sang with Ken during the interval and Shirley sang a solo with Ken accompanying her on the piano. When they left in the company of Ken and one of his friends, greeting each other with light, friendly kisses, Joseph watched as the two men walked off with Shirley and Janet chattering happily between them.

A letter arrived for Shirley with a London postmark and the address of an agency on the corner. As before, Hetty hesitated before giving it to her, but this time she guessed that a disappointing response would not be as hard to take. Now the two girls were starting rehearsals for the panto Shirley wouldn't be so hurt. She handed it to Shirley when she went down to relieve her for her mid-morning break.

'They've been a long time making up their minds,' Shirley remarked as she tore open the envelope. She frowned as she read it. 'Mam, I don't understand. They're asking why I didn't accept their previous offer of a part in the chorus of a new musical. I didn't have any offer. What can have happened to it?'

Hetty's hands flew to her mouth, a universal expression of shock and dismay. 'I — oh Shirley, I've been so stupid!'

When Hetty told her daughter about the previous letter and Joseph taking it away without showing her, they both knew what had happened.

'He lied, didn't he?' Hetty said.

'I wonder if that was the first time?' Shirley mused when the anger had left her. 'I've always been puzzled about the time Janet won over me. Both Janet and I thought the decision was phoney. She didn't sing well that night. The range was wrong for her, it wasn't one of our rehearsed numbers and she even forgot the words at one point and Ken helped out.'

'Keep well away from the man,' Hetty warned.

Later Hetty asked Bleddyn to have a word with Joseph, which he did, his burly strength and aggressively jutting yaw unnerving Joseph for a while, but not for long. He was convinced that Shirley belonged to him and he would marry her. Once she had got this foolishness out of her system she would turn to him for protection and comfort.

–

Myrtle Copp didn't really enjoy delivering groceries on the big carrier bicycle after school, specially now the evenings were so cold and dark. Most of the customers were friendly but there were a few who grumbled about the few biscuits that were broken and regularly blamed her for dented tins or a bacon ration that looked less than perfect.

The call she most feared was to the run-down shop premises where Alice Potter lived with her father. Colin Potter regularly complained to her for one reason or another and every time she knocked on the door she held her breath, waiting for the angry, shouted words. He would look at the box of groceries and poke the bags and packages, frequently handing back an item he didn't think they should buy and demanding that she make a note on the bill explaining the reduction.

Because she wanted to finish early and go to help Hannah in the gift shop, she carried three small orders instead of making three journeys and the bike was top-heavy and nearly toppled over once or twice.

Getting used to the weight, she began to hurry and when she knocked the wheel against the kerb and lost her balance, falling into the road on top of the laden bike, she was angry with herself, knowing there would be a delay.

A lady took her inside and washed her cuts and bruises but all the time she was aware that she would be late delivering to Colin Potter and she grew more and more afraid. He always complained if she arrived later than he expected. The other worry was that biscuits would be broken and what if the eggs were too? She knew she would have to go back to the shop to get them replaced and that would make her later still.

To her relief the two eggs were unharmed and she carefully repacked them in their paper bag, tucked for safety in tissue paper and placed between soft items like the packet of tea and a loose-wrapped bag of sugar.

Knocking on the door she listened nervously for the slow, dragging footsteps as the man walked down the long passageway, leaning against the wall to maintain his precarious balance. Since being injured in a boxing match he had never been able to walk unaided, and his temper was far from good. The wild-looking man snatched the order without a word and slammed the door. She was so relieved she was smiling as she set off for the next call. Thank goodness that ordeal was over for another week, she thought as she heaved the heavy carrier bike away from the wall.

–

Once the beach activities were finished until the following year, Marged and Huw and the rest of the Castle family usually looked for work to see them through the winter months. Bleddyn kept his usual job of running the fish-and-chip café in town and Beth helped him. This year Beth also managed to work in the new handmade gift shop with Hannah for several hours on most days. In between serving customers she would sit working on new items to offer for sale, her fingers guided by the patient Hannah.

Several people had brought handwork good enough for them to sell and Eirlys had devised a numbering system to enable them to know who needed paying for what had been sold at the end of each week. They weren't making much money but they had hopes that with Christmas approaching, they would soon sell all they could make.

Hannah still did her dressmaking, taking the work to the shop when it was possible, to enable her to spend more hours there. Dashing off to meet Josie and Marie from school curtailed the time spent selling their handcrafts except when Bleddyn was free. When he could he took the two girls home or to the park.

Eirlys and Beth often went to the shop on Sunday to clean and redress the window. Time was precious for everybody and with both of them working five and a half days a week, Eirlys at the office, Beth in Janet's café, they needed to show the others they were doing their fair share.

One Sunday morning in late October, Eirlys was painting a design on the window of the shop door, when Evelyn, Taff's widow, called to speak to Beth.

'Do you know that Taff's father is planning to marry Hetty Downs?' she said as Eirlys opened the door for her.

'Yes, I think it's great news, don't you?'

'Not really. Taff was very fond of his mother and he'd have been hurt.'

'Rubbish!' Eirlys snapped. 'What is it about you and weddings, Evelyn? You hated it when I was going to marry Johnny and you weren't any happier when Johnny married Hannah.'

'That isn't true. I didn't think it was right for you to marry Johnny when your father and Johnny's mother were — you know — seeing each other.'

'Carrying on?' Eirlys suggested. 'Having an affair? Go on, you can say it!'

'If Bleddyn found out that your father was the one who'd led her away from him, he'd kill him.'

'Led her away?' Eirlys gasped. 'What world d'you live in? Irene Castle wouldn't go or do anything she didn't want to.'

'Took advantage of her unhappiness, that's what I think!' Evelyn snapped. 'But whatever — Bleddyn would still want to kill him.'

'He won't find out though, will he? Unless you want to tell him.' Eirlys stared at Evelyn and wondered if that was on her mind. 'If you do it'll be pure mischief. No good can come of it, not now Irene's dead, so you'd be deliberately making trouble for the fun of it,' she warned.

'I don't believe in secrets. Best the truth is known.'

'Why? Don't you think it wise to protect innocent people? Or can't you resist telling secrets for the malicious pleasure you get from revealing them?'

'You've no right to talk to me like that! Your husband is out gallivanting with other women, going dancing as though he was single, and you don't seem to care. And there's me a widow, my husband not even allowed a funeral!' She sobbed, but Eirlys didn't attempt to comfort her. Evelyn was a difficult person to befriend, there was always disapproval in her conversations.

'This has nothing to do with the tragedy of Taff's death. Evelyn, this is you wanting to upset people. You should wish your father-in-law luck and welcome Hetty Downs into the family,' Eirlys said firmly.

'The Castles aren't my family any longer. I'm Mrs Taff Castle in name but I no longer belong.'

'That's up to you. Bleddyn will treat you like a daughter-in-law for as long as you behave like one.'

'How can I behave like one with Taff dead and Bleddyn carrying on with his chip shop as though nothing's happened? He should feel as bad as I do but he doesn't. He's indifferent to the loss of his son.'

Eirlys's voice softened. 'Go and see him, Evelyn, at least share your grief with him. He holds up for the rest of us but he's finding it hard. I know him well enough to see that even if you don't.'

Pushing the door open and almost upsetting the tins of paint Eirlys was using. Evelyn ran down the street. Eirlys frowned. She hadn't handled that very well, she thought sadly.

Evelyn's remarks about Ken going dancing as though he were single hadn't registered. If she had thought about them she would have put them down to Evelyn's spitefulness, nothing more.

Evelyn went to Brook Lane and knocked on Bleddyn's door before walking in, calling, 'Dad? Are you there?'

Bleddyn came out of the living room carrying an empty coal scuttle. 'Just lit the fire, I have. You've timed it well for a cup of tea if you've got time.'

She nodded and watched as Bleddyn went outside and refilled the scuttle, washed his hands meticulously and started to set the tray for tea. Her face wore a sullen look. He didn't seem to be grieving. If Eirlys thought he was hiding it out of concern for others she was wrong. He was getting on with life, lighting fires, making tea, cooking chips as though that awful message hadn't come. She could hardly stop the words coming; she felt an uncontrollable urge to shock him, hurt him.

When the tea was poured and the formal politenesses were done with, she said, 'Taff was so proud of you, Dad.'

'Proud of me? What have I ever done to make anyone proud? All I've done with my life is have fun on the beach like an overgrown kid!'

'Well, the way you coped with Mam being so ill.'

'That was easy, you marry for better or worse. Anyone would have done what I did.'

'And keeping control when you found out about her and Morgan Price, that takes a strong man, Taff said.'

'What about Irene and Morgan Price?'

'Oh, I thought you knew. I mean, I must have been mistaken. Sorry, I misunderstood something that was said. Stupid of me, eh?'

Bleddyn was thoughtful as they sipped tea and touched the tops of a dozen subjects trying to make a conversation. His head was buzzing with half-remembered incidents and half-said words. When Evelyn had gone, he grabbed a coat and went to find Morgan.

On the way he passed the shop where Eirlys was finishing her painting, and stopped to ask, 'Where's that father of yours?'

'At home I think. Why do you want him, Mr Castle? Anything I can help with?'

'Not this time. I have to see Morgan and I just might kill him!'

'Did you see Evelyn?' Eirlys asked as the man hurried on. When he called back over his shoulder that he had, she knew exactly why he was looking for her father. What an unpleasant girl Evelyn could be. So pompously certain of herself, never deviating from her own rigid rules, never accepting that she could be wrong.

Hastily locking the shop, she ran through alleyways and over waste ground, determined to get there first. Perhaps one day, Evelyn might make a mistake herself or, even more unlikely, she might make allowances for someone else's. Eirlys thought as anger simmered.

When she burst into the house she found her father reading the Sunday papers.

'Get out, Dadda. Bleddyn Castle's on the way to find you, and he knows about you and his wife,' she gasped.

—

Bleddyn walked fast, his hands bunched into fists. He was longing to push his fist into Morgan's face. The man had made a fool of him. His jaw tightened as he realised that others must have known and had been laughing at him. His pace slowed a little as he thought of Hetty and how happy his life had become since Irene's death, and of the loss of his eldest son. His temper calmed as he put the affair between Morgan and his wife into the past. But he still needed to relieve his fury.

Morgan ran down the garden, jumped over the fence into next door and leaped two more fences, making his way to the allotment shed where he locked himself in and sat, shivering, as he waited for Bleddyn to appear. He always knew this day would come but had hoped to delay it until both he and Bleddyn were too old to fight. As he sat in the dark musty-smelling shed, his imagination saw Bleddyn grow taller and fiercer by the minute.

When the knock came he felt his muscles become liquid.

'Come out, Morgan Price! Come out and face me like a man!'

Morgan cringed, making himself as small as possible even though he knew he couldn't be seen. He'd stay here as long as it took, until Bleddyn gave up and went away.

'I know you're in there, and I can wait all today and tomorrow. I am a very patient man, Morgan Price.' He said nothing more and the minutes passed. On a nearby allotment a man could be heard rooting out a few parsnips, the fork digging into the soil, hitting stones as the earth was smoothed over the empty space, the man calling across to a friend nearby. Morgan sat on the floor hardly daring to breathe for fear of being heard.

In a more casual voice, Bleddyn said, 'Its all right, you know. I knew there was someone. I just didn't know it was you. Irene was unhappy and sick. She tried to find happiness but it always eluded her. Perhaps I should thank you for giving her some excitement, some fun. What d' you think, eh?'

Morgan said nothing and didn't move a fraction of an inch even though something hard was sticking into his leg and his arm was stiff.

'You were the worst off, weren't you, ruining your daughter's happiness. She turned my Johnny down because of your carrying-on and there she is, married to Ken, and even I can see she's very unhappy. You've got that to live with, so you're the worst off. No, I don't feel any bitterness towards you for the trouble you caused. Irene's death wasn't really down to you. And my son Johnny is very happy with Hannah. It's Eirlys's life you've messed up and you have to see her every day and know what you did to her. Live with that, can you?'

Inside the shed Morgan's heart was racing. He knew what his affair with Irene Castle had cost his daughter and hearing someone else saying it was more than he could take. He stood up and opened the door.

'I regret what I did more than you know. But I've suffered too. Losing Annie, then Teresa and the three boys was a punishment. I miss them all terribly. And you're right. I've suffered bitter regret seeing Eirlys so unhappy, knowing I caused her to leave your Johnny.'

'Sorry, but you'll have to suffer some more,' Bleddyn said as he swung a fist at Morgan's face, then stomped off.

The man working close by called, 'Hey, what's going on? I'll call the police, mind, if you don't stop.'

'It's all right,' Morgan shouted back with a voice that sounded different from usual, echoing around in his head like the railway announcements in an enclosed station. 'It's all right, Arthur, I only bumped into the door.'

'A right hook from a shed door? That's a good 'un! Haven't heard that one before.'

Eirlys said nothing as she bathed her father's face and put a plaster over a cut on his cheekbone. Neither did she mention it when she next saw Bleddyn. Her father had it coming and in her opinion he'd got less than he deserved.

—

Beth had a letter from Peter telling her he was coming home for forty-eight hours' leave. She showed it to his father. 'We don't usually know when to expect him, so I wonder what this leave means?'

'Don't look for problems, Beth love. Be thankful he's coming.' They both knew that his leaves usually meant he was off on a dangerous mission behind enemy lines.

'The last time he was home he looked so ill, I hated seeing him go back before he was fully recovered,' Beth said.

Scrounging oddments of fat from her parents, swapping some tea for some extra sugar and offering a few duck eggs in exchange for some marmalade, Beth made a cake, the marmalade plus grated carrot and a few prunes being a substitute for fruit. Not the usual Christmas cake but it would have to do and they would celebrate Christmas when Peter came home, whenever that was, in case he couldn't get leave in December. She decided to decorate the room too and spent some time gathering holly, ivy and branches of the blackthorn bushes which she painted white in place of a Christmas tree and on which she hung baubles and glitter.

One of the people making gifts to sell produced fine quality hand-knitted ties and she bought one, wrapped it and put it in the corner where they intended to place the tree. Christmas — their first Christmas together — would be early, but it would be as perfect as she could make it.

With a month to go to Christmas Day, Peter arrived and, to her relief, looked fitter than when she had last seen him.

'Good news.' he said after kissing her and hugging his father. 'I'm staying in this country, at least for a while. Training others to do what I've been doing, hoping to give them the skills I've learned, to keep themselves alive.'

It was a celebration far more exciting than any other even though they weren't allowed to tell anyone else the reason for their happiness. For the foreseeable future Peter would not have to face the danger of being dropped behind enemy lines working to help flyers and others to make their way home through occupied country. Beth hoped that his new appointment training others, sharing the knowledge he had gained over the past three years, would keep him home, safe, until the war ended, no matter how long it took to defeat Hitler.

–

Huw and Marged were kept busy catering for the flood of weddings continuing to take place that year. Marged opened the café on the cliff high above the beach on these occasions, even though the weather was often cold and damp. It made the poorest of wedding parties more exciting having the unusual and beautiful setting for the wedding breakfast. Huw made sure that the black—out for the windows was kept in good condition because even when the meals were arranged for the afternoon, the celebration sometimes went on until darkness had fallen.

Alice Potter, who helped in the seaside rock and sweet shop on the promenade during the summer, sometimes came to help. She was shy and still had to be coaxed before she would tell Marged she had heard from Eynon. Teasing, probing, nothing would persuade her to give a hint about how she felt about him. Her face would redden and even Huw felt sorry for his teasing and gave up on it.

Secretly, Marged wondered whether Alice and her youngest son would be the next wedding the Castle family would celebrate.

–

Eirlys had watched Ken storm out of the house. He had arrived late the previous evening and when he announced his intention to go and see Janet and Shirley, she asked him not to go. 'Surely it isn't unreasonable to expect some of your time?' she had complained.

'Shirley asked me to go and see them, it's something to do with a charity concert. You know,' he'd said sarcastically. 'the war effort?'

The argument increased and had ended with Ken storming out while Eirlys stood on the doorstep staring after him, wondering how he could have changed into a bad-tempered stranger.

With rehearsals every day except Sundays and Mondays, Shirley and Janet were very busy. Beth was running the market café and enjoying the experience and Shirley's boss had been persuaded to allow Hetty to take her daughter's place at the newsagent. So when they were asked to sing at yet another concert, they had to refuse.

That evening, straight from the row with Eirlys. Ken went to see Janet on the excuse of asking her to take part in the concert. She had been thinking about Max. Ken was fresh from a row with Eirlys, and comforting each other got out of hand within minutes. They made love, each one acting to punish the one they loved: Janet felt both regret and anger with Max for being outside during that air raid, and Ken hated Eirlys at that moment, for what he considered such a lack of understanding.

They both went separate ways and arrived at Shirley's fiat a few minutes apart to plead for her help with the concert. It was for the victims of air raids, to buy them replacements for their lost possessions.

The two girls agreed to ask permission from their producer and after careful consideration he agreed. 'Nothing once we're into production.' he warned. 'but as it's for such a worthy cause, you have my permission.'

Ken spent a little time rehearsing with them, then he had to go away to appear in a concert at an RAF camp in Yorkshire, promising to try to get back in order to take them and escort them home.

As the day of the concert approached, there was no sign of Ken. Janet blamed herself for becoming involved. He had to stay away, how could they face each other? He was married to Eirlys. What they had done was inexcusable.

'Pity Joseph hadn't been born with more sense.' Janet sighed. 'Pain that he is, we could do with him sometimes.'

'I hope I never see him again,' Shirley said angrily. 'He tried every way he could to ruin our chances of a career in show business and I hope he rots.'

'From the feet up. Slowly,' Janet added.

Shirley hadn't seen Joseph to speak to since his outrageous behaviour had been discovered. He had tried several times but she ignored him. When he came into the shop she threatened to call the police and, if there were customers in the shop, she begged them to get him out. For the sake of his reputation he had to stay away. But he had been seen skulking in corners at the dances she and Janet had attended. She sometimes wondered whether he went to every dance advertised in the hope of her being there. Otherwise, how did he know when and where they were planning to go?

The concert in which they were to appear was held at a large hall not far from the centre of town and the seats were all taken. To Shirley's irritation when she peeped around the curtain before the performance began, sitting in the centre of the front row was Joseph with his mother. She didn't want to embarrass Mrs Beynon, realising that she would be unaware of her son's activities — which was probably why he had brought her — but she hated performing in front of Joseph. Imagining his strong disapproval would inhibit her and she knew she would give less than her best.

Janet looked around for Ken. If he could be found he would somehow get Joseph shifted. It was almost time for curtain-up before she spotted him and leaving Shirley backstage she ran down to explain to him what had happened.

Ken was not performing and sat in the third row with Eirlys.

'Eirlys, excuse me but Shirley and I need Ken's help,' she said as the band began to play the introduction. She quickly told them about their unwanted guest and Ken left Eirlys to speak to the manager of the hall.

The result was Joseph and his mother being apologetically moved to the back row and a refund of their ticket money offered, plus the explanation that an important agent from London was there to see some of the acts.

'An important theatrical agent who tried to get in touch with her by writing to her — several weeks ago!'

Joseph stung under the words. Ken was making sure he understood about the agent's letter. Without a word of complaint, he and his mother moved, magnanimously refusing the refund.

The Two Jays were near the end, but instead of rushing off when their spot ended, they waited hoping to meet Ken and Eirlys after the finale. They were both still wearing their long, white dresses as they stepped towards the stage entrance. This was usually easier than trying to get through the crowd at the front doors. From voices coming back to them they learned that it was pitch black and raining heavily. They caught a glimpse of Joseph obviously waiting for them and turned away from the exit; instead they went out through a rarely used delivery door at the back of the hall. The rain and the darkness was startlingly and frightening. They couldn't see a thing.

'It's like we've stepped into the final scene of a horror film,' Janet said nervously, 'cutting us off from everything that's bright and busy, leaving us alone and helpless in the gloomy night.'

'Stop it,' Shirley said, laughing. Then exasperated, she exclaimed, 'This was a stupid mistake. Damn Joseph for making us skulk around like villains! Why do we let him do it to us?'

'Shall we go back in and use the front?' Janet suggested.

'If we don't hurry we'll miss Eirlys and Ken.' But the door had closed behind them and couldn't be opened from outside.

'Which way do we go?' Janet asked. 'I can't remember where we were to meet.'

'I'm not sure. It's so dark, and coming out of a different entrance I've lost my bearings,' Shirley said. 'Damn this rain. My hair will need washing and curling tomorrow morning after this.'

Feeling their way, following a wall, bumping into unseen objects, sending a metal bin clanging away, and tripping over their skirts, progress was slow and the rain was soaking into their clothes. 'I'll go this way, you go that way and if we miss them we're bound to meet up at the main entrance and then we'll get a taxi. Right?'

'Right.'

Both girls set off and Shirley moved slowly to the corner of the building. Having no light to help, she clung on to the wall as she felt her way around the first corner. Why hadn't they used the main entrance like the rest? It was usually quicker to use another door and avoid the audience's departure but not on a wet, dark night in December when she wasn't sure of the way, she thought as she worked her way along the seemingly endless wall.

She heard the sound of cars starting up and moving off as she approached the second corner which she hoped would bring her in sight of the front of the building and the car park. Then a shadow, barely discernible in the night, loomed upon her and Joseph's voice said, 'Shirley, please let me talk to you. I can explain why I did it. It was for you.'

'Go away,' she shouted, hoping someone would hear her.

'I was only thinking of what's best for you,' he said.

'Rot! Rubbish! Get away from me!' She felt his hand on her arm, holding her back, and she pushed him hard and ran to where the sound of voices represented safety. She ran without thinking straight across the tarmac towards the pavement and a car suddenly came towards her, close, very close. As it was reversing, the driver couldn't see her and she backed out of the way, desperately shouting. She reached behind her with a hand, trying to find the wall, afraid of falling in the high-heel shoes she was wearing.

The car came on slowly, forcing her towards the wall of the building in which she had just been a performer, and voices continued and laughter rang as the sound of the engine filled her mind like a nightmare. The dull glow of the car's lights were too weak for her to be seen by the happy crowd so close by, her shouts lost in the excited chatter.

'Janet!' she screamed, then the car hit her. Mercifully the driver had risked getting his head wet and looked out of his window to check his position. He saw the white of her dress and jumped on the brakes.

Shirley collapsed over the boot of the car. Her screams went on and on. People gathered around. The driver shouted his innocence. Janet cried. Unknown voices asked questions and others tried to reassure her. But the sound of the engine was still in her head and the voices came to her muffled as though through an echoing tunnel.

The next few hours were never fully remembered. She had flashes of scenes in which she was carried, remembered voices filled with concern, and in her head she heard Janet crying. Then there had been an ambulance taking her on a journey with Janet beside her, and a trolley taking her through hospital corridors that seemed to go on for ever.

She awoke in bed in a ward with other beds either side of her, coming out of a nightmare filled with fear, in which she was shouting at the driver of the car that had hit her. When she opened her eyes, the occupants of the other beds and the nurse sitting at her desk in the centre of the room were all staring at her. Then the nurse smiled and came over.

'Glad to have you back with us, Miss Downs. Your mother and Janet are outside. Would you like to see them?'

'What's this?' For the first time Shirley noticed the high mound of bedclothes covering her legs.

'You hurt your legs, I'm afraid, but we'll soon have you up and about. A few months and you'll be on your feet again. Don't worry about anything. That's what we're here for. We'll do the worrying and you concentrate on getting well.'

'My legs? But I'm a dancer!'

'Not for a while. Miss Downs, not for a while.'

Shirley tried to move, get out of bed, prove to herself that the nurse was wrong. The pain was followed by paralysing fear, causing her to scream.

'No more of that, now,' the nurse admonished severely. 'Screaming and making that dreadful noise won't help you or anyone else. Stay calm; your mother and your friend are upset enough without you making a fuss.'

'A fuss? But I'm a dancer!'

'We'll see,' the nurse said with kindly intent. 'Not being able to dance isn't the end of the world. Just for now think about how fortunate you were not to have been killed.

Another few inches and this could have been far worse. You've broken your leg and damaged the muscles of the other. You'll mend, given time.'

'I've broken my leg?' Another scream welled up but died unheard.

Janet and Mrs Downs came in and they seemed unable to speak. Janet stood allowing tears to slide down her cheeks and Hetty sat down and put a hand on her daughter's face and tried to smile.

'It was Joseph,' Shirley sobbed. 'He tried to talk to me, tried to grab me and I ran away and—' She turned to Janet and said, 'That nurse, she seems to think I won't dance again.'

'You will. She doesn't know you like I do. Nothing will stop you taking part in that panto in three weeks' time. Or if not this one then definitely the next one and that's a promise.'

'Nice try, Janet,' Shirley said, and turned her face away to hide the tears.

Ten

Guilt and remorse made Joseph want to run away, hide from everyone, imagining the whole population of St David's Well would be pointing a finger and accusing him of Shirley's injuries. He phoned the office and told them he was ill and wouldn't be at work for a few days, then sat in his room and stared at the walls. On the evening of the second day he braved the outside world and went to the hospital. It was visiting time and he buried himself in the crowd of visitors standing armed with magazines and flowers and other gifts, and when the doors opened he walked in.

He lost his nerve before he had taken two steps into the ward. Seeing the lines of beds down each wall and the assorted patients looking hopefully towards the arrivals, he backed away.

Using the excuse that he had forgotten the flowers he had intended to bring, he asked a nurse to point out Shirley Downs. He was distressed when he saw her lying there. Her face was as pale as the pillow on which she rested, and with a complicated traction apparatus looming over the bed. He hurried away, bumping into people in his haste.

How could he face her? What could he say? He knew he was really going there to insist she accept it was not his fault. What if she agreed to see him, and could forgive him for the pestering that had resulted in this dreadful injury?

What would he do then? After Dolly, how could he face another sick wife? Ashamed of his feelings he went home to hide once more in his room. He couldn't even talk to his mother. She too would be ashamed of his conditional love.

The following morning he took flowers to the ward and said, 'Tell her they are from a friend.'

–

Shirley was depressed and nothing anyone said comforted her. She asked her mother to write to the producer of the pantomime and explain that she would not be able to take part. The doctors told her she was likely to be in traction for six weeks and after that would have to use a wheelchair to get around.

When Janet was told about her resignation, she too withdrew from her place in the chorus.

'Why?' Shirley demanded. 'I'm the one who's injured, you shouldn't let this spoil things for you.'

'I won't enjoy it if you aren't there. Being together, sharing it all, then travelling home talking about the performance, that would have been the fun,' Janet explained.

Janet was there when Ken came to see Shirley and after a few nervous seconds there was no uneasiness to spoil their meeting. They joked and laughed and cheered her, but once outside the doors, Janet felt the tears well up and Ken's arms were a comfort and his lips touching her cheek were both soothing and exciting.

She knew she had no right to be in his arms, even though they were there because of Shirley's accident. She moved away, dried her eyes and, walking as far away from him as the pavements allowed, hurried home. She didn't prolong their parting; she just promised to inform him of Shirley's progress and closed the door firmly against him. She and Ken. It wouldn't do at all. Then he knocked and she foolishly answered. He stepped inside and held her in his arms.

Then a voice called, and they broke apart to see a figure running down the dark street materialise into Eirlys.

'Ken?' she called as she neared them. 'I'm glad I caught you. I went to the hospital and guessed you'd have seen Janet safely home. It's Marged's fiftieth birthday on Saturday and they want you to come for supper. Can you come?'

She was speaking to Ken, but they both answered. 'I'd love to.' Their enthusiasm might have surprised Eirlys if she thought about it, but parties were a welcome change from boring routine and she would have recognised their pleasure as nothing more. She was unaware of how relieved they were that the message was so innocent and that the black-out, cursed so often, had prevented her from seeing them moments before.

Janet was shaken at the speed with which she had been able to accept the comfort of Ken's arms. She was trembling as she closed the door against them and didn't move for a long time. The precipitous situation, then falling over the edge of dishonesty, cheating on her friend in the most unkind way, hadn't been a considered plan. It had happened so suddenly she couldn't remember who had made the first move although she suspected she hadn't protested, not for a second.

She was undressed and ready for bed when there was another knock at the door. This time Ken pushed his way in and claimed her lips with his and slowly led her to her bed.

Bleddyn walked home from the hospital with Hetty a few days after the accident. At a convenient shop doorway, he stopped and pulled her into his arms. 'This might not be the right time to discuss this, love, but with Shirley needing help, why don't we get married now and share the responsibility?' He smiled, and Hetty felt the movement of his cheek caress her own. 'Everyone knows we plan to marry so it won't come as much of a surprise. Shirley is happy about the idea and I, well, I'd be the proudest man in St David's Well.'

'Yes, Bleddyn. I'll marry you, of course I will. As soon as you want.'

They walked the rest of the way slowly, arm in arm, the promise of a good future stretching out before them. No grand ceremony; because of Shirley's condition they decided on a quiet affair with very few people present. Then while they waited for Shirley to recover they would get Bleddyn's house ready to welcome her there.

'We'll go the hospital tomorrow and tell Shirley, then we can tell the few who need to know.' he said. 'I'll do everything I can to make sure you and Shirley don't regret it.'

—

While Shirley continued to stay in hospital, Janet had time to think. She was falling in love with Ken Ward and, as he was married to Eirlys, she knew she had to get away – temptation was strong. Besides being aware that Ken and Eirlys were not really compatible, it was the general attitude of people in these dangerous times to grab happiness at the expense of others, convinced that it would be short-lived. She was tempted, so she had to leave.

Being alone, with no family, she clung to St David's Well and her friends as a substitute for the sisters, brothers and cousins that she lacked. Now she would have to pull up her roots and leave, start again, make new friends. The prospect was frightening.

It wouldn't be easy, but it had to be soon. Once Shirley was out of hospital she would become involved with her convalescence, become a support for her through the tedious months of recovery. And all the time, Ken would be there. They would visit Shirley, probably take part in concerts together and grow closer and more dependent on each other. There would be opportunities for love. She had to leave but where should she go?

Women were being conscripted for the first time in history from the present month of December: unmarried women from twenty to thirty years old. While she was running the café she would probably be exempt, but if she were not, then to have a choice of what she would do, she would have to make a decision soon. Another reason not to delay.

She considered the options. Land Army? No, she didn't think she had the stamina for heavy work. Wrens? She liked the uniform, but was that enough? There were posters everywhere inviting women to join the ATS, the WAAF, become a nursing auxiliary, go into factories to make munitions. Then a poster caught her eye.

Get into a good war job now.
Join the NAAFI.

Catering for the armed forces seemed the perfect choice. The more she considered it, the more it became clear that the NAAFI was the place for her. With her experience of running the café single-handed, she would be able to take on a good position and do a good job. She went at once to the recruiting office and filled in the necessary forms, then went to tell Shirley her decision.

Shirley was in the hospital bed, a magazine in front of her face and when Janet approached she saw her friend was not reading but using *Woman's Own* to hide her tears.

'Come on, Shirley Downs, this isn't the way to get well,' she encouraged. 'Don't you know that laughter is the best medicine? Haven't the nurses told you that?'

'I'll laugh when I find something to laugh at.' Shirley smiled sadly. 'I'm lying here thinking about the dances we did, the songs we sang, knowing I'll never do them again.'

'Rot! If the doctors have told you that then they don't know you. I've never met anyone more determined than you. Even if the chances of you dancing were less than fifty-to-one I'd back you.'

'Last night I dreamed we were dancing and I tried to get out of bed. The nurses had to call the doctor to get me back in position. If I've disturbed the leg it might mean another operation.'

'Does it hurt?'

'No more than usual.'

'Well, it's probably all right. You're fastened in there so tight I doubt if you could escape without half the army coming to help!'

'What's new in the outside world?' Shirley asked, putting down her magazine and drying her swollen eyes.

'Well, you know that women can be called up as from this month? I've decided to get in first, before I'm told where and what to do. I've applied to join the NAAFI. You have to agree it's what I'm best suited for.'

'You're leaving St David's Well?'

'Only for a while. Once the war's over I'll be back.'

'But why? You're needed in the market café. Feeding the fighting force isn't the only way of helping win the war! Women need a cuppa!'

'Beth is doing all right. I think I can persuade her to stay and run it for me until this is over.'

'She'll be working on the beach next summer. What will happen to your café then?'

'Next summer?' Janet laughed. 'This'll be over before next summer! And you and I will be back on stage, singing our little hearts out!'

'I don't think so.' Shirley sighed. 'The doctors don't seem very hopeful of me jumping around in the near future. I'll be in traction for weeks yet, and even then I'll need a wheelchair to get around. Crutches in the house, wheelchair if I want to go outside.' She looked at Janet and asked, 'Has something happened to make you want to leave?' She wondered whether Janet had been offered a part in a musical and was afraid to tell her.

'Nothing except my need to do something to help end this damned war.' Janet was tempted to tell her friend about her feelings for Ken, but decided that the best kept secrets were in the head of only one person; it was the only safe way of keeping them.

'I'll never dance again. I – I don't even want to go out, so the wheelchair will be wasted on me.'

'Of course you'll want to go outside!'

Shirley's face seemed to collapse as she whispered, 'What a mess, eh?'

'I know a few people who've broken a leg and I don't see them in wheelchairs. It'll only be temporary. You're talking as though it's for life.'

'Might as well be for life, Janet. I'll never dance again, not like I used to.'

'A few months from now, you'll be dancing. Let's face it, Shirley, you could dance using crutches and still be better than me!' She was rewarded with a weak smile.

'Don't tell anyone about the wheelchair. I need to accept it myself before I can talk about it.'

Janet promised, wondering why the thought of a wheelchair was so frightening. Perhaps Shirley was convincing herself that it would be a permanent necessity, that if she accepted it, she would never live a life without it. If that were so, she ought to tell someone, so they could convince her otherwise.

But who?

The nurses reassured her that Shirley and her mother would be given all the facts, but the break had been a serious one. The doctors were more encouraging and she felt better after speaking to the doctor and then Hetty and Bleddyn. They were all more determined to treat the injury as a temporary setback. Making plans, dreaming dreams, would help Shirley's recovery as much as the other aspects of the care.

–

In Brook Lane, Bleddyn looked through the post, relieved to find a letter from Johnny. Since the death of his elder son, Taff, he felt a rush of panic every time he saw the telegraph boy in his area and every postal delivery was treated as a threat. If a letter came with unrecognised handwriting, he thought it was from a commanding officer to tell him the worst possible news.

But today was another reprieve. Johnny's letter was cheerful and contained a hint that he was on his way to North Africa, with his reference to the sand that worked its way into every article of clothing. The reason it hadn't been blue-pencilled as too revealing and a possible help to the enemy, was explained by the fact that the whole letter was full of reminiscences about the previous summers and their work on the sands of St David's Well.

In some ways it was a comfort to know where his son was going but at the same time an extra worry when news was given of fierce battles between Rommel's forces and the British Eighth Army under General Auchinleck.

Marged and Huw heard from Johnny occasionally and, in the way of wartime, they showed their letters to Bleddyn. With everyone there was a thirst for news and even news of other people's sons was welcomed.

Alice heard from Eynon, Marged and Huw's younger son, and reading between the lines, it appeared that he was waiting for a posting, but no one knew where it was likely to be. She scanned the newspapers daily wondering if a new offensive was likely and shared her anxiety with Beth and Eirlys. She couldn't talk as easily to Marged and Huw and she certainly couldn't share Eynon's most recent letters with them. They were love letters, telling her of his feelings for her and talking about a future in which she would be his wife.

On 7 December the Japanese attacked Pearl Harbor. A day later Britain declared war against Japan, and America entered the war. They had supported the British throughout with lease-lend food and in many other ways, but knowing that the strength of their forces was to stand beside their own men gave people heart. With other countries like Finland, Hungary and Romania standing against Britain in the almost global war, and with most of the Continent under German control, for most people it was heartening news. With America on their side, many believed it would soon be over.

Bleddyn put Johnny's letter aside to show Hannah. They had always shared what news they received. He would show Evelyn too, he decided. With Taff dead, Evelyn was still his daughter-in-law and he wanted to convince her of it. On this occasion he went to Evelyn first.

After reading the letter and agreeing with him about the hint of where Johnny was heading, she handed him another letter, this time in unfamiliar writing. It was from Taff's commanding officer.

Bleddyn's hands shook as he read about the qualities his son had possessed, and of his bravery under fire. And of how he had once saved the lives of at least a dozen others by wiping out a gun emplacement on the cliffs above the battlefield.

St David's Well citizens could no longer feel they were immune to the difficulties and tragedies of war. Too many families had suffered the loss of loved ones.

'I have something to tell you.' Bleddyn said as he sat down near the dining table, the table he had helped his son to carry from his grandmother's house, a gift for his new home. He was hesitant, dreading Evelyn's reaction to his news, specially now having just received such a letter. He knew that in spite of ill timing it had to be said, otherwise she might hear from someone else and be more upset.

'You know about Shirley's accident?' he began.

'Of course. I wrote her a letter wishing her a speedy recovery.'

'I don't know whether speedy recovery will be possible,' he said sadly. 'Imagine her distress, just starting to become successful as a dancer and singer then losing the use of her legs. It's the most cruel thing.'

'She's alive, isn't she?' Evelyn said harshly.

'I know it doesn't compare with what happened to our Taff, but she is alive and she's having to live with the fact that she'll never dance again.'

'What can we do? She'll have to face it, live with it, like hundreds of others. After all, she only needs to look around her at the men crippled by war, men with artificial legs, or wearing a jacket with a tied-up, empty sleeve.'

This was definitely not the time to talk to her. Not with the letter about Taff's death in her hand. Bleddyn stood up and said, 'Don't forget where I am, Evelyn love. You're still my daughter-in-law, Taff's much-loved wife. I'll always be glad to see you.'

Folding the letter, Evelyn put it back into its envelope and slipped it into a drawer. Inside, Bleddyn saw a pile of letters – all she had left.

'Well, I'll be off. I'll go to the shop and show Johnny's letter to Hannah. We always exchange news. I'll tell her about your letter too. Perhaps one day you'll let her read it.'

'Perhaps. I'm glad Johnny is safe,' Evelyn added. 'I want him to survive in one piece. I'm not really religious, but I do pray for his safe-keeping, just as I used to do for Taff's, and Ronnie's when he was away, and Eynon's.'

'Thank you for that, Evelyn love. They need our prayers.'

As he was walking through the door, Evelyn called, 'Dad – I can still call you Dad, can't I?'

'Of course you can! You'll always be my daughter-in-law. Taff's wife.'

'Dad, what was it that you had to tell me?'

'Oh, nothing important. It'll wait.'

'Please. Don't push me out.'

Bleddyn hesitated a moment, his heavy frame filling the doorway as he made up his mind. Closing the door, he went again to stand beside the table.

'All right. The situation is this. Shirley will be in a wheelchair for a while when she comes out of hospital. She can't really go back to the flat above the newsagent.

She'd have to be carried up there and she'd be a prisoner, unable to manage the stairs. Hetty and I are getting married and preparing a home for her in Brook Lane.'

'I'm glad,' she surprised him by saying. 'You need someone to look after. Hetty and Shirley will be a way of helping you cope without Taff, and when Johnny comes home he'll be glad too.'

The response was so unlike the usually prickly girl that Bleddyn turned and hugged her.

'Thank you, Evelyn. You don't know how much I value your approval.'

Just having held the letter telling of Taff's death, she was afraid of the emptiness that faced her if she didn't continue to be a part of Bleddyn's family. She still felt the inexplicable jealousy that had damaged her friendship with others but she forced it aside and smiled. 'Have you chosen a best man yet?' she asked brightly. 'That's something Taff or Johnny would have liked, but I suppose your brother will be the one.'

'Well, no,' Bleddyn said. 'I don't intend to tell the family until it's over. Hetty and I want a quiet ceremony. You, Beth, Ronnie and Bernard Gregory are the only ones to be told, although most people have guessed it was likely.'

'Bernard will be best man?'

'Yes, and Ronnie will stand in for Taff and Johnny. Beth will be there for Hetty.'

'Can I be there?'

He shook his head. 'Neither you nor Hannah. The more we invite the worse it will be for the others. Do you understand?'

She nodded, and wished him luck as he left her.

–

The gift shop was doing good business. Christmas, with the increasing difficulties of finding presents, had brought customers in their dozens. The small shop was packed all day. The problem was getting supplies. Sometimes Eirlys felt she had been without sleep for a week as she worked long into the night getting work finished ready for the following day.

She wasn't the only one. Hannah worked long hours too and Bleddyn still helped by taking Josie and Marie out whenever he could. They still went to the park during the afternoons, not to play but to feed the birds. Twice Bleddyn had seen Lilly there with an older man, to whom he was introduced.

When he mentioned this man to his brother, Huw told him that the man's son, Sam, seemed to be a serious contender for Lilly's hand. Lilly was another young woman heading for marriage after a short courtship. 'Marry in haste, repent at leisure' was a saying that made people laugh. Old-fashioned and a nonsense. More relevant today, with its undertones of sadness, was 'Gather ye rosebuds while ye may, Old Time is still a-flying. And this same flower that smiles today, tomorrow will be dying.'

–

Letters were spasmodic in arriving from those serving in the forces and Shirley's mother arrived at the hospital one day bringing three letters for her from Freddy Clements, her dancing partner of earlier days. Shirley put them aside until her mother had left, then read them once, twice, three times, irritated by the blue-pencilled lines in which the censor had obliterated something that might conceivably assist the enemy. He was a different Freddy from the selfish, smartly dressed gents' outfitters salesman she had first known. This new Freddy was serious and, on paper at least, more thoughtful.

She had written to tell him about the accident and explained that her dancing was finished and she might spend a long time in a wheelchair. His response was surprising and short, his only reference to her accident being. 'Sod the dancing, you don't need legs to sing! And we can still go to the pictures, can't we?'

Apart from Janet and her mother, Freddy's was the first positive reaction she'd had and she laughed at the pithy and brief letter, standing it up on her bedside locker.

–

Eynon wrote to Alice and to his parents with an occasional note to his Uncle Bleddyn. In one of these he asked Bleddyn to look out for Alice for him, explaining that Alice's father was disabled and with an unpredictable temper.

After a word with Huw and Marged, Bleddyn dropped a note through Alice's door inviting her to visit them.

Alice was anxious about her father. He was becoming more restless, unable to sit for more than a few minutes and unable to sleep through the night no matter how late he stayed up. Alice had been to the doctor to get pills for him but these he had irritably thrown on the back of the fire.

He was often up during the night and early one morning she had been woken by the smell of burning, to find that he had gone back to bed leaving a frying pan containing bacon on the gas cooker. The tea towel, then peeling wallpaper had caught fire and she had battled alone to prevent the whole room being destroyed.

She kept most of the worries to herself, but he threatened the postman, who then refused to make any more deliveries, then punched her when she complained. Bleddyn saw the bruises on her upper arms and persuaded her to tell him what had happened.

'He wasn't always like this,' she excused sadly. 'So kind and gentle he was, except in the ring of course. Then that blow to the head changed him and now, I don't know what to do to please him.' She choked against tears. 'I want to please him but I don't know how.'

Bleddyn had a word with the doctor but Colin could be calm and lucid when he needed to be, and gave the impression of being in control. The doctor told him that unless Colin did something really violent, or they could see that his life or the life of Alice was in danger, they couldn't do anything. Bleddyn made Alice promise to let him know if things got out of hand again. He was helpless, at present, to do more. He wrote and explained the situation to his nephew Eynon.

—

Once the shock and the shame of Shirley's accident began to fade from his mind, Joseph considered the situation. He talked to the nurses and the doctors, telling them he was Shirley's fiancé and trying to assess her recovery. Somewhat reassured, imagining that once she recovered her mobility she would be ready to forget the stage, settle for being a wife and mother, he began calling at the hospital every day and, although she refused to see him, he left gifts of flowers and sweets and an occasional cake.

One day, convinced she was strong enough emotionally to cope, Shirley told the nurse she would talk to him.

He walked in almost hidden under the parcels he carried. Handing them to the nurse, he bent over Shirley's bed and kissed her lightly on the cheek. 'Thank you for agreeing to talk to me,' he said as he sat beside her. 'I didn't blame you for refusing, but I desperately need to explain.'

'You almost had me killed,' she said harshly.

'I wanted to talk to you, nothing more. I wouldn't have hurt you, Shirley, you know how I feel about you. I thought I was doing what was best for you, I really did.'

'Oh, you weren't thinking about yourself? Me giving up all ambition and spending my life looking after you?'

He looked down, reached out for her hand. 'Would that be such a terrible thing?'

'Yes, it would!' She didn't intend to give him an inch. 'I have a talent and you can't live with that.'

'I love you and I want to look after you.'

'I'm not ready for love. I want to get out of this bed and get on with my career.'

He looked startled. 'Get on with what? Surely you can't still expect to sing and dance? Not after this? You'll have to forget short skirts! Any ideas you had of a stage career were destroyed when you crushed your leg!'

The words, a cruel reminder of what she had lost, made her rage spill over. 'The injuries *you* caused! No, Joseph, nothing will stop me! And your determination to make me change my mind just gives me more determination to get strong again.' She rang the bell for the nurse and shouted. 'Go away and don't come back! You might as well have killed me. I hate you as I've never hated before.'

The nurse ran towards the bed and Joseph didn't need a repetition of Shirley's angry shouts to know he had to leave.

Maude and Myrtle came soon after and were alarmed to see Shirley is such a state of despair. Nervously they sat, one each side of her, offered her the flowers they had brought and slowly she calmed down.

They talked to her about the jobs they were doing, Maude in the factory canteen and the undersized Myrtle delivering on her huge bike.

'You don't look strong enough to ride one of those,' Shirley said, trying to take an interest in the chatter when all she wanted to do was bury her head in her pillow and cry.

'I am too small really, but I'm getting better. I ride downhill now with my feet off the pedals an' all,' Myrtle said proudly. Even in her depressed mood, the vision made Shirley smile.

'I'm more afraid of Alice Potter's father than riding the bike,' the girl went on. She described the man's behaviour, more to make Shirley laugh than because of her worries.

'You make sure you tell Bleddyn,' Shirley said. 'Mam told me he was a bit strange. Eynon asked his uncle to look out for Alice.'

'He can deliver there for me if he likes,' Myrtle said cheekily. 'He's a bit bigger than me. Just a bit!'

–

Bleddyn and Hetty had arranged their wedding for Friday 12 December and they met at the register office at eleven o'clock in the morning. Hetty was wearing a simple cream dress under a camel coat, with a spray of tiny button chrysan-themums on her lapel. The cream dress was summer weight but she didn't have anything warmer that was smart enough for this special day. Beth had chosen a forest-green suit under which she wore a smart cream blouse. Over her arm was a coat in camel the same as the bride's and they laughed at the coincidence as they approached each other.

In the fashion of the time both women wore hats. There was a dry-cleaners in the town where hats could be reblocked and remodelled and they had both used this service to great effect. Long feathers taken from an aban-doned hat had been set on a turned-back rim to make Beth's into a 'Robin Hood' style and Hetty's had a spray of flowers covered by a short veil. Bleddyn told them he was proud of his two special women on his special day.

The small wedding party walked back to Bleddyn's house in Brook Lane and had a snack before separating to go on with their daily routines, Bleddyn to open the chip shop for the lunchtime session, and Hetty to continue preparing the downstairs front room for her daughter's arrival.

Beth and Ronnie returned to the market, Beth to the café where she had left her sister Lilly in charge for the short time she would be away. Ronnie made his way to the greengrocery stall where his wife, Olive, and their baby were holding the fort.

There was no sign of Lilly when Beth reached the café. A long line of impatient customers were waiting and a harassed Sally, from a nearby fruit stall, was trying to cope. Without waiting for an explanation, Beth thanked her and took over, swiftly dealing with the queue. In a lull, and after making tea for Ronnie and Olive and for Sally to thank her for her help, she asked what had happened to Lilly.

'She asked me to look out for five minutes while she went somewhere,' Sally told her. 'That was an hour ago and we haven't seen her since!'

Beth fumed silently. Her sister Lilly had never been enthusiastic about work but she hadn't expected her to walk off and leave the café unattended.

For the next hour she was busy preparing the meals she had planned, thankful that she had put a casserole and a fish pie in the oven to keep warm while she had been away. A huge pan of potatoes chopped small was soon boiling ready to mash, and tinned carrots and tinned peas were simmering.

Lilly came in breathlessly at one o'clock full of apologies.

'I was rushed off my feet,' she said before Beth could speak. 'I ran to fetch Mrs Denver to help me.' She gestured behind her to where Mrs Denver was hurrying towards them.

'I was only gone an hour. What did you want Mrs Denver for?' Beth demanded, as she juggled with dishes, serving two people at once.

'Desperate it was. I couldn't possibly manage on my own, not with dinners to watch an' all,' Lilly said, holding out her hand for customers' payments as Beth served meals. Behind them in the confined space. Mrs Denver squeezed in and began sorting out the dishes.

'Thank you. Mrs Denver, but we can manage now,' Beth said kindly. She could hardly blame the woman for coming when Lilly had asked.

'It's no trouble and hardly worth the rush if I don't do something to help.'

Irritable now, Beth thought that if she expected payment it would come out of what she had promised Lilly.

Mrs Denver seemed to know instinctively where everything was kept and what was expected of her. She knew where to find the utensils and managed to wash dishes as they went along, so they didn't pile up as a long tedious task at the end of the busy lunch hour. Beth often found a plate in her hand before asking for one. If only Lilly were like that, what a boon she would be. Before she left, the efficient lady even mixed batter using duck eggs from Ronnie's stall and made some drop scones to sell during the afternoon.

-

Over past weeks, Freddy's letters had been more regular and Shirley guessed he was home rather than abroad. When he turned up at the hospital to visit her she understood why. He wore a large bandage on his shoulder which, he told her, had been shattered by a bomb fragment.

'A right pair of old crocks we are,' he said as he bent to kiss her. 'We'd look right on a mantelpiece, like a pair of comic bookends.'

That visit and others over the days that followed lightened her spirits like nothing else had. And once, when Joseph tried to see her. Freddy told him loudly and with complete authority to 'Clear off!'

'Cheeky sod, coming here,' he muttered as Joseph left. 'Don't know how he's got the nerve.'

When he went back to camp, Shirley was stronger in spirit and looking forward to going home. It was only then that her mother told her about her marriage. Shirley had been so depressed that Hetty had been afraid the news would upset her. Now her only complaint was that she had missed the occasion.

'D'you know, Mam, I haven't used one of my clothing coupons yet and there's you letting me miss the chance of buying something new!'

'I might have to borrow some,' Hetty teased. 'Mine have almost gone. Stockings, some underwear and handkerchiefs on top of a new coat. I used the same dress I bought last summer, mind, so I wasn't too wasteful.'

'Take as many as you need,' Shirley offered. 'I won't be buying clothes until I can walk into the shop and choose them.'

Hetty kissed her, hoping the sadness she felt wasn't visible on her face. No one could be certain yet, but Shirley might be in a wheelchair for a very long time.

The room in which they planned for Shirley to sleep had been repapered in a bright floral design. The single bed was covered in a Welsh blanket in cream and greens, the rug on the floor had been specially made by Eirlys to match, and the addition of some pictures gave the place a cheerful ambience that they thought Shirley would appreciate.

–

Hannah wrote letters too. Besides writing to Johnny, she wrote to her parents although they lived in the same town. She called on them regularly, sometimes with the children and sometimes alone. Her parents made it clear they didn't welcome her visits and would look up and down the road as though embarrassed at inviting her inside. No matter what she said, or however she steered the conversation, they did not want news of Johnny and reminded her frequently that she was a wicked woman living in sin. She determinedly persevered, believing that one day they would forgive her for not being the kind of daughter they wanted. Surely they wouldn't deprive themselves of their granddaughters for always?

Every Christmas she hoped that the good will would soften their hearts but this year was going to be like all the rest, with not even a card to wish Josie and Marie a happy time.

–

Christmas passed pleasantly enough for Shirley, with Hetty, Bleddyn and the rest of the family doing what they could to share it with her but she was relieved when it was over.

January, with its ice and snow, was welcomed as the month in which she would go home.

On the day of her homecoming Beth and Eirlys had both brought flowers, cut and potted: Chrysanthemums, a sweet-scented daphne and a scented stephanotis for outside her window, plus a pot of daffodils already spearing their way through the soil. These had been recommended by Beth's father-in-law Bernard Gregory, a keen grower of flowers, besides the vegetables with which he earned his keep.

Janet was due to present herself at the NAAFI canteen just a few days before Shirley came out of hospital. Leaving the café had not been easy. She knew she was pulling up her life by the roots and had nowhere else to begin to set them down again. Unless Beth could keep the café going for her, there would be nothing to go back to. And where would she spend her leave when it came? She hadn't be able to afford to pay rent on the flat, and it was now someone else's home. So where would she go? She had kept her worries to herself. She knew several friends would be sympathetic and offer their homes as a base but she didn't want to be a nuisance. Somehow it would work itself out.

Since she had left the children's home she had managed on her own, so this wasn't as difficult as it might be for others, she told herself. Independence was a hard lesson learned young. She was leaving good friends, but she would make others. Everyone she met from now on would be in the same position and as anxious to become friends as she was. She tried to imagine it as a great adventure, and planned to write amusing letters to Shirley and Beth and the others and make pretend she was having fun. She wouldn't think of Ken at all.

Beth had been so kind taking over the café and keeping it going for when she returned, if she ever did. Beth had promised to keep in touch and report to her on the progress of the café.

'When you come back I'll find a place for you,' Beth had promised. 'Us Castles know everybody. You won't have any difficulty finding somewhere to live and when you're on leave you can stay with Mam; she told me to invite you. She'd love to have you. She hates rattling around in the empty house, she said.'

Janet thanked her but thought she wouldn't accept. Once she went away she'd stay away until the war ended and she was demobbed along with everyone else. Trying to cling on to the town and her friends would only make the parting worse. And she daren't risk meeting Ken.

She left early one morning after packing away all her possessions and giving them to be sold to raise funds for Red Cross parcels for prisoners of war.

She was stationed at an aerodrome which was home to a squadron of Spitfires. She was introduced to the manager who gave her a set of keys, showed her where the stores were kept, pointed out the importance of keeping the books carefully, and left her to discover the rest for herself.

As she later wrote to Shirley, she then spent an hour fidgeting and poking until she knew where everything was kept and what utensils and stores were available. The rest of the staff soon arrived and looked to her to do the cooking, pointing out that the first break, at which the men and women would expect tea sandwiches and cakes, was at eleven o'clock. 'I then made the fastest rock cakes on record,' she reported to her friends. There were counters to fill and the tea trolleys with the urns of tea, which a couple of the counter hands usually took to the hangars, to be filled and made ready. At the end of the first day, Janet realised that she would not have a lot of time to grieve for Ken and everything else she had left behind. For this she was grateful, she told herself as she fell, exhausted, into her bunk.

Eirlys was surprised when Ken arrived a couple of days after Janet's departure, unaware of her leaving.

'She's joined the NAAFI? Why has she done that?' he demanded. 'I thought she was going to join our concert party?'

'She's obviously changed her mind,' Eirlys replied irritably. 'Look. I have to go. I'm on duty at the ARP station at seven.'

'A nice welcome home! Can't you spare a few hours out of your busy life to spend with your husband?' he asked with equal irritation.

'I might have if my husband had greeted me like a wife instead of demanding to know where Janet is!'

'I went straight to the market café because I have a booking next week and thought she'd help.'

'Sorry, but I don't sing or dance.'

'No, more's the pity,' he muttered. 'Well, if you're off out I might as well go and see some of my friends.'

'Good idea,' Eirlys said sharply as she picked up her thick winter coat and left. She walked around the street for a while to hide her distress. What had happened to their marriage? It wasn't fair to blame Janet; she was responsible for her own marriage. If she and Ken had drifted, she had allowed it to happen. And Ken had to take some responsibility too.

The meeting place was in the school and, although they had suffered few air raids and those nothing more frightening than seeing enemy planes flying overhead, they were meticulous about fire-watching and making sure lights were extinguished at sundown. Recognising one town would help navigators to find others.

She went in and when the others had dispersed to their various look-out points, she filled the water boiler ready to make cocoa later on, then began to deal with some of the paperwork. A knock at the door interrupted her.

Adjusting the black-out curtain, she opened the door and Ken stepped in and took her in his arms.

'Sorry, Eirlys. I'm very sorry. It's been a terrible week. Two friends have been killed, another wounded, and I can't forget Max.'

Her feelings were mixed as she held him and comforted him. She wanted to believe that everything was all right but a part of her wondered with concern whether his distress was not for lost friends, but the loss of Janet.

Ken spent all the following day trying to find out where Janet had been stationed.

—

Shirley found life bearable once she had settled into her new home. Friends visited often and two regulars were Maude and Myrtle.

They both entertained her with their observations. They had an amusing slant on life and chatted non-stop about the people they met and described the antics and attitudes of people so she could almost see them. They talked about summer days on the beach and life with Marged and Huw Castle. They had been accepted as members of the family and Shirley was pleased to see that her mother had lost all anger against them and entertained them with ease and pleasure. She was pleased too to see how happy her mother and Bleddyn were.

If only she hadn't been injured, had been able to take part in the pantomime and go on to the greater things she knew had been awaiting her, Janet wouldn't have gone away and life would have been wonderful.

'Damn Joseph Beynon and his jealousy,' she said aloud.

–

Beth was happy now she knew Peter wouldn't have to go abroad any more. He didn't come home very often but he wrote, long, interesting letters mostly about the past and the future. The present was troublesome and best ignored.

When he did come home, they treated it like a holiday. Whenever she was free from running the market café they spent a lot of time helping Bernard around his smallholding and in any spare time they walked through icy fields, stopping at a country pub to eat and talk. Beth thought they would never run out of things to say to each other. She didn't help in the gift shop when he was home; Eirlys and Hannah didn't expect her to, understanding how precious the time with Peter was to her.

Peter said nothing about his work and she didn't ask. She knew he was involved in training men and women to go behind enemy lines; people who risked their lives to help escaped prisoners achieve a home run. Thankfully the training took place at home; he would never again have to face the dangers of working behind enemy lines. She could cope with anything now she knew that he was safe.

Eleven

Shirley continued to have letters from Freddy and his support was casual, just the odd reference to her injury and the certainty of her full recovery. She felt better for receiving them and she kept them to read over again. There was no false sympathy; he instinctively knew she had more than enough of that and his letters made her smile as no others did.

There were letters from Janet too and hers also cheered her. Her introduction to serving the RAF seemed fraught with disasters and her observations on those who served them with snacks and others supplying their daily needs like cigarettes, shaving cream, writing paper, pens and sweets were always amusing.

There was another side of course. She told her of the boys who didn't come back and those who came back badly injured. These incidents obviously distressed her but after the shock and pain she suffered at the beginning, with the need to tell Shirley of her tormented dreams, she described these tragedies briefly, not dwelling on the cruel waste of young lives. The simple words and brief sentences she used were enough to portray the horror of life and death at an RAF station.

Later, Janet told her she had applied to serve overseas, which meant she would be wearing the uniform of the ATS

Expeditionary Forces Institute and would have to undergo some intensive training. Shirley envied her. Danger aside, it was better than sitting in a wheelchair day after day.

Shirley spoke pessimistically of her mode of transport but, although the wheelchair was still essential, she was learning to stand and to walk around the furniture. She told no one except her mother and Bleddyn, who encouraged her proudly. '

'Like a baby again,' she said to Hetty as she boasted of her success at walking a few steps with first the crutches then a stick.

-

Lilly Castle and her baby no longer went to the park. The weather that January had been very cold, with ice on the roads and snow settling and building up into dirty, misshapen mounds that marked the edges of the pavements for days on end. She had occasional letters from Sam, but he was not a good correspondent and she called one day to see his father in the hope of news.

Mr Edwards welcomed her enthusiastically and when she went inside, dragged the pram into the hallway. She took out her most recent letter to show him. It wasn't very long, just a few words along the lines of 'I'm well and I hope you are'. Mr Edwards smiled and handed it back.

'Not the best reporter, my Sam,' he said sadly, 'but he obviously wants to keep in touch. I'm sure he values your letters very much.'

'I don't suppose there's much he can say,' Lilly excused. 'What they do say is sometimes pencilled out. I tell him about little Phyllis and about my brothers and sister. Plenty to tell, although I doubt if he's really interested, mind.'

'Tell me,' Mr Edwards coaxed. 'I am interested. Your sister is married and helping to run a gift shop. Is that right?'

Lilly sat in the kitchen while Sam Edwards prepared a tray of tea and some biscuits. She noticed how competent he was as he attended to the simple tasks. He had been a widower for several years and had obviously taught himself the necessary skills needed to run the house.

She knew he worked in the food and supplies stores used by army personnel, keeping note of what was in stock and which items needed to be replenished. The hours were sometimes long and, he had told her, the work tedious. All that was needed was an orderly approach. Running the house and dealing with a garden filled with vegetables besides must have kept him very busy, yet whenever she called, the house was neat and orderly. Just the sort of husband I'd like, she thought with a smile. She hoped Sam Two, as she referred to his son, had inherited his father's talents.

When Sam came on leave at the end of January, he invited her to spend the evening with him.

'Dad will cook for us and we can play cards after if you like.'

'Wonderful.' Lilly replied, wondering how she could get out of the boring card games. She had enough of those at home when her mother invited friends in. Card games needed concentration which she lacked. 'What about the pictures?' she suggested. 'Your dad doesn't go out much, I bet he'd enjoy it.'

'But we couldn't take Phyllis.' The disappointment on Sam Two's face was almost comical.

'Oh no.' Lilly tried to share his dismay. 'But we could take her out tomorrow?'

'Pictures it is.' He smiled. 'You, me and Dad.'

–

Joseph still visited Shirley when he could. He usually waited until Hetty and Bleddyn were likely to be out, working out the evenings when they would be at the chip shop until past ten o'clock. He would knock on the door and when Shirley called, he would go in before she realised who it was and could tell him to go away.

The door was never locked. Shirley was unable to move fast enough to answer a knock so it was impossible for her to stop him walking in. He never stayed long, just asked how she was getting on and warned her about doing too much.

'I walked right across the room with only a stick yesterday,' she told him on one occasion.

'You shouldn't do that. It's too soon,' he exclaimed. 'You should still be in the wheelchair. Why don't you let me take you out? We could walk around the shops and even go to the park if you dress up warm. If there's anyone you want to visit we could do that too. It would be refreshing to get out and talk to people and you wouldn't be so anxious to do more than you should.'

'You don't want me to get out of this chair, do you? You want me stuck here, dependent on you. Well, sony, Joseph Beynon! But it isn't going to happen. Now go away, I need to do my exercises!'

Joseph left but he was smiling. He had loved her since he had first seen her and his love for her was a jealous love, he admitted it. She was beautiful and he wanted that beauty to be for him alone; he had to keep her away from the admiring glances of other men. She belonged to him and, one day, his patience would be rewarded.

While Shirley was disabled she couldn't think of singing, and dancing was no longer a possibility. He was determined to make her accept the curtailing of her ambitions. Then, when she was mobile again, he would persuade her to marry him. The injury was far less serious than he had first thought and having a wife who had to spend a lot of time at home would suit him perfectly. He would love her and care for her and she would want nothing more, and neither would he, he thought happily. With Shirley as his wife, life would be just perfect.

Until then, his mother would continue to look after him perfectly well. He was preparing for the time when she was no longer able to. Then Shirley would care for them all.

At the beginning of February, his plans were cruelly disrupted. Mrs Beynon woke one morning and when she tried to get out of bed a pain across her chest stopped her. She called Joseph who ran to the telephone box and asked the doctor to call. An hour later he was told that his mother had suffered a heart attack.

–

Eirlys had more time on her hands now the winter had closed down so many aspects of her work. Plans were going ahead for the entertainments during the following summer but there was nothing urgent about the preparations. Ken was still away for much of the time and when he was home they were uneasy with each other, more like strangers than they had ever been, in spite of the months of marriage.

She remembered the casual friendship they had enjoyed and wondered how it had been lost. Surely marriage should lead to greater closeness, not this feeling of being trapped with a guest who had outstayed his welcome? She tried to take an interest in what he was doing as she once had, coaxing him to tell her about the concerts they were giving, and the audience's reaction to his songs.

'I don't write songs like Max did,' he told her one day. 'I try, but he was inspired.'

'Perhaps being in love with Janet had something to do with it. Emotion can't be turned on and off, can it?' She looked at him as she spoke, wondering if his love for her had died and whether it would ever be revived.

Perhaps he guessed her thoughts or maybe he needed reassurance himself because he turned and put his arms around her and kissed her with greater passion than usual. 'I love you, Eirlys, and if loving someone was the key, I'd win every award in the business.'

For a while she basked in the joy of his words.

She was still making rugs and wall-hangings and more recently embroidered pictures from the wool they had in stock. Her father framed them and they sold moderately well, with the never-ending demand for wedding gifts. The stream of hasty marriages continued unabated and it seemed that every day there was at least one happy couple among their acquaintances who were celebrating their union.

–

Marged and Huw Castle wondered if their daughter Lilly might have found her future husband. At twenty-eight she was approaching the age at which marriage was unlikely. They knew Lilly wrote regularly to Sam and also spent a lot of time visiting his father. 'It looks hopeful,' Marged said to Huw, more than once.

When Hetty and Bleddyn called one Sunday afternoon, they shared news of the family as they always did, discussing any letters that had been received from Johnny or Eynon and the activities of the other members of the family.

'That Sam who Lilly's going about with seems a nice enough young bloke,' Bleddyn said, referring to a day when Lilly and Phyllis had brought the young man to meet her uncle and step-aunt Hetty. 'He seems very fond of the baby too. D'you think Lilly might have found someone special?'

'We wonder that too,' Marged replied, glancing at Huw.

'I only hope he's hard-working, because if he marries our Lilly he won't get much work out of *her*!' Huw said with a grim smile. 'I don't know who she takes after; she's a damn sight cleverer than the rest of us. I've never known anyone so nifty at avoiding work as our Lilly.'

'If this Sam is as besotted as he seems, then I don't think she'll have much trouble persuading him she needs looking after and spoiling,' Hetty smiled. 'Why not? Good luck to her.'

At the kitchen door, Lilly listened and smiled.

–

Shirley wasn't feeling well. She had woken with a heavy feeling in her chest and when she coughed it hurt. She lay back on her pillows and tried to sleep. Both Hetty and Bleddyn were out. They had risen early to go to the wholesalers for fish, an occasional visit to check their regular order and to see what was available. They intended to go into Cardiff later and Shirley would be on her own until lunchtime.

She found herself thinking about Joseph. He hadn't called for several days and although part of her hoped her continuous requests for him to stay away had worked, this was one day when she would have been glad to see him. She needed a doctor and there was no way of calling him.

She managed to sit up and between bouts of tiredness she wrote to Janet. It was a sad letter, telling her she was unwell and that her chest was painful, and it probably meant she wouldn't sing again.

Joseph called an hour later and contacted the doctor.

'It's probably pneumonia,' he told her as they waited, adding, 'Don't worry, it's probably because of the time you're spending in the house. If you'd listened to me and got some fresh air, you might have avoided this.'

'I don't like people seeing me like this,' she protested, gesturing towards her leg with a wave of her hand.

'You should have listened to me.' he repeated, patting her hand affectionately. 'I know what's best for you and one day you'll realise it.'

'Will it affect my singing?' She needed reassurance but Joseph gave her none.

'Try not to think about that now,' was all he said, but with implications of doubt in his voice. He sat and held her hand. He said nothing about his mother's illness. 'Dogged by illness. It seems to be my fate, caring for the ones I love, dealing with their ill health. But I don't mind. Shirley. I'll care for you as I cared for Dolly, with love and devotion.'

Her already low spirits deepened with every word.

The doctor had just arrived when Hetty and Bleddyn returned.

'Joseph thinks it's pneumonia and I'll lose the power of my voice.' she said to Hetty. At once Hetty asked Joseph to leave, thanking him briskly for his help.

She took Shirley's hand and said to the doctor, 'Now, will you tell us how she is, Doctor? I'm sure she's making good progress, isn't she?'

Taking on the cheerful tone she presented, the doctor smiled. 'She looks very well to me and the reports I have from the hospital are all encouraging, Mrs Castle.' He took out his stethoscope and a few minutes later said, 'I think you have a heavy cold and there's some infection in the chest, but it isn't anything like pneumonia and we'll make sure it doesn't get any worse.'

A more cheerful Shirley listened to Hetty warning her about Joseph's determination to undermine her confidence. 'It wasn't just the dancing and singing he tried to stop. He wants you dependent on him so much, that he wants you to consider yourself an invalid,' she said grimly.

'He won't come here again,' Bleddyn said warningly. 'I'll see him and make sure of that.'

'I wrote a miserable letter to Janet. I don't think I'll send it,' Shirley said.

'Too late,' Bleddyn told her. 'That Joseph took it when he left. Why not write another one to tell her you don't feel as though you're at death's door now old joyless Joseph has gone?'

'He really is best avoided, Shirley love,' Hetty warned, and Shirley agreed.

'I have to work harder and get out of this room as soon as possible.'

'And get back to your singing lessons as soon as you're able,' Bleddyn added.

That evening, with the medicine the doctor had prescribed already taking its effect if only psychologically – she wrote to Freddy, telling him about Joseph's attitude and her weakness in allowing it to affect her. Putting it into words helped and she promised herself she would write a similar letter to Janet very soon.

–

Joseph's mother didn't go into hospital. With the help of neighbours she continued to look after Joseph and he was hardly aware of any change. His meals were ready when he went home after work and his washing and ironing were dealt with without any apparent problems. She didn't ask for his help, except for dealing with the fire, carrying in the coal and making sure the fire was lit before he left for work each day. Thinking it better not to worry her by making her fear she was unable to manage, he didn't offer further help.

Gradually, as the days passed and she seemed to be back to normal, he forgot the fright and pushed it to the back of his mind. Shirley filled his thoughts through the day and his dreams at night. Her accident had been tragic but perhaps it had been a benefit too, he reasoned. Once he could persuade her that her career prospects were gone for ever, she would see how foolish she had been to expect it. With Janet away and Ken busy with his concert tours, there was no longer anyone to encourage her.

Filled with buoyant hope he called on Shirley, When she answered the door, standing with the support of a walking stick, he smiled and stepped forward. He managed to step back just fast enough to avoid the slamming door.

–

Unlike Joseph, Lilly's romance seemed to be making excel-lent progress. When Sam was on leave they went out in a threesome, or four if Phyllis was included. When Sam was away she spent a lot of time with his father, making herself at home in the neat little terrace house, listening to the wireless or reading the magazines Mr Edwards bought for her.

Phyllis would be put down on a warm blanket to play and it was Mr Edwards who spent the most time with her, enjoying the small measures of progress as the child gurgled happily and struggled through the various stages of mobility, 'walking' when held, pulling herself up and walking around holding on to the furniture, strengthening her muscles ready for her first unaided steps.

Mr Edwards often cooked them a meal, mashing the food and helping to feed Phyllis, who stared at him with her dark eyes, laughing occasionally as though they were sharing a joke.

--

Eirlys knew her father still wrote to Teresa and the boys but whether the letters ever reached them she couldn't tell. There were never any replies. Christmas had come and gone without a word. On the rare occasions when he spoke of them, Morgan told her he knew the boys would get in touch one day. 'I might not know their address as they move about such a lot, but they won't forget ours.'

'I just hope they're safe,' Eirlys said. 'London is still being bombed. The Blitz might have ended but the bombs still fall.' She missed them too. Not Teresa: she blamed her for the death of her mother and the unhappiness suffered by her father, but the three boys had filled the house with laughter, and now there was just her unhappy father, an unhappy husband and nothing to look forward to except an unhappy future.

Ken came home for one night and he went out in the evening, this time not even asking her to go with him. 'I'm going to the dance to search for talent for the shows,' he told her vaguely. 'We've so many bookings we've cut the acts into two groups and we're a bit light on singers. There's usually plenty of talent in the interval entertainment.' She knew that it wasn't the search for new singers that took him to the dance; it was the need to get away from her.

She called on Hannah as she went home from work the following day and told her of the sad state her marriage had reached.

'I just don't know what to do.'

'Do nothing. I think everyone is finding life difficult, all the normal day to day habits and routines are gone. The expectations are no longer the same. One day they will come back and things will settle. Ken is frantically busy, and even when he's at home with you, his mind is still wrestling with problems of transport, booking acts, writing songs, and all the other things he has to organise.'

'Perhaps you're right,' Eirlys said doubtfully. Then she spoke of something she had been trying to block out, a suspicion which had been growing like an evil cloud. 'You don't think he's like this because he misses Janet, do you?'

'Nonsense.' Hannah laughed. 'They worked together occasionally, but he wouldn't have married you if he felt anything other than friendship for Janet Copp!'

The derisory tone made Eirlys smile at her suspicions but didn't succeed in wiping them completely from her mind. Something Evelyn had once said: the unhappy girl's need to poison other people's relationships had not bothered her at the time, but had surfaced when other people had casually mentioned the amount of time Ken spent with Janet. She had been telling herself it was nonsense, but the fear gnawed away at her.

That night she wrote Ken an affectionate letter telling him how much he was loved and how much she was looking forward to the war ending so they could build their lives together in the way they wanted to live. She flattered his ability as a songwriter and told him how she saw them working together to develop his talents, making London their base if that was what was best for him. She ended by saying she would travel the world with him in pursuit of his career if necessary because she had utter faith in his ability to succeed. As she slipped it into the letter box, she felt like a cheat. Deep in her heart she knew that her happiness was in the wrong hands.

Far away, in Yorkshire. Ken read the letter and felt sick and guilty. He screwed it up and put it into the bin. It was a letter he couldn't face answering. He had just found out where Janet was stationed and had written a similarly loving letter to her.

—

Janet hadn't received the letter from Ken. The sad note from Shirley in which her friend had sounded so depressed had persuaded her to apply for leave and visit her. She was on her way to St David's Well as Ken's letter was placed on the counter of the canteen.

When she knocked on the door of Bleddyn's house, Shirley called, 'Hang on a minute,' then the door opened and she stood there, propped on a stick, make-up adorning her lovely face, her long hair falling to her shoulders in curls, looking the picture of health.

'Janet! Hi yer!'

'There's no need to ask how you're feeling,' Janet said, hugging her. 'And there's me thinking you need cheering up!'

'Come in and tell me what you've been doing.' Shirley limped back to her room where a bright fire lit the room with a red glow. Papers were spread over the bed and the armchair was facing the fire with a table beside it covered with more paper.

'What's been going on? Haven't you heard of saving paper for the war effort?' Janet teased.

'Promise you won't laugh. I'm trying to write some songs.'

'That's wonderful. Get me a cup of tea while I have a look.' Janet picked up one of the sheets of paper on which Shirley had carefully written the words and another on which the notes were carefully marked in pencil with the words underneath them.

'Hey, I'm the invalid, why should I wait on you?'

'Rubbish. You can't pull the wool over my eyes, Shirley Downs. You're fine, so get that kettle on!'

Shirley pretended to grumble as she went into the kitchen and set a tray. Leaning on the table she managed to get everything together and only when the tray needed carrying did she admit defeat and ask for help.

Janet hummed the melody, and they began to add the words as the tune was learned.

It was a lively number and when Hetty and Bledd'yif came back from the lunchtime session at the chip shop they were delighted to hear the two girls singing loudly and strongly,

'Don't be sad 'cos the world's gone mad, let's dance.

Kick those heels, shake those hips, let's dance, dance,
dance, dance.
Have some fun 'cos the Hun's on the run, let's dance.
Kick those heels, shake those hips, let's dance, dance,
dance, dance.'

Janet was dancing and Shirley was managing to move
around with the aid of a stick. Both were laughing helplessly.
Within minutes, the girls were rearranging the words into
verses and chorus and making up fresh verses. Hetty was
singing with them and Bleddyn was tapping an accompaniment with the poker and the coal scuttle.

'I don't think Ken would give it much praise,' Shirley said,
laughing, as they collapsed exhausted into chairs and on to
the bed. 'But it's done wonders for me!'

'I think you should show him,' Janet said seriously. 'It
needs work but he might be able to do something with it.
It's certainly a lively tune.'

'Do you keep in touch with Ken?' Hetty asked. 'You
and he worked closely together, didn't you?'

'No, when I moved away from St David's Well I left
behind everything, apart from a few good friends.'

They changed the subject then and Janet told them of her
application to serve overseas. That seemed to bring the war
closer and the happy mood left them.

When Janet left for the train that would take her back
to camp, Shirley felt stronger and more in control of her life
than she had for weeks. By the time winter ended she would
be on her feet, on a stage, and she would be singing.

–

Joseph's mother began to feel weaker, less able to do the daily tasks that had once seemed so easy, and during February it became apparent to Joseph that his life was undergoing a change. The meals were not always there when he got home and there were occasions when the clothes he needed would have to be hastily ironed by his clumsy and inexperienced hands. The assistance willingly offered by kindly neighbours faded as the need increased and he finally faced the fact that for the first time in his life, his mother needed his help.

Concern for his mother was secondary as he once more bemoaned the fates that had handed out such cruel deals. If only Dolly hadn't died. If only Shirley would accept his love. If only—

Following the advice of one or two of his mother's friends he arranged for someone to come in twice a week and clean the house. The weekly rations and whatever else was needed were delivered and it was up to him to note their additional needs, such as household cleaning materials he hardly knew existed, and add these to the weekly order.

Arranging to leave the money for the milkman and the baker every Friday and for the insurance lady each Monday was simple: he put it under a flowerpot behind the gate. Finding someone to deal with the washing and ironing solved the laundry problem. Then there was only the cooking. Mrs Beynon was not bedridden and between them they somehow managed to prepare and cook their meals.

Joseph hated the inconvenience of it all but comforted himself in the belief that once Shirley and he married, everything would revert to normal. The fact that she was still refusing to see him seemed nothing more than a minor hiccup.

Letters and telegrams still brought comfort and fear to the town. Johnny was in North Africa with the Eighth Army and, so far as they knew, Eynon was still somewhere in England.

Alice still wrote to Eynon and, overcoming her shyness, she would sometimes share the snippets of news she had gleaned from him with his family. When a couple of weeks passed and she hadn't heard from him, she went to ask the family if they had been more fortunate.

With her husband Wilfred, Marged's sister Audrey lived in the big house that had once been the home of their mother, known to most as Granny Molly Piper. Ronnie and his wife Olive lived there too with their baby girl. So when Alice called, there was usually someone home. On this occasion there was not.

Not being married or even engaged to Eynon, meant that any news of him being hurt or captured would go to Marged and Huw and it was a foolish superstitious fear of bad news that made her call on Audrey rather than his parents, Marged and Huw.

Receiving no reply to her knock on that evening, she forced herself to knock on the house a few doors down to ask Eynon's mother if there was news of him.

She was welcomed and offered tea but she stood anxiously waiting for an answer to her question. 'Have you heard from Eynon?'

'Two letters yesterday,' Huw told her. 'I should have called round to tell you, but I've been too busy. Sorry, love.'

'It doesn't matter, Mr Castle. As long as he's all right.'

'He'll be fine. Our Eynon has shown us how capable he is of looking after himself. Imagine all those months on the run and surviving unscathed.'

'I'm sure you're right, but I do get a bit anxious when I don't hear for a while.'

'Come here any time. Treat this as a second home,' Marged said. 'Eynon's friends are always welcome, specially you.'

Alice thanked them, drank the tea and went back to her sad little home.

-

It was Myrtle who delivered the weekly order for Joseph and his mother and she was the one to tell Shirley about his mother's illness.

'He brings the order into the shop now, and it's him who calls again to pay, so I've heard. Heart attack they say, poor woman.'

'Is she in hospital?' Hetty asked.

'No, home she is, but resting a lot of the time, not able to do much.' Myrtle giggled then as she went on. 'He mops the kitchen floor and shakes the mat at night, hoping none of the neighbours will see him, would you believe! Shamed he is, having to do women's work.'

'You had a lucky escape there, Shirley,' Bleddyn said.

'He's the sort to expect you to take over and run the house while he carries on just the same as before.'

'Lucky escape? You must think I'm daft. I only used him as an escort to see Janet and me safe home. No chance of my marrying someone like Joseph Beynon. I've never pretended, mind: I'm sure I haven't ever let him think there could be anything serious between us.'

'Poor man. Besotted he is. I think he still hopes to marry you one day.'

'Yes, one day, when I've given up on a career and I'm willing to settle down to be a dutiful wife!' Shirley's expression made it clear what she felt about that idea.

Myrtle stood up and said. 'I've put it off long enough, I have to deliver the order for Alice's father now. I hate going there, but there's no one else to do it today.'

'Want me to come with you?' Bleddyn offered. Myrtle thanked him but declined.

'He's harmless, just a bit frightening, that's all, him being wounded in the head an' all. I'll be all right. I've only got to hand over the box without dropping it.' She giggled again. 'Biscuits and eggs, they're the worry of my life!'

As she drew closer to the neglected shop the humour of the situation left her and she wished more and more that she had agreed to Bleddyn going with her. Big he was, that Bleddyn Castle, and even Colin Potter at his worst wouldn't start making a fuss if he were around, she thought anxiously.

She was unaware that as she headed for the old shop premises, walking alongside the carrier bike rather than riding it, Bleddyn had followed and kept up with her with ease. He was smiling as he watched her, her skinny legs in their black woollen stockings straining in a knock-kneed stance as she fought with the heavy machine to keep it upright as she turned a corner.

She propped the bicycle against the wall and knocked on the door before walking back to collect the boxed groceries. Her hands were cold and the box slipped as she stood there and, as the door opened, Colin saw a tin of baked beans slide out and fall to the ground. In seconds his temper had exploded.

He pushed Myrtle, making her stagger, and grabbing the box of groceries, he threw it on to the path and with a hand on each of her shoulders, began to shake her.

'The eggs! You've smashed the eggs,' he snarled.

'No, no eggs this week,' she shouted, her voice wavering with the violence of his attack. Then Bleddyn was there, pulling the man off, holding him against the wall warning him to be still.

Myrtle was crying. Then Bleddyn said, his voice surprisingly calm, 'I'll hold him here, Myrtle, you go and fetch the police.'

Two hours later, Colin was locked up. Leaving Myrtle with Hetty and having sent for Maude, Marged and Huw, Bleddyn went to find Alice.

Seeing her father in the police station was upsetting for Alice, yet she nursed a hope that perhaps now, the doctors would find a way of helping him. He hadn't always been like this. Until the blow to his head during that final boxing match had caused damage to his brain, he had been a loving, affectionate father. Looking at him drooped and defeated, his hands over his face, she forced herself to remember how he had been, not what he had become.

'Dad, I'm here and I won't let anything bad happen to you.' Whether he heard she wasn't sure. He looked up and stared at her but didn't seem to know she was there. 'If only Eynon was here,' she said aloud. 'I'd be so glad to have him here to help us.'

'No men in the house!' Colin said sharply.

'Oh,' she smiled, 'so you do know I'm here.'

It was decided that Colin Potter should go into hospital and remain there for the foreseeable future. Instead of relief, Alice was alarmed. How would he cope in a place he didn't know and with strangers running his life? What would happen to her? Without the money her father contributed from his savings and his pension, she couldn't afford to stay on in the rooms behind the shop. Besides, she didn't know whether she could live there alone. It was an unfriendly, frightening place.

Ancient woodwork creaked and groaned, water dripped like tiny footsteps and plaster dust dribbled in brief showers on to the bare floor.

In the days her father was absent she had slept in the room next to the kitchen, afraid to face the dark staircase and the empty rooms above. She had to find somewhere better to live, but with the small wage she earned, it was an impossible task. If only Eynon were here, she thought time and again.

She didn't know what he could do that she couldn't, but was certain he would find a solution. At least she would be able to discuss the few alternatives open to her. Cleaning the place and renting out another room was a possibility but she didn't think she could do that alone. There were repairs to do and it wasn't as simple as wallpaper and paint; the dilapidation had gone too far for that.

She wrote to Eynon, trying not to sound too miserable. She wanted him to know the situation but not to worry uselessly when he was unable to help her deal with it. To her delight, Eynon wrote back telling her to telephone him at a call box at seven the following Friday, which she did. He had found a solution, although it wasn't one she had expected.

'Let's get married,' he said.

After a short, frantic conversation, she emerged from the telephone box, flushed, her eyes glowing with happiness. Tonight she wouldn't be afraid to sleep alone in the awful house. She was going to marry Eynon, be Mrs Eynon Castle and live happily ever after, just like in the films.

The euphoria lasted as she approached the old shop but then began to fade. When a figure stepped out from the darkness she almost screamed, convinced that her father had come back and was in a rage.

'Alice?' Marged said, 'Sorry to frighten you, love. Have you spoken to our Eynon?'

'I thought it was Dad,' Alice whispered, 'afraid he'd be in a temper.' Then Marged was hugging her and leading her away from the dilapidated doorway and back to Sidney Street.

Lending her a few clothes was not a problem, although they were all too large for the slender girl, and she slept in a clean sweet room and was woken at seven o'clock by Huw bringing her a cup of tea.

'I'm not making a habit of this, mind,' he said with mock severity. 'Just for your first morning as Eynon's fiancée and my future daughter-in-law, to let you know how pleased we are. Right?'

'Right.' She smiled. 'And thank you.'

Marged and Huw went back with her later that day to help her clear her belongings from the rooms she had shared with her sick father. Marged noticed the girl's efforts at keeping the place clean, seeing the attempts at washing the black mildew from the walls and the well-scrubbed floors in the part of the house they used. She saw the clean curtains which hid the shelves where food was kept and the old, battered saucepans gleaming with constant care.

Everywhere there was dust. Windows didn't fit and cloth had been ineffectually stuffed around the sides to keep the weather at bay. The plaster was blown, and was bulging away from the walls and in many places trickling down as they watched. Gaslight fittings were hanging precariously and it was obvious that the only light, apart from one or two places, would have been from candles.

'Eynon said we were lucky the place hadn't blown up with us in it,' Alice said as she saw the horror on their faces.

'I only wish we'd known before,' Huw said gruffly. 'Damn it all, Marged, no one should live like this.'

'I couldn't have moved out before. I wouldn't have been able to leave Dad.'

'He's safe now and he'll have proper care.' Marged hugged the solemn girl. 'Look after you, we will, until our Eynon comes home.'

–

At the RAF camp, Janet was free to leave camp once the work was finished, although it was usually after nine thirty before everything was cleared away and the floors scrubbed, and the place was as spotless as the manager demanded. There was often a dance held locally and whenever she could, Janet would go. The girls in the NAAFI canteen became friends and usually travelled together, sometimes cadging a lift from one of the lorries when there were no officers around: sometimes there was a bus and on other occasions they walked.

Going into the village hall where the local dances were regularly held, the first person she saw one night was Ken.

'I was hoping you'd come,' he said as casually as when they met in St David's Well. He led her on to the floor where the record was playing a polka to which everyone was dancing in a very exaggerated and humorous manner. The mood was one of highly charged excitement and before their first dance was over they were laughing and having fun with the rest. At first they were too breathless to speak. They stared at each other as though unable to believe they were there together.

Another record began, this time the slower Jerome Kern's 'All The Things You Are', and at once the mood changed, became quieter as the dancers sang the words dedicating them to their partners. Janet and Ken stared at each other: neither had said more than a few words. There didn't seem the need.

One of her friends came to find her and dragged her to the stage, where she sang, this time looking at Ken and singing to him.

The last waltz played, the lights were lowered and the murmur of softly whispered promises and words of love were spoken. As the crowd dispersed. Janet began to look for the rest of the girls who had come with her.

'I have to go, there's a lorry promised us a lift.' she said. But Ken led her away from the dark shapes issuing out of the doorway, to where a group of trees promised privacy, although in the darkness of the night it was hardly necessary, just the lovers' need for solitude. He kissed her deeply and with longing. She had no will to resist even though she knew she had no right to be so happy with a man who belonged to someone else.

'How did you find me?' she asked, knowing it was no coincidence that had brought them together.

'It doesn't matter. Why did you leave without telling me or keeping in touch?'

'You know why.'

'Because you feel the same as me, that I shouldn't have married Eirlys?'

'Forget it, Ken. You did marry her and you and I shouldn't be talking like this.'

'Write to me, Janet. Keep in touch, then we can meet sometimes, see if our feelings fade or whether it isn't too late to do something about it.'

'No, Ken. Please, stay out of my life. I left St David's Well because I wanted to leave you. Don't you understand? I don't want this. I don't want to see you again.'

'Janet?' a voice called. 'Hurry up or we'll have to walk back!'

'Run more like,' her friend Elen's voice added.

Pushing him away she ran to where the lorry driver was revving the engine impatiently. With a foot on the tailboard, she raised her hands and was pulled up, then she turned to help others. In the unlit back of the vehicle, laughing as the lorry lurched and toppled them against each other, they began to sing popular choruses. She didn't join in and hoped no one would see her tears.

The lumbering movement of the lorry and sitting side-ways made her feel sick and she still felt a bit queasy the following morning. It would be a good excuse to miss a few dances, pretending that the travel upset her.

Letters arrived from Ken and at first she didn't answer them, determined that having left home she had to go through with her decision to give Eirlys and Ken's marriage a chance. One she read over and over. He had made up his mind, he knew where his happiness lay and he wanted to divorce Eirlys and marry her. It was too late, she couldn't agree. Loving and losing seemed to be her fate.

She stayed in camp when her friends went to the next few dances, hoping that if Ken were there he would realise she had meant what she had said in reply.

A few days later she wrote again and told him news he didn't want to hear.

–

Alice settled happily into Marged and Huw's home. For Lilly it was an advantage having the girl who was so anxious to become part of the family so conveniently near and anxious to be her friend. There was a family of which she wanted to become a part too. She made use of Alice as a babysitter when she went to see Sam's father to talk about weddings.

A letter from Sam told her he was being sent overseas. She showed it to her parents. He explained about his embarkation leave and asked her to marry him.

'And what will your answer be?' Marged asked, her fingers tightly crossed.

Lilly surprised them all by saying. 'I'm getting married next Saturday. And before you start fussing, it's already booked.'

At once Marged began to talk about food.

'Oh forget all that, Mam!' Lilly spoke sharply. 'We don't want any fuss. In fact, we'd like to go to the register office and not tell a soul.'

'Lilly, love, don't do that. People will—' Marged was about to say that tongues would wag, people would suspect the reason for haste was a baby on the way. But with an illegitimate child already, she doubted whether Lilly would be concerned about gossip.

'All right, tell us where and when and we'll gather the family and make it a small celebration. But I hope our Eynon gives us the chance of a proper do. We need a good knees-up and that's a fact.'

'Next Saturday at three o'clock. We'll meet you here.'

'You mean here, at home?'

'Right here in this room. Right?'

'So we can go together to the register office you mean?'

'We'll all meet here, Mam.'

With that, Marged had to be content.

Hannah made a coat and hat for baby Phyllis, Huw booked cars to take the family to the register office and back again. Marged raided the Christmas decorations for silver balls, with which she made table decorations with the addition of some ribbons.

No one was sure what to buy for a wedding present. Marged and Huw presumed that, until the war ended, Lilly would continue to stay at home, sharing her room with Sam when he came on leave.

'Cash would be best,' Huw said. 'Then they can save for when they get a place of their own.'

The news spread and Eirlys's gift shop supplied many of the congratulation cards made by Hannah, to mark the occasion. Marged spent all her clothing coupons and Huw's on underwear to give Lilly a decent trousseau, and found a suitable dress and coat in a second-hand shop for herself. Ignoring Lilly's insistence that a sit-down meal was unnecessary. Marged went to see Bernard Gregory and managed to buy two chickens with which she planned a roast dinner for the fifteen or so guests she expected.

Amid the shoal of wedding day cards and good wishes that arrived by every post, there was a letter telling them that Eynon was missing in action. Marged stared at it as though willing it to disappear. When she showed it to Huw and later to Bleddyn, they decided that they would say nothing until after the wedding.

'A small affair this wedding is anyway and it would be utterly miserable if we announced this. Our Lilly deserves a happy day at least,' Marged sobbed as she read the message for the fifth time.

'We'll have to tell Alice, mind,' Huw said in a choked voice. 'Can't just blurt it out without warning her, can we?'

To their surprise, Alice took the news calmly. 'I know he's safe,' she insisted. But whether she believed it or was trying to cope in her own way, they couldn't decide.

Eirlys was invited to call at the house at three o'clock on Saturday 14 March, to expect a meal but not to refer to it as a wedding breakfast.

'You know our Lilly, awkward is her middle name. Says she and Sam don't want a fuss. I ask you, how can you expect to get married and not have a bit of a fuss?'

'Perhaps Sam is a bit shy.' Eirlys suggested. 'He hasn't had the chance to get to know you very well. Being in the army most of the time he and Lilly have been friends.'

'Maybe that's it. Well, he'll soon learn that you can't belong to this family and not enjoy a good party!'

'Where are they going to live?'

'She's that vague you'd never believe. I presume she'll want to live here until Sam gets out of the forces. She can hardly do otherwise, can she?'

Eirlys gave her the neatly parcelled cushions she had made as a wedding gift. 'Tell her that if the colours aren't what she likes I'll change them.'

'Thank you, Eirlys. She'll be thrilled for sure.'

Eirlys smiled. It was hard to imagine Lilly excited over anything as mundane as two cushions!

Guests began to arrive at two thirty and Lilly was nowhere to be found. Huw, looking distinctly uncomfortable in a suit, declared that if she didn't show soon he was going to change into a sports jacket and damn the conventions.

'You'll suffer like the rest of us,' Marged warned. 'How d'you think I feel in second-hand shoes that are a half size too small?'

'This collar's so stiff with starch it's threatening to cut my throat and how smart would that look with blood all over the place, eh?'

At five minutes past three the door opened and Lilly walked in with Sam's father. She carried a small posy of flowers and wore a hat with fresh flowers sewn on to the brim. Marged had to admit that her daughter looked lovely for her wedding.

'Come on then, get into the cars, we're late as it is,' Marged said, swallowing tears of emotion and pride.

'We aren't going anywhere, Mam,' Lilly said. Taking Sam's father's arm, she said, 'Sam senior and I were married half an hour ago.'

Twelve

Marged and Huw pretended that the wedding was a happy joke and encouraged the other guests to think the same. Deep inside, hidden by their smiles, they felt humiliated. Marrying a man the same age as her father would have been difficult enough to explain, but to marry him secretly, while giving everyone the impression she was going to marry the son, made it impossible. How could they face people, knowing they were talking about them, laughing at their embarrassment?

The party atmosphere was strained, only Lilly seeming unaffected by her announcement. The food was excellent but no one tasted it; they were all wishing the occasion was over and they could leave. There was the threat of an approaching row in the air that no one wanted to witness.

Ken sat next to Eirlys wishing he were a hundred miles away, with Janet. A letter had arrived that morning and he had taken it from the postman without Eirlys seeing it, the handwriting telling him it was from Janet. It was unopened and he hoped it was an answer to his own, telling her he wanted to divorce Eirlys and marry her.

As the talk went on around him he fingered the letter, wanting to read it but unable to get away from Eirlys. He needed privacy, a pleasant place and the time to relish what he hoped was the promise of a new beginning, a happy future.

'I do think Mrs Denver should have told them – you know – what was going on,' Eirlys whispered.

'Going on?' he said, half hearing what she was telling him and alarm stiffening his jaw. 'What's going on?'

She pointed at Mrs Denver, who had apparently been present at the marriage. The poor woman looked close to tears. She was trying to help Marged as the meal progressed, hovering as though waiting for an opportunity to explain her involvement, but Marged didn't want to hear. Every time the older woman opened her mouth to speak, Marged pushed her angrily aside. Why hadn't she told them what Lilly planned? How could she condone such a wicked plan?

Everyone was trying to make conversation but trying to avoid certain subjects made it hazardous. The present wedding was taboo, the weddings of others were no better, and the war, with the fall of Singapore and ferocious bombing raids of Germany which would certainly bring reprisals, was too gloomy to mention.

Marged and Huw were thinking about how they had protected their daughter's special day by keeping to themselves their worry about Eynon, and unanimously they agreed it was no longer necessary. Why should they pretend everything was a huge joke when their son was somewhere fighting for his life?

As they were finishing the wedding cake and holding up their glasses for the toast, Huw stood up and instead of wishing the couple a life of happiness, he said solemnly, 'We weren't going to mention this today, out of consideration for Lilly and her – husband. But Marged and I heard a few days ago that our younger son, Eynon, is missing in action somewhere in France.'

There was a gasp of horror that brought tears to Marged's eyes. Lilly's hands flew to her face and Ronnie hugged Olive as the words were spoken. Beth and Peter held hands, looking at each other. Peter knew better than anyone the danger Eynon faced if he were behind enemy lines.

'Do we know any more, Dad?' Ronnie asked, his voice shaking.

'Only that he's missing, son. We didn't even know he was over there. So that's what I want us to drink to. That wherever he is, our Eynon is safe.'

The toast to the happy couple seemed unimportant after that.

Peter and Beth talked together in low tones, Beth asking him if he could somehow find out where her brother was.

'I'll try,' he promised, 'but I'm no longer in the field and it's difficult. Secrecy is imperative to save lives.'

In the absence of a best man, the other witness being a neighbour who hadn't been invited to the wedding breakfast, Sam stood up and said a few brief sentences. He promised to look after Lilly and Phyllis, and told them all how proud and happy she had made him by becoming his wife. Then he asked that their prayers would be for the safe return of Eynon, whom he had never met, but hoped to meet very soon.

Ken seemed to have distanced himself from the atmosphere surrounding the newly-weds. Whispered conversations went on around the table, cake and drinks were consumed, and he stared into space unaware of anything. When Eirlys spoke to him he hardly seemed to hear. His answers were brief and vague.

'Wake up, darling,' Eirlys said, laughing. 'You don't seem to be with us at all. Writing a tune in your head, are you?'

He chose a moment when Eirlys was talking to Beth to slip away into the garden, where primroses crowded under the bushes, their buds filled with promise. Leaf-buds were bursting on the trees in which birds sang melodiously, creating a cheerful scene. He opened the letter and stared at the page for a long time without moving.

Eirlys was commiserating with others on the worrying news about Eynon and didn't notice his absence or, on his return, the look of concentration in his eyes, a brightness that hadn't been there before.

When the meal and the somewhat empty toasts were over and people began to leave, Marged let her guard slip and to Mrs Denver, she hissed, 'You knew about this and didn't tell us.'

'I didn't know.' The woman was tearful. 'I arrived at the register office early and looked for the family. Puzzled I was when there wasn't a sign of any of you. I didn't know Lilly had given you the wrong time, and I didn't know about Sam senior until they walked in.'

'Rubbish! You must have known. You must have realised the discrepancy in the time.'

'I had no idea. When Lilly and Sam's father came, I looked around for Sam, and Lilly said, "He's here, meet my future husband. Sam." That's the first I knew. Went cold I did. I thought of you and the shock it would be but it was too late for me to tell you, or even warn you. I'm so sorry. I was there as a witness and I'm ashamed. I just hope they'll be happy, and I can still see little Phyllis.'

Marged didn't believe her. It was better not to: she had to have someone to blame.

'I don't think much of Sam for doing this to us,' Huw muttered as Sam waved goodbye. He was carrying baby Phyllis, with Lilly hanging devotedly on his arm. 'Not much of a man to agree to such a cruel joke.'

'Our Lilly can be very persuasive, mind,' Marged admitted sadly.

'The only way to deal with it is to pretend it was a huge joke,' she said as Ronnie and Olive tried to comfort her later that evening. 'A big huge joke, that's what it was, and Huw and I were in on it, sharing it with her.'

Over the next few days, she told the story with great exaggeration to everyone she met, making sure she got her version in first as often as she could. Huw did the same, and it was only when they were alone that they said what they really thought of their daughter and her new husband. None of it was polite.

–

Eirlys wondered how much Lilly had told her parents. She and Ken had been surprised and when she had looked at Marged and Huw, they seemed to be as shocked as the rest of them. They recovered quickly but she thought the whole thing had been an unkind surprise to them all.

As they walked home, she thought Ken was still unusually quiet. Glancing at him she saw he was frowning deeply.

'Why the glum face, love? Is anything wrong?' she asked, stopping and turning to face him. 'Perhaps I can tell you something to make you smile.'

'There is something I have to tell you,' he began.

She put a hand over his mouth playfully and said, 'Let me tell you something first. Something that will take away your sad expression.'

He gently pulled away her hand and protested, 'No, let me talk first.'

'Ken, I can't wait another moment. Darling, you're going to be a father!'

He pulled her to him, trying to hide the shock of the unbelievable words. In the letter from Janet, crumpled and hidden in a pocket, she had just told him the same thing.

Eirlys was unaware of Ken's dismay and the following day she went to see Beth to tell her the news.

'Peter and I want to wait until the war's over before we start having children,' Beth said after congratulating her. 'It's been going on for two and a half years, it can't last much longer, can it?'

'At least Peter is safe now.' Eirlys smiled. 'Thank goodness he won't have to go abroad again. That must have been very frightening for you as well as him.'

'Yes, it's a relief. I just hope we hear good news about Eynon soon. Mam and Dad look quite ill and I know they aren't sleeping.'

'The thing is, Beth, although I'm thrilled to be expecting a baby, I want to go on working. Is that very terrible? Ken's work is hardly well paid and we won't be able to manage on the little he earns.'

'He won't carry on with a concert party after the war, surely?'

'I think he hopes to make a career in the music business. Song writing and some performing. Like Shirley and Janet, but with different talents.'

'Shirley's voice is wonderful. I hope she recovers from the accident and gets back to her career,' Beth said. 'I think she lost confidence for a while.'

'Janet going away didn't help. I wonder why she left so suddenly?' Eirlys mused.

'She knew she'd have to do some war work, and made a move while she still had a choice. Pity though. Shirley could have done with her being around these past weeks.'

Eirlys reached home that Sunday to see a police car outside and two policemen standing at the front door. Her father was opening it as she ran down the path and she followed them in demanding to know what had happened. She was frightened: they might have found out who was responsible for the robberies her father had carried out with the evacuee, Stanley, after all this time. A glance at their faces reassured her.

Offering them tea, she waited to be told the reason for their visit.

'You had three evacuees,' the constable said. 'Stanley Love and his brothers Harold and Percival. Right?'

'Yes. Are they all right?' Morgan asked anxiously.

'Poor little fellers, they've lost their mother.' He glanced at Eirlys, as though not wanting to talk while she was there.

'We'll have that tea now please, Mrs Ward,' the sergeant said politely but pointedly.

'Not until I know what's happened to the boys,' she said firmly.

'Well, it seems,' he began hesitantly, 'that their mother was in the habit of going out at night and leaving them alone. Only young she was, poor girl. Probably liked a drink and a bit of company. You know how it is.' He was still eyeing Eirlys, hoping she would leave them. 'Well, it seems that she was in a bombed-out building – er – probably sheltering from an air raid or the rain or something. And, well, it seems that the building collapsed and killed her and – er, some man who happened to be sheltering with her.'

Eirlys moved to her father and held him as the sergeant went on. 'The boys were taken into care, together with others who had been orphaned by the bombing but they insist that they live here, in St David's Well, and gave your name and address, sir.'

'Our address you say? What could they mean?' Eirlys said, teasing her father in her delight. 'Well, they're right. They came as evacuees and lived with us until their mother took them away. Twice she did it, mind! But we'd be happy to have them back, wouldn't we, Dadda?'

'I've missed them so much,' Morgan said, unashamedly tearful.

–

Janet waited anxiously for a reply from Ken. Telling him she was going to have his child had been a difficult letter to write, but she felt he ought to know, even though the decision about how she dealt with it was her own.

She was fortunate that the morning sickness that was usually such a nuisance in early pregnancy didn't happen. The only sign was the constant visits to the lavatory and the loss of the monthly 'curse'. At this moment she wouldn't regard it as a curse, more a welcome visitor.

She hadn't been at the camp long enough to make any strong bonds, but being away from home for the first time the girls were very friendly and the closeness that might have taken months was already growing. Sharing the living accommodation created an intimacy as nothing else had, and helping one another, going out as a group during their free time, had all added to the camaraderie and encouraged trust.

The ability to share confidences, particularly about their love life, was an essential part of it. Because of this, when her friend Elen, who was also from Wales, asked her what was wrong. Janet told her.

'What will you do? You'll have to leave the moment they find out.'

'I can't make a decision until I've heard from Ken,' Janet told her.

'But you have your medical for working overseas in a month. You don't have time to wait for a letter that might not come.'

'I can't do anything until Ken knows and tells me what he wants me to do.'

'Call me cynical if you like, but he's got a wife, hasn't he? His loyalty will be with her.'

'You don't know Ken.'

'I know men! When it comes to the nitty-gritty of life, they take the safe option, believe me.'

'I know he loves me.'

'I'm sure you're right, but what's that got to do with anything? He'll stay with his wife and pretend this never happened.'

The letter arrived, and Ken told her that much as he loved her he couldn't help her. The circumstances were just too complicated and would be too distressing for Eirlys. He filled a page with reasons but to Janet they were nothing more than cowardly excuses. He was unable to face the responsibilities of what had happened. Janet read it twice then showed it to Elen.

'Sorry, Janet. I really am. I was right, but don't think I get any pleasure from that. I would prefer to have been wrong. I just wanted to stop you expecting roses, roses all the way. Life isn't like that.'

She held Janet while she cried, then added, 'It happened to me. That's why I'm so cynical.'

'What did you do?'

'Said goodbye to the man and to the baby.'

'How?'

'There are ways, if you're determined. There's this woman in our village. Years ago she'd have been burnt as a *gwrach* – the wise woman, or witch. But she's helped a lot of women avoid a baby they can't afford, for various reasons.'

'What does she do?'

'Gives you a dose of this stuff, gin, and herbs like penny royal and others. Boils it till it's a reduced to couple of tablespoonsful and makes you swallow it.'

'Dangerous, is it?'

'I suppose so. I felt quite ill for about a week. But if you're desperate—'

–

Ken read and reread Janet's letter in which she had told him about the child. She told him she expected nothing, that the mistake was as much hers as his and she didn't want to force him to leave Eirlys, whom she considered a friend.

She was unaware of the fact that Eirlys too was going to have a child. Perhaps she wouldn't have told him if she had known. Janet loved him for what he was and would have done what was best for him. She didn't want to change him as he suspected Eirlys would, once the realisation of an irregular wage began to be a problem.

Now he'd been told that the house would be filled to overflowing with the three boys from London coming once more to stay.

He felt obligated to Eirlys, whom he had married, but in his heart he wanted Janet. She would have been a partner for the whole of their life together, sharing a love of music, and giving him the support he needed to continue with his career once the war was over. With Janet he could have taken chances, gone all out for the career he wanted. Even with a child they would have persevered and chased success.

Marrying Eirlys had been a stupid mistake and he felt a cheat, a confidence trickster like the spivs in the big cities selling unsatisfactory goods. He'd married her under false pretences, telling her he loved her when he knew that his feelings for Janet were stronger.

He wrote again to Janet, begging her to ignore his previous letter, telling her it had been written before he'd thought about it properly. He told her lovingly he had changed his mind, and as soon as she wrote telling him she would agree, he would tell Eirlys about them and ask for a divorce. To convince her of his decision, he wrote a second and a third letter, reaffirming his promise.

–

Once she had made up her mind, Janet didn't delay. On their next day off she went with her new friend to see the lady who promised an end to her problem. The woman who opened the door to them was smartly dressed and quite young, probably no more than thirty. She certainly wasn't the ancient crone Janet had expected to see. When she reached camp that evening, she went straight to bed, and in the morning reported sick. She hinted that she'd had too much to drink the previous evening and, threatened with a cut in her wages, was left to sleep it off.

The letter from Ken in which he told her he had changed his mind and wanted to leave Eirlys, and live with her and their child, she didn't read until much much too late.

—

The Castle family had further news of Eynon a few days after the unfortunate wedding. He was a prisoner in a German camp. Huw said they could relax, holding on to the hope that for the rest of the war he would at least be safe. 'Unless he tries to escape,' Peter warned Beth when she told him. 'Many men just can't cope with being locked up and I think your Eynon might be one of them. On the run for months then imprisoned by the army, he'd find it hard to accept locked doors, but for his sake I hope he does.'

'Can't you find out?' she pleaded. 'Mam and Dad are sick with worry.'

'So are thousands of other parents. No, love, we have to sit and wait; the hardest part of the battle, some say.'

A week later, two men succeeded in making a home run and from these Peter learned about Eynon, but it was news he didn't pass on to Beth.

Eynon had been one of a small group to walk out of the camp wearing German uniforms and carrying the relevant forms, but he had been picked up only hours after he had passed through the gates. He had been beaten, his arm was broken and he had been placed in solitary confinement. It was while he was being taken to hospital to have his arm treated that he escaped again. At present, all that was known was that he was in a small village somewhere in occupied France. Peter decided that once there was more definite

331

news, he would go and bring him out. Something else he didn't tell Beth.

–

Shirley was getting stronger and when she was asked to sing at a small party to celebrate an ATS girl's twenty-first birthday, Hetty and Bleddyn persuaded her to accept.

Joseph called a few days later when Hetty and Bleddyn were out.

'What's this about you singing at a birthday party for a lot of soldiers?'

'It's nothing to do with you.'

'How can you say that? I love you, I want to marry you, look after you until you're fit and well.'

'I don't want to hear this. Please, Joseph, go away.'

'How can you be so stupid? You aren't strong enough. You shouldn't put such a strain on yourself. This will set you back weeks, and you won't have the voice you once had. Not any more. Not after sitting about for all this time, and the bronchitis. You're finished as an entertainer. Why won't you accept what I say?'

Shirley raised her walking stick threateningly and told him to leave, but his words had done their damage. When the moment came for her to sing in front of a crowd mostly in uniform, and accompanied at the piano by a friend of the birthday girl – who didn't play all that well – she lost her nerve.

Her voice, usually so strong and sure, came out tremulously and she faltered and left the stage. The pianist continued to play and gradually the crowd joined in and the impromptu sing-song ended the evening happily.

For Shirley the evening ended differently. She went out on two sticks and waited at the door of the small hall for the taxi she had ordered for an hour's time. A figure loomed out of the darkness and Joseph said. 'Shall I phone for a taxi?'

'No, Joseph, I don't want you anywhere near me. I've ordered a taxi and when it comes I'll go home alone!'

'But you need me.'

'Keep away from me, d'you hear? Or I'll talk to the police.' The stick was raised and this time she brought it down not more than inches away from his head.

She wrote to Freddy and told him exactly what had happened, and as before, his reply was far from sympathetic.

> My dear, dear girl.
> I reckon that was a good thing, you drying up at that party. You can see now what an idiot you are to let someone like Joseph affect your plans. Now you'll be strong and never let it happen ever again. Wait till I get home and I'll kick his 'whatsit' so hard he'll find himself in Somerset. Until then, book a proper concert and sing for yourself, not anyone else, just yourself, and you'll be a wow. I can't wait for the day when I'll be there cheering you on.
> Good luck. God bless, your loving friend. Freddy

A few days later she wrote to Ken and asked him to arrange for her to take part in a concert when there was one planned in the town. Freddy was right; she had to take responsibility for herself. Joseph had damaged her confidence but she had to accept that she had allowed it to happen. Facing that as Freddy had intended, she determined never to let it happen again.

–

The shop opened by Eirlys and Hannah to sell handcrafted gifts continued to be busy, although since the frantic rush at Christmas time, it had slowed down to a steady trickle of business that Hannah could cope with easily on her own.

Bleddyn had bought a treadle sewing machine and delivered it to the shop and it was there Hannah did most of her dressmaking. When she wasn't making clothes – usually from other unpicked ones – she made smaller things to sell. 'Make Do and Mend,' the posters told people and that applied particularly to clothes. Large jumpers were sewn into smaller ones, coats became trousers and jackets for children, men's trousers became skirts. Unpicking seams and pressing the material took time, and the use was limited by the odd shapes, but it meant inexpensive garments could be made and sold without using the precious clothing coupons.

Hetty and Bleddyn looked after Josie and Marie after school and usually brought them to meet Hannah at five thirty when the shop closed. There was usually a meal waiting for her and she had never felt so cared for or so loved. She still contacted her parents but there had not been any softening in their resolve to treat her like a wicked and ungodly woman.

One evening, when rain had shortened the day and made the afternoon gloomy, she was sewing sequins on a dance dress. It had originally been made for someone much larger than Shirley Downs but now the long skirt and the simple top, decorated with sparkling sequins in deep-forest green, would make an elegant gown for her return to the stage.

Hannah had managed to find some specialist wadding that she had sewn inside the hem to make it stand out at the bottom, emphasising Shirley's wonderful figure.

When the door opened and a customer walked in, she didn't look up, but continued to concentrate on the small needle coming up in exactly the right place for the next sequin.

'Still busy I see,' her mother said quietly.

Jumping up, Hannah went forward to greet her mother but hesitated. Her mother didn't like outward displays of affection, and besides, as she had hardly spoken to her since her marriage to Johnny Castle, she probably wouldn't consider the slightest show of emotion appropriate.

'Yes,' she said after a pause. 'I'm still busy and loving it. The variety means there aren't two days alike and it's fun dealing with the customers, helping them with a new garment from old, or choosing a suitable gift.'

'The girls, they're well?'

'Why don't you come and see them?' Hannah asked softly. 'They often ask about you.'

'Do they?' Her mother seemed surprised.

'I've told you often enough. And they've written to you and sent birthday and Christmas cards.'

'It isn't easy—'

'Oh but it is, Mum. All you have to do is come to Brook Lane and walk in. You and Dad would be welcome.'

'I don't think so.'

As she turned to go, Hannah said, 'Mum, it's my birthday soon. Why don't you bring Dad? Perhaps you can make us a cake.'

'You don't have to remind me when your birthday is!' The harsh tone was back and Hannah instinctively stepped back.

'It would be nice to share it with you, like when I was a child.'

'We'll see.' Without another word she left and for a moment disappointment shadowed Hannah's face, then she remembered. When she was young, as with many other families, 'we'll see', usually meant yes.

–

Eirlys was a little worried. Peter hadn't been home for several weeks and she had received no letters from him. She had the feeling that, in spite of his reassurances, he had been called to return to France and work in occupied territory. His knowledge, built up since 1938, as well as his ability to speak French and German, meant his skills were of great value.

Hiding her fear from his father, she wrote to Peter regularly and made a joke of his failure to get in touch.

'He's so engrossed with his latest group of trainees he's forgotten us,' she said to Bernard one morning as they watched the postman once more passing by without stopping.

'Do you suppose they're young women this time and that's why he can't tear himself away?'

'Highly likely.' Bernard said. 'Another week and he'll have forgotten us completely.' He smiled then, knowing that the mild banter was an attempt to hide their worries and was failing to do so. 'Try not to be alarmed at the absence of a letter.' he said. 'This is one time when no news is good news. Bad news travels fastest.'

'We haven't heard anything more about Eynon.' she told him.

'Same rule. You'd hear if anything bad had happened.'

'I keep dreaming that Peter has gone over there to rescue him and they'll both walk in together, laughing at our fears. You don't think he really is in France, do you? Looking for Eynon?'

'From what I understand, your young brother can take care of himself.'

–

In a partially burned barn, twelve miles from the northern French coast, Eynon was trying to do just that.

Fifteen miles north-east of him, Peter was walking along a country lane, a farm labourer by his side, both singing bawdy songs and obviously very drunk.

A German sentry stopped them, and warned them to be quiet or they would be arrested as it was almost time for curfew. Thanking him, laughing like only the inebriated can, they climbed a fence and crossed a field towards some woods. As soon as they were out of sight, their 'drunkenness' left them.

–

Janet finally read Ken's letter and wept for the loss of her baby and for the loss of Ken. Now it was impossible to ask him to leave Eirlys. Too much pain had been caused by their love for it ever to work out happily. She had written telling him what she had done and she wrote again, this time giving her decision that their love was well and truly buried in the past. It had been a foolish mistake, an indulgence, something that

337

should never have happened. When the letter was posted, she felt marginally better but wondered if she would be as strong if they ever met again.

Ken struggled to cope with the news of the abortion when Janet's final letter reached him. Janet's words hurt him but in a way were also a relief. He couldn't sleep, and surreptitiously reread the letter while Eirlys slept beside him. Janet was right about the pain their love had caused. Prolonging it by making it known to everyone, would have added to that pain. Watching Eirlys sleeping contentedly beside him, he knew that she didn't deserve the treatment he had been planning to hand out.

It was two am, and sleep was far from his mind. Sliding out of the bed, he went downstairs and began to write letters to the artistes whom he wanted to appear in the grand concert to raise funds for Red Cross parcels to prisoners of war. He wondered whether Shirley would be well enough to take part. If she had recovered her strength and her voice, he would give her top billing to end the evening for him, but he doubted whether it were possible. The accident had mined her confidence and without that she was unable to let her powerful voice ring out.

It was going to be the largest entertainment he had organised and, as usual, he wished Max had been there to help him. His invariable good humour and patience had made everything easier, and more fun. Thinking of Max brought his mind back to Janet and he stared at the paper for a long time without writing a word.

Eirlys went with him to look at the stage of the theatre he had booked. It was daunting, seeing all those seats and knowing he had to fill them. With the assistance of the manager they worked out the finances and went away sobered by the task he had given himself.

'So many tickets to sell. You don't realise how large these places are until you see them empty,' Ken said.

'Come and buy me a cup of tea and we'll make lists of what we have to do,' Eirlys said, pleased to be involved with his work. Usually his concerts took place miles away. This one was on home ground and organising large-scale entertainment was something she had experience of. Ken gratefully accepted her help; his concerts were usually arranged by several people and played to readily available audiences. This large-scale public offering was dauntingly different and his alone.

Taking a notebook from her bag. Eirlys began to list their various tasks. 'It comes under the heading of Holidays at Home, so I can use some of the facilities at the council offices,' she said.

'Does it?'

'It does now!'

They worked out the various ways of advertising the event and the cost of the tickets and where the tickets would be sold, and decided that was enough for one day. It was when they were coming out of the café that they bumped into Janet.

'Janet! What a lovely surprise,' Eirlys said, hugging her. 'What are you doing home?'

'I came to see Shirley and give her a pep talk. It seems she's allowed that Joseph Beynon to make her feel useless and I'm here to talk sense into her.'

Janet seemed uneasy, talking to her but with her eyes looking ahead of her as though anxious to be off.

'We've been planning the Grand Concert for the eleventh of April. D'you think Shirley will be ready to sing?' Eirlys asked. Then she looked at Ken, about to ask him to explain more fully. But when she looked at his face, then back at Janet, she had a chilling feeling. The way they were looking at each other, eyes filled with longing. It wasn't friendship; there was something else.

'I – I'll leave you to explain to Janet. I'll go and see Hannah.' she said. She had to get away. She couldn't face what their eyes were telling her.

She didn't go to the shop but instead went home. Locking herself in her room, she began to think about the times Ken and Janet had worked together. Was she imagining it, or were they in love?

She heard Ken come in only moments after her and as he climbed the stairs so her heartrate increased. He was going to tell her goodbye. She would be alone with a baby. She'd be looking after her father and the three boys, but she would be alone.

'You've guessed.' Ken said as he came and stood beside er

'I've guessed.'

'You've only guessed a part of it. Janet and I did have a brief affair but it's over. Believe me, Eirlys, it's over. It probably happened because we were together so much, working together, mourning the death of Max. It happened and we both regret it, but it's over and it won't happen again.'

'How can I believe that? I saw the way you looked at each other.'

'The look we shared was guilt for deceiving you when we both love you.' He took a deep breath and said with as much meaning as he was capable, 'Eirlys, I love you, deeply and for ever.'

She didn't believe him but knew that somehow she had to face this, accept it as another casualty of war, and eventually put it behind her. The alternative, if he was speaking the truth, was misery for them all.

–

Ken went to see Shirley and together they went to a hall Ken had been given as a rehearsal room and she sang for him. She had Freddy Clements' latest letter in her pocket and she held it tightly, like a talisman, as she went through three numbers with Ken playing accompaniment. By the third she was singing with all her power, the room echoing with the final note making the hair creep on Ken's neck. She hadn't lost her talent.

'Will you take top billing and end the concert for me?' he asked, grinning widely. 'Vera Lynn and Anne Shelton are busy and there's no one else.'

Clutching Freddy's letter tightly she nodded. 'Yes, I'm ready now.'

Ken wanted to phone for a taxi to take her home but using a stick she determinedly walked to the bus stop and allowed him to help her on to the platform. People kindly made room for her and she sat, smiling, knowing that her life was back on course.

When she alighted not far from Brook Lane Ken walked with her as far as her gate. The sound of voices singing reached their ears and they stopped and waited as a small group turned the corner. Morgan was striding along with Stanley singing enthusiastically, 'Run, Rabbit Run', with the low voice of Harold accompanying them. Singing a few words now and then was the solemn Percival, making no attempt to keep in tune, just about managing the rhythm but all on the same note.

Forgetting his dismay at the thought of the noisy trio sharing the house, Ken laughed as he turned to follow them. 'What a comedy act those three would make, eh?'

–

The day of the concert was overshadowed by the continued absence of Peter and the lack of further news about Eynon. A young airman knocked on Bernard's door one evening and gave them a message purporting to come from Peter. 'Buy two extra tickets for the concert on the eleventh of April,' was all he said. Doubtfully, but with a hope so strong it became a physical ache, Bernard agreed. Eirlys block-booked twenty-six tickets.

All the Castles would be there including Lilly and her new husband. Mrs Denver had willingly offered to look after baby Phyllis and Olive and Ronnie's Rhiannon; she would put them to sleep in her home, using drawers in the absence of cots.

Alice was there and Maude and Myrtle with Auntie Audrey and Wilf. Eirlys's father arrived early and waited outside proudly accompanying the Three Musketeers. Beth and Bernard got ready, choosing to go on their bicycles. Others used the bus or walked, to wait outside until the doors opened.

Joseph sat in a back seat and waited for Shirley to appear. From the conversations going on around him, he knew that, for most, Shirley Downs was the draw. He was ashamed to realise that he was hoping for her to fail, so she would come to him, need him, admit that her happiness lay in the role of wife and not performer. How could someone with no background expect to reach such heights? Poor, foolish girl. She was bound to fail and she had to know he was there for her when she did.

—

Ken stood giving final instructions to the orchestra and performers, wanting to make sure that the timing was precise so there was no break between the acts.

Mainly due to the efforts of Eirlys and her friends and the Castle family, particularly Bleddyn, the concert was sold out. If Ken was nervous it didn't show, except perhaps in the way he shouted more loudly than usual, and the way he clenched his jaw. This was what he wanted to do for the rest of his life. The agony was excruciating, the excitement unbeatable. As the audience began to troop in, many uniforms present among the suits and dresses, with children's voices piping above the rest as they found their seats and searched pockets for sweets, he could think of no greater happiness. He blew a kiss at Eirlys as she walked along the aisle and slid between the rows with her father and the boys. Together they'd be a perfect team. He was certain of that now.

Eirlys saw him as he slipped behind the curtain, nervous but fulfilled. She mused on the many hasty marriages the war had encouraged. Marriages wouldn't fail for lack of love but perhaps because there was no time to strengthen that love with anticipation and long-term plans, and by setting down memories. Living for the moment had its drawbacks. With no yesterdays, the tomorrows lacked a certain joy.

Bleddyn looked along the row of faces: all his family plus those he cared for were there. Hetty anxiously watching the curtain, knowing her daughter was backstage, hoping she would cope. Hannah and her girls, taking in the atmosphere ready to write and tell his son Johnny about it. His brother Huw with Marged, trying to forget their fears for their son. Eynon. Their daughter Beth, afraid for her husband Peter and being brave for his father's sake.

He hugged Hetty and said softly, 'What a fortunate man I am, Hetty. Thank you so much for the happiness you've brought me.'

'Shirely and I have never been more content, my darling. Never.'

Beth sat with an empty seat either side of her. She knew there wasn't a chance of Peter timing his arrival so precisely that he could appear in time for the concert, but she had to keep faith with him. A seat apart from her, Bernard understood.

The acts were well received. Everyone there had come with the intention of enjoying themselves. The comedians had never had such encouragement and the dancers and singers and acrobats and conjurers never more appreciated.

Only Beth was distracted. She glanced towards the aisle time and again, foolishly hoping for a miracle, when for a miracle to happen was a chance in millions.

The last act was announced and enthusiasm grew. When the curtains opened to an empty stage, with only a piano to be seen, the crowd fell silent. This was their girl, their local lass. The one they had been waiting for.

'Ladies and gentlemen, please welcome our very own star, Jane Downs!'

As Shirley stepped out, using just one stick, and walked to the piano, the audience welcomed her to their hearts.

As she sang the first few words, something in Joseph died. She was wonderful and he must have been stupid not to realise it. He looked around him at the faces rapt in admiration. She was world class, not a silly amateur as he had tried so hard to pretend. She was touching hearts with her voice. What a fool he'd been to imagine she could love someone like him. Trembling, ashamed, he sat there wanting to run away. He had to leave St David's Well, he couldn't face her now he had come to his senses. As the first song ended to tumultuous applause, he pushed his way out of the theatre and ran home.

–

It was as she prepared to sing her third song that curtains swished and the doors at the side opened and two men walked in. At once Beth recognised Peter, then she realised that the second man was her brother Eynon. She had been right, Peter had gone to bring him home.

Shirley recognised them immediately as they moved along the front row, even though the stage light distorted her vision, and she began to clap. Then the whole family stood up and began to shout and cheer. The rest of the audience didn't know what was going on, but if there was a celebration they were determined to be a part of it and they stood and cheered too, as Peter and Eynon moved along the row, kissing the family and shaking hands until they were sitting, one each side of a joyful Beth.

When the tumult had settled down, Shirley began to sing again.

She sang two more numbers, and when the clapping showed no sign of diminishing, she announced an encore. Clutching Freddy's latest letter in her hand, she no longer wished for the return of yesterday as in Max's beautiful song.

She sang instead, 'It's a Lovely Day Tomorrow, Tomorrow is a Lovely Day'.

For her and for many others who were beginning to join in, it would be true.